The Breaking of Mona Hill

Christy Aldridge

ALSO BY *Christy Aldridge*

Weeping Willow
Rogues
Six Months
Kill, My Darlings
Seth
These Ghosts Bleed
All The Pretty Hells You See

This book is a work of fiction. Any reference to historical events, real people, or real places are used fictitiously. Other names, characters, places or events are products of the author's imagination, and any resemblance to actual events, places, or persons, living or dead, is entirely coincidental.

Copyright © 2023 Christy Aldridge
Cover Design by Grim Poppy Designs
Editing by Heather Miller
First Edition
All rights reserved.

ISBN: 9798374560190

PRAISE FOR 'THE BREAKING OF MONA HILL'

"There is a darkness in the pages of THE BREAKING OF MONA HILL, a darkness that taints the light long after you finish the book. This book reminds us, quite rightly, to be scared of the dark."

Anthony Creane
Author of TERRORFICTION: THE COLLECTION

"Christy Aldridge is a sweetheart... And one of the scariest writers writing today."

Judith Sonnet
Author of CHAINSAW HOOKER

"Christy Aldridge's writing hits you where it hurts. With her newest book, you'll find yourself breaking alongside its main character, but you'll love every excruciating second of it."

Lucas Mangum
Author of SAINT SADIST and GODS OF THE DARK WEB

"A rustic, bible belt nightmare of biblical proportions. Mona shines a visceral light on the horrors of womanhood."

Otis Bateman
Author of MAGGOT GIRL and MEDUSA'S SON

"Bleak, heart wrenching, and raw, Aldridge pours pain across every page with her captivating characters and powerful prose."

Candace Nola
Author of BISHOP

For those of us who are wallpaper.

Chapter One.. 15
Chapter Two...55
Chapter Three..81
Chapter Four. 107
Chapter Five...143
Chapter Six...177
Chapter Seven...................................201
Chapter Eight...243
Chapter Nine...271
Chapter Ten...285
Chapter Eleven.......................................299
Chapter Twelve..315
Chapter Thirteen....................................327
Chapter Fourteen....................................337
Chapter Fifteen.....................................351
Chapter Sixteen......................................375
Chapter Seventeen....................................393
Chapter Eighteen....................................421
Chapter Nineteen....................................437
Chapter Twenty.......................................461
Chapter Twenty-One..................................491
Acknowledgement.....................................497

Trigger Warnings....................................500

The Breaking Of Mona Hill

The Beast with Ten Horns and Seven Heads

"See, I think there are roads that lead us to each other. But in my family, there were no roads- just underground tunnels. I think we all got lost in those underground tunnels. No, not lost. We just lived there."

Last Night I Sang to the Monster
Benjamin Alire Saenz

Part One

Chapter One

Genesis 3:16

To the woman he said, "I will make your pains in childbearing very severe; with painful labor you will give birth to children. Your desire will be for your husband, and he will rule over you."

There was an overwhelming feeling of shame and despair washing over the teenage girl as she stood in the driveway of the abortion clinic. She knew they offered different options. The brochure outlined a lot of good services that the people inside could help with. Things like healthcare, treatments and vaccines, cancer screenings, exams, amenities for both men and women.

Most of the things in the brochure seemed like they were more helpful than harmful.

The building itself even looked different than what she imagined. She expected a place that gave her the same feelings a bar did. Maybe not flashing neon signs and promises of alcohol, but the same inviting exterior. The same temptation waiting inside. A place that screamed, *'Come and sin with me.'*

But the outside of the clinic looked normal. There were posters in the windows of smiling girls, some with babies, and bright, happy colors. There was still the sense of inviting, but not in a sinister way. There was something calming about the building. It didn't make her feel like she was about to enter a baby killing factory.

It was not the heathen hell Mona had been brought up to believe.

Some of the bigger churches in the area would come here and picket sometimes. She watched it on the news. Her mama would all but applaud them for doing the Lord's work, stopping those poor girls from killing their unborn babies, but Mona always wondered if it was so simple. She never felt like applauding them for what they did. It never felt sincere when they claimed they were trying to save the babies.

Her focus would land on the girls. The ones that looked terrified to walk in and be judged. They would decide to walk away. The church people would clap for those girls, but Mona felt sorry for them. It didn't seem right that someone should carry something they didn't want. Sure, they might have laid down and had sex, but it was still their body. And Mona had to imagine they had other circumstances that kept the news from being joyful.

She did.

Her palm rested on her stomach. She imagined a bump but knew there wasn't one there. She wasn't more than six weeks pregnant. She knew the exact day. Based off the book she read in the library, her baby wasn't even the size of a sweet pea. Their eyes, nose, and ears weren't even fully formed yet.

But it had a heartbeat. She didn't know how something so small could even have a heart yet, but she knew it was there. She wondered if she would hear it today.

She did hope that the pregnancy test she had taken was wrong. The shame the girls on TV showed was the same one she felt. She didn't want to kill a baby. The book called it an *embryo*. A *fetus*. Those words made her feel better, but not completely. She kept thinking about that heartbeat.

If she was quiet enough, she felt that she could feel it beating. At night, when she slept, she imagined it was beating so loud that everyone in the house could hear it. The whole night within those trailer walls, there would be the steady beating, a rhythmic terror that would reveal all of Mona Hill's sins. It would put them right on display for everyone to see, and she knew what would happen if anyone found out about it.

A car pulled in behind her and she realized she had to decide.

Standing out in the parking lot was really going to make her look suspicious. If someone she knew drove by, they'd tell her parents. She couldn't have that.

Fear made her go inside.

She opened the doors and heard children playing. When she looked to the waiting area, she could see a couple gathered around the toy with the beads, moving them along the metal lines and clashing them together to make the loudest sound. That toy was in every doctor's office Mona had ever been in.

That could be her in a few years. She could be one of the women sitting in the chair watching her child play. A growing human, something with a personality and a drive to make as much noise as possible. Something with a laugh and a smile. A pulse.

A heartbeat.

"Can I help you?" a soft voice asked.

Mona turned to see an older lady sitting behind the glass. She looked at the kids again. That sinking, uncomfortable feeling came back. One worse than the shame she felt. The one that overpowered the shame and made her decide abortion was the only option.

"Yes ma'am," Mona said, coming up closer to the glass. She didn't want to speak too loudly. She didn't want to see anyone look at her with judgment.

The lady gave her a comforting smile. "Do you have an appointment?"

Mona nodded.

The woman reached behind her and pulled out a clipboard. She handed it through the opening in the glass to her. "Go ahead and take a seat and fill this out. What's your name?"

"Mona Hill."

"Okay, Mona. I'll call you when your appointment is ready," she said, offering a smile and then looking back to her work.

Mona wondered how many girls she saw in a day. How many abortions? This wasn't some big city like New York or Los Angeles. This was the South. Bible Belt country. Everyone preached against this sort of thing, yet Mona knew some had done it anyway and kept it a secret. That was how most things were. You did one thing behind closed doors and preached about another. Did the woman with the sweet smile go to church every Sunday and raise her hands in the air when the preacher preached against abortion, but then come to work and smile pretty for the women that came to get one? Did she keep their names written down so she could remember the ones that wouldn't end up in Heaven with her?

Mona was worrying a lot about that. If she chose to believe it was a baby and not an *embryo*, she was committing murder. Murdering one of God's children. Surely, that had to be one of the biggest sins there were. The Bible said that God viewed all sins the same, but the church seemed to preach that some sins were worse than others. Her murdering a child and her stealing gum just didn't seem to be on par with each other.

She sat down in the waiting area with the rest of the people there. Looking around, they were all women. Most looked much older than she was. They were here to get birth control or take advantage of the other services offered. The ones that didn't damn your soul to Hell. They didn't have to sit in the chair and feel the shame and guilt that she did.

This is necessary.

She kept reminding herself of that. Sin or no sin, this was necessary. She had to get rid of this fetus inside of her. If she didn't, she might as well be committing suicide, and based off what she had been taught, God didn't like that either.

If she got caught being here, she was basically committing suicide too. Her parents would kill her or worse. She would wish that she was dead.

She bounced her feet and tried to distract herself as she waited for her name to be called. One by one, the other women disappeared into the back with their children or by themselves. Mona would look at the clock and watch the time pass, convinced it was moving slower than it was. She made an appointment to keep from risking her parents noticing she was gone for longer than she was supposed to be. She told them she was babysitting for Owen's mom. Gave them a time she would be home. Even though she still had plenty of time, she worried it would go by too quickly and she would get caught.

"Mona Hill."

Her eyes looked toward the door where a young woman in scrubs waited. She got to her feet, dropping her backpack on the ground like the clumsy idiot she was, and drawing more attention to herself. She quickly pushed it higher on her shoulder and grabbed the clipboard before going with the nurse.

"I'll take that," the woman said. Mona handed her the clipboard and followed behind her. They walked down a series of tiny booths before she presented a seat to her and walked around to sit in the chair opposite.

There were more flyers and papers with smiling couples and happy people. Mona envied them. The last thing she felt she would ever do again was smile.

"Okay, Mona. What are you here for, darlin'?"

Mona's throat felt dry. She cleared it and licked her lips, but her voice still cracked as she said, "Ab-abortion."

The girl across from her looked her over. She tilted her head. "How old are you, sweetheart?"

"Fifteen."

There was a softness that crossed her face. "Do you have a parent here with you?" she asked.

Mona shook her head.

The girl laid down the clipboard. She looked at Mona longer than was comfortable. Mona looked away and when she looked up, the woman was glanced around quickly, as if to make sure no one was around. When she leaned in closer, Mona knew for sure that she was trying to make sure no one could hear them.

"Listen, sweetheart. In the state of Alabama, abortions aren't exactly the easiest to get. And if you do get one, you must have a parent's signature. Judging by the way you look scared to speak, I'm going to guess the last thing you want is your parents to know," she said.

Mona nodded.

"Even with a signature, you wouldn't get one here. I guarantee it. Too many Bible humpers to ever go through with it, even with you being so young. They don't care how you got pregnant, just that you have a baby inside you and getting rid of it is murder," she told Mona.

She was repeating Mona's worst fears, words she had heard in her head repeatedly. She knew this was a possibility and it filled her to the brim with fear and panic. She couldn't carry this baby. She couldn't have this baby. She just couldn't.

"But I get it. It doesn't matter what your circumstances are, honey. You made the decision. If you really want to go through with it, I know someone that can help, but she has a price and it's not going to be as safe as it is in a clinic. She does her best to make things as safe she can, but she is just a woman on her own trying not to get caught by police. You understand?"

Mona nodded again.

The girl nodded and pulled a piece of paper out. She wrote down a number and an address, folded it, and handed it to her. "That's her number. Call it. She'll give you all the details. I'm going to cancel your appointment and remove your name from the computers, that way you shouldn't have to worry about any mail or follow up phone calls of any form. Just call her number and get yourself settled."

Mona took the paper and clutched it in her hand. This was a way out. A 'GET OUT OF JAIL FREE' card. The amount of relief that flooded over her as she touched the paper was immense. It was a feeling the lady in front of her wouldn't understand. In fact, Mona expected to see judgment, but when she looked at the girl, all she could see was kindness.

"Thank you," she whispered.

"Not a problem. It really is a shame. Your life matters too," she told her.

And those words glued themselves to her memory. Mona couldn't remember a time when anything in relation to her had mattered, let alone her life. Here was a perfect stranger telling her that her life mattered. The woman didn't even know her, yet Mona felt like her words weren't any less sincere because of it.

"Now go on. Have that taken care of. And take care of yourself," she said.

Mona nodded, standing up. She held the paper tight between her thumb and pointer finger, starting to leave before stopping herself. She looked at the girl again.

"What's your name?" she asked.

The girl smiled. "It's Jill."

"Thank you, Jill."

Jill smiled and Mona turned around to walk away. She didn't make eye contact with anyone she passed. She held onto the paper and walked out of the building, determined to put as much distance between her and it as she could.

She folded and unfolded the paper as she walked. The number and address were written with beautiful script. Jill was a pretty name, Mona decided. Jill was the name you gave a girl that was pure and genuinely kind. It was the name of pretty girls with lots of friends and a loving family. Mona decided that Jill wore white cotton skirts when she wasn't working and had a golden retriever. It was trained and sweet, lying beside her and her boyfriend when they watched TV together.

Mona wished she had been born as Jill. To a different family. In a different body. Be a different person. Have a different life. She wished she could be the one to offer kindness to a stranger and wish them the best. She wished she was able to be sweet and generous to people she didn't know.

Mona looked at the paper. She had to keep a close eye on it. If someone found it and decided to call, she didn't know what the woman would say. She didn't know how she'd explain it either. It was best to call from somewhere else and commit the address to memory, but she also didn't want to forget it.

She walked away from the building, deciding to call the number from the same place she had made the appointment. It still wasn't the best option, but the house was close by, and her boyfriend wasn't home.

She walked through town, heading to one of the slummier parts. There were two types of poor people in the south. Those that lived in government housing and those that lived in the trailer parks. The only thing poorer than that was being homeless, and in towns as small as theirs, there was only one man that was poor enough to have no place to live but the woods.

Her boyfriend lived in the projects. Holt's Square was the name, but most people called it the Slums. The Slums were the lowest of the low. If you lived in the Slums, you were always one paycheck away from homelessness. There were always more kids than bedrooms and often, only one parent was around.

Mona walked along the streets, something she usually didn't do alone. Drug dealing was one of the main forms of work for people in Holt's Square, her boyfriend included. It was one reason her parents didn't like him, though they had nothing to confirm it. Her brother would get drugs from him all the time.

She hated it.

She walked up to his house and knocked on the door. She knew who would answer. Carrie, with her third child on her hip and a cigarette in her mouth opened the door and scowled at Mona. Not because she didn't like her. At this point, after a life of disappointments, her face just looked like that. She couldn't erase the frown any more than she could erase the past mistakes that had led her to this life she hated.

I'll end up looking like that if I don't get out of here.

It was a thought that sent her stomach into a horrible twist.

"Oh, hi, Mona. Owen's not home right now. He's over at the shop working with Joe," Carrie said.

"Oh, really?" Mona said, feigning surprise. "It must have slipped my mind."

"Yeah, I'm sorry, sugar. You want to wait here for him? I'm sure he'll be here any moment and can drive you home. I would, but I got the kids," Carrie answered.

"No, it's okay. You think I can use the phone though? See if I can call a friend to come pick me up?"

It was a lie, one Carrie might realize if she actually took the time to listen. The idea of Mona having friends was as believable as Carrie using birth control. Or liking her kids.

"Sure," she said, moving aside and letting Mona through. "Go ahead and make your call. I've got to finish cooking for these heathens though, so just come to the kitchen when you're through."

"Yes ma'am. Thank you," Mona answered. She walked into the living room to the landline and waited for Carrie to disappear into the kitchen. When she did, Mona unfolded the paper again and dialed the number. She looked toward the kitchen one more time to make sure Carrie wasn't listening in while the phone rang.

"Hello?"

Mona's attention snapped back to the phone. "Um, yes. Someone gave me your number to call about. . . uh, helping me with a problem," she said. She felt like a complete idiot speaking. How did one call to have an abortion? How did you strike up that type of conversation?

The lady was silent for a moment. The silence was tense. Like she didn't believe her, but if what Jill said was right, she understood why she wouldn't. "Who gave you my number?" she asked.

"Jill. From the clinic. She said you could help me," Mona answered. "I need an abo- "

"I know what you need," the woman said, cutting her off. "She give you my address?"

"Yes ma'am."

"Be there at nine tomorrow morning. I'll help you with that problem."

The line went dead, and Mona was left feeling empty. She didn't know why there was so much dread filling her body, but the way the line went cold made her think she wouldn't meet someone like Jill tomorrow. The lady on the phone was unemotional. Mona didn't feel like she was empathetic. She worried about what tomorrow would bring.

She rested the phone back against the receiver. She took in a deep breath before turning around to find Jimmy staring at her.

Jimmy was seven years old and Owen's half-brother. In Mona's opinion, he was a brat. He and Owen shared a room, a fact that was awful most of the time when she came over. He would insist on coming in the room because 'it was his room too.'

He just looked at her with a mischievous grin. Mona didn't like it. You couldn't trust seven-year-olds, especially little boys. And especially boys like Jimmy.

"Mona's gotta a problem," he said.

"Shut up," she told him. She walked past him and toward the kitchen. Jimmy followed behind her. She didn't like it. She didn't know how much he had heard of her conversation either.

Carrie was in the kitchen. She was cooking, but when Mona entered the doorway, she turned around. She raised a brow. "Someone coming to get you?" she asked.

Mona nodded. "Yeah, I'm gonna head to the end of the block and wait for them," she told her.

"Okay. I'll tell Owen you stopped by."

"No," Mona said, masking her hesitation with a smile. "I'll just see him tomorrow. He'll want to come over if you tell him I stopped by."

Carried smiled. "Yeah, he would," she said. Her smiled faltered a bit. "I guess he's still not welcomed in the blessed Hill household."

Mona didn't like to talk about her family much, especially to Carrie. But Owen's reasons for not being allowed over weren't a secret. And Mona couldn't hide that her parents hated her boyfriend. They certainly hadn't hidden it anytime they'd been around him.

"No."

His mother gave her a rueful smile. "Well, probably for the best anyway. Owen's gotta learn when to stop talking back at some point," she said. "That boy snaps off at the drop of a pin. Like his daddy, that one. Someone'll put him in his place one day and he'll stop."

"Yes ma'am."

"You sure you don't want to wait for him?"

"No, I really do need to get home."

"Okay," Carried answered. "Be careful, honey."

"I will. See you later," Mona said, waving before turning around and heading to the door. Jimmy followed her all the way to the door. When she opened it and let herself outside, he was still smiling at her with a grin that made her uneasy.

"Have fun," he told her, then shut the door in her face.

She rolled her eyes and sighed. Owen detested the kid. Mona did too. But even Jimmy wasn't as bad as her family. She'd rather have a brother like Jimmy than have the ones she had.

She started her walk home. It would take her at least thirty minutes to get there. She dreaded the walk, but hitching a ride was not something she liked to do. Usually, she didn't have to worry about it, but she was already doing very sneaky things. She didn't need to draw more attention to herself and her growing web of lies.

The walk would help clear some of her thoughts before she got home. With the warm air and the late-night summer breeze, she could try to clear her mind before she got home and lost all semblance of control she felt she had in her life.

Owen was control. Owen was something she could have, no matter how her parents tried to ruin it. Because Owen also wanted her, even if just to spite them. Bad boy with the church girl. That was how he viewed it.

Mona just viewed him as a means of escape.

It was strange to be with someone you knew you didn't want to be with for the rest of your life. Owen was a nice distraction, and she was hoping that he would be her way out, but she didn't want to marry him and build a family. She'd never be any better off than her parents were if she did.

She just wanted out. Wanted to leave. But she didn't know how to do that.

It wasn't that she didn't love him. She did. But then again, she wasn't sure she even knew what love was. She didn't see love when she looked at her parents. Or at Owen's parents, or whatever man his mother was dating at the time. She didn't see it in any couple around her. She didn't even see it in the relationship she and Owen had with their parents.

Steve said that God was the perfect image of love, but she wasn't sure how that was possible. The God he talked about sent angels to kill hundreds of thousands of people, including the Egyptians' first born. She didn't know how that constituted as love but would never ask. Asking was blasphemous and blasphemy sent you straight to hell.

But apparently, so did abortions.

It seemed like no matter what way she turned; she was bound to die a sinner. A place in Hell was reserved for her and there was nothing she could do to change it. That sense of helplessness followed her wherever she went.

But, to Mona, she wasn't sure which was worse. Knowing God was there, and she was not living up to His word, or the idea that He didn't exist at all.

Owen didn't believe in God. Owen called it fear-mongering. He said it was how they controlled the less intelligent. Not that Owen was very smart. He wasn't even in school anymore. The day he dropped out, he was escorted out of the school for cussing out the principal. He called him some bad names, even an ugly racial slur. It seemed like everyone around her used it, no matter what skin color the other person was, but it gave Mona an uncomfortable feeling. She didn't like it.

She walked until she got to the trailer park. If Holt's Square was the lowest you could go, the trailer park she lived in was only one step above it. There was another trailer park in town, but it was much nicer. Mostly because there were far more people living there. Whispering Oaks was smaller. It was mostly lots you rented. You needed a place to put the trailer you bought? Whispering Oaks was where you did it. Didn't pay your lot rent? You had to pay to have your trailer moved. That cost a lot more than the lot rent did.

There were five trailers in Whispering Oaks right now. One was empty. One might as well be empty, given that the man that lived there was a truck driver and never seemed to be home. One housed an old woman, practically senile. One had a young couple and their baby, but she was often being kicked out and then coming back when the fighting subsided.

Then theirs.

The Hills of Whispering Oaks.

There was a sense of dread that came over her as she walked toward the trailer at the end of the park. She watched the old woman, Mrs. Pratt, lift her blinds as she passed. Mona almost wished she was walking into that trailer instead. She knew Mrs. Pratt was snobby and nosey, but she was also half deaf and losing her marbles.

Inside her home was the family she wanted to escape. The life she wanted to leave behind, and every time she had to walk back up the road to her house, she felt that urge to run creep over her. It was a feeling she had to push aside constantly, but it was always there.

She was desperate to run away.

She could hear the TV going as she got to the area that was

considered their yard. When she opened the door, her dad, youngest brother, and Birdie were watching it. The nightly news was on, telling her father how bad the world was so he could, in turn, tell them how bad it *really* was.

The news was biased.

Her mother was in the kitchen, cooking chicken on the stove. The fan above was on full blast, pulling out the smoke as fast as it could, but the house still looked a little hazy. The chicken would be dry and flavorless. The mashed potatoes on the counter would need more butter. The green beans would be fine because they came from a can. Everything would need more salt.

The screen door closed first, making a louder sound than what she had anticipated. They all looked at her, but the three in the living room quickly looked back at the TV. Her mother was the only one that didn't ignore her. Her mother was the one she wished would ignore her.

"Dinner will be done in fifteen. Go get washed up," she instructed her, before also ignoring her and resuming her previous task. Her words were straight to the point, but always said in a tone that made Mona think she was angry with her. And maybe she was. It seemed like she was always doing something to make Mama mad.

"Yes, ma'am."

Mona walked through the kitchen and into the living room. She thought she would make it through without getting her father's attention, but that was a hope quickly crushed. He didn't even mute the TV to speak to her. Because it didn't really matter what she said.

"Did you stop by that bum of a boyfriend's house?"

"Yes, sir. But he was working," she told him. She knew it was better to tell the truth as much as possible. It was a lesson frequently being learned to avoid punishment.

Not that she would tell him what she had been doing before then.

"I'm sure," he grumbled. "Go get washed up."

"Yes sir."

She continued her journey toward the bathroom. The trailer only had two. One in the master bedroom at the other end of the house and one between the two bedrooms. She and Birdie shared the bathroom with Clyde and Beau, the latter of which jumped from his bed as she passed and stood in the door of the bathroom after she walked in.

"You were gone for a long time," he said.

Mona didn't answer. She didn't even look at him. Beau was her twin brother. She didn't think they resembled each other at all. Not physically, but especially not mentally. Beau was just as bad as the rest of them. In fact, Mona knew him to be worse.

She turned on the sink and began to wash her hands. In her peripheral vision, she could see him leaning against the entry way with his arms crossed. He wasn't going to leave her alone. He had something on his mind. She hoped if she ignored him for long enough, he would leave, but as she dried her hands and started out, he did exactly as she assumed and stood in place.

"I need to get through."

"Have you thought about what I said?"

Mona's eyes snapped up to him. His face was too smug for her to feel any sort of confidence or strength. Something about Beau always stole that from her. Sometimes, she wondered if he had gotten those traits from their father, and she had gotten the submissive traits from her mother. Was it hereditary or was it the environment?

This was something Mona thought about a lot. Nature versus nurture, she believed it was called. It was the debate over whether human behavior was determined during a person's life or because of their genes. Was she submissive because it was something inherent, or was she that way because of the environment in which she was raised?

And Beau? Was he born bad? Or was it their lives?

And if so, either way, was there help for either one of them? For any of them? At some point was a person irredeemable?

Was she?

Mona shook her head to answer Beau's question but found she couldn't answer her own. She wasn't sure if anyone would ever be able to answer her question. Maybe not even God Himself.

"You need to," Beau told her. "This place around here isn't

getting any better. So, you're either with me or against me."

He moved from the doorway and walked back into his room. He closed the door behind him, and that made Mona feel more secure. She liked walls and doors. They were there to keep things out. She liked when they were closed.

But she also liked windows. She liked having a way to escape when the lock was on the opposite side of the door.

She walked into her room, the room she now shared with Birdie. Birdie had lived with them for a while now. She was practically her little sister at this point, despite having no actual relation to her. Birdie was an orphan. A stray dog. Her mama left her with them and never came back.

She took off her shoes. She laid her backpack on the bed. There wasn't much inside other than a couple of books. School was over for at least another month, but she liked the bag. It was easy to hide things in.

She reached into her back pocket and pulled out the note. She should have tossed it, but she was afraid she'd forget the address. She opened her bag and pulled open a part in the fabric that was unstitched. She shoved the note inside and then pushed the bag under the bed.

Mona hated how sneaky she had to be. It was nothing new for teenagers to hide things from their parents, but she felt she had to hide everything from everyone. She had no one to confide in and it was lonely. No one to tell about her pregnancy. No one to tell about her conflicting spiritual thoughts. No one to go with her and hold her hand after the abortion. She would have liked to tell Owen, but he wouldn't like it. He would get angry and not be there for her. They weren't that close.

There was absolutely no one.

She was alone.

The sounds of the TV and her mother yelling that dinner was done reminded her that, though she was alone in all the ways that mattered, she was never physically alone.

She walked back into the living room, Beau opening his door right after she walked past it. He was behind her as they went into the kitchen and grabbed their plates. Only Mona, Birdie, and Mama had to grab plates though. They made the boys plates first and then their own. Birdie had Clyde, Mama had Daddy, and Mona had Beau because he was her twin.

She made Beau's plate and then her own. She walked back into the living room and sat down on the floor as everyone began to eat. Beau sat down beside her. She wished he hadn't. She hated the way she felt next to her twin brother. How small, how vulnerable, how pathetic even. She wished he would give her space. Leave her alone. They may have shared the womb, but that was the last thing she ever wanted to share with Beau. Of all the people in the world, she wished she was invisible to Beau.

The TV was still on, but a gameshow was playing now. It was the same one that had been playing every day since she was a child, and she had no interest in it. She didn't have much interest in anything.

They ate in silence, but then her mother started to talk. She was always the one to start talking. She liked to have conversation going, something Mona didn't understand.

"Do you think you'll go to church with us Sunday?" she asked their dad.

Mona braced for yelling. Church was an arguing point between them sometimes. Although her Daddy liked to quote the Bible and throw the verses at his children and wife when needed, he did not like the church. Not just the one they went to, though he and Pastor Steve had conflict, but church in general. His philosophy was that you didn't need to be seen to worship God.

Her mother's philosophy was if you weren't in church, you were immediately damned to Hell. No ifs, ands, or buts. The Bible said to go to church, so she went to church. There were few things that the Bible said to do that her mother didn't.

But now, Mona wondered if she did all of it to repent for her sin. Her devotion to God and attending church so religiously now was a punishment she enforced on herself. Her own way of trying to make right the sin she still lived.

Not that Mona could confirm that.

"And be surrounded by those bunch of heathens? I can stay here and get as much holy rollin' as I'd like," he told her.

The only commandment Mona knew Mama would always break

would be honoring her husband if he had told her she wasn't allowed to go. Since they both knew this, Daddy never told her she couldn't. He just refused to go himself.

Mona wasn't sure which one she believed in. She felt she *needed* to go to church, but she wasn't sure if she *had* to go to the building for it to be real. Truth was, she went to church every single time she was told, and she still felt just as lost as she would have if she didn't know what church was at all.

Mona felt Beau move closer to her. Instinct made her want to move away, but she didn't want to make a scene, not when the air was tense with Mama's exchange with Daddy. Any distraction and things could escalate. Mona wanted to avoid that.

"We'll be late coming home then. After morning service, we're going to deliver some food with Pastor Steve, so we'll just stay until after evening service too. I'll make you some black-eyed peas, collards, cornbread, and some porkchops before we go so you ain't gotta worry about what to eat," she told him.

"That takes all day?"

"We're going door to door, dear. No sense in wasting the gas coming back home when we can just stay at the church."

"How much you wanna bet the old man slaps her before the night's over?" Beau asked her.

Mona didn't say anything. She hoped this wasn't where the conversation was heading. And she didn't like that Beau seemed excited for it. Wanted it. She hated that this was even a possibility.

Or that she seemed to be the only one ashamed of that.

"So, I have to stay here without a way to go all day, is that what you're saying?"

"Unless you'd like to take us to church and come back home," Mama answered, her voice calm and collected, despite how their father's voice was rising.

Mona didn't want a fight to start. Her heart was beating faster with each word out of their mouth, waiting for them to start arguing with each other. She hated arguing. She hated conflict. All she wanted was peace. Even a little happiness, if that wasn't too much to ask for.

But looking around her, she realized she was the only one that cared. Beau and Clyde seemed to thrive on the fighting. They liked when Daddy got angry with Mama. It was the show of control he gave them. Showing them how to be the man of the house, the head of their household. It was displays of dominance that made them feel more like men. It gave them a blueprint of what to do in their own lives, Mona would guess. They had no control over Daddy, but any woman was fair game.

Birdie just ignored it. Of course, she had been living with her mama until a few years ago when her mama went to jail for trying to sell her to an undercover cop. A couple months of reminding her that she could go back to being sold for some crack and Birdie suddenly thought her life was good here. Like a dog being adopted by a family only to be put on a heavy chain in the snow but still feeling like it was better than the streets. A woman being verbally abused but saying, "At least he doesn't hit me now."

But Mona, she couldn't help but notice it. She noticed all of it to the point that she constantly felt on edge. The lack of control was something that plagued her day-to-day life. She was always scared and aware of the reaction each action could cause. She felt she had to play mind reader to every little detail of her life to try and minimize the damage.

No one else seemed like they did.

It felt like every other person in the house wanted to be louder than the next. Sometimes, Daddy would let this pass. He'd let Beau throw his temper tantrums with everyone, bossing them around, being cruel, but when Beau's attention turned to Daddy, that was when things would change. Mama, Clyde, Birdie, they could all be ugly and mean to each other, and her, but once something threatened Daddy's control, that was when words were said, or things were broken.

Be it a glass or an arm.

She could see that control being tested now. Mama questioning his choices. Mama putting him on the spot to make one. Daddy was seeing red.

However, Mona was now aware that Beau had his hand on her leg. She had her legs pulled up, her plate resting between her thighs and stomach, and Beau's hand was right in the crevice of that. His fingers were rough, and they were gripping her.

Her eyes caught his facial expression. He was excited. He could feel the energy in the air just as much as she could, but rather than fearing the outcome, he was waiting for it. Hoping for it. His nerves were set on fire while hers were on edge. Beau would get off on the turmoil. Mona would die a little more.

When she looked back to her dad, she realized he was now looking at her. Everyone else seemed to be looking at the TV, including Mama, but his eyes were now on her and moving toward Beau. She had no doubt that he could see Beau squeezing her thigh. Nor did she think he could miss the rising excitement on his face as he waited for their dad to explode. It was all so clear. Spelled out for him to read it.

But when he looked back at Mona, there was disappointment on his face. She didn't understand it. Was he disappointed with Beau? Or was it her? Although he was short-tempered and liked to hit things, and people, when he was angry, there were times when Mona could swear she saw something more in his eyes. Something close to love, but not quite. There were times she didn't absolutely hate her father, when she doubted her own misgivings instead.

There was something different now. Another expression that Mona didn't understand.

Recognition.

And after the disappointment left his face, there was a cold, but embarrassed expression that followed along with that recognition. "Yeah, I'll drop y'all off," he said.

Their mother, Clyde, and Birdie seemed to not notice that last shift. They didn't notice that this would have been a prime time for him to go off the rails. They didn't notice that he consciously chose to be agreeable instead.

But Mona noticed.

And Beau noticed.

Beau gave her thigh another squeeze. This one was meant to inflict pain and it did. She bit down on her tongue to stop herself from making a noise and looked to her daddy to see if he had noticed. His eyes were now trained on the TV, as if he were forcing himself to not look away for any reason.

Shunning her.

And Mona could sense that Beau was angry. Whether it was caused by their father's judgment or his lack of response, Mona couldn't be sure. The only thing she knew was that she could *feel* her brother's anger and resentment. It radiated off him like heat, sinking into her own pores and making her feel just as bad as he did.

When she and Beau were little, people used to make statements about the fact that they were twins. They would say that the bond between twins was different than normal siblings. Special. Someone once said that twins were on their own wavelength and in tune with each other. Connected.

It was that connection that scared Mona. She wondered and feared that it was true. She was connected by blood to her family, but Beau was different. He had always been different, and Mona could sense that. She could sense every foul and ugly thing about him.

Over the years, it was that sense that made her put as much space as she could between them. She wanted nothing to do with it. She didn't want to be close to that nastiness inside of him that she could sense.

But to Beau, that only seemed to make him try harder. Because they were linked. He often went on about them being different. That they were forever stitched together in a way most people would never understand. As little kids, they even had their own language, but Mona wanted nothing to do with it anymore. She wanted nothing to do with Beau.

Living in a house with him, surrounded by his emotions all the time, was driving her crazy. She knew that if she could sense these things in him, he had to be able to sense her hatred and distrust of him as well.

She wondered if that meant he could sense the guilt she felt around the baby inside her. She hoped not. She prayed not.

The last thing she needed was for Beau to know about that. She didn't want him to know about the abortion. She needed him to keep his distance so she could work through this without things blowing up in her face. The last thing she needed to deal with was a vindictive twin.

"I think it's time for everyone to scatter," their dad said. It was then that she knew something was up with him. It was still early in the night. Usually, he made them sit through everything but the evening news before telling them to get to their rooms.

"Girls, go do the dishes," her mama ordered.

"Yes ma'am," both girls said in unison.

"Go make sure the lawnmower and weed eater are back under the house, Beau," Daddy instructed, his eyes still on the TV.

"I already did," Beau answered.

Their Daddy snapped his eyes toward Beau. It was more in the way he said the words than his choice of them, and everyone knew it. Especially Beau.

"Then go make sure," he told him, this time with more force. "Clyde, grab the keys from the truck while he does."

"Yes, sir," Clyde answered, like the dutiful son he was. "Come on, Beau."

Mona watched Beau get up, but that anger between her brother and dad was still there. The room seemed alive with that feeling.

As he passed, he made eye contact with her. A look he shared with only his sister and one she could decipher with no issue. She felt she could almost read his mind at times, and this was one of those times.

He was going to kill their dad one day. Slice his face from ear to ear so they'd finally see the old man smile for once. And once he was dead, bleeding out on the floor, Beau would take his place and things would be different.

Not better, but different.

Beau and Clyde walked outside, even though Beau closed the door harder than what was necessary. Mona instinctively looked toward her dad, but he didn't even turn. His grip on the arm of the chair seemed tighter, but he himself didn't jump up and grab Beau by the hair like she would have expected.

Beau lived to see another day.

"You wanna wash or dry?" Birdie asked.

Mona turned back to her and shrugged. "Doesn't matter," she answered.

"You wash then. I hate washin' the dishes," Birdie answered, grabbing a towel from under the sink and getting into position.

She and Birdie started washing and drying the dishes. Mama was outside, getting up the laundry. She'd come back in and go through the it, hanging and folding her and Daddy's laundry before separating the rest for them to grab and put up. Not that Mona had any trouble with that. All her clothes were shoved into a storage box so Birdie could have the closet. Birdie was more focused and particular with her clothes than Mona was. Since Mona had no use for the closet, when she and Birdie began to share a room years ago, she told Birdie she could have it, something that she seemed grateful for.

Beau and Clyde came back inside, and Clyde handed Daddy the keys. Beau was still sour, evident by not only his face but his entire demeanor.

"Thanks, son," Daddy said. "Go on and start getting your bath while the girls finish up. Beau can get one after you. First, he and I are gonna have a talk. Man to man."

Mona was trying to focus on washing the dishes, but her eyes were also moving up. Watching their dad stand up and grab his cigarettes. Although Clyde looked intimidated, Beau didn't look fazed at all by the fact that Daddy wanted to speak to him alone. When Daddy walked to the back door, Beau followed without fuss.

She turned her attention back to the dishes, but she could see their daddy through the window. She could see his cigarette light up each time he took a drag, but nothing else. Birdie had taken it upon herself to start humming a song from the radio. If there was a chance for Mona to hear what was being said, it was lost as soon as she began to hum.

They continued cleaning the dishes even as Clyde finished in the bathroom and Mama came in from getting the clothes. When the backdoor opened and Daddy walked in, Mona couldn't help but look confused. Despite the humming, she hadn't heard any fighting at all. No banging or yelling. No voices raised loud enough to hear. But Daddy was inside and sitting down while Beau was still outside.

"Birdie, go on and get a shower real quick," he told her.

"But Beau- "

"I said get a shower, Birdie. Let Beau worry about himself," he snapped.

"Yes sir."

Mona watched Birdie go. She started cleaning the rest of the kitchen, wiping down the counters. She was putting the leftovers away when Beau finally came in. Her attention went straight to the door as he came inside. Through the doorway, she watched his eyes wander straight to her again. Nothing but pure anger seething on his face.

Mona didn't like it. But she couldn't look away. It was cold. Vengeful. He was livid. The energy radiating from him let it be known that no one should speak to him. Especially her.

Birdie came out and seemed to sense that as well. She quietly moved past him to go through the living room to the laundry. Their dad was the only one brave enough to really acknowledge him, especially when he looked up and saw the look between Mona and Beau.

"Go get your shower, Beau."

Beau broke his eye contact with her, and she felt relieved. His eyes held her captive, and she was happy to be set free. She turned her attention back to sweeping while Beau left to get a shower.

Once she finished sweeping, she went into the living room and grabbed her clothes. Both Birdie and Clyde were gone and in their rooms. Mona would be the last one in the shower, which meant it would be a quick one for the night. She doubted there was any hot water left at all.

She was going to head to her room and put her clothes up before getting a shower. When she walked through, her name was spoken. She turned to see her daddy staring at her.

"Come here, baby girl. Come talk to your old man for a few minutes," he told her.

Mona felt uncomfortable. She didn't like being put on the spot, especially when they were virtually alone. She didn't trust being alone with anyone really. She hated how vulnerable she felt.

But she went to him anyway. She walked to his chair and then knelt in front of him. She felt small and weak in front of her daddy and his intense stare.

Mona didn't want to make eye contact, but his finger found a place beneath her chin and lifted her face to look at him. His eyes searched hers, then looked elsewhere, as if he were seeing her for the first time. As if he were searching for something, something Mona didn't want him to find.

Her guilt was in full force under his stare. How much of *her* could her see? She wondered this with most everyone. Out of the people in her life, could any of them see *her*? Not just the façade she put on for them. Not the walls she built to protect herself from them. Could they see who she was beneath all of that?

Was she ugly?

Because Mona had no clue who she was. She never put down the mask. She never let down her guard. She had no clue what was under all the fear and the survival. Maybe she was just as ugly as her family. Just as cruel and senseless. All her judgments of them were just a reflection of who she truly was as well.

Nature versus nurture.

She hoped she was wrong. She prayed she was different than them. That she was better. As conceited as it may appear, she wanted to be so much better than they were. To deserve the high horse they would say she sat on. She didn't want to be like them.

But it wasn't any of these things that her Daddy was looking at. When he tilted his head, the words that came out were, "I don't think I've noticed how beautiful you've become."

Mona felt a chill run down her spine. His hand left her face, and she couldn't help but see the mistrust on his. He had questions. Doubts. He was trying to mask them with feigned love. But these questions were rolling along the entire spectrum.

"You've really blossomed into a woman, Mona," he said to her. "But you're still my little girl, right?"

She could read between the lines, despite the lines in front of her being easy to see. They flashed like warning signals that her answer had to be one of two things.

The truth.

Or the best lie she ever told.

She couldn't tell the truth. The heartbeat beating twice inside her ears let her know she couldn't tell him that. A part of her wondered if he knew the truth and that was why he asked. He was trying to catch her in a lie. Trying to make her slip.

But there was no way he could possibly know about the fetus.

Because if he did, he would have had to be there. He would have seen.

Beau.

No. He didn't know. No one knew but her and Jill. And Jill didn't really know her. Jill didn't actually matter.

"Always, Daddy."

For a moment, he looked at her with his accusatory stare again. Waiting for her to slip up. Searching for something to tell him she was lying. Waiting for her guilt to set in. But Mona was already full of guilt, and she had already been acting this long. Nothing would make her slip up because this was for survival, she reasoned. Slipping up meant consequences she didn't want to face.

His face softened, and his finger turned into the palm of his hand against her cheek. It was warm, but Mona longed for it to feel comforting. Loving. It felt like every other hand that had touched her.

Possessive.

Controlling.

"I worry about you, Mona. I worry about people taking advantage of you. Soiling you. You would tell me if someone ever tried to hurt you, wouldn't you?" her father asked.

Mona nodded.

"That boy you're with. . . I don't trust him any farther than I can see him. Boys like that only want one thing and they'll knock you up and leave you. They all got that bug in their brain. They think with the wrong head, baby girl. Your brothers too. And when they see a pretty girl like you, well, they just lose all sense of control. It's not their fault. They just can't control themselves, which is why you shouldn't do anything to provoke them, right?"

Mona nodded again.

"Good. And Beau? I swear that boy has so much of me in him, he don't know which way to go. Probably why we butt heads so often. You'd tell me if he was ever messing with you, wouldn't you?"

Mona nodded, but the truth was, she wouldn't tell her father anything.

His words reaffirmed it. It didn't matter what the situation might be, she would be the one blamed. This was a fact she had known for years. It was always hers, and any other girl's, responsibility to not provoke a man. Not in anger or in lust. Consensual sex, the woman was the aggressor. Rape, the woman was teasing. Anger, the woman was taunting. Men couldn't control themselves.

So, no matter the answer, Mona would always lie and nod.

She wasn't sure if that lie was convincing enough. If it wasn't, it was forgotten when Beau walked into the living room with his dirty clothes. She didn't have to turn and look to know it was Beau. Perhaps that was a twin thing.

Her father looked at Beau, and Mona didn't turn her head at all. She made sure to keep her head forward as Beau walked through and headed to the washing machine. He turned to look at her as he did, and she wished she hadn't looked up to meet his eyes.

She could clearly see the accusation on his face. He wondered what she told their dad. He wondered what they had spoken about. Maybe because of what their daddy took him outside for. Mona didn't know. She didn't want to know. She just wanted to avoid Beau at all costs and go to bed.

When Beau disappeared, her Daddy removed his hand from her and resumed his normal position, staring at the TV. "Go get a shower and get to bed," he told her.

"Yes, sir."

She stood and left the living room promptly. She walked into her room and grabbed her clothes, paying Birdie almost no mind, just as the young girl was doing to her. She walked into the bathroom and closed the door. She wished she could lock it, but there wasn't a lock on it. The only lock was on the master bedroom door, so Mama and Daddy could have privacy when needed. Not that they needed it much anymore. In fact, it seemed like they weren't interested in anything to do with each other now.

Mona showered quickly. She didn't care much about relaxing. The less she had to be around her naked body, the better. Anytime her clothes were off, she felt disgusting. Ugly. Her hands would immediately reach for her belly and then retract. She didn't want to acknowledge it. For the last few days, she had hoped pretending it wasn't there would make it go away, but she could still feel it.

A heartbeat.

Even when she finished and crawled into bed, she listened for it. It was there, beating just as faintly as ever. So soft, but deafening. When the trailer fell into silence, it was the only thing Mona could hear. That monotonous bump throughout the night reminding her that she still carried a secret with her.

A secret she would have to keep until her own heartbeat was gone.

Chapter Two

Job 31:15

Did not he who made me in the womb make them? Did not the same one form us both within our mothers?

Waking up was easy because Mona didn't sleep. She thought the night before had been rough, knowing she had an appointment with the clinic, but this was worse. Stressful. She knew she had to keep her location a secret for the second day in a row. Her mind was also troubled with the night before.

She didn't like her father pulling both her and Beau aside to speak to alone. She didn't like Beau casting her looks that only she could decipher. She didn't like Beau cornering her when she got home because he wanted to talk about his secret.

Their secret.

She guessed it was their secret now too. As far as she knew, they were the only ones to know. But the seams were beginning to unravel around her, and she wondered what exactly was a secret anymore and what was the truth?

And his proposition. He wanted her to think about it, but Mona didn't want to. It didn't help her, even if on the outside it looked like it might. It only made things worse.

She was up before everyone else. She snuck out of the bedroom and into the bathroom to get dressed. She slipped out of the house and sat down on the steps outside. It was about five in the morning. The sun wasn't fully risen yet and the breeze was still cool from the night air. In a couple of hours, everything would be muggy, and the heat would be the stupid kind that made you sweat while you were standing still.

She hated the South.

Sometimes, when she was in school, she would borrow library books that were about traveling. She had read one about Alaska. Something about the Northern Lights and the way things would go dark for so long spoke to her. She wanted to leave Alabama and buy a cabin in the middle of nowhere. She wanted to own a dog, a huge, fluffy dog, and read books by the fireplace.

If she was going to be alone, she wanted to be completely alone but with a dog. A companion. Something that didn't know judgment and only knew love.

She'd get a job. A real job that paid her. She wasn't good at anything, but she would work. A waitress maybe. Except waitresses had to be social and Mona didn't like speaking to strangers. She didn't know how to be flirty or extroverted. Her tips would be horrible.

She could get a job in a bookstore or as a librarian. Something where things were quiet, and people did their own thing. That would be nice. A job where she could sit and read more. The only issue was librarians were smart. Smarter than all her teachers, Mona had come to realize. She doubted she had the smarts to be a good one, and libraries didn't deserve less than the absolute best.

No matter the job, she was sure things would change if she were on her own. Living life without needing to answer for every little thing she did. No one that owned her. No one to control her. She could leave when she wasn't comfortable. She'd even learn to speak up for herself. She could be like the other women she read about, women that went toe to toe with whoever was bothering them. Women that stood up for themselves and refused to change for anyone. Maybe one day, Mona could be that type of woman.

She closed her eyes and imagined herself. Somewhere in her twenties, sitting on her porch in a rocking chair, a cup of hot chocolate in her hand and her dog beside her as she rocked to the cool, brisk morning air. She was happy. She didn't think about the trailer in Whispering Oaks. She didn't think about the Hills. She'd change her name. She'd cut her hair. She'd get tattoos or piercings. Wear clothes that didn't come from neighbors or the church.

She'd be happy.

That was what she wanted most in the world. To just be happy, no matter what that meant. She'd give or do anything to have it. Anything at all.

But out of all her dreams, it was that one that felt the most out of reach.

Could someone be happy with a lifetime of bad memories constantly hanging over their shoulder? She could run away from the trailer park and her family, but could she ever escape the memories? They weren't things you could hide from, only suppress, and suppression wasn't something she was good at.

She sat outside and enjoyed the peace and quiet until she heard the bedroom door open. She looked behind her just as the front door opened and her mother stepped outside. She looked surprised to see Mona there, but quickly smiled instead.

"You're up early," her mother told her, closing the door behind her. Mona moved as close to the rail as she could, so there would be enough room on the mobile home steps for both of them.

Her mama sat down and sighed as she closed her eyes. Mona took the chance to look at her face. She thought her mama was pretty, but she looked tired. Older than what she was. There weren't any pictures of her before she gave birth to Mona and

Beau, but those earliest ones showed a woman that was beautiful, not pretty. She could have been more than just their mama and a wife, but she chose this life.

It hadn't been kind to her. She didn't have smile lines and crow's feet because of joy. The lines in her face were caused from pain and misery. She rarely smiled anymore. Even in church, the one thing Mona was convinced brought her joy, didn't make her smile. It made her cold. Everything about her mama felt cold, like she was made of ice. One hard blow and she'd break. She couldn't have warmth without disappearing completely.

"I'll be glad when summer is over. This heat is ridiculous," Mama said. She looked over at Mona. She reached out and touched a strand of her hair, pulling at the curl with her finger. "Having all this hair isn't nice when it's so hot and humid. We'll both be frizzy before the day is over."

Mama never let her cut her hair. Mama never cut hers either, and since Birdie had moved in, her hair had never seen a pair of scissors either. A woman's hair was her glory. This was from the Bible and something Mama lived by religiously. At this point, Mona wasn't sure how long her mama's hair was because she kept it always braided and in a bun. In her oldest photos, her hair had been to her shoulders. Mona guessed that was the last time she had ever cut it.

Mona's hair was now to her butt. She usually kept it in a braid, because in the Alabama heat, it would get hot and wild fast. She didn't like buns or ponytails though. They gave her headaches.

But sometimes, when she was alone, she let it loose. Like now, in the morning breeze, she liked the feeling of letting her hair down. Let it blow and move along her back. Let it be wild and free.

Her mama let go of her hair and looked out across the trailer park again. Mona waited for her next sentence. Mama couldn't sit and enjoy the silence. She always had to have noise and Mona didn't like it. She preferred the silence. She longed for it.

She heard more movement and her mama turned around. She sighed in defeat. "Sounds like your daddy is up. Let's make breakfast," she told her, smacking her thighs and standing up. Mona stood up behind her and followed her inside.

They started on breakfast while her daddy watched the morning news. They were the only three awake because of it being summer. Beau, Clyde, and Birdie could sleep in for a while because there wasn't any school. Mona could too, but early mornings were her only time fully alone.

Mona washed the dishes after they finished her daddy's eggs, grits, and toast. He and Mama ate in the living room, but Mona didn't have an appetite. She rarely did in the mornings, but this morning particularly. She had nervous twinges in her stomach, not only from knowing where she was going, but also from trying to find an excuse for why she was gone again.

When she was done with the dishes, she walked back into the living room and sat down. They watched the rest of the news and then Daddy got up to get ready for work. Mama was already dressed and pulled out her sewing machine. Mama didn't leave much unless it was for church things, but she'd sew and mend clothes for people for extra cash. Sometimes, Mona would help, but not today.

"Is it okay if I go to Owen's house?" she asked.

"You gonna be spending time with that boy today?"

Mona shook her head. "His mama wanted me to babysit today. Owen won't be there until later," she told her, which was true. Minus the babysitting part.

"Go tell your daddy. But tomorrow, I need you here."

"Yes, ma'am."

Mona walked into the bedroom with her father and stood in the doorway. He noticed her right away and raised a brow. "What is it, Mona?"

"Mama said to ask you if it was okay for me to go over to Owen's house. He won't be there until after work, but his mama needed me to babysit today," she told him.

"What time will you be home?"

"Before five at the latest."

He looked her over. Mona was sure he was examining her outfit, but Mona hadn't dressed yet. Her hair was pulled back to cook, but that was it. He wouldn't get his reassurance from how she looked now.

But he sighed and finished putting on his work boots. "Go

ahead. Just be back before five or you won't be walking anywhere for a while," he warned her.

"Yes sir," Mona told him and left the room. She walked into the back half of the trailer and found some clothes. She went into the bathroom, brushed her teeth, and braided her hair. She changed into a white T-shirt and a knee length denim skirt. She hated her clothes. Not because she was fashionable or desired to be, but because it was the only thing she was allowed to wear.

Maybe 'allowed' was too strong. It was the only thing she could wear because it was the only clothes she owned. Her closet only had clothes from the church, donated there by older devout Pentecostal ladies. They only wore T-shirts and denim skirts, so the clothes they gave away were the same. Even the shoes: they were always white tennis shoes. Only the brand changed. But they all looked the same.

This was one of the few things she wouldn't devote much time to. They were just clothes. Just shoes. She didn't want to stand out or be noticed anyway.

And most days, that was enough. But some days, like today, she couldn't help but see the clothes for what they were.

A uniform.

She walked out of the bathroom and made her bed. She cleaned her side of things before grabbing her backpack. Daddy was already gone, and Mama had the TV on trash talk shows. Mona gave her a kiss on the cheek and left the house. She walked through the trailer park, the sun having risen and casting a bright light on everything now.

The park was dead. No one had flowers or any signs of life outside their trailers. Cars were parked, some porch lights were still on, but there was nothing else that gave off a sign that there was life, real, vibrant life inside. Everyone's yard looked like a mess except for the truck driver and the old woman. One because he was never home, including now, and the other because of age. She had no reason to leave her house most days to make a mess in her yard.

Once she was outside the trailer park, Mona pulled her backpack off. She searched through to find the piece of paper Jill had written the address on. She didn't know exactly where it was, but things weren't so big that she couldn't figure it out. She'd just ask someone the street name and find her way there.

She got on her bike and rode into town. She stopped at the gas station, bought a bottle of water, and asked the cashier about the street. The cashier didn't know, but she pulled it up on an app on her phone. She showed it to Mona and Mona found a street she knew that was close to it. She memorized the other street names after and even drew part of it on a piece of paper before getting on her bike and heading out.

The location was at the edge of the county line. It was deep into the woods, but Mona expected that. She doubted the woman behind it wanted to have a location that was easy to find. If someone ever ratted her out, she'd be screwed.

As she rode her bike, Mona wondered if she should feel more apprehensive than she did. The day before, fear had wracked her brain. Guilt too. But today, she wasn't feeling much of that. In fact, a burst of indignation was coming over her instead.

She wasn't going to carry this baby. Religion, guilt, fear, none of it was stronger than the growing hatred she felt for her situation. The fetus wasn't responsible for that, but it was the result. It was a chain, a lock bound to keep her where she was forever. And though most of her reasons for not wanting the baby were selfish and painful, she *would not* bring this child into the world she lived in. *That* was a mercy to her unborn baby.

And if God knew any mercy, he would understand her choices. Mona had to believe that.

Because if she didn't believe that, if she chose to believe that God would hate her and send her to Hell for aborting the fetus inside her even after knowing her reasons, she wasn't sure she could still love Him. It wouldn't matter whether He loved or forgave her. She wasn't sure she could feel anything for someone that would think it was better for that child to be born, knowing everything that He knew.

And how could she be okay with someone that thought it was okay for her to have that child? For Mona to give birth to someone she would never be able to love?

She couldn't consider any other option. She'd never be able to hide a pregnancy. She would have to tell her parents and that would end one of two ways. She'd either be kicked out or punished. If she was kicked out, she'd be back in Beau's grips, exactly where he wanted her to be, desperate and hopeless.

If she was punished, she'd be forced to carry and keep the baby. Adoption would not be an option, no matter what the circumstances were. Her parents would consider that as part of her punishment as well. To care for the thing she had laid down and spread her legs to get.

And she would be stuck. Stuck the same exact way she was now.

Abortion was her only answer. Staring at the shack she rode up to, she realized this was the only place that could help her now. This rickety little mobile home in the middle of nowhere was the only place that could offer her the help she needed.

Mona put the kickstand down on her bike and walked up to the door. She found herself hesitant to knock, but not because of what she was there to do.

She didn't know this person. They could be horrible. This could all be some awful set up. And if not, she was faced with someone that might want to know why she was there. Know the story.

Mona wasn't ready for anyone to know the story.

She didn't want anyone to ever know.

Reaching forward to knock on the door was a struggle, but she did it. She knocked and waited, feeling more and more antsy in the time it took for someone to come to the door. When they did, they didn't open it. A rectangle opened from the other side to show it was a small door itself. The eyes behind it were dark and tired. The voice that came out was annoyed.

"Who are you?"

Mona licked her lips. "Mona. Jill from the clinic- "

The door closed. Mona felt worried that she had said something wrong, but the sounds of locks unlocking quashed those fears. The door opened and the woman in front of it moved to allow Mona entry.

"Get in," she ordered. Her voice let Mona know she didn't want any nonsense. What she said was what she expected right then.

Mona walked in and the woman closed the door behind her. Mona didn't know what she expected, but a kitchen full of kids coloring was not it. They each looked up at her as she stood there, and Mona felt very aware of how she looked to them.

"Kara and Casey, get my things. Follow me," she instructed and began to walk toward the other end of the trailer. Mona followed quickly behind her as the two girls she assumed were Kara and Casey stood and went to the other half.

The woman led her into a bathroom. At least, Mona assumed that was what it once was. The sink was still there, but the toilet and bathtub were missing now. There was a surgical table at the end now. It had stirrups for your feet and looked adjustable, but it did not look comfortable. It looked like a torture device.

There was a sickening lurch in her stomach. The room was cold.

It made things worse. The walls didn't fit right with the cold steel of everything else.

Mona stared at the wagon wheel wallpaper and decided she didn't like it. She didn't like any of it.

"Change into the gown on the bed and then get up there. I'll be back in just a minute," the woman said. She didn't wait for Mona to say or do anything. She left the door before Mona could even turn to look at her.

The room felt so small. It lacked personality. There was no warmth, not even within her own body. She felt just as cold and distant as everything around her. Everything was so metallic. It gave no comfort, peace. There was nothing here to judge or care for her, and in some ways, that was worse.

She stripped her clothes off and folded them. She put on the gown and got onto the bed. It was freezing beneath her. Her brain tried to focus on that instead. On the feelings around her rather than the process she was about to go through.

She hoped the process would be quick. She didn't want to lay there and think about it for too long. All her nerves were dancing beneath her skin, making her feel like she was being shocked. She couldn't relax. It seemed like she might forget how to breathe if she thought about it for too long.

The woman came back in the room dressed differently. She was wearing a paper dress over her clothes. It was like the one Mona was wearing now.

The two girls came in behind her with two baskets and cleaning supplies. They didn't stay in the room. They left the stuff and walked back out, closing the door behind them. Mona preferred that. They were too young to know about any of this. Too young to witness it.

"Lay back and put your feet in the stirrups."

The woman was stern. Cold, like Mama. But there was a difference to her coldness. She was trying to detach herself rather than be cruel. Mona could respect that.

Even if it did nothing to help her.

Mona did as she was told and stared up at the ceiling. It was a popcorned ceiling, just like at home. Mona tried to focus on the grooves and patterns instead of the woman between her legs. If she focused too long on any one thing, she feared she'd start to cry. Or that she'd get scared and leave.

Out of everything, she couldn't do that.

"People feel different things. Some say it's painful, some not so much. I'll give you a shot to numb it, but you'll still feel it to an extent. You don't have any second thoughts before I start, do you?"

Did she?

Mona searched her brain. She searched her heart. She found she didn't have any reservations about having the abortion. No second thoughts. No remorse. That scared her in a lot of ways. Shouldn't she? She'd been taught this was a baby growing inside her. A living, breathing child. Shouldn't there be a little reservation about killing it?

She just wanted to get it over with.

"No, ma'am."

The woman looked at her and Mona saw something in her eyes that she quickly masked. Not pity, but a sadness. Whether she was sad over the circumstances or Mona's decision, she wasn't sure, and she wouldn't ask.

"Okay, just relax. I'm just going to examine you first."

Mona wanted to relax, but she felt so vulnerable. It was bringing back images to her head that she had been pushing away for weeks now. Images she tried to forget completely of being spread open and exposed. Him there, him telling her to relax, enjoy it. Him constantly in her ear, trying to make her enjoy herself. Memories she wanted to force away for the rest of her life.

She couldn't force them away.

"I'm going to insert a tool to see better, so you'll feel something cold and hard."

And she did feel it. But it wasn't a surgical tool that came to Mona's mind as she did it.

It was him. She could feel him inside her again. Moving slowly at first, staring down at her, careful to keep her stare so he could see it. Control. Ownership. Mona didn't have a choice. No options in this or anything. She was his. Always had been.

Once he got what he wanted, he was quicker. Rougher, even. She cried, but it did nothing to deter him. It made him go harder, take what was his without remorse. He'd forced this thing into her without remorse, but she was supposed to feel remorse for getting it out of her.

It was unfair.

It was painful.

She hated him.

She hated herself.

She felt the needle and realized she hadn't been able to hear the woman. She had been squeezing her eyes closed so tightly that when she opened them, black spots bounced everywhere in front of her. They were even on the woman as she looked at Mona.

"Is everything okay?" she asked, but Mona couldn't really answer that.

She could only feel everything. Feel him inside her again. Feel him raping her. Feel him impregnating her. Feeling him take that control from her over and over again. Trapping her. Keeping her glued right where she was forever.

When she did speak, she couldn't control the high pitched sound to her voice. The stress. The pain.

"No! I just want it out of me."

"Okay, I'll remove the tool and we- "

"Not that. The thing inside me. The fetus, his baby, whatever it is. I just want it out of me," Mona cried.

And she really cried. She could feel every single tear as it fell down her cheek. And her emotions were everywhere. Once they started, she couldn't get them to stop. She hadn't realized how much she had been holding in until she let it all go.

She hadn't realized how much of her pain wasn't linked to the baby inside her at all. None of her guilt or shame had to do with getting rid of his baby, but everything to do with how she had been impregnated in the first place.

The woman in the room touched her hand. Mona looked at her and saw a calmness on her face. "Calm down, baby girl. I know this is uncomfortable, but I will get it out of you. You just have to calm down first, okay?"

Mona nodded.

"The numbing should be going into effect now. You tell me when you're ready. It'll take a few minutes and it'll be uncomfortable, but we can start any time. I just need you calm," she said.

Mona took in a deep breath. She wiped her eyes. "I'm sorry."

"Don't apologize. You're not the first girl to cry in front of me."

And Mona could tell that was true. Truer than even that woman wanted to admit. She had probably seen hundreds of girls, all with their own stories, their own pains, and she just had to do the procedure and send them on their way.

Maybe that was why she hadn't shown much emotion when Mona had called. Or even when she showed up. Maybe being cold and aloof was a coping strategy for her too. It must be hard to deal with someone else's pain and shame. Mona didn't know how many girls she had helped, but even one had to be something that stuck with you.

"I'm okay now."

"Okay. You tell me if you want me to stop."

But Mona wouldn't. No matter what, she would grin and bear it now. She would sit through it no matter how painful it was. Emotionally or physically.

And it was both.

The emotional she could shut off. She could keep her mind focused on the physical pain to get through it. Divert it to other things. Focus on the end result.

The physical was a little more difficult to bear. The numbing shot didn't feel like it had done anything. She couldn't be fully sure if most of the pain was real or just her overreacting, thinking there was pain and in doing so, creating actual pain.

But she didn't cry again. She laid there and counted. Stared at the ceiling and focused on it. Counted each groove above her head. Counted the wagon wheels on the walls. Thought about how warm the bed was now.

She kept her mind on anything else until the woman stood and Mona felt everything removed.

"I want you to lay here for a little bit. When you sit up, be slow. I'm going to leave a maxi pad in here for you to put on too. You'll probably be cramping and bleeding for a while. Shouldn't be much worse than your regular period." The woman stopped. She stopped herself from thinking whatever was on her mind and went back into her explanation. "Just take ibuprofen for the cramps. Try to take it easy."

Mona nodded.

"Get dressed when you feel capable. Feel free to lay there if you need to. I'll be in the kitchen if you need anything."

And then she was gone. Mona decided to lay there for a few minutes before sitting up. She thought about what it looked like. The fetus. The baby. The clump of cells. If she saw it, would she feel guilty? Would it make her feel justified? Was there a way for her to feel okay with this? Maybe it was better to not know. Maybe it was even better for her to feel guilt. It had to be better than feeling absolutely nothing.

She didn't feel lightheaded, so she moved from the bed. When she took off the gown, she looked at her stomach. There was no difference on the outside, but she felt different. She ran her hand over her belly and felt relief wash over her.

No more heartbeats.

She was free. She found she could look at her body for the first time in weeks without feeling horrified. She was able to appreciate that it was gone. It was over with now. That one lock was broken. The chain gone. He didn't have this control over her now.

Mona finished getting dressed and made sure to put on the pad the woman had given her. She grabbed her things and walked out the door and down the hall. The woman was sitting in the kitchen, just as she had said. She stood when Mona came in and walked to the door.

Mona made her way there. "Do I pay you or something?" Mona asked, her voice low.

The woman opened the door and shook her head. "I don't charge the girls Jill sends. You're good," she told her.

Mona walked out the door and onto the porch. She didn't stop to say goodbye or anything like that. She got the feeling that the woman wanted her to be gone as quickly as possible. She didn't even blame her for that. She understood.

Until she spoke.

"How old are you?" she asked, catching Mona off-guard.

She stopped at the rails and looked down. She didn't feel comfortable meeting her eyes. "Fifteen," she answered, suddenly feeling very ashamed of her age.

"You look even younger," the woman said. "Babies shouldn't have babies. Don't feel guilty. Don't be ashamed. I'm only sorry I can't hurt him the way he hurt you."

Mona looked up. She caught a knowing gaze. A woman that understood exactly what had happened. No judgment, only sympathy. Mona wanted to cry.

It was the first time she had ever felt seen in her entire life.

"Take care of yourself, Mona," the woman told her. She closed the door behind her, and Mona listened as she locked each lock again. She never wanted to leave that spot.

She wasn't even sure what time it was now. The only thing she knew was that she was hurting, and it was a long way back to town. She wanted to get to Owen's house, and she was hoping he might drive her back home. She wasn't even sure if she could ride her bike at this point.

Mona started walking with her bike, back the same way she had come. She was already feeling the effects that the lady had told her about. She was cramping like she was having a period. They weren't the worst that she had ever experienced, but they were still noticeable. They were still painful. Cramps always were.

But the worst part was still the procedure itself. Because all those things that she had tried to push away and force back since they had happened had risen to the surface. And now all she could do was think about them. Remember them. Remember her part in them.

No one had ever shown her the same sympathy that this stranger had. Maybe because Mona would never tell anyone. She would never hurt him like that. Even though it would be justified, she would never hurt him the way he hurt her. Despite the feelings that she had for every single man in her life, she would never hurt anyone the way that he had hurt her. Because that would make her a bad person. Just as awful and mean as they were.

Wouldn't it?

Mona didn't want to think about it. She wanted to shove it down again. Forget it ever happened. Now that she was rid of the result of her-

Rape

-shame, she could move on. It was possible for her to go about her normal life now. She didn't have anything to keep her feeling guilty or shamed about. She didn't have to worry about concealing a pregnancy. It was gone. And no one would ever know what she had done. No one would ever have to know what had happened. She had no reason to fear anyone. She had no reason for anyone to hold anything above her head. To take her control again.

Mona wasn't too far away from the trailer when she heard a truck coming up behind her. She moved to the side of the road, as was obligatory, and then turned around to make sure she could see who was coming. She didn't immediately recognize the truck until the driver stuck his head out and called to her.

"Hey, moan, moan, moan, Mona!" Jerry Cardwell called from his driver's seat. Jerry was bad enough, but when he pulled up beside her, she realized that if Jerry was driving around, her brother Beau was with him.

Sitting in the passenger seat was her twin brother. And though his friend was being rude as usual, she could see the wheels turning inside his head.

"What are you doing out here?" he asked her.

Mona didn't like the accusatory way he asked her. Beau might have been a lot of things, but he was not stupid. And being her twin, she guessed that gave him even more reason to see when something wasn't right with her.

"I had an errand to run for Owen's mom," she told him as she walked. She never stopped walking. She didn't want to talk to them, but she knew that Jerry wasn't going to drive away until he felt ready.

"How is Owen? You still dating that loser?" Jerry asked.

Her brother was twisted, and that meant that his friends were usually equally as bad. Mona didn't know why, but ever since Beau started hanging out with Jerry, Jerry had always made it his mission to talk to her. He went out of his way to find excuses to speak to Mona. When she started dating Owen, he found reasons to bring his name into the conversation. Usually, to call him some bad name.

Once, Beau had even pointed this out. But his reasonings were that it was her fault. And that she was doing it on purpose. Because his exact words to her were that she needed to stop flirting with his friend. That he didn't want Mona trying to have sex with his friends and being a slut.

Mona knew that she had no interest in Jerry. And she knew she hadn't intentionally done anything to make Jerry like her. But she knew that it was still her fault, nonetheless. She'd grown up hearing how it was always her fault for the thoughts of men.

Because she was a woman. Because women couldn't stop themselves from being a temptation to men. Because men lacked self-control. That was what Daddy told her. Men couldn't help themselves when they were around a pretty girl. They were incapable of resisting those urges. That was their curse for Adam doing what Eve said. Men no longer had any self-control.

Mona didn't understand. She was able to control herself. In fact, it wasn't even hard.

But she was a woman. And, they didn't have the same impulses as a man. Even Mama and Birdie, they never seemed to struggle. She had never heard either one of them talk about how they had to restrain themselves with any man. They just kept their heads down and went about their business.

And who was Mona to question any of it? Because her parents were supposed to know right and wrong. They were supposed to have the answers. And she was supposed to honor her father and mother, to respect them. Because no matter what was said or what was done, they would always be right.

This is what the Bible said.

"Of course, you stupid ingrate," Beau answered. "Now just drive."

"You need us to give you a ride back?" Jerry asked her.

Mona took one look at Beau's face and knew her answer had been decided before she even had to make it.

"No. I'm okay."

But she wasn't okay. And honestly, if it hadn't been Jerry, if it had been someone else, a woman, Mona might have considered hitching a ride. Because the last thing she wanted to do was walk all the way back into town. To walk to Owen's house. Last thing she wanted to do was even to get on her bike.

She just wanted to go home and sleep, but that wasn't going to happen either. She couldn't go home just yet. Because if she did, her mom would want to know why. And Mona knew that she could tell her that she started her period, and her cramps were really bad, but that would end up being just as much of an issue.

Because her mom would tell her dad that she had come home early and it was because of her period, and her dad would tell her that that was the curse she had to bear as a woman and when you gave someone your word you were supposed to keep it.

If Mona were lucky, that would be all that was said. However, Mona knew better. He would end up grabbing his belt or making her go outside and get a stick so that he could hit her with the switch.

Because punishment was always needed.

That was how you learned.

And now that her brother had seen her running errands for Owen's mom, she felt that it was best to head straight there and just grin and bear it. Go and actually help Carrie with her kids, even though she hadn't asked her to.

It wasn't like it would be a surprise. Carrie seemed to like when Mona would come over and help her with the kids. Maybe it was the reason she didn't care too much about her son dating someone she deemed a Bible thumper. She had a built-in babysitter sometimes.

"You sure, Mona? You look like you're hurting," Jerry said. The sincerity that suddenly flooded his voice was almost touching. It was unlike Jerry to sound concerned about her. It was unlike anyone to be concerned for her.

Mona looked over and she realized that Beau was now looking at her even harder. Like he was realizing that Jerry was right about something. That this something was worth looking into.

"He's right. Want us to give you a ride to Owen's?" Beau asked.

But she didn't trust him any farther than she could see him. And even then, she knew that Beau couldn't be trusted because you would never fully know what was going on inside his head.

"No. I'm okay."

"Fine," Beau answered. "Suit yourself. Let's get going, Jerry."

Mona kept walking, but even over the loud exhaust, she could hear Jerry when he sighed in defeat. Maybe, for even a moment, he had concern for her. Real, genuine concern that stemmed beyond his own selfish existence.

"See ya, Mona," he said.

Mona didn't acknowledge him. He revved his truck up and sped past her, but she saw Beau's face in the rearview mirror. Even as they got further away, she could see the trouble brewing in his mind.

Even now, she wasn't safe.

Chapter Three

Galatians 5:19

The acts of the flesh are obvious: sexual immorality, impurity, and debauchery.

The walk to Owen's house was long and painful. In truth, the last thing she wanted was to actually help Carrie with the kids. It would only be for a couple of hours, but Mona just wanted to rest. She'd give anything to find a bed and lay down. Sleep away the emotional and physical toll she felt on her body.

She was surprised when she saw Owen's truck in the yard. That was better. With Owen there, she could hang out with him. Maybe she could get some rest, just relax and wait for him to take her home.

She knocked on the door and Carrie answered. She grinned. "Here to see my boy?" she asked.

"Yes, ma'am," Mona answered.

"Good. Owen!" Carried called out, moving for Mona to come inside. "Your girlfriend is here!"

Carrie left her, so Mona shut the door and walked the rest of the way in. Owen came out of the living room and smiled as he walked to her.

"Hey, gorgeous. I didn't know you were coming by today," he said.

"I'm going to be helping Mama tomorrow, so I figured I'd drop by today and hang out," she said. She was honestly surprised at how easily lies were coming to her now. Perhaps that was the sin settling in. She had opened the doorway and now they all would begin to infiltrate her soul.

He took her by her hand and started toward his bedroom. Mona was actually relieved. If she had to stay in the living room with his brothers, she might lose her mind. Especially with the way she felt.

They walked into his bedroom where Jimmy was playing with his toy cars, making them crash loudly into each other.

"Get out, Jimmy," Owen ordered.

When Jimmy looked up, Mona knew the words that would come from his mouth before he said them. "It's my room too!" he whined.

"Come on. Not today," Owen complained. "I'll give you ten bucks to leave us alone."

Jimmy stood, gathered his toys, and stood in front of Owen with his hand out. Owen handed him the money and watched him leave the room. Her boyfriend closed the door behind him.

Mona wasn't so sure she liked that. Usually, Owen closed the door when he wanted to make out or try to have sex with her. Mona didn't like feeling locked in, and she definitely didn't want to make out with Owen today. All she wanted to do was rest.

"I thought you had to work today?" Mona asked, sitting down on the bed as Owen walked to his TV and turned it on. He flipped through before finally landing on a music channel and shrugging.

"Got off early. Wasn't much to do."

Owen laid on the bed and stretched out, throwing his hand behind his neck and relaxing. He looked at Mona and motioned his head for her to lay next to him, which she did. She crawled up beside him and rested her head against his chest and stared at the TV.

Moments like these were what she craved. Intimacy. Safety. She longed for someone to hold her close and just enjoy her presence. To just feel secure and relax.

To feel loved.

She couldn't get all those things from Owen, but she could get the action. The feel of a body against her, a soft embrace, a strong and steady hand. She could feel what that might be like with Owen, but never get the emotional side.

She didn't love him.

In all honesty, she knew he didn't love her either. She was just there. She was available. There wasn't any love from him, not really. Nothing about her that made him want and need only her. What he got from her, he could get from any girl. There was no way he'd ever be able to love her.

How could you love someone you didn't even know?

Not that it was his fault. Even Mona didn't know who she was. No one did. And she felt like she knew who he was, and she didn't love him. He wasn't her person. He was just available.

Then again, how could she ever know if she could love him if she never pushed to know him more than she did now? She wouldn't allow herself to love him. Couldn't.

"What's got you out and about today?" he asked her.

"Nothing. I was going to see if your mom needed my help with the kids."

"She always needs help," Owen told her. "The woman can't do anything for herself. She can't even pay her own bills. That's the only reason she keeps that prick around."

Mona knew he was referring to his mother's current boyfriend. Owen didn't like him and often referred to him only as a 'prick'. Mona couldn't even remember what his real name was. Not only because Owen referred to him as a prick but because he referred to all of them like that, and Carrie wasn't known for staying with a man too long. Carrie didn't make connections with men. She just used them for what she needed.

Maybe Mona was doing the same thing.

She wished that she could tell Owen what she had really done that day. She wished that they were loving rather than just together. She wished that he was her person. That he was someone that she could confide in, really confide in. She wished she could tell him everything.

How she felt.

What she'd been through.

When she looked at Owen, she didn't see a safe place. She didn't feel trust. He couldn't handle all that was dark, all the ugly that came with her life.

The truth of the matter was, without love, at the first signs of ugliness that he would see in her, he would leave. Because that was what love did. It helped make the ugly, bad, and painful easier to bear. It made all of those things that most people couldn't handle able to be handled. It gave a reason for forgiveness. For grace.

But she didn't have that with Owen. And she would never have that with Owen. In the end, it was better to keep it all to herself. To hide yet another part of who she was for someone else.

Mona was used to that.

Owen was still holding her, but she could have guessed, if she really wanted to, that holding her was not the only thing he wanted to do. It was never the only thing he wanted to do. Owen wanted to go further. He always wanted to go further. And Mona didn't.

Truth was, Mona wasn't sure if she ever wanted to go further with anyone. All those feelings and attractions that she had been warned that she would have for so many years, Mona just didn't have them. She wasn't sure if that was because of the warnings or if maybe something was wrong with her. It wasn't like she was attracted to girls. Her parents and Pastor Steve seemed to think that was the absolute worst that a person could do. To be gay was a sin, they said.

Mona just didn't feel an attraction to anyone. But Paul hadn't married in the Bible. And he said that it was better devote your life to Christ than to get married.

But Mona was a woman. And things were always different for women. Because the Bible said that she was meant to be a wife. To be submissive, to honor and obey her husband. To be silent. So, if a man wanted to marry her, as long as he was a God-fearing man and saved by the blood of Christ, Mona would guess that she wouldn't have much of a choice in whether she wanted to be married or not.

Owen was reaching for her now. Different than the comforting and safe hold that she had wanted. His hand was moving down. Moving to the hem of her shirt and moving it up to touch her skin. She didn't want to lose the comforting embrace that she had gotten moments before. She tried to be quiet because of that.

But when it became apparent that he was not going to just stop with touching her, she realized she had to say something.

"Owen, stop."

Owen's hands moved forward. It was on her belly now. She knew that he was moving toward her panties. Part of her wondered if she should let him move there. She wouldn't even have to give him an excuse this time. If he moved forward enough and touch the pad that she was wearing or happened to touch blood if he went inside, she doubted he would want any after that. He'd probably even be mad at her that she hadn't told him.

Instead, she cramped when his hand touched the lower part of her stomach and she moved from him. She turned to the other side and cupped her stomach as she took in a deep breath. She barely heard Owen's disappointment through her own stab of pain.

"I swear, Mona," Owen huffed. She could tell that he was mad before she even turned around. But when she did turn around, she could see that he was very mad.

There was something that seemed to rise up in her too. She was in pain. Physical and emotional pain, and he was angry at her? Mad because she wouldn't let him rub her in a sad attempt to turn her on? How selfish, she thought.

How inconsiderate.

"I'm on my period," Mona said with a small voice. Any other time, she might not have said anything. She was good at being quiet until they told her what she had done wrong. But this time she felt that she had an excuse. A very valid excuse.

"And every other day of the month?" Owen asked. "You know, we've been together now for a few months. Most other couples have been together even shorter than we have and are already having sex whenever they want. I've tried to keep in mind that you go to church, and you believe in all that God stuff, but it ain't even about that. You just don't want to have sex with me. Not because of God or because of your parents or anything like that. You don't want to have sex with *me*."

He wasn't wrong. Mona didn't want to have sex with him. She didn't want to have sex with anyone. She was only fifteen and she was already sick and tired of all the things that came along with sexuality. Tired of being told every Sunday that sex before marriage would send her to hell. Tired of being told that if a man lusted after her that it was her fault. Just tired of being an object. Whether it was in church or with the godless heathen, as her parents like to call Owen. It seemed like no matter what they believed, it was the same everywhere.

Men couldn't be trusted.

But despite this revelation, she didn't want to argue with Owen today. She just wanted to relax and enjoy him. Give herself time to recuperate before she had to go home.

She tried to think of something that she could say that would calm him down. She couldn't think of anything right off and everything she thought of sounded like just another argument to her. She could hear each rebuttal he would make with everything that crossed her mind. She just wanted to minimize the damage.

But her silence didn't help either. Owen got up from the bed and rolled his eyes. "You can't even deny it," he told her. "I would just accept it if you denied it. But you can't. I don't even know why we are dating at all."

"Because I love you," Mona said. The words weren't completely true. She suspected that he knew that. But they were the words that he wanted to hear. She knew that. They just weren't enough.

"If you loved me, you would have sex with me sometimes. It's what people do in love," Owen said.

Mona wasn't sure what caused the snap inside of her. Never in her life had she ever been assertive. She couldn't even say that she had ever been emotional in an outward way. But something about what he said elicited a response from her that she was not used to.

Anger.

"So, it's only love if we have sex? Sex equals love and that's all that I'm good for when it comes to you and anyone else, right?" she asked him. She also stood up from the bed. She was feeling indignant. Her cheeks felt hot. Her neck was burning. Mona wasn't used to this emotion.

And when Owen spun around on her, that emotion seemed to slow down a little. Because she saw the same look that she had seen constantly on her dad's face. A look her brother shared with her all the time. The righteous fury. Because how dare she question anything he said.

It was the shock that she didn't understand as much. Because she had never spoken up against anyone else. Their anger was always from something else. Her forgetfulness, her mistakes, her existence. This was because she spoke up. She spoke out. He hadn't expected her to. Like everyone else, Owen expected her to submit and beg for his forgiveness. He had hoped to send her on a guilt trip and get his way.

"Don't turn this around on me. You know what I mean," he told her.

Mona grabbed her bag. "You're right. I know exactly what you mean," she told him.

Owen's temper flared. "Oh, and you think you just know everything, don't you? You're just-…"

"What?" Mona asked. "A prude? A tease? Spiteful? Mean? What word do you want to use to make me feel bad about not screwing you, Owen?"

Owen crossed the room and shoved her against the door. She watched him lift his hand to hit her, but she didn't flinch. This was nothing new. Never from Owen, but she was used to being struck. Pushed. Yelled at.

It was just that, usually, she didn't feel she had done anything to deserve it.

This time, she might understand being struck. She spoke out. She snapped at him. If he hit her, she figured this was as good a reason as any. Owen might as well join the list. Mona had no reason to be scared of that. She expected it would happen sooner or later. Why would she ever believe that her relationship with Owen would be any different than her relationship with any other man?

But Owen didn't hit her. He stopped. Mona kept his eyes, confused at what was going through his mind. Why he was misdirecting his anger into the wall instead, choosing to bang his fist against it. He hit the wall so hard that a picture in the hallway fell and shattered outside his door.

But he didn't hit her.

Mona would swear that it shocked both of them. Because she did expect him to hit her. And maybe he had expected to see fear in her eyes. And neither one happening managed to confuse them both.

Not being afraid confused Mona.

It seemed that not hitting her confused Owen too.

"What the hell is going on in there?" Carrie's voice yelled. It sounded like she was at the end of the hallway. "Why is my picture broken?"

Her footsteps were moving closer to the room. Owen moved away from Mona and turned his back on her. Mona wasn't sure what was going on in his head until he said, "You need to leave."

With her anger fading, she felt the need to apologize. She said the word, but it didn't seem to affect Owen. It didn't change his mind about her leaving either. He just shook his head and turned around to look at her.

There was remorse on his face. Mona hadn't expected to see it there. She didn't know what she expected to see from Owen at all, but this was not it.

"Just go home," he said.

"But…"

"We'll talk."

Mona wasn't sure what that meant. She wasn't sure when he meant it either. But he wanted her to leave, and she now had to walk back home. It was best to just do what he said and leave.

She opened his bedroom door and was almost face to face with Carrie. She didn't stop to speak to her. She looked away as quickly as possible, shamefully, and kept walking, moving past Carrie even when she said her name. Mona kept walking until she was out the door and headed to the road. She could hear Carrie yelling behind her, yelling at Owen, but she didn't stop. Maybe Owen wanted her to leave before his mom started yelling at him. Maybe it was a kindness.

Either way, she was heading home. She had hoped Owen might drive her there, but that wasn't happening. And now she was in some serious pain. All she wanted to do was stop and rest.

She looked at her watch. She had time to take it slow. She wouldn't stop walking, but she could take her time.

Taking her time only meant that she had more of it to think of

Owen now.

    She didn't understand what had happened. She had been dating Owen for four months. They had been partners for a science project. Mona liked science, but Owen hated school completely. However, while they worked on the project together, he seemed to try to like it. He helped and they ended up with a B plus.

    She had been truly shocked when he asked if she wanted to hang out. He was older than her. He'd been held back a grade, but Mona couldn't remember which one. He was notoriously considered a bad apple. She understood that he likely was only asking out of pity or curiosity. It wasn't a secret that she was a 'good girl'. That was either a turn on for him or something he felt sympathy about.

    She told him she couldn't date. He said he would come over. Mona suggested church instead and he agreed. He attended church with her, and Mona introduced him to her parents. Birdie was the only person that seemed to like him, and Mona was sure that was because she thought he was cute. Birdie liked any and all boys.

    He came over after that. But it was quickly made known that no one liked him, and Owen let her know he didn't like them either. Rather than deter her, it made Mona more determined to have a relationship with him. If he didn't like her family, she didn't have to worry about him being like them.

    But that wasn't how things worked. And time was making that more apparent. Owen wasn't any better than them just because he was different. He was just a different kind of bad. And maybe she had always known that, but it hadn't mattered. He was just a means to an end. Someone she was hoping would help her escape. But it was looking more and more like she was going to have to find a way to leave on her own.

Today though, today she had seen something different. A man behind the boy she didn't care to know. Someone with his own story. One she had never pried into just like he didn't pry into hers. They just hung out and watched TV. Or around his friends. They listened to music. They did things to distract them, and they didn't push to get to know each other. Not the real people they were rather than the personas they had around everyone. Neither of them was vulnerable with the other, but Mona hadn't realized that until today. Until she had looked at him stopping himself from hitting her.

There was so much she didn't know about him, and it was sitting on the surface. Someone with a past. Someone with feelings. Mona tended to forget that people around her could have emotions and feelings. She watched everyone around her be so distant, so self-absorbed, that she forgot they had emotions too. She forgot they were just as human as she was.

And she wondered if it was Nurture versus Nature again. That maybe she forgot people could feel because she often felt as if she felt nothing. As if she were numb and hollow. Just a shell moving through life. Because she didn't care if she hurt anyone's feelings. Not the people she was around day in and day out. She didn't care if she hurt them. She doubted she could. Was that something that came from being a Hill? Or was that something she adapted to from being raised by one?

She thought a lot about who she was. Who she would be. Because she didn't know who Mona Hill really was beneath her family. Without her family. Who was this girl that felt nothing?

That wasn't true. She felt a lot of things. She just didn't dwell on them. If she did, she wouldn't survive. She couldn't survive if she had outbursts like she did today. Crying or screaming, she'd be eaten alive by those around her. It was easier to shove that to the side and pretend she didn't feel anything at all. Pretend she was numb. Pretend she was okay until it was actually true. Until she didn't have to pretend anymore.

She was so tired of pretending.

She didn't pretend to hear the sound of someone yelling. She heard it clear as day. Something was going on beneath the bridge she was walking across, and it didn't sound pretty.

Mona walked to the edge of the wooden bridge and peered over. She could see a couple of guys moving at the bottom and a four-wheeler sitting on the muddy bank. It was possible that they were drunk, and just acting stupid. In any case, Mona knew it wasn't smart to make herself known. She needed to get away as quietly and quickly as possible.

Then she heard a dog yelp and a man's voice scream. Mona's entire body broke out in goosebumps. Were they hurting an animal? A poor, defenseless animal?

Beau liked to be cruel to animals. He and Clyde would sometimes take slingshots and hit the squirrels around the trailer. Not because the squirrels were being pests or damaging anything. Just because they liked to see them fall. Mona knew, for Beau anyway, he just liked to see them die.

He had killed their cat a long time ago. Mona guessed it wasn't really their cat, but she had snuck it home and fed it under the trailer. It stuck around for the food and Mona liked feeling the way it purred against her. She'd make excuses to go outside and hold it.

She had only been eight. When her daddy saw it, and saw how much she loved it, he didn't make a fit about it. Instead, he began to bring home cat food. It was really cheap, but Mona realized he was okay with her having the cat. She let it stay outside and would pay attention to it every chance she got.

Beau didn't like how much time she spent with it. He didn't like the attention it got from Mona. She could see him seething with jealousy every time she would play with it and not him.

She knew she needed to get it away from the house, but she loved it. Selfishly, she didn't want to make it leave. It was the only thing she had that was hers.

But one morning she went outside to feed it and it was laying in the yard with blood coming from the mouth. There was a bit of foam too. Their daddy said it looked like it had been poisoned, and that was the end of the conversation, but Mona knew who had killed it.

Beau stood on the porch and just stared at her. His eyes did all of his speaking, just like they did now. She knew he killed her cat. And his eyes told her he would do it again. To anything. Or anyone. If something took her away from him, he would kill it.

Maybe subconsciously, that was why she wasn't close to Owen. Because Beau would know if she was, and he would have an even bigger problem with Owen.

She wondered if Beau might be beneath the bridge. Maybe him and his friends were hurting an animal. If so, it was another good reason to run away now. But she didn't sense Beau around. Call it a Twin Thing, but she could usually tell when Beau was somewhere close.

If the dog hadn't yelped again, she might have walked away. Despite it all, her heart hurt with the sound, and she knew she wasn't capable of just walking away and leaving it there. The situation was dangerous, but honestly, Mona wasn't sure if she cared much.

Death didn't scare her.

Mona moved to the end of the bridge and looked down the path heading down to the creek. A bicycle was laying on its side and a backpack on the ground. All the contents were scattered about, and Mona could tell that most of it was clothes.

She moved slowly down the side until she could see what was

going on. There were four guys. Two were holding one by his arms against the ground and another one was tying the leash of the dog to the beams of the bridge. Its feet were still touching the ground, but if she didn't do something, they were going to strangle the dog.

Mona looked around for something she could use. She didn't want to risk making the situation worse, but she had to do something to distract them.

She wasn't sure what possessed her, but when she looked at the four-wheeler, she knew that was as good a distraction as any. She wanted to see if they were looking her way. When they weren't, she moved toward it. She put it in gear and pushed it toward the creek. When it started moving, she moved back to her spot, out of sight, and waited for it to make the sound of it going into the creek. She watched as the water helped it move and began to push it downstream.

"Jack! The four-wheeler!" one of them yelled.

"Well. get it!"

Mona moved closer to the bridge when one of them moved into the water. They tried to grab the four-wheeler, but the water was steady enough to keep it moving. He couldn't stop it and he fell into the water trying to get on it to start it.

"Dude, it's going downstream!" another one yelled.

The one that told them to get it, Jack, was the one to speak next. "Idiots. My dad is going to be pissed off if y'all mess that up!" he yelled at them. Mona heard something else splash and she peeked around to see the dog in the water. It quickly ran up onto the shore and away, but Mona could clearly see the two guys now and the other guy they had pinned.

The one that had been holding the dog walked up the guy, presumably the dog's owner, and knelt down. "That mutt bark at me again, and I'll kill it. Got that, hobo?" he asked. When he stood back up, he swung his foot back and kicked the guy on the ground hard. Mona even jumped back in fear. She covered her mouth and stayed perfectly still, hoping they hadn't seen her.

It wasn't until she saw the other boys run past her that she realized they didn't know she had been there at all. They went running down the creek after the four-wheeler and their friend. Mona waited until she couldn't see them anymore before coming out and rushing to the man's side.

"Are you okay?" she asked him, helping him to sit up. He wasn't paying any attention to her though. He was looking around.

"Biscuit? Where's Biscuit?" he asked, getting to his knees. "Biscuit! Come here, boy!"

"He ran off," Mona told him, realizing he was talking about the dog.

"Biscuit!"

Mona stood up and looked the direction the dog had run. She looked back at the man. "I'll see if I can find him. Wait here," she told him. She wasn't sure if the man said anything after she started running in the direction the dog did, but if he had, she didn't hear him.

She followed the paw prints in the sand, watching them disappear into a bunch of underbrush. Mona got down to her knees and peered into it. She knew the dog was spooked. Spooked dogs could turn on you in fear. Mona wanted to avoid scaring him too much if he was close by.

"Biscuit," she called softly.

She listened for movement. She called the name again and the dog finally moved. She could just see its eyes peering through the briars. Mona followed the eyes down to see the leash and that it was stuck.

Mona smiled and held out her hand to the dog. "Come here, boy. It's okay," she assured the dog.

She thought about reaching for the leash, but she didn't know the dog. She wasn't sure how he'd react to that, and she didn't want to be bitten.

Biscuit moved out of the briars more. He kept his eyes on her, but his demeanor wasn't untrusting. He was just scared. When he sniffed her hand, Mona scratched his nose softly. He moved closer to her without hesitation and began to pant.

"You poor baby. I won't hurt you," she told the dog.

She wasn't sure what a dog's comprehension level was or if they could just sense the good in people, but the dog seemed to trust her without much more than a few nose scratches. He tried to come closer to her, but his leash was caught in the underbrush.

Mona made the decision to trust the dog too. She moved her hand to the back of his ear and gave him more scratches. He seemed to like that and began to kick his back foot in pleasure. Mona smiled at the display and used the distraction to pull the leash toward her. It came loose easily, and the dog's demeanor didn't change.

"You're a sweet little boy, huh?" she asked the mutt. The only breed she could tell by looking at it was that its bloodline likely hadn't known a breed for a long time. He was big, fluffy, but his hair was coarse. He was a bunch of different shades, but there was a big white blotch on his face and chest. The rest of him would be considered brindle. His ears flopped over, his snout was long, and his paws were massive. He was a massive teddy bear and made his stance clear when he decided to attack her with kisses.

"Biscuit," a man's voice said. Mona turned to see the homeless man walking toward them. He was limping, but his backpack was on his shoulder, and he was pushing his bike toward them.

The dog bolted from her to the man without warning. Mona looked at them both and watched the dog search over his owner before jumping up to smother him in kisses too. It was obvious that the dog loved his owner very much. It was also obvious that the owner loved his dog too.

"Who's a good boy? You are," the man said, his rough voice going into a babyish tone as he showered the dog in love too.

Mona looked toward the underbrush again and saw she could

walk up that way to get back on the road. She started that way when the man stopped talking to the dog and decided to speak to her.

"I saw what you did back there," he said. "Thank you. From both me and Biscuit."

Mona felt uncomfortable with the words. She offered a small smile in her nervousness. "It was nothing."

He shook his head. "No, it was a lot. Poor Biscuit," he stopped, rubbing the top of his head. "Well, it's not worth even thinking about. He got spooked by the four-wheeler. They kept on until he barked at them and that's when they attacked us. I thought they were going to kill him."

Mona looked him over. "It looked like they were going to kill you both," she told him.

He looked at himself. "I guess they were. No one would care about a bum and his dog though," he confessed.

She knew exactly how that felt. If something were to happen to her, no one would care about another piece of trailer trash being gone. They likely wouldn't even notice. Her existence didn't matter to anyone but her.

"They stole some of my stuff," he said. When Mona looked up, he wasn't looking at her. He was looking at the dog and shifting his legs. "What money I had left for his dog food, my medicine. I don't know what I'm going to do now."

Mona wasn't sure why he looked so shifty telling her, but she reached into her pocket without hesitation. She had eighty dollars: money she had been sure she was going to give to the lady that performed her abortion. Money she had saved in secrecy from Carrie's random babysitting days for months. Originally, it was money to run away with. Then, an abortion fund. Now, it was his. She immediately handed it out to him.

"It's not much, but it's eighty dollars. It might help," she told him.

He looked at the money first. "Oh, you are kind. A fine Christian girl," he said, taking the money.

Mona stopped smiling, even though the smile had already been small. She wasn't sure if she liked being called that when her day had started with lies and an abortion. It only seemed to make her guilt more apparent to herself when he called her a Christian.

She swallowed hard and looked up to see he was looking at her. He was perfectly still now, but he looked as if he were having his own revelation. Something was going on in his head and Mona wasn't sure what it was.

She had been so willing to give trust to the dog, but she would never do that with a human being.

"I really need to be headed home," she told him. She began to move again, walking up the embankment and onto the road before she heard him behind her.

"Wait!" he yelled. She turned around the see him pushing his bike up the embankment.

She wasn't sure how she should feel and decided it was best if she got to her own bike. Just in case his intentions weren't good. She wasn't sure if she'd be able to ride it away fast, but she could throw it at him and try to run if he made any sketchy moves toward her. It was better to have something in plan.

But he was holding her money out to her. Mona narrowed her brows in confusion as he refused to look at her again.

"Take it back. I don't need it," he told her.

"But you said..."

"I lied," he said. Beneath his scruff, his cheeks seemed to be red. He looked ashamed and kept his eyes on the dog. "They didn't take my money and I would have just spent this on a bottle of Jim Beam. Biscuit has food in my backpack, and I've got my whole check of disability if he needs more."

Mona tilted her head. "Why are you telling me this?" she asked him.

When he looked up, he narrowed his own brows. "I don't know. Maybe because I'm hoping it'll help you. You shouldn't just give what you have to people because they ask for it. You shouldn't let people take advantage of your kindness," he said. He rubbed his hand over his face. "And I know I'm a lot of things. But even I have my morals. I can't take advantage of some little girl like that. Especially one that just saved the life of my best friend. I'm a lot of things, but contrary to popular belief around here, I'm not a bum. I'm not a completely bad person."

Mona felt bad for him. She felt bad about her own trepidation toward him. It was funny to her that the one person she should have the most fear over was probably one of the few people to be honest. Honest even though it made him look bad.

"Thank you," she told him.

He looked up with confusion again. "Thank you?"

"For being honest," she told him. "But please, take the money. The Bible says to give. I could use all the blessings I can get."

He took back his hand, but it was slow. Not because he was glad he could keep the money. She could tell that he understood she really wanted him to have it for her own reasons. He seemed to accept that and do what he could to help.

"You deserve them all. Not for this alone, but for what you did for me and Biscuit too. Most people wouldn't have risked that for a bum and his dog," he told her.

The sad truth was, she knew it to be true.

"So do you. Most people aren't honest even when it makes them look good," she told him. "Doesn't matter what label they put on you if you're a good person."

"My name is Paul, by the way," he told her.

"I'm Mona," she told him. Maybe she should have been more cautious about giving him her name, but she didn't feel threatened.

"Thank you, Mona," he told her. "We both should get out of here before those idiots come back."

She nodded. She looked at Biscuit again and smiled. "Make sure you get him some treats. He was a good boy," she told him.

He nodded and smiled, patting the top of the dog's head. "He always is. Be safe, Mona," he told her.

"I will," she answered. She watched him turn and start walking away. The dog trotted along beside him but turned around to look at her. There was joy on its face and Mona found herself envious of a homeless man's dog named Biscuit.

Chapter Four

Jeremiah 17:9

The heart is deceitful above all things and beyond cure. Who can understand it?

As the days passed, the pain grew less intense. Like her period, it faded with each day, the cramps diminishing in pain and her bleeding turning into nothing more than a couple of drops. What was left of her baby slowly expelled itself from her body and stopped existing to anyone but her.

The heartbeat left and she managed to sleep. Life wasn't good, but it was bearable again. She no longer feared that someone was going to know she was pregnant because she no longer was. No one would know her secrets.

She did worry that someone was going to find out about her abortion, but as the days passed, she was sure even that fear would pass. After a while, there would be nothing left to prove it. She would be completely free to move on.

Sunday was the day she didn't look forward to. She hadn't been excited for church at all. Not only the fact that they were going to be there the entire day, but because her spirituality was wavering.

She had been aware of this for a while. She was questioning things, so that had to mean her faith wasn't secure. No one questioned things in the church. The Bible was Law, and you didn't question the Law. You didn't question the words inside it or the people that preached it.

And although they said to ask questions, some questions were off limits. Those questions were the ones circling Mona's head and she had no one to ask about them. She couldn't talk to Pastor Steve because he was the type of person to tell her to pray about it. But praying about it didn't answer her question. The only thing she got when she prayed was radio silence. Most of the time, she didn't even feel like anyone was listening.

Sometimes, she would even go far enough to say it felt like nobody was there.

Too often she wondered if God was real. If He was, He had turned a blind eye to her family. He had given up on them and left them in the dark. And she didn't blame Him. At some point, maybe people were also unlovable. Past forgiveness. Past grace. And she felt like she was past those things. She had always felt like she wasn't worthy of those. But she wondered if she had ever felt them.

Was she ever loved?

Forgiven?

Blessed?

Or were those things another facet of life that people made up? Were things like love real? Was there such a thing as good and evil or was it all a gray area? Was everyone just judging things according to their own set of rules? The things they deemed good, passed down from generations of people beating it into their heads. Did everything exist as it was because of one set of parents passing their own judgments from generation to generation?

Nature versus Nurture. Were people born this way or raised in it? Did they come with these morals already programmed into their head or were they taught? Were people born bad or good?

Beau was a good example. Maybe she was too. She didn't necessarily feel bad, but she felt Beau was. Was he? Or was she passing her own judgments? Was she right? Was there anyone out there to let her know if she was right or wrong? Was there someone that *did* know what was right? And if so, why did they get to decide?

Every time she found herself alone with Beau, she wanted nothing more than to be away from him. The day after her abortion, she managed to avoid him because he left. She stayed home to help her mama, and Beau went off with their daddy to work. Clyde and Birdie had to work around the house while Mona helped her mama with the sewing.

But when night came and showers were had, Mona found herself taking a shower second, only after Beau. When she finished her shower, he was in her bedroom, laid out across her bed and looking suspicious. He met her eyes as she walked in and looked as if he were trying to figure something out.

"Have you thought about what I said yet?"

Mona felt the hair on the back of her neck stand up again. "No, Beau," she told him. "Please get out of my room."

Beau scoffed but didn't move. "Well don't you just think you're high and mighty. Got that crooked old hypocrite to reprimand me so now you think you're something special, huh?" he told her.

"I didn't get him to do anything," Mona told him.

"No one can touch his precious little princess. I guess he figures he created it so the only one that can touch it is him," Beau said.

His voice always held so much animosity when he spoke to her. Because he didn't have to pretend or appease her. There wasn't a façade in front of her. He wasn't on survival mode like they all were with their parents. He wasn't on big shot mode like he was in front of Clyde or Birdie too. He wasn't trying to impress her because he was willing to show Mona exactly who he was. He wasn't scared of her either.

In their family, everyone acted and reacted a certain way. No one was ever themselves because you were always in survival mode. Mona knew she was, and though Beau was the most rebellious, he was too. The only person he was ever himself with was her and she hated it. She didn't like who Beau was beneath all of it.

"You let Daddy touch you, Mona? Or do you just dangle the possibility in front of him like you do everyone else?" Beau asked her.

She almost felt hurt by the look he gave her. Contempt. Maybe even hatred. And he believed what he was saying. He fully believed what he was saying, and it was sick. He was sick. And yet, it still managed to hurt her.

"No."

Beau jumped up from the bed and was in front of her before she could move. He pressed her up against the wall and wrapped his hand around her throat. He didn't squeeze, but instead used the pressure to hold her in place.

She grabbed his wrist, attempting to pull him away, but Beau held his grip and sneered at her. He even laughed at her and her attempts to get away from him. And when his free hand moved lower, touching her thigh beneath her night shirt, Mona went still. His calloused hand moved up and then squeezed her flesh, pinching her hip.

"You can play the tease, but you're mine, Mona. We both know you belong to me," he said, moving his lips close to her ear. It sent a shiver down her spine, but not in an excited way like Beau hoped.

Mona's head replayed this scene again. It replayed all the scenes again, all of the times this had happened within the last two months. Only this time, they were at the church storeroom in her mind. The first time. Beau had her in the same position, but in her church clothes instead. She remembered hearing the door lock and turning around. The distance between him and her took no more than a second for him to cross and pin her up against the wall. His forearm was placed against her throat and his other hand worked her skirt up over her hips and then he ripped her panties off.

The memory replayed over and over. Scene after scene as he pinched her in the here and now. As his breath hit her ear the same way it did six weeks ago. As she felt him pressing against her as he *raped* touched her in places she didn't want him to. Felt her, moved inside of her, impregnated her, all within minutes. And then he just dropped her on the floor and moved away.

"You're mine, Mona. Not that trash you date. Not Dad's. Not any man's. Mine," he growled. Mona couldn't ignore the possessiveness of his voice. That dare it made to question him. To go against what he said.

But Mona couldn't. She couldn't speak at all. She didn't want to speak either. She wanted him to *rape* get what he wanted and leave. She just wanted to be able to breathe again and be away from him. For his entire presence to just disappear and leave her with herself. Let her go to sleep. Let her cry. Let her feel anger again. Real, unbridled anger and then let it fade.

The floor down the hall creaked and he moved away. His eyes never left hers, but she knew why. He was daring her to scream. To let whoever was coming down the hall know what he was doing. Maybe he was even curious to see if she would.

But Mona wasn't going to. She was sure he knew that.

She knew it was Clyde or Birdie. If it was Birdie, she'd walk into the room and Beau would have to explain himself. But when she heard the door open, she realized it was Clyde. He was going to get clothes for his shower.

Beau smiled. He continued to smile triumphantly until Clyde went into the bathroom and closed the door. He then tilted his head. "You need to the think about what I said, Mona. Right now, I'm patient. Make me keep waiting though and things aren't going to end well," he told her.

Mona stood still as he walked past her. She waited until his bedroom door closed before she finally took a breath. Once she took her first breath, she slid down the wall and found that they were coming quickly. Quick and shallow and she realized she was hyperventilating.

Panic attack?

She closed her hands over her mouth and told herself she needed to get a grip. She tried to focus only on breathing. She didn't know what she was supposed to do to calm herself down. All she knew was that she *couldn't* have a panic attack right now.

But her mind could only focus on Beau and his words to her. Beau and his revelations that he had told her while she sat crumpled on the storeroom floor at the church. The words that echoed after she asked him why.

"Because this is how it's supposed to be. You belong to me. Just like Mom belonged to Dad. The only difference is, they weren't twins," he told her.

Mona was confused, looking up to meet his eyes with pain and disbelief. "What are you talking about?"

And she could tell he enjoyed telling her. This secret he knew was now added to the list of secrets they shared. Each just as bad as the next. Each one just as painful for Mona to bear.

"Mom and Dad are related, Mona. Brother and sister. They tried to hide it, but Dad let it slip when he was drunk. He said when they're pretty and willing, it doesn't matter who they are. He said Mama was a tease and you know what he said after? Go ahead. Ask, Mona," he taunted her.

Mona wouldn't. She didn't want to know what he said. All she wanted was to stop hearing Beau speak. To forget what he said. To pretend nothing was true and all of this was a dream. Not only from what Beau had just said to her, but from what she feared he would say next.

Beau kneeled down to get eye level with her. He cupped her chin with his hand, squeezing roughly. He forced her face to look at him and only him.

"He said you looked so much like her at that age. That at your age, they're ripe for the picking. Begging to be taken. Waiting for the first man willing to come along and give you no time to say no," he said, then narrowed his brows and zeroed in on her. "The old pervert wants you so bad, he's losing his mind. He finds ways to touch you. To get you to be around him. He's afraid someone will get you before he can. And someone did, because you never belonged to him. You've always been mine."

And Mona feared he was right. In that moment, looking into his eyes, she realized that was her biggest fear. That she was his. That she belonged to him. Maybe even that he belonged to her. That being twins, being who they were, they were forever tied by some invisible line, never able to depart from one without destroying the other.

He let go of her face and stood up. Mona didn't move as hovered over her. She wanted to look away from him, maybe in defiance, maybe just in disgust, but she lacked the will to do either. She could only watch him as he relished in his victory. He picked up her torn panties and shoved them in his pocket before grinning at her.

"For later," he said. He walked to the door and unlocked it, leaving the room.

Mona found she couldn't cry about it. She wanted to. She wanted to curl into a ball and cry, but she feared him walking back inside. She didn't want to give him the satisfaction of knowing how hurt she was. He didn't get to know how he had affected her. Mona wouldn't allow it.

She stood up and cleaned up. She made sure she looked presentable, got what she came in to get, and then left. She went about her daily business. She didn't go anywhere near Beau and did her best to avoid him.

But Mona thought about what he said from that moment on. Playing it over and over in her head. Thinking about how such a secret could be kept for so long. How they could live every day with this huge lie hanging over them. It seemed like one of them would have regrets. Feel shame. Get caught.

And she wondered if Beau was even telling the truth. Because Beau liked to lie. And Beau had just done something awful to her. Maybe he had thought that giving her that reason would have helped in some way. Give some kind of reason for why he had done what he had done to justify it for himself.

But Mona knew that the only way she was going to know for sure was if she did some digging of her own. She couldn't come out and ask one of them about it. Beau said that Daddy had gotten drunk and told him, but he wasn't going to let it slip to Mona. And Mama wasn't going to either.

Her next best option was the internet. She wasn't sure if they had changed their names or not, but she took a guess and tried it anyway. She didn't get many results. So, she just decided to try another way. A couple of days after the

rape

incident, she took out the pictures of the family. She looked back for any pictures from their childhood. But there were no pictures of Mama and Daddy before they had her and Beau.

She asked Mama about this. She asked Mama if she could see a picture of her when she was a kid, because she wanted to know if they looked alike.

Mama grew cold and told her that she didn't have any pictures from her childhood. And when Mona asked if she could see some of Daddy, Mama said they didn't have any of those either. All of their pictures were lost.

That could have been true. She couldn't prove otherwise. However, that night, her mama did her best to find thing that would anger Daddy at Mona. When Mama left the food on too long and it burned, even though Mama was cooking she managed to blame it on Mona, and Mona received the back hand to the face for burning dinner.

And while she lay on the kitchen floor, she looked up to see Beau staring at her with a knowing smile. Because he knew that she had been trying to find out whether Mama and Daddy were brother and sister or not. And he knew that this was a result of her snooping. They both knew Mama had made it clear to stay away from the topic or things would get worse.

It was a few days later when Beau found her again. This time it was in the house. While she was in the bathroom, he came inside. Mona barely had time to realize that he had come in behind her before he had her on the floor and was unzipping himself. Mona found it best to disassociate from what was happening.

Beau didn't even have to tell her not to scream. Because years of knowing not to fight back gave him an advantage. Even in a house full of people, he would be able to get what he wanted without anyone knowing what he was doing. With no one to stop him.

After he was through, he didn't leave the bathroom. Instead, he just sat against the door and looked at her as she pulled her knees to her chest and covered as much of her body as possible in the pose.

"We could run away from here," he told her. "We could do just like they did. I'm the only person in the world that knows you, Mona. I'm the only person now that's ever going to be able to satisfy you. No matter where you go or what you do, you'll always belong to me now."

"You're sick," Mona said. She wished she could have added some animosity to her voice. Some venom that would strike him and let him know exactly how much she hated him. Something in her voice that would scream to him that she thought he was horrible. That he was demented. Something that would go through his brain and convince him that Mona wasn't afraid of him.

But there was nothing. Just the feeble words from a girl trying her best to keep it together. From a girl that was struggling to not lose her composure in front of him. A girl trying to keep whatever pride she had left as he put her in the most vulnerable position that she could ever think of.

"If I am, so are you. We're just a couple of inbreds, you and I. Poor white trash living in a trailer in some podunk Alabama town with two inbreeders as parents; we never had a chance. We are the poster children for the South. But I have got to get out of here. And I'm going to leave one way or the other. And I want you with me. One way or another, I'm taking you with me and there won't be anyone around to stop us," Beau said.

Mona stared at him and realized that those weren't just words to him. He truly meant that no one was going to stop them.

He didn't have to tell her for her to know exactly what he meant. He would kill them all. Because if he killed them, who would be able to stop them from leaving and doing the exact same thing that their parents had done?

And every day since then, Beau had either raped her, threatened it, or asked her about what he had told her. And she knew that her time was limited. That eventually she was going to have to do something. She was going to have to leave or die.

Beau wouldn't stay patient forever.

And then she missed her period.

Mona wasn't sure if she was just late or if there was something else going on. Although the only thing that could be going on was that she was pregnant.

Mona was going over and over in her mind over how she was going to get a hold of a pregnancy test. She had limited money and she really was not looking forward to stealing, but she managed to get lucky one day at Owen's house. In the bathroom of their apartment, Carrie had a pregnancy test box. One test was missing, but there was another one inside. And Mona, although she still knew that it was stealing, figured that it was less risky for her to use Carrie's extra pregnancy test than to steal one from the store. She took the test at Owen's house, telling him that she was cramping badly so that she had time to wait.

And then it came back positive. Mona stared at the test until she was sure that it wasn't real. The test itself had to be fake. She didn't pee on a stick. There wasn't a pregnancy test in front of her. It wasn't real. None of it was real and everything was a dream.

She realized that Beau was trying to get her pregnant. This had been part of his plan. Beau wanted her to get pregnant. Beau needed her to get pregnant. Because if she was pregnant, he would have more of a hold on her. He would be able to give her a reason to go with him. To run away.

Because if she was pregnant, she had two choices. Let everyone know that she was pregnant and have them send her away or make her life absolutely miserable until she decided to go with Beau, or just leave with Beau to begin with and avoid all of it.

Mona was sure Beau considered these to be her only options

because he thought he knew Mona. He thought any other option would be ghastly to her, but it was the first thought she had. It was the first thing to pop into her head once she realized he had done it on purpose.

It was the only option.

She was only lucky Beau hadn't raped her tonight. But she was sure he would try again soon. He would keep trying until she was pregnant.

Mona had to do something. She had to get away somehow, but she felt trapped. She could run away, but then she left Birdie to possibly be Beau's new toy. Or she left her family to be killed. Without any money and being only fifteen, she doubted her chances outside were much better than they were inside the trailer with her brother.

She was stuck. She didn't have a job, other than the little bit of money Carrie would sometimes give her to watch the kids. She had given all that she had to the homeless man a couple of days before, but even that wasn't enough to run away on. Her biggest hope was Owen, and she hadn't heard from him since he told her to leave.

She wondered if she could start birth control without needing a parent. God knew her parents weren't going to let her start. Her mama said it was against the Bible. Daddy said it was a scapegoat to go off and be a slut. Neither one was going to entertain the idea of her starting it.

Abortions were not something she wanted to start. She didn't want to get pregnant again. She didn't want Beau to mess with her anymore. She just wanted to leave.

She heard the bathroom door open and realized Clyde was done. Birdie would be getting her bath and coming in the room soon. Mona got up and crawled into her own bed, pulling up the blankets and closing her eyes so she could try to go to sleep. Birdie finished her bath and came into the room without disturbing Mona.

Mona didn't get much sleep that night. She wondered if Beau might come back. And she was afraid to get up at all. Because she couldn't be sure that Beau wouldn't listen for her to get up and attack her then. And the last thing she wanted was to have to deal with Beau again.

The next day, Mona stayed home again. Not only so she could get more rest, but because she honestly had nowhere else to go that day. She wasn't off trying to get an abortion and she wasn't sure if she was supposed to even speak to Owen at this point. She had no idea what was going on between her and him.

Beau left. Clyde and Birdie stayed around the house for most of the day before Mama sent them to the store to grab groceries. And Mona stayed home and helped her clean and do housework.

Mona grew worried when Beau wasn't home before dinner. Everyone knew that that was not acceptable. You always had to be home before dinner or tell people that you weren't going to be home before dinner was done. Beau had done neither.

In fact, Beau didn't get home until Sunday morning. As everyone else was getting dressed and ready for church, Beau and Jerry pulled into the yard. Mona heard them when they came in and she heard the door shut as Beau got out and headed to the house. She knew, just like everyone else did, that a fight was about to break out.

Mona finished getting ready and walked into the living room in the middle of Daddy yelling at Beau. Beau was standing there, so cold and almost lifeless. Mona could smell the alcohol before Daddy yelled at him for coming home drunk.

"I'm not drunk anymore," Beau answered. "Now I'm just hungover."

The words were smart enough for Daddy to backhand him across the face. Beau hit the wall and then crumpled to his knees. Mona could almost feel sorry for his feeble state when he was on the ground.

But she didn't. She would never actually feel sorry for Beau.

"Take these kids to church. Beau and I will meet y'all later," Daddy instructed.

Mama was already holding the keys. "You know we're going to be there all day, remember?" she asked.

"I know!" Daddy snapped. "Now get out of here."

Mona grabbed her things and joined everyone as they got out of the house as quickly as possible. She tried not to make eye contact with Beau as she passed. She could feel the hatred rolling off him the same way the smell of booze was. Both were making her sick and uncomfortable.

The rest of them climbed into the truck and Mama drove them to Sunday morning service. At the end of service, Beau and Daddy still hadn't shown up. Mona knew she shouldn't be worried, but the feeling was there and prevalent. She hated not knowing what was going on.

"I bet Uncle Ray tore Beau's butt up," Birdie told her later as they were walking the streets. Most of the church had volunteered to deliver meals after the service. Mama had been one of the first ones to volunteer, and that meant that the kids did too. It was supposed to be that Mona and Birdie would partner up, and then Beau and Clyde would also walk together, but now Mama was walking with Clyde and it looked like that wasn't putting her in a very good mood.

Mona had a sneaking suspicion that Mama had a crush on Pastor Steve. If not, she idolized him. Because Mama did everything in her power to constantly be around Pastor Steve as much as possible. Anytime that something happened at the church, and Pastor Steve needed help, Mama was there. Mama did things for him that the pastor's wife was supposed to do. But Pastor Steve didn't have a wife. To Mona's knowledge, Pastor Steve had never been married at all.

And Mona was pretty sure that Pastor Steve might have a thing for Mama too. She also was sure that Daddy might know about this. She sometimes wondered if that was why Daddy was so against church. Maybe it wasn't church itself but the specific church that Mama went to instead. Maybe it was one of the things that made him so angry. Because he knew his wife had a thing for the pastor. And the pastor had a thing for his wife.

But Mona wished that Mama hadn't made them do this today. She didn't like the idea of walking around with Birdie for hours. Especially now that Beau had come home and was in trouble. That meant that Birdie had gossip. And once Birdie started talking, you couldn't get her to be quiet. And Mona so loved her silence.

"He likes getting on Uncle Ray's nerves. I sometimes think he does it on purpose. Like he enjoys getting in trouble," she said. Birdie had been calling Mona's parents Aunt and Uncle since moving in with them years before. Once, she had tried to call Mama by that name and Mama had slapped her and told her she wasn't her daughter. After, Birdie had never tried again.

"I don't know why he likes that though. I hate getting in trouble. The last time I got into trouble, I couldn't sit down for a few days. And that was just for forgetting to dry a blanket! Beau always does things much worse. He's gonna…"

"Birdie, can you tell me what that address is again?" Mona interrupted. She didn't need to know the address, but she really wanted Birdie to talk about something else. She didn't want to talk or think about Beau.

Birdie looked at their list of addresses and called out the address again. Mona thanked her and kept on walking toward it, hoping

Birdie might shut up for a while. She should have known better though. The only time Birdie was quiet was when Daddy was around.

"How's Owen?" Birdie asked. "I wish I could have a boyfriend. Clyde says I'm never gonna get one unless he's blind. I really don't like Clyde sometimes, but the Bible says you're supposed to pray for people like that, but I really don't wanna. So how is your boyfriend? Aunt Ann says there ain't enough prayer in the world to help that boy."

"Owen is fine."

Not that Mona knew for sure. She hadn't spoken to or seen him since Thursday. He had made no attempt to come see her and Mona hadn't left the house until today. She wasn't even sure if he was still her boyfriend, but she wasn't going to divulge such information to Birdie of all people.

"Are you okay? You've been quieter than usual. Which isn't that noticeable because you're always so quiet, but I can't remember the last time we actually talked. You used to talk to me sometimes, and even if you didn't really care, you at least tried to pretend you were interested. And now you don't even listen. You just do your chores and go to sleep," Birdie told her.

Mona looked at her and wondered how obvious it was to everyone else. Birdie would say a lot without thinking, her sentences always being quite a few before anyone had a chance to join the conversation, but Mona wasn't aware she could notice anything outside of her own existence.

But Birdie had noticed, and Mona didn't have a reason she could share with Birdie. Despite Birdie being younger than her, and not really at fault like the rest of her family, Birdie wasn't her friend. Birdie couldn't keep her mouth shut and if she got in trouble, she'd spill to save herself.

Mona didn't blame her for that. That was how life was for them. When things turned bad, you found a way to make it less. No matter who you had to throw under the bus. Birdie was just trying to survive like the rest of them.

Somewhere in the time Birdie had come to live with them and up until her

rape

incident, Mona had tried to give Birdie a place to be herself. Annoying as she could be, Mona knew what it was like to be shamed into submission. Mona felt like she had no one she could be herself with, but Birdie was able to talk about whatever she wanted to with Mona.

Mona didn't think this made her a good person, or that it wiped away how bad she was inside, but didn't it count for something? She wondered that a lot and prayed about it. You wouldn't get into Heaven by works alone, the Bible said that, but didn't they still count for something?

"I'm sorry," Mona answered.

Birdie shrugged. "It's okay. Clyde said you're probably just PMSing. He also says that I'll start soon, and him and Beau said if you're old enough to bleed, you're old enough to breed. Beau said I'll probably be just like my mama, but I'm not going to. Mama always said I would too, but I'm not gonna. Not until I have a boyfriend. A real boyfriend that Aunt Ann and Uncle Ray like," Birdie said, continuing to walk and talk like they were just discussing cupcakes and not the sexuality of a twelve-year-old.

Mona wouldn't comment on it, but she realized she had to keep a closer eye on Clyde too. She had to watch both of her brothers around Birdie.

She had a sliver of hope that Clyde might not be the same as Beau, but Clyde was glued to Beau at the hip. He tried to do everything he could to emulate his older brother. It was becoming apparent that it was working too. If Clyde was repeating phrases Beau liked to use, he needed to be watched too.

"Hey! It's a doggy!" Birdie exclaimed, immediately getting to her knees and whistling.

Mona looked up to see a dog she recognized. Biscuit was running toward them, tail wagging, tongue flopping, and he stopped at Birdie. He sniffed her, getting a laugh from her, but then came to Mona. He jumped up on Mona and tried to give her face plenty of kisses.

"I'm so sorry!" Paul said, running up to them.

Mona recognized him with no problem, except he was carrying some bruises on his face now. Mona assumed they were from his incident a few days prior, but she couldn't be sure.

Birdie stood up and moved away a bit. Mona understood that she was nervous. The only thing she wasn't sure about was whether she was nervous because it was a stranger or because she was afraid someone might see her speaking to a man.

Paul's brows narrowed. "I know you," he said, smiling. "You saved Biscuit."

Mona grew tense. She could feel Birdie's eyes on her. She didn't know what Birdie was thinking, but she didn't like the situation.

"You must have me confused, sir," Mona answered. She looked at Biscuit and gave him a pet before trying to push him away. The dog didn't care and continued giving her kisses.

But Paul seemed to understand. "I'm sorry. Biscuit just ran to you, so I assumed. My eyesight isn't all that great," he told them. "Come on, Biscuit. Let's leave these nice young ladies alone."

Biscuit moved away but reluctantly. Mona felt sadness at not being able to really pay attention to the dog, but it was better if Birdie chalked the event up to just a random encounter with a half blind homeless man and his dog. The less of a situation Mona put herself in, the better.

Because she couldn't trust Birdie.

When Paul and Biscuit were far enough away, Birdie nudged her. "That was super creepy, right? I bet he was going to try to steal from us, or rap…"

"Not everyone is a bad person," Mona interrupted. She looked at Birdie, who looked confused. "I'm sure he was just confused. And dogs are good judges of people. If he was bad, I'm sure his dog wouldn't go with him."

Mona hated that she felt the need to say something, but not saying something felt like an injustice. Like Birdie would fall into that same trap as everyone else if she viewed everyone as bad, especially based off how they looked. She hoped her reasoning helped Birdie.

Birdie just shrugged. "Still gave me the creeps. But the dog was cute," she said.

Mona had to accept that this was as good as she was going to get with Birdie. The best she could hope for was Birdie losing interest in the event and never speaking of it again.

They finished out their route and met up with Mama and Clyde. Everyone gathered into the church's van and headed back.

When Mona got back to the church, right before Sunday night service was to begin, Mona realized that Beau and their daddy were sitting on the steps. It surprised Mona as much as it did her mama.

"How did you get here?" her mother asked.

"I called up an old buddy to drop us off. Beau and I had us a nice little talk, didn't we Beau?" her daddy asked.

Beau said nothing, and Mona wasn't sure if that was better or not. The only thing she could really focus on was the fact that Beau seemed to be stewing with something. Like he was gnawing on a wound, unable and refusing to let it heal. He had a bone to pick with someone, and that meant the wound had to stay bleeding.

She knew without a doubt it was her he had the problem with.

"Does that mean you're going to stay for the service?" her mother asked him.

"I might as well," her daddy answered. "Y'all have Sunday School? Right?"

"Yes, sir," the three of them answered in unison. Beau was the only one to remain silent.

"Well, let's get on inside," her mama answered.

They all walked inside the church and sat down in the pew that their family always sat in. Technically, they were still a little early for service, but that didn't really matter. Mama was busy talking Daddy's ear off about their afternoon, and Birdie was talking Clyde's ear off about something to do with food. Mona wasn't even sure if Birdie knew what she was talking about half the time.

And Mona was trying her best not to focus on Beau. And she had a feeling that Beau was also trying to avoid looking at her. Or talking to her. Maybe he didn't even want her to know that she was in the same universe as he was.

Mona preferred it that way. She wished it could be that way all the time, but she had a feeling that Beau was just biding his time. Waiting for that perfect moment to blindside her. Maybe he would

rape

attack her again. Maybe he would have to take out his rage from getting in trouble on her. Maybe he'd find some way to blame it all on her. Because it seemed like that was Beau's thing. To blame everything on his twin sister. She was the reason he was the way he was, and vice versa.

Church started. A little while into the service, they told the children that they could go off to their youth group, and the four of them did. They each followed the youth pastor into the room and began their own church.

Mona tried to focus on what was being preached, but she struggled. Because no matter what the sermon was about or how they tried to explain it all to her, Mona felt like she was missing the point.

What was the point of all of this? What was the point of going to church if church couldn't save you? What was the point in being a good person if your good deeds didn't save you? What was the point in existing when your entire goal was to not be here? What was the point in being alive when everyone was so focused on what would happen after you were dead?

And she didn't understand how you could be saved but then need to be saved again. How when you did something bad, that negated the fact that you were saved. Or how some people believe that if you were saved then you were always saved, and it didn't matter the bad things that you did. Did it even matter? Did anything matter?

The Bible also said that God judged all sins the same. There was no sin worse than the other. Mona felt like maybe some sins really were worse than others. Because if you lied on a test, how was that ever equal to murdering someone? How was that equal to raping someone?

Did her

rape

incident equal to the same as her abortion? Was Beau equally damned as she was? Because Beau chose to do something out of selfishness and cruelty. Mona felt her reasons were much more noble. She chose to do something out of fear and survival. Beau took what he wanted because he wanted it. Mona got rid of something to protect it.

But she also did it to protect herself.

Maybe her reasons were just as selfish. Maybe that meant she wasn't any better than Beau. Maybe it even meant that she was playing judge by trying to convince herself that she was better than Beau was. Because in some ways, she wondered if the Bible would be fair and kind to Beau more than it was to her. Because there were men in the Bible that raped women and then were called godly. Men that murdered other men so that they could have their wives and were considered holy. Men did awful things in the Bible, and they were still told to be respected and looked up to. Because they were saved.

Mona felt more like it was because they were men.

And all of this boiled down to the unconditional love they preached about so much. But unconditional meant that no matter what, you were loved. That wasn't the same thing being preached. Whether you were gay, a murderer, smoking, drinking, raping, or just stole a piece of bubblegum, God was supposed to love you no matter what. But what they preached was that if you didn't fit into a certain group, you were damned until you were saved by the Blood of Christ.

She had a lot of questions and a lot of doubts.

When service was over, the kids in the youth group always went outside. It was one of the few joys that Mona had. You could go outside and play basketball or just sit around and enjoy the nighttime. You could stare up at the stars and just enjoy the breeze. Mona hated when it turned to winter because then no one would go outside. The youth pastor would make sure they all stayed indoors, and Mona preferred going outside and being alone.

But when she went outside with the rest of the group on that night, Beau grabbed her wrist and pulled her to the side of the building. Mona tried to pull away from him, but Beau was walking fast and almost dragging her behind him. She looked to see if anyone noticed, but no one was looking their way.

Beau didn't release her. Even when he got to where he wanted to be, Beau kept his hands on her. He grabbed her upper forearms and pushed her against the side of the brick building.

She felt the back of her head hit the wall. Pain exploded from there and gave her an instant headache. His grip on her arms was tight and painful.

Mona was sure that he was going to attack her again, right outside with the risk of everyone coming around and seeing him because he had gotten in trouble. He was throwing another temper tantrum and she was his punching bag, so to speak.

But instead, he shoved her against the wall again. He didn't try to lift her skirt or unzip his pants. There was nothing but pure anger on his face. In fact, Mona couldn't recall if she'd ever seen Beau as angry as he was with her. This was the purest emotion she'd ever seen cross Beau's face.

"How dare you kill our baby!" he scolded her, the words coming out angry but in a low tone. As if he also did not want anyone to know what was going on.

But Mona couldn't focus on the fact that he was trying to be as secretive as possible. The only thing she could focus on was that Beau knew. Beau knew that she had had an abortion. And she had no idea how, or why. Her mind was replaying every single altercation she had with Beau ever since having her abortion. She was replaying every word that was said, every look, every action she had taken for where she had slipped up. Because she thought she had covered her tracks so well. She thought that she had done everything in her power to make sure that Beau of all people didn't know. And she hadn't even gotten through a couple of days before he knew what she had done.

"How did you…"

Beau moved one of his hands to his back pocket and pulled out a piece of paper. Mona's heart sank as he unfolded it to show her the number and address that Jill had written down for her. She knew he must have gotten it the night he was in her bedroom. Maybe he'd had a sneaking suspicion after seeing her on the road that day.

"Didn't think I would find out, did you? Course you didn't. Because you're nothing but a stupid little slut. You wanted to hurt me. You didn't care about anyone other than yourself."

Mona wasn't aware of where the emotions that she was feeling lately were coming from, but the same anger that filled her when Owen had pushed about having sex came over her as Beau was speaking.

And honestly, she wondered if Beau did have a point. Perhaps the only person in the world that had ever known Mona was Beau. And perhaps that was the reason why it came even easier for her to strike back at him now. To let that anger overtake her and just snap.

"You raped me!" she yelled at him. She shoved back against him, but it wasn't her strength that made him let her go. It was the surprise. It was that shock again. Shock that she would even dare to speak up. To say something against what he had done against her. To have an opinion or a voice above a meek whisper.

"Don't even act like that's what it was," he told her. "You know you wanted it."

"Wanted it? What in the world would make you think that I

would want anything to do with you, Beau? I can't stand you. You say that we are twins and that we're the only ones that will ever understand each other, and you're right. I understand you perfectly," she told him, her voice filled with as much disgust as humanly possible. "I understand you completely. And I cannot stand you. You are ugly and you are horrible. You are disgusting, Beau. And for you to think that I would want you, that I would want to carry your baby, and run away with you?! You must be deranged."

Mona wasn't sure if Beau was more shocked or just angry. Because the look on his face was almost murderous. Beau looked as if he would strangle her if she kept on.

And Mona almost wished he would. Because life with Beau was only going to get worse. She knew this. She could tell just by looking at him. Him knowing that she had had an abortion was only going to make things worse. It was only going to make him more persistent. More watchful. He was going to monitor every single move she made from now on.

Death would be a release. If he strangled and killed her right now, she would at least be free. And that was all she ever wanted from life, to just be free. And if she couldn't have that while alive, then maybe she could get it when she was dead.

Beau just stared at her, as if he were trying to put pieces together inside of his head. And maybe that's exactly what he was doing. Maybe he was determining what was going to be his best course of action. Maybe unlike her, he wanted to use his head rather than his heart to speak.

Twins were supposed to be so much alike, but Mona wondered if they were complete opposites instead. Because she was convinced that Beau didn't have a heart and she knew that her decisions were never made with her head. Not the decisions that she wanted to make.

"Do you feel righteous now?" he asked her. "Do you suddenly feel better about yourself? You want to tell me how horrible I am as if you aren't exactly like me? You can deny it all you want, but we're the same. You know it. And you can act like you're disgusted with me and everything I've done and say it's just horrible, but you're no better than I am. You killed our baby."

"I killed your spawn! I did that child a mercy. Because maybe you are right. Maybe we're exactly the same, and guess what? We're just two inbreds created by some sick twisted love affair between a brother and a sister. A brother and sister that ran away to keep their sick twisted secret from anyone knowing. Look at our parents, Beau! You're honestly telling me that you want to emulate them? You want to create a child just like us? A child that will one day grow up and learn about his parents' secrets too? You want to do that to someone else?"

"We would be different," he told her.

"You're just as bad as they are," Mona replied. "Actually, you might even be worse. Because we don't know if Daddy had to rape his sister in order to have her."

Beau slapped her. His hand connected with her cheek and knocked her to the ground. The entire side of her face lit up in pain. It tingled and her ears began to ring. Her eyes watered.

She looked up anyway. Whatever it had been before that kept her submissive when it came to Beau seemed to be gone for the moment. Because the only thing she wanted to do was stand up to him.

"You'll get what's coming to you," Beau told her.

"I'm not scared of you," she told him between gritted teeth.

"You should be," he said.

He walked away from her, rage seeming to shake inside of him. Mona couldn't help but feel all that anger directed toward her, and she directed it back. Because if she could feel how angry he was with her, she knew that he could feel how angry she was with him.

But she knew he could feel that other emotion she was full of, despite how she wanted to shove it away. Fear. Because she was also scared. Because walking away was not something Beau did. Beau acted. Retaliated.

As she watched him walk away, her anger couldn't help but subside and let terror in as she wondered what Beau planned to do to her.

The Great Whore of Babylon

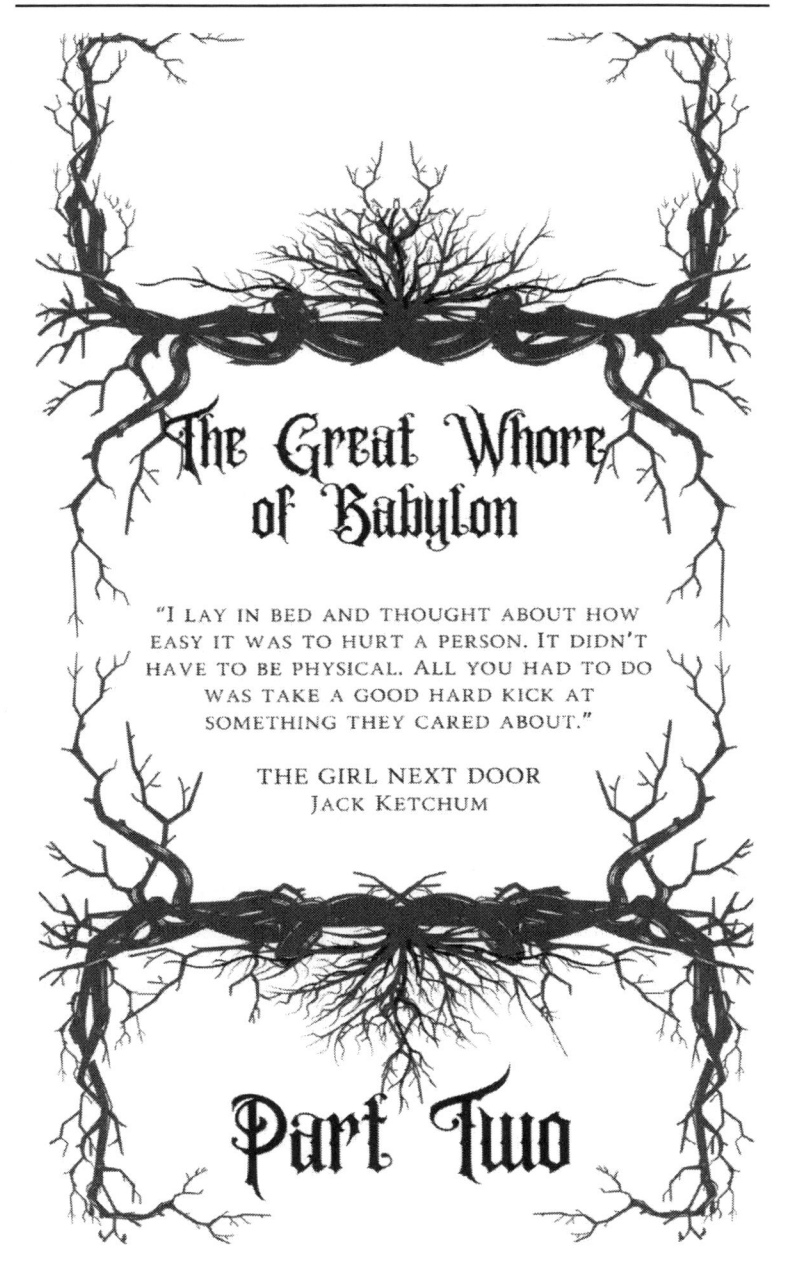

> "I lay in bed and thought about how easy it was to hurt a person. It didn't have to be physical. All you had to do was take a good hard kick at something they cared about."
>
> THE GIRL NEXT DOOR
> JACK KETCHUM

Part Two

Chapter Five

A fool gives full vent to his anger, but a wise man keeps himself under control.

Proverbs 29:11

Most of her life had been spent against the wall. Pushed against it to be yelled at, hit, molested, backed into corners to keep from escaping. When your entire life was spent against a wall, it wasn't a crazy thing to begin finding ways to blend into it.

She remembered a story, a very important story for women, her English teacher had said when she made them read it in class. It was about walls. It was a story about a woman and the wallpaper.

Yellow wallpaper, and women were trapped inside it. At least, that was what the woman in the story was convinced of.

Her teacher explained the story was a good discussion piece on women and their roles, particularly in marriage. It was a story of depression and a woman's descent into psychosis, but her teacher said she felt it was also a story of how man could control and aid in the mental decline of their spouse. That was off the record, she joked.

However, Mona was stuck on the wallpaper. It was the most important aspect of the story and as much a character as the narrator was. The narrator's lack of a name also stuck with Mona in ways the rest of the story did not. Her and the wallpaper, the two most important characters, entwined and forever linked together.

For the woman, because she had no other mental stimulation, she focuses on the wallpaper. In the story, the pattern became bars to her, and she began to see a woman inside them. Trapped. Because in the wallpaper, she could see herself. Trapped as well. By the end of the story, the woman believes the woman has escaped. Mona's teacher explained that this was an indicator that she had finally settled into her own psychosis and discontentment with her marriage role.

For Mona, she felt it was a little more than that.

The woman became one with the wallpaper. She became the wallpaper. Maybe the woman she had seen behind the bars was some version of herself, a version she had been before she was married. The only way to let her out was to paint herself in. The only way to survive was to become the prison you painted yourself, that way, you held the key. For Mona, the narrator had a name.

It was Yellow Wallpaper.

Mona was part of the wallpaper, too. She stood against the wall she knew so well and painted herself into it. Her wallpaper had covered wagons and was only yellowed from time. Sometimes it wasn't wallpaper at all. In some rooms, she was the wood grain in the paneling, but the purpose was the same. To survive the hell she was in. If she was confined to four walls, she would become one with the walls to keep from going crazy.

But Mona was sure her viewpoint wasn't what the author intended. Maybe she was trying too hard to fit her own narrative in, but in a lot of ways, fiction gave you the permission to do that. Mona found purpose in the way she viewed the story and its characters. It gave her a reason to blend in. A way to protect herself.

The last thing Mona wanted was for anyone to notice anything about her. But when you were walking around with a giant bruise on your cheek, it was kind of hard for the people you didn't want to notice you to not notice.

"The hell happened to your face?" her daddy asked the next morning when she came in from the porch. She hadn't heard him up yet, but today was one of the rare days that he woke up before

Mama did.

Another thing Mona really didn't want to do was tell anyone exactly what happened. Because Beau had information on her now. If, and, most likely when, Beau decided that he wanted to share that information with everyone, Mona wanted to avoid the consequences at all costs. Or at least delay it, for sure. She didn't know if he ever would or if he was just waiting for the perfect moment to tell everyone.

The last thing she was going to do, though, was provoke him into doing that early. She hoped that she would be able to find some sort of way to escape. Some magical way of getting out of all of this. Because she wasn't going to get out of it with Beau. That much was known to herself. There was no way that she was going to leave with Beau and live out the sick incestuous fantasy that he had created in his mind.

But for now, she just had to lay low. She had to bide her time until she could figure out what she was going to do. Even if she had to leave and be homeless. Live on the streets. At this point almost anything sounded better than her current situation.

"I don't know," Mona told him. "I'm not sure if I might have slept on it wrong."

"Nobody sleeps on their face so wrong it ends up with a huge bruise, Mona. Why are you lying to me?"

"Because I don't know why," Mona said with a shaky voice.

"It was that boy of yours, wasn't it? That scuzz you date," her daddy said.

"No, sir."

"I don't want you seeing him anymore, Mona. I mean it. He's bad news and has been bad news since the day you met him," her daddy said. He kept walking because that was the end of the conversation.

Not that it really mattered at this point. Her daddy would find no argument from her because she was pretty sure that she and Owen were over anyway. She hadn't spoken to him since he had told her to leave his house and part of her figured that he told her to leave because maybe something she said rang true. Maybe he really didn't want to just be with her. Maybe his interest had always been of a sexual nature. Maybe she had finally said something that went through his head, and he realized that it was better just to cut his ties now.

Mona went in the kitchen and began to make her daddy's breakfast. Mama wasn't too far behind, and she helped make the rest of it as Mona left and got dressed for the day.

She stared at herself in the mirror. It had been a long time now since she had done so. For the last couple of weeks, she couldn't stand to look at herself. She was afraid of seeing exactly how ugly she was. Afraid that Beau would be right. That she would be just as ugly as he was, and her reflection would show that back to her.

But she looked at herself today. She turned her cheek to look at the bruise Beau had left. Her hand reached up to touch it but retracted quickly at the first sign of pain. She didn't know what would be best to make a bruise go away quickly. But if she found out, she would try it.

She brushed her teeth and changed into her normal clothes. She braided her hair and took one last look at herself. She wished she was pretty. That natural sort of prettiness that came from girls that were good. Like something inward made them pretty on the outside too. You just looked at them and knew you'd never find someone prettier than them.

But she was plain, sad, and bruised. Inside, she wasn't much different. She would never be pretty. Not in a way that mattered. On the outside, she would always be ugly. On the inside, she would always be much worse.

When she left the bathroom and walked into the living room, she saw that Beau was already awake. That was a surprise. Beau usually tried to sleep as long as he possibly could. The only time he woke up was when there was something important for him to do or Daddy had him working.

Mama and Daddy were in the living room eating breakfast. Beau was eating too. He was sitting on the couch right beside them.

And he paid her no mind as she walked through.

She wished that she could say the same about Daddy.

"You seen that bruise on her cheek?" Daddy asked Mama.

Mama looked at her and then narrowed her brows. "Where in the world did you get that from?" she asked Mona.

"I'm not sure," Mona lied.

"I know it was that boy," her Daddy said. "I told her I don't want her seeing him again."

"Well, she ain't seen him since Thursday," her mama said. "So, I don't think that he's the reason. As bummy as he may be."

For once, her daddy seemed to realize that someone else was right. And he thought the information over, realizing that Mama was right about that. Mona had only left the house for church since Thursday. Mona almost wished that they hadn't remembered, because that meant that he was going to ask her about who had actually done it, which he did.

"Well, if your boyfriend didn't do it, then who did?" her daddy asked.

Instinctively, Mona cast a look toward Beau, then quickly the other way. She realized that they might assume from her gaze that it was him. The only thing she knew for sure was that Beau was listening. He was going to see if she ratted him out like he assumed she would. And when she did, he would have a reason to tell them exactly what she had done.

But he should have known that she wouldn't because she was scared. She feared what would happen if she did. Not only of what Beau would do, because she knew what Beau would do, but of what Mama and Daddy might do. Would they take her side over what Beau had done to her, or would none of that matter because of what she had done?

She was almost willing to bet the latter.

It wouldn't matter if Beau had gone into the church, burned every Bible and wrote, "Jesus sucks cock," with the ashes after taking a piss on them. The moment they heard the word 'abortion' it would be over for her. They wouldn't care what Beau said or done: nothing would ever come as close as her having an abortion.

"I don't know how it happened. It just popped up," she told them.

Her mama looked her over again. "Might wanna take you to the doctor then. Could be something," she said, resuming her normal eating routine as she turned her attention back to the news.

"Ain't no sense in wasting money on the doctor for a bruise. It ain't that serious," her daddy answered. "Go in there and eat breakfast. Your mama made a fresh pitcher of tea, too. Your lemonade is by the sink."

"Yes sir."

Although jokes were made, there was one thing that Mama did for Mona that she considered considerate. When Mama made everyone else sweet tea, she always made a pitcher of lemonade for Mona. Mona was the only one that didn't like tea and Mama wasn't going to spend money on things like Coke. Not that Mona really liked it either. She liked water and lemonade.

She grabbed a glass from the cabinet and poured her lemonade. Once she made her plate, she walked back into the living room and sat down with them, putting distance between herself and Beau.

Usually, she didn't like paying attention to the news. Mona disliked the constant negativity, and it seemed the news only covered the bad. At the end, they would throw in one human interest story, as if the one story would suddenly make everything else better. One tiny sliver of hope before thirty minutes later when they covered the bad news again and reminded you that Earth was a hellhole.

Today, her attention was grabbed the moment the scene popped onto the TV screen.

"We bring to you today a story we covered last night. Police are still after the people responsible for starting a fire in Redwood, Alabama. Now, the perpetrators can add homicide to their list because forty-two-year-old Margaret Hansen and her four daughters were also found inside the residence. Police are saying that their deaths were not in relation to the fire, but that the fire was set as a preventive measure instead. So far, the police have few clues, but are confident that they will find the people responsible."

On the TV screen, the camera panned to their local sheriff and the reporter began to interview him. But Mona was staring at the screen for another reason. The reason that made her head slowly turn to Beau when she realized that it was him.

It was the same trailer she had gone to the week before. It was where she had gotten her abortion. The place was almost completely ash, but Mona recognized it. She recognized the yard, the road, the car, the scene was seared into her memory forever. It was the place that got rid of her problem, the problem Beau now had with her.

Beau had killed that woman and her kids.

But it was her fault. She couldn't deny that she had led him straight to her. That if Beau hadn't found that stupid piece of paper, he wouldn't have known about her. He wouldn't have gone there and figured out what she had done.

And how had he gotten the information out of Margaret? She didn't know Mona's name.

Maybe he had brought a picture. Maybe it didn't take much information if she was the only girl to show up on that day. Maybe Margaret didn't even have to confirm it for him. Maybe he only needed to know why anyone would come to her house.

Did he have help? Maybe him and Jerry had driven down there, and they had probably tortured her and her daughters until they got the information they wanted. Mona could see them promising them that they'd be okay if they just answered their questions honestly. And then when they did, and they gave up the information that he wanted, they killed them.

She wondered how he had killed them. Because Beau was not the type of person that would just murder somebody quickly to keep them out of their misery. She knew that if Beau had killed them, and she knew he had, that he had done so in a gruesome way. He had hurt them all badly, including her daughters. Her daughters that had only shown Mona kindness. Even the woman, that Mona now knew as Margaret Hansen, had only shown her kindness. And because she had helped Mona, she and her family were dead now. And it was completely Mona's fault.

Mona looked at Beau. He was now looking at her, still eating his food and giving her a smug stare that told her that he knew that she knew that he was the one that had done it. That he had gone to that address on the piece of paper she had, and he had found out what she had done. And then he had killed them and gone off and gotten drunk. Went off all night and just stewed on what he had done. Thought about what he was going to do.

Maybe he had thought about finding Mona and killing her. Maybe his anger had been so bad that he had considered offing her, too. That it would be easier to. It would make him feel even better if Mona was dead too.

But then he didn't do anything. Maybe this was also part of his plan. He would just let her wallow in her own guilt. Because she could only blame herself for these people being dead.

Or maybe he had some of the reason for not killing her off. Maybe he was going to use this to get his way. Maybe, even though he was angry that she had killed their baby, he still had plans to get her to go with him. Those plans might be more elaborate now. Or maybe he was just going to go back to doing what he had been.

Either way, Mona had to stop him. She had to get out. Find some way to escape here before something terrible happened. Before Beau decided to tell people. Before everything would go to crap, and Mona would never be able to leave. She had to do something.

She resumed eating, but her appetite was gone. She was thinking too much about Beau. Too much about what she had to do. And trying her best to figure out what in the world he was planning.

When Daddy stood up to go to work, Beau stood up as well. That confused Mona, but it seemed like Mama had already known.

"You two have a good day at work," she told them, taking their plates and walking into the kitchen.

Mona wasn't sure if it had been punishment or part of Beau and Daddy's talk yesterday, but it appeared that Beau would now be going to work with Daddy.

Mona wasn't sure how she felt about that either, but she did like the fact that he wasn't going to be there at the house. It gave her time to think. It gave her time to plan.

She helped Mama clean up after breakfast. Clyde and Birdie woke up a little bit later. Mama sent Clyde outside to clean up the yard. She wanted it raked and the grass cut. Clyde or Beau always got outside duties because they were boys and Daddy's back wasn't what it used to be.

She put Birdie and Mona on house duty. The wonderful thing for Mona was that she didn't put them together cleaning one room. She gave them both the list of what she wanted them to do, and Mona was able to clean up in silence while Mama went in the living room, turned on her daytime TV, and began to sew.

Being able to clean on her own gave her time to think. And she had a lot to think about. The main thing she had to think about was how she was going to get rid of Beau and his threat.

The thought that kept going over and over in her mind was that if he was in jail, maybe that would help. She didn't know if the police would figure out who exactly had killed Margaret, but if she could somehow point them in the right direction, maybe she could get rid of Beau. If Beau was in jail, convicted of murder, he wouldn't be around anymore making her life a living hell.

But doing that came with risk too. Because Beau might try to take her down with him. Maybe he would say she was there. And if that didn't work maybe he'd say she was the one that sent him.

And he would definitely tell her parents that she had an abortion. He would tell them that that was why he had done it. He would turn it all around on her and because he would be away, all of their anger and torture would come back on her. And he would sit in jail away from it all and probably still end up getting away with it because it was Beau. Beau usually managed to get his way no matter what.

Beau always got his way in the end.

So, if she went this way, she had to be very careful about it. She had to make sure that Beau didn't suspect a thing. She had to put the police onto his trail, and then get away before Beau was caught. She had to find some way of getting out of there. Some way to get as far away from her parents and this town as possible.

Mona was convinced now that there was absolutely nothing Beau wouldn't do to get his way. Even if it meant killing their family. Even if it meant killing her. If he could kill a woman that had done nothing to him personally, he could kill people he had been around his entire life.

She didn't think Beau cared about any of them. She didn't even think Beau really cared about her. The only thing Beau cared about was himself and whatever he wanted. And apparently the thing that he wanted was her.

Mona wasn't sure what she was going to have to do, but she knew that she had to make a plan. She had to do something. She had to come up with some sort of way to get out of there. Beau getting in trouble for what he had done was one thing, but she also had to have a plan of how she was going to run away. How she would escape her family. But she had no idea how she was going to do that.

She didn't know how to make it on her own. She didn't know how to get away and not be dragged back the moment someone else saw her. She didn't have things like a passport or even a driver's license. She wasn't sure if you could buy things like a plane ticket or bus ride without one. And she was very unsure about hitchhiking. Getting into cars with total strangers, no protection, nothing that would keep her safe from whoever might be behind the wheel. It all seemed very risky.

Because the last thing she wanted was to escape one hell only to be put in another.

But she had to do something. And if that meant she had to walk until she could find shelter, live under bridges and do whatever she had to survive, at least she would be in control of that. At least it would be a chance.

After Mona finished her rooms, Mama sent her to the store. Birdie was taking longer than usual, and Clyde was not one to send to the store. Clyde had a penchant for stealing. If you sent him to the store, it was almost a sure thing that he was going to buy himself something sweet while he was there. Mona wasn't sure if she quite considered that stealing, seeing as he didn't hide it, and it wasn't the money. It was to get something he couldn't get at the house, but it wasn't his money, and his parents would really bear down on him because of that.

So, it was Mona that was trusted to go to the store, and that was okay. The only issue was that they only had one car and Daddy and Beau were in it to go to work. Mona's bike had a basket, but it wasn't going to be enough to hold everything that Mama needed. She could ride it into town, but she would most likely have to push it back home with the bags on the handlebars.

Not that Mona minded as much. She'd have time alone. She liked her time alone. She enjoyed space to think, or just breathe. She enjoyed just existing without worrying. These times completely away from everyone else was prime time to just be. To simply exist without repercussions.

She went to the store and got Mama's groceries without any trouble. As she was coming out though, Biscuit came running up to her. She smiled as the dog jumped up on her and wanted attention. She sat the bags down beside her bike and gave him some.

Animals really were the purest beings to exist, and Mona loved them for it.

"Where is your owner?" she asked the dog, as if she actually expected the dog to say something back. Obviously, it wouldn't but it still felt obligatory to ask. She looked around but didn't see his owner.

She picked up her bags again, put the bags on the handlebars and began to push it as she moved out of the parking lot. Right as she was rounding the corner of the store, she saw Paul coming around with a bag of his own. It looked like he had been in the dumpster around back, but there was a look of worry on his face. Wondering where his dog, his only true companion, had gone off to.

When he saw her, and more importantly when he saw Biscuit, that look of worry vanished, and Mona could swear that it took ten years off the man's face. Seeing him see his dog almost made Mona think that he was probably a lot younger than the scruffy beard and dirt and grime made him look. That his clothes that needed washing and his beaten-up shoes actually made him look a lot older than what he really was. Because Mona might have aged him at fifty when she first met him, but looking at him now, she wondered if he was even at forty yet. Either way he looked just as pleased to see her as he had been to see Biscuit.

"Hello, you," he said, rubbing Biscuit's ears. He then erased the look of pleasure as he looked around and lowered his voice. "You alone?"

Mona wasn't sure if she should feel alarmed by that question, but she wasn't. She didn't feel as if she couldn't trust Paul. Though she knew next to nothing about him, there was something about him that reminded her of safety. Something that felt comforting. She felt no need to be cautious, despite everything in her life telling her she should be. Her entire existence had only proven that you couldn't trust anyone.

And yet, when he asked her if she was alone, she didn't feel as if she should tell him that she wasn't in case he had any perverse ideas. She nodded. Because she knew the reason he was asking was because he had known that if she wasn't he needed to leave her alone.

He smiled. "I'm sorry if I caused any trouble yesterday. Seems like Biscuit is just good at finding you," he said with a laugh, scratching the dog on the top of the head.

"It's okay. Dogs have a good sense of people, but not situations," Mona said with a smile.

He laughed. "Yeah, I'd guess so. My mama always said that animals had the best judgment about a person. But it does seem like they can't tell, or don't care, about situations like we do," he answered.

"I think your mama was right," Mona said.

He laughed a little and grabbed his bike and began to walk. Mona began to walk with him. "I think some people are the same way. Able to see a person for who they are better than others," he told her.

"Some people just pay attention," Mona told him, to which he smiled.

"Maybe so. You're a young girl, you don't even look like you're older than thirteen or fourteen, and yet you're still here talking to me. And you don't feel scared at all, do you?"

She needed to. That was what her head told her. It said not to trust anyone, especially grown men you didn't know. It told her that everyone had an agenda, and no one could be trusted because they all were wicked and evil.

But he was right. She didn't feel scared at all. And she knew what fear felt like when you were around men of any age. Men that you had to worry about. Men that looked at you because you were young and thought impure thoughts about you. But Mona didn't feel that way around him. If anything, she felt safe around him. She told herself to be wary, but she didn't feel wary.

"Not really," she said.

"And it's because you can just tell. You just know. I wouldn't hurt you. When we met the other day, I felt a connection with you instantly. Which is the real reason I didn't want to lie to you. You reminded me of my baby sister. Not in appearance or anything, but in your soul. There's such a pureness, a sweet, but tortured little girl. I could just tell, and it drew me to you. Call it intuition or instinct or something but it's different than that," he said.

She could almost tell that he wanted to get off on this tangent. He wanted to explain this, because maybe he had even been thinking about it. She didn't know why, but it seemed like he needed to say something.

"My mom could take one look at me and know exactly when I was lying and usually what I was lying about. She always knew. Whether I told her or not, she always knew exactly what I was feeling. She could always tell when I was around. She called it her Knowing. I don't know what it is, but she said everybody has a little bit of it. And animals have a lot of it. Which is why I think Biscuit is able to tell exactly where you are. Because every time I turn around now it seems like he's trying to guide me to you. And I have to remind him that that's not what grown men do around young ladies."

Mona smiled as she looked at the dog. Biscuit looked up at her with his tail wagging and his tongue hanging out as he kept pace with them. Mona loved the dog. She knew the dog loved her too.

"I know it's a weird thing to talk about. But I felt like I needed to share it with you, so you'd know that I understand. It's a strange thing, and maybe it's not even real, but there was just a connection here and I was hoping to explain it, so I didn't come across as a creep for speaking to you," he answered.

Mona looked up from Biscuit. She could see that Paul felt very conflicted. She wondered what that was like, to question your own politeness because of the stigma around you.

She then realized she didn't have to wonder.

In the same way Paul was worried anything he said might come across as creepy or misconstrued, Mona worried that anything she said or did would be viewed as inappropriate or teasing. She was constantly worried she was being sexual in the same way Paul was worried he was being inappropriate, even though they both knew their intentions were pure. They weren't being the things they thought they were, but the fear of someone else believing they were was stronger than reason.

Mona liked him. She liked Biscuit more, but she liked Paul. She liked that he could talk without needing input, but also without speaking just to speak. He had things to say when he spoke. Reasons for saying them. And Mona liked listening. She was a great listener.

"For what it's worth, I know you're not a creep," Mona told him.

He smiled. "For what it's worth, that's all that matters."

They walked most of the way in silence. At first, she wasn't sure why he was walking with her, especially when he had nothing to say. But she slowly realized he was watching over her. Protecting a young girl as she walked home alone.

Once the trailer park was within sight, Mona stopped and gave Biscuit a head scratch. He looked less like a happy dog and sadder now, realizing what was going on.

"I better get on home," she told them both.

Paul nodded and patted his leg for Biscuit to come to him. Reluctantly, the dog did. He didn't look very happy about it and Mona contained the laugh that this threatened to bring out.

But then Paul suddenly looked at her with disappointment. "I know it might not be any of my business, but are you going to be okay? I can't help but feel like you need help," he told her.

Mona shook her head. "I'll be okay," she told him.

"You sure about that?" he asked.

It took Mona only a moment to realize that he was looking at her face. Mona had forgotten that she was still bruised. She'd forgotten that Beau hit her the night before like it was nothing more than a slight inconvenience. She forgot that it led to her cheek being an ugly shade of purple and noticeable to people around her. She was so used to being invisible, she wasn't used to people looking at her.

For a moment, she wondered what Paul might see when he looked at her. What did he really see? He said he saw her the same as his baby sister, but setting that aside, what was it that he really saw when he looked at her?

The first time he met her when she cowered in the bushes to save his and Biscuit's life, or a little while later when she was being loved by his dog and he thought he would swindle some cash from her… What did he see in her face that told him that he shouldn't do that?

What about when he saw that one moment of fear when he had approached her and Birdie? Or even when he had found Biscuit with her again just minutes before? What had he thought when he walked up on them and her face was bruised, but Biscuit's happiness was evident?

And what about now? What was it that Paul saw now as he looked at her? Did he really see a sad little girl? Did he see her pain? Did he actually see her?

It was these questions that seem to be going over and over in Mona's mind lately. She wondered who actually saw her. Who was she to them? What was her role in their lives?

Because Mona had no clue who she was. She didn't know if she was good or bad. She didn't know if she was just like Beau, evil at the core and only out for herself. She didn't know if she was a good person. She didn't even know if she was morally decent. She had absolutely no idea who she was, and she wondered how people around her looked at her. What they thought she was. What they saw when they looked her way.

To Beau, she was a prize. Property. She belonged to him and only he saw who she truly was. Mona knew that he saw the same thing that he saw in himself. That he was good. Maybe not as good as most people would think, but good in his own opinion. Beau looked at her as the result of his unhappiness and the chance of his new happiness. He saw her as a way out. An outlet for his own pain.

She was sure her parents saw a disappointment or possession. Especially her dad. She sometimes thought that her mom saw a lot of herself in her and maybe she was a little jealous of Mona. Jealous because of how Daddy kept his eye on her. And Daddy was exactly as Beau said. Possessive of her because he saw her as his. Because he wanted her in the same way he had wanted Mama so long ago. But because that made him feel bad, he instead kept close tabs on Mona to make sure no one took what he wanted.

She sometimes felt that Beau was a lot more like their mother than she thought. That Beau had that same possessive, but jealous streak that their mother had.

Clyde looked at her and saw just another thing. Just an object. Because she was a woman. She was no more important than anyone else. Clyde was not free-thinking. He didn't question things. He just took what he was told and ran with it.

Birdie saw her as competition. Because Mona was the daughter and Birdie wasn't. And she could tell how much Birdie wanted to be loved and accepted. And she could tell that Birdie wanted her mama to look at and treat her as a daughter. She wanted that connection, and it was Mona that should have it. Because Mona was their child.

Owen saw her as something. Mona wasn't sure what. Maybe before their argument, he had seen her as his girlfriend and that meant something to have sex with. Something to unload his frustrations in. A vessel really.

But now she wasn't quite sure.

In the same way that she wasn't sure what Paul thought of her. And she wasn't sure if anyone actually saw who she was and not just their idea of her. Did anyone truly see Mona, and if they did, was she good? Was she lovable? Or was she damned?

Mona wondered if she were to really look at herself, stop for a minute and just stare at himself in the mirror, what would she see? Would she see something that she liked? Would she see someone worth saving? If she looked into her eyes long enough, would Mona want to save herself?

And maybe that was why she didn't. Maybe she was afraid that if she took too long of a look, she would understand that she deserved nothing more than what she was given. That she might stare for long enough to realize that she was exactly where she needed to be. That she needed to be punished. Not so much for anything that she had done but for things that she would do. That maybe, outside of this family, outside of their control, she would be even worse, and she would deserve all the pain and misery that would come her way. That maybe this was God's way of keeping her contained. This was His way assuring that she didn't go out and hurt anyone. That she didn't do like Beau did. Maybe this was His attempt at saving her soul.

Or maybe it was a pile of horse crap and Mona was tired of buying into it.

"I'll be okay," she told Paul.

He offered a small smile. "I hope so," he said. He looked down at Biscuit and gave him a good scratch behind the ears. "Come on, boy. Let's get you some food ready."

Mona smiled at the dog and watched him turn with Paul. Tail wagging, tongue out, she could tell the dog loved his owner. She watched after them, almost wishing she could follow them. Wishing she could just turn around and go with them, hide out from the rest of the world and just love on Biscuit.

Why don't you?

She looked toward the entrance of the trailer park. She knew why. She would be found out quickly. Not only would she be found, but Paul would be in trouble because of her. And if Paul was in trouble, Biscuit would have no one. Mona couldn't ruin two lives because she decided to be reckless.

She would bide her time and find a way that didn't get anyone in trouble for her. She'd find a way to get away from them and not have to look over her shoulder constantly.

There's only one way you'll do that.

Mona forced the voice of reason from her mind and pushed her bike into the trailer park. She walked past the other trailers and into her own yard. She carried the bags inside. She and Birdie put away the groceries because Mama told them to. She was cooking and Clyde was cleaning up his and Beau's room because Beau was working now.

When Mona saw Clyde, he had a red welt across his cheek. Mona didn't even have to guess to know that he had likely popped off about Beau not having to clean. Probably something was said about it not being fair, and that word was almost a trigger for their mother. She'd backhand you faster than you could fully say the word.

Or maybe she was tapping into that *knowing* that Paul mentioned.

Or maybe she was tapping into that survival instinct she needed.

Daddy and Beau came home while Mama was still rolling dumplings. Beau gave Mama a kiss on the cheek and then went ahead and took a shower. He seemed like he was in a cheery mood, and that was very unlike Beau.

And he was completely ignoring her.

Mona wasn't complaining, but she was suspicious. She was waiting for him to do something. She didn't know what he was going to do, but she knew this wasn't it. He wasn't going to just ignore her as revenge. He was planning something. Plotting.

Or maybe he was already acting on his plan.

All of it just made her even more nervous. She didn't like these moments of limbo. It was the not knowing that was really bothering her. It kept her on edge, and she was sure Beau liked that. It was probably something he was counting on.

Or maybe he just had no clue how else he could make her suffer.

Or maybe it was all talk.

Everyone ate dinner and then they watched TV until Mama told them to start getting showers. Mona helped in the kitchen and Beau stayed in the living room and discussed work things with Daddy. Mona was going to keep track of what they were saying, but the sudden pain she was feeling in her stomach kept her mind focused elsewhere.

It was sudden and sharp. They felt like cramps, but not in the same area. It was higher up, and it felt like someone was poking and twisting her guts inside. They were coming and going, and making Mona break out in a cold sweat.

"Mona?" her mother asked from nowhere.

Mona spun around and caught the look of concern on her Mama's face. She narrowed her brows and crossed her arms as she stared at her daughter but made no movement toward her.

"You're looking a little green around the gills, girl," she mentioned.

"Period cramps," Mona said quickly. Maybe a little too quickly. But it was the first thought to enter her mind, and she was wondering if it was coming soon. She didn't know when her cycle would begin again. She hoped soon, but the feeling she was feeling could be more intense because of the abortion.

At least, she was hoping.

Mama didn't look convinced. But she also didn't look worried. She looked at the dishes. "Go get some ibuprofen. Birdie will finish your chores tonight," she said, her voice snappy. Mona knew she was disappointed that Mona was hurting enough to not do what she was told. She was disappointed that Mona would let her pain inconvenience anyone else.

"It's okay. I can finish," Mona told her. She turned around and started on the dishes again. She worked even faster and with more focus. It seemed to be enough for her mama to go about her business and save Mona from any repercussions.

She took her shower last. By then, the water was cool, but she wasn't feeling as bad. She wasn't bleeding, so she hadn't started her period. She passed it off that maybe the food didn't agree with her and that was where the cramps had come from. They were past for now and she got ready for bed.

She managed to fall asleep, but before midnight came, Mona woke up in a cold sweat. Her stomach was twisting again, but this time there was more than just pain.

Mona had to get up fast and cover her mouth the keep from throwing up in the bed. She swallowed some of it before she could get to the bathroom. She didn't even bother to close the door as she got on the floor in front of the toilet.

She wasted no time leaning over the toilet and throwing up. She realized there was nothing she hated more in the world than to vomit. And since it was rare that she ever got sick, it was rare that she ever vomited at all. There wasn't much compassion in their house for when you were sick. You just had to suck it up and keep going or get in trouble. The passive aggressive attitude was enough to make you avoid telling someone when you didn't feel well.

But here she was, keeled over the toilet, and puking for no reason that she could see.

She didn't know what caused the sudden need to throw up, but it was burning for her to do it. She felt so sick and so disgusted. Her stomach felt like her period, but much worse. It felt like the cramps that she would get, magnified by a hundred. Her throat and nose were burning, her eyes watering. When she reached over to the toilet paper and rolled some off in her hand to wipe them, she finally looked in the toilet and felt scared.

There was blood. Blood and her vomit. Mona fell back and moved up against the wall. That couldn't be right. She didn't want to look again, but she was hoping that she could find the strength to look and that the blood would be gone.

Because it wasn't real.

Vomiting blood wasn't a good sign. She didn't know what it was a sign of, but her first thought went to her abortion. Was it something to do with that? Was she throwing up blood because it wasn't escaping between her legs anymore? Was that blood part of the baby? Was it even normal? Was it caused by the abortion?

And if any of those questions were yes, what in the world was she going to do about it? Because she couldn't tell her parents. She was afraid to tell anyone and have them take her to the hospital and find out what she had done. But she was also afraid that if she didn't say anything that things would only get worse and that she might die.

And Mona was so close to getting away now. All she had to do was play her cards right. Someone finding out that she had had an abortion before Beau was long gone and she was able to save up enough to get out of town, she couldn't do that. She couldn't allow that to happen.

She finally found the willpower to get back on her knees and look inside the toilet. It was blood. Blood splattered all over the bowl, probably from where she had coughed up the last bit. The rest was just food, it looked like.

But that blood, that horrible, awful blood reminded her she had so much left to lose.

Mona flushed the toilet and then flushed it again just to make sure that all the blood was gone. She was sure that someone had heard her throwing up, the walls were thin, but she didn't want to give them a reason to find out about the blood. She could just tell them that she had gotten sick to her stomach all of a sudden. It might even get her in trouble, but it was better than being found out.

She stood up and looked at her face in the mirror. She looked pale, but she wasn't sure if that was because of her throwing up or if that was just the reality that had set in when she had seen *what* she threw up. Because she was scared. She was always scared, but she was really scared now. Scared that everything she had been trying so hard to escape from was going to keep her trapped forever. Maybe this was just a foreshadow of the things to come.

A sign that she was never going to get away. Because she would always have something getting in the way of her leaving.

But she had to keep hope. She was so close she could taste it. All she had to do was just keep quiet long enough to find a way out. Long enough to find one little thing that could help her escape and not get caught. She didn't know what that thing was, but she would figure it out. She had to. Her life depended on it.

She threw some cold water on her face and then patted it dry with the towel. She opened her mouth and looked inside, looking for any traces of blood, and then decided that she would just brush her teeth. She brushed them two times before telling herself that she was overreacting. She had to calm down and she had to think about this.

Because if she reacted rather than stopped and thought, it was only going to get worse. She was only going to end up making a mistake and ending up stuck. Ending up just as she had always been.

The first thing she knew she was going to have to do was figure out what was going on. She was going to have to get by to the library.

She was going to test the waters in the morning to see when she would be able to go to the library. Even if she had to take Birdie and Clyde with her, she had to get there and figure out what might have caused it. Most importantly, find out if her abortion could have anything to do with it.

But she wondered if maybe she was overreacting about that too. She was throwing up blood, but this was the only time. She hadn't been throwing up blood for the last few days. There wasn't even anything that said she was going to throw it up again. It was just this one time.

But Mona knew that it was better to be safe than sorry. If she could rule out that it was her abortion, perhaps she could say something if it happened again. If someone else happened to figure out that she was sick, she could feel a little better about telling them and possibly seeing a doctor.

Although she was hesitant about seeing a doctor. She wasn't sure how pregnancy or anything might affect things like blood levels or other things that she wasn't thinking about. She couldn't be sure that a doctor wouldn't take one look at her and realize that she had been pregnant a week before. And then she would be in trouble, because the doctor would surely tell her parents that something wasn't right. Or they would even hint around, and her parents would get the idea that something was going on.

And that was all they needed to get suspicious about anything. That was all they needed to be angry at her and have a reason to let loose their anger. And then she would be on the bed, sore and flinching anytime she moved for a week.

She wasn't sure if she had a week to spare. Because she had to make sure that she was gone soon. And she had to make sure that Beau was being seen as a suspect. She had to get to a phone. A phone where nobody would be around to hear her when she called the police and gave them a hint. A phone that couldn't even be traced back to her house. Either that or she had to find another way of guiding the police to him.

She didn't trust them to do the job themselves.

With all of these questions circling in her mind, she turned off the light. She crept quietly back into her bed and stared at the ceiling, hoping she'd be able to figure out what to do before it was too late.

Chapter Six

Isaiah 13:11

And I will punish the world for their evils, and the wicked for their iniquity; and I will cause the arrogancy of the proud to cease, and will lay low the haughtiness of the terrible.

"Is Mona home?"

Mona hadn't expected to hear his voice. When she saw a familiar car pull into her yard, she knew who it would be, but she still didn't expect to actually hear his voice.

"You're not welcome around my daughter anymore," her daddy told him.

Mona was standing in the kitchen. She could just see Owen's

face as he stood off to the side of their mobile home steps. Her daddy stood in the door, the big, brute force that he was, and blocked out the rest of him. She doubted Owen could see her in the kitchen watching him.

"I just need to talk to her. It won't be more than ten minutes."

He looked stressed. It was funny how Mona could see that now, how she was starting to see him. She had known Owen almost her entire life, but only from a stranger's perspective. Then, they had begun to date, but she still was nothing more than a stranger to him, and him to her. She didn't bother to learn much about him other than what she saw. He'd been nothing more than a distraction. A small beacon of hope had risen in her that he might be her way out, but she now knew that even if he could do that, he wouldn't do it fast enough for her.

"I said you're not welcome here."

That one moment of vulnerability between the both of them had started her thinking, though. Started her looking. Seeing what was hidden rather than what he had shown her. Maybe even started her feeling, because with Owen, she had cut off all feelings that she could. The walls between them had been thick and wide and tall. Because she could control herself completely around him, it was easy to shut off all feelings and emotions.

"Just tell her I stopped by."

But now, she was feeling something. She was very unsure of what it was, but it was something. She wouldn't call it love, because she knew for sure that wasn't what it was, but maybe compassion? Sympathy? She knew there was more to Owen than she had given him credit for, and she was a little upset with herself for not understanding that sooner.

Her daddy didn't answer back. Mona walked into the living room and headed toward the bathroom as he slammed the door. She looked out the window in the living room as she passed, watching Owen get into the car.

He'd be back. Mona feared for him when he came back, but he would be back.

Owen happened to glance up as he closed the door. He looked at her; tempted, it seemed. But he cast a soft smile her way and started the car up. Mona watched him leave before heading into the bathroom.

Things were only getting worse. She knew it. The sick feeling she was keeping was bad enough, but now her tiny act of rebellion was being shut down for absolutely no reason at all. They knew Owen wasn't responsible for the bruise on her cheek and they still ordered her to not see him.

Soon, it would be more. They would continue to find other things to control until Mona was scared to breathe. It would never end, and Beau knew that.

He knew and that was why he wanted to run. He saw his offer as kindness, but Mona knew better. It was not a jail break, just a new prison cell. She was just giving someone a new key to keep her captive. And this cell came with more repercussions than Mona wanted.

She hated Beau. She might be willing to say she hated all of them. Either way, she wanted to be gone. Distanced from them completely and able to be herself.

That was the one thing she would never get with her family. No matter what, she would never be able to be who she was around any of them. She always had to be on alert. She always had to watch every move she made.

But she didn't even know who she was to begin with. She had no clue. All she knew was that she wasn't this person. This version of wallpaper she had to be in order to survive. If she wasn't around them, she could find out who she was. She wasn't sure if she'd ever truly find out, but she'd have a chance.

A chance was all she was asking for, really.

Mona got dressed and braided her hair. She walked into the kitchen and did her morning rituals of cooking, eating and cleaning before asking if she could go to the library. As expected, her mother assured her that she could as long as she took Birdie and Clyde. It wasn't ideal, but it was expected. She was told the thing that she knew she would be told. If she was going to the library, because everyone knew that when Mona went to the library she liked to be there for a while, she could take Birdie and Clyde with her. That way they could get off Mama's nerves for a while and maybe grab a book or two.

The only problem with that was that Clyde wasn't allowed to grab any more books from the library. After the librarian had to keep reminding Clyde over and over to bring back his books, they eventually just revoked his library card.

Birdie hardly ever checked out library books, because she didn't really like to read, but she was still able to get them if she wanted them. Mostly, Birdie would just look around the library for any boys that were roughly in her age range and try to look cute. It was a tactic that Mona would not rat on her for. Mona knew as well as anybody that, really, the only way that they were ever going to be able to leave Mama and Daddy's house was if they were married.

Or if they got knocked up.

The only way they would leave is if they had another house to go to, and the only way they were going to find that was if they found a man. Birdie was only twelve, but she already knew this. And Mona guessed that she was just trying to go ahead and shoot her shot as a way to eventually escape.

Mona wished she didn't have to take them, but it was better than nothing. She could do what she needed to do while they played around and did their own thing. Birdie would flirt and Clyde would see what trouble he could get into.

Honestly, Mona didn't think that she would have to deal with them at all while she was at the library. And that was good. That meant that she could look for the things that she needed to look for.

Because Mona was going with Birdie and Clyde, they all took their bikes. They rode their bikes into town and then parked them at the library. Mona wished she had an actual bicycle lock, but the next best thing that they could do was use the chain that Clyde brought along with his. They chained their bikes up to hopefully keep from being stolen and then went into the library.

Mona brought back the books that she had checked out two weeks before, and Birdie disappeared immediately. She told Mona that she was going to look in the young adult section, but Mona knew that she really was going to look at the young adults of the male gender.

Clyde stuck around as she returned her books but then disappeared to go outside, which didn't bother Mona at all. She immediately turned to the computers and got online. She purposely chose a computer that faced the wall when she sat down. That way she would be able to keep an eye on Birdie and Clyde if they decided to come and see what she was looking at.

She also opened two tabs. One with pictures of books that were mysteries, like Mona usually got, and then one for the actual reason she was looking online. That way if someone did come near her, she could hurry up and switch the tabs to keep them from seeing what she was looking for.

She had to do these things. She had to take these precautions. Her entire life felt like she was walking in a minefield. She had to watch every step. She had to try to anticipate each next step she took. She had to try and figure out what the outcome was of the actions she' Of what actions would lead to what situations. And most of the time she could keep herself safe. She could keep herself protected.

But sometimes things would happen that she hadn't accounted for. Things she would kick herself over later. She would realize that she should have thought about this before she had done it. Realize that she had missed it completely and she would kick herself for missing it. Like the paper in her backpack. But she still had to try her best. She still had to try, and it was exhausting.

All the sneaking was even more exhausting. She was anxious. Her anxiety was through the roof. Because this wasn't something to just survive. This was a full-on lie. It was something that they could never know about. Because if they did there was no telling what would happen to her. This was something that she had to keep up until she could be gone, and that was nerve-racking. She didn't want to have to spend her entire life lying.

Lying.

Of all the sins in the world, she hated that this was the one that she had to commit on a daily basis. She wanted to be a good person. She wanted to be filled with the light of God and be pure and precious, to be filled with the spirit, but she didn't know how she was ever going to do that when she had to lie just to make it through a day. She didn't know how she was going to survive when her entire survival depended on her lying and sneaking and cheating and doing all the things that the Bible said not to do. Because the Bible said to trust in Him, that He would save you from all your troubles. But it was hard to believe that when He was also the one that put you in your troubles.

Mona couldn't honestly blame herself for the position that she was in. Because she was born into this family. She didn't have another choice. It wasn't like she had gotten into a bad relationship or that she was dealing with normal parents that she just didn't agree with. Mona knew deep down that her situation was not normal. It was not something that she could just blame on herself. She wasn't the one that put herself in this position.

And she knew that if she was to tell someone else this, especially someone from the church, they would tell her that she was being a little selfish. Or that she wasn't taking responsibility for the role that she played.

And she wasn't completely sure if that was true or not. She didn't know if she was putting too much blame on everyone else and not enough on herself. Because she had felt guilt when she had been researching abortions and trying to figure out how she was going to get one. She felt shame while she was there. And she'd had to lie about it ever since she had had one.

But the reason that she had one was because of her situation. Because of the family that she was born into. Because of Beau. Because he had taken away her right to say whether she wanted to get pregnant or not. Because it had been her body, but he had decided to use it to his own advantages.

He had raped her and raped her again and again to intentionally try to get her pregnant. Because he wanted her to be pregnant. Mona hadn't laid down and had sex out of marriage. She hadn't been reckless about any of that. She'd been dating Owen for almost as long as Beau had been raping her and she had never tried to have sex with him. She never even thought about it. Because she didn't want to. And that was a choice that she had made.

But Beau had taken away her choice when he got her pregnant. So, if there ever was a time for her to have an abortion and not feel wrong by anyone's moral code, wouldn't now be that time? Couldn't she stop feeling as if she had to lie about it when it was justified?

Or maybe it wasn't justified. Maybe she was just hoping it might be, so she didn't have to feel so scared. Or so judged.

Or an even bigger, more dangerous maybe was that it was justified no matter what and people just made their own judgments because that was what people did. They passed blame onto one issue to avoid their own. It was a way of diverting the attention to something else so they could justify the sin they committed.

That was what Beau did, after all. He made a big deal about the abortion but neglected the rape he had done to cause her to get pregnant in the first place. He measured that the abortion was worse than the rape. By his own moral code, she had no doubt that he didn't think what he had done was bad at all. In fact, she'd go as far as to say that he considered it okay and wasn't worried about his soul being eternally damned at all.

After all, Mona knew Beau considered himself an atheist. He pretended to pay attention in church, but it was mostly to avoid trouble. Like Owen, he had issues with the people that went. Unlike Owen, he also had issues with the idea of a god controlling anything.

Mona, however, still didn't know what she thought. Unlike her parents, who thought anyone that didn't believe in God was eternally damned to Hell, and her brother and boyfriend, who thought people that did believe in those things were eternally damned to bondage, Mona didn't care who thought what. Because on both sides of the spectrum, it boiled down to control. Her parents used God to control them. Beau used the lack of God to control himself.

Mona was using her doubts and confusion to gain back some control.

She searched for the side effects of abortions, but found that vomiting and nausea were only one for a couple days after. There were no mentions of blood or vomiting after those few days being a sign for concern. Most of the things that were reasons to see a doctor immediately were dealing with vaginal bleeding, and Mona wasn't having any issues with that.

With that put aside, Mona was fairly certain that she hadn't vomited blood because of the abortion. That lifted a huge weight off her shoulders. With that ruled out, she looked up causes for vomiting blood. She was met with a ton of different things. Anything from cancer to liver failure. But most of these things said it was prolonged vomiting, not one time.

Mona closed out the tabs and got up. As long as it wasn't caused by her abortion, she felt better. She wasn't sure if she would throw up blood again, so maybe it was a one-off thing. She ate something bad. Maybe even a tear or an ulcer. But right now, it seemed like she had nothing to worry about. She just had to wait and see what would happen.

She walked into the crime and mystery section of the library and found a few books to take home. She didn't like checking out too many at a time because she wanted to be sure she didn't lose any of them. For all she knew, Beau would hide enough of her books until she was banned from the library. He hadn't done so, but it was a possibility and Mona tried to keep her eyes out for those.

She found Birdie in the Young Adult section, but there were no boys around. She was thumbing through a dystopian romance, but not really reading it. She looked bored and Mona felt bad for her. She probably was hopelessly bored. Not only here in the library but in her life as well.

Mona knew that Birdie longed for excitement. Birdie longed for romance. She wanted to feel the thrill of being kissed or taken out. Someone holding your hand, cupping your face, telling you they loved you. She was even sure Birdie was thinking about things like

THE BREAKING OF MONA HILL

sex. Mona hoped she wasn't, but Birdie was maturing fast.

Too fast.

Mona worried. She looked at Birdie like a sister. It was why she told Birdie little things. Things about Owen, things about boys. She discussed those things, to a certain extent, with Birdie. She knew Birdie was a tattletale and she could always flip Mona's words just to get a little attention, but for the most part, Birdie was okay. Birdie was innocent.

But Mona watched the world around her, and she found Birdie to be a little too flirtatious with Clyde. It scared her. Not only because she could be right, but because she could be wrong.

Her daddy saw bad everywhere he looked. Her mama saw the Devil. Mona didn't think the world was all bad, but it was easy to see it if you looked. She was afraid that she was becoming like them. That nothing was going on at all between Birdie and Clyde but because of Beau, she now assumed there was. She saw what she wanted to see and couldn't trust her own judgment anymore because of her trauma.

Or maybe Paul was right, and she just knew. Nothing was wrong with her instincts. If anything, they were finer tuned to what was going on around her. And if that was true, something was definitely going on, or just beginning to, with Clyde.

Clyde wanted to be like Beau. He idolized him. From the moment Clyde had been born, Beau had been an attentive big brother. He did everything with Clyde, showed him all he knew, and they talked all the time. She sometimes thought that it was one of the reasons Clyde was so distant with her. She was the only person closer to Beau than he was.

But Mona would give him that total access if she could. Or she would shut him off completely. Because she worried Birdie was going to end up in her position.

She didn't know if anything had happened or if they had just flirted around with the possibility of something happening between them, but she made a mental note to keep a closer eye on them. Just to be safe.

"Are you ready to go?" Mona asked in a quiet whisper.

Birdie turned around and nodded. She put the book back on the shelf. Birdie didn't borrow any books and simply followed Mona to the counter.

Mona looked around as she checked out her books, but she didn't see Clyde. When the librarian finished, Mona put the books into her backpack and walked outside with Birdie. They were halfway to their bikes when Mona finally caught a glimpse of Clyde.

"Ew, Clyde! That's gross," Birdie said, but continued to walk toward him.

Mona started, but a sharp pain in her stomach made her stop and clutch it. Even still, she knew she didn't want to get any closer to him anyway. She really was going to throw up if she did.

Clyde was messing with a dying squirrel. Part of its intestines were on the ground and Clyde was poking at them with a stick. He was laughing every time the squirrel twitched.

"It's still alive! Maybe we can save it," Birdie said, squatting next to him.

"Its guts are out. You can't save it, idiot," Clyde told her with a nasty tone. His next poke was to its face where it really began to twitch. Clyde laughed at that and even Birdie managed a giggle.

"Shouldn't we put it out of its misery then?"

Mona could almost see the joy fill Clyde's body as he stood up. He didn't even wait for Birdie to move before he slammed one foot down on its head. Mona heard the cracks in its tiny skull splinter and break as parts of its brain and blood splattered out of it. Some of it got on the hem of Birdie's skirt and she was angry, but Mona's stomach turned. She had enough time to turn around, thinking about the bush, before she threw up on the grass.

"Now look! You made Mona sick," Birdie exclaimed.

"What a pussy. It was gonna die anyway!" he yelled at her, seemingly disappointed that him splattering a squirrel's brain across the road would make her sick.

But it wasn't the squirrel. It helped, but Mona was already feeling sick before he did that. It was just that the action gave her the last little nudge her stomach needed to expel her breakfast.

She didn't throw up as much as she had the night before, but she had only eaten breakfast. She didn't have much to throw back up.

She heard Birdie coming toward her, but she couldn't stop

herself from dry heaving and gagging. When Birdie asked if she was okay, Mona couldn't really answer. Not that Birdie would have wanted her to if she could. She would have been very tempted to give her the same smart aleck tone Clyde had with the squirrel.

She could tell that Birdie, and even Clyde, were beginning to grow a little nervous. Maybe even concerned. And one of the last things she needed was for them to start questioning why she was throwing up. Because they would go home and tell Mama and things could only go downhill from there.

Mona didn't even comment on the fact that Clyde had killed that squirrel the way that he did. She didn't want to have any of that interfere with whatever she was doing. She couldn't risk pissing Clyde off. She honestly couldn't risk pissing anyone off at this point. With Beau already angry at her, she figured her free passes were limited.

She wiped her mouth and stood up. Birdie looked at her strangely, but she managed a small smile for Birdie's benefit. "I'm okay. Just made me sick."

"It was gross," Birdie said, then cast a sour look Clyde's way.

Clyde shrugged. "It was going to die anyway," he said, as if what he had done wasn't gross on its own. Or inhumane. Sure, maybe it needed to die so it wasn't suffering, but Clyde didn't do it because he was thinking about the animal. He did it because he saw a chance to kill something and took it.

It was things like this that worried Mona. She had read enough crime books to know people that killed animals as kids, in brutal or sadistic ways, were often bad news. She couldn't remember if the term was psychopath or sociopath, but it was scary either way.

And Clyde was already so much like Beau. If he had the chance, he would become exactly like Beau.

Was he already planning to kill all of them? Just like Beau?

Was it Beau's fault that Clyde was this way? With how Clyde tried so hard to emulate Beau in every way possible?

Mona knew for a fact that Beau had to have these thoughts. There was no question that he wanted to kill them all. In fact, Mona knew for certain that it was the way Beau would make sure that they never came after them. He would kill them before they left. Mona wasn't sure if she could also be complicit in that. She wasn't sure if she could live the rest of her life with that any more than she could live the rest of her life with Beau and his sick fantasy.

"Let's just go home. Mama is probably wondering where we are," Mona said.

They each climbed onto their bikes and Mona put her books in her basket. She was hoping the nausea would ease off, but she found herself feeling worse as they biked their way home.

When she did get home, Mona didn't eat lunch. She could get away with that, but she couldn't get away with skipping dinner. So, she took her chances with skipping lunch and spent the day in bed, saying she was reading, but really trying to get the uneasy feeling in her stomach to disappear.

She was cramping badly. The pains were sharp and intense, and she found herself cradling her stomach, close to tears. She was almost relieved that Birdie was somewhere else, so she didn't have to fake being okay around her. She could try to push the pain away if Birdie wasn't there to question her and keep tabs on her.

When it came time to start dinner, she had it numbed. The pains had subsided for a while, and she was at least able to get up and help with dinner. She even tried to get in Mama's good graces by cooking dinner for everyone so Mama could rest instead.

Mona cooked for everyone and prepared the plates. She was feeling okay. She managed to get through dinner, but after she had taken a few bites of her food, she began to feel sick again. She wasn't sure why her stomach felt so bad, but there were sharp pains followed by intense cramps. The only thing that had ever come close to feeling the same way as this did was her period when it was really bad in the first few days.

She wasn't sure what she was supposed to do in order to make herself feel better, but she knew she had to fake it. She couldn't let anybody know that she wasn't feeling good, because that would just get her in trouble. She had to do the rest of her chores, get her good nights said, and then go to bed. After her shower, where she could cry or cower down in the shower until she felt better, she'd be fine. She could have those few moments to help herself, readjust so that she could go to bed without anybody knowing how she was feeling.

She washed the dishes and cleaned up the kitchen with Birdie's help. Mona made sure not to let it show that she was in pain. They managed to clean the kitchen entirely before Birdie had to go and take her shower.

Mona helped with the laundry, separating it out and then grabbing her own to put up. After she had hung up and folded her clothes, Birdie came out and Mona almost ran into the bathroom.

She turned on the sink so that she could brush her teeth, but the only thing she could do was grip the counter and take deep breaths. The pain was excruciating. It felt like something was at war with her insides. She didn't know what was causing it.

She felt pretty certain that it didn't have anything to do with the abortion but that was the most recent thing she had done. It could have been her actual period coming and maybe this was God's way of punishing her. Maybe He was letting her know that she had gotten her period back when it came back at a cost. The cost of her not having a baby was that she would now have to endure some of the worst cramps of her entire life.

And Mona figured this was just what she would have to do then. She would have to deal with it. It wasn't like she could do anything else. She couldn't complain about it to anyone. She couldn't talk to Pastor Steve or even her own mother about this. She didn't have any friends to confide in. She couldn't see a doctor or even go to the clinic. And she had already been to the library and that was about her only access to the internet. It was her only access to information when school wasn't in session.

She was just stuck.

Mona brushed her teeth, but only for a few seconds. She really just wanted to get into the warm shower and hope that the hot water might ease her discomfort. She wasn't sure if it would, and a nice long bath might have been better, but if anything could at least ease it off she'd be okay. That was all that she really cared about. Just easing some of it off.

But as she turned on the water for the shower, the cramps turned into nausea. Suddenly, dinner decided to come back up, and Mona rushed to the toilet and vomited. She threw up until her nose was running and tears were coming from her eyes. And when she looked into the toilet, it was blood again. She quickly flushed it only to start throwing up again.

Mona had never vomited with as much force or pain as she did now. And although the night before she had managed to throw up without disturbing anyone, there was a knock at the door this time.

"Are you okay?" Birdie asked from the other side.

"I'm…" Mona couldn't even get the last word out without vomiting again.

She heard the door open, and panic began to set in. Birdie was probably the worst person that could come into the bathroom while she was throwing up. Because Mona knew that if she got close to the toilet, she would see the blood and freak out. And that's exactly what she did.

As Birdie came further inside, she looked at the toilet, and Mona heard her gasp in fear. "Aunt Ann! Aunt Ann, hurry!"

"No," Mona tried to protest but then vomited again. She wiped out her eyes as she pulled her hair back, but she felt so weak. Mona felt like she might pass out if she wasn't able to stop throwing up soon.

"What in the world are you back here yelling about?" she heard her mother complaining as she came down the hall. Mona had really hoped that she could avoid her mother at all costs. Because she knew that her mother was going to be angry about her throwing up. She was going to be angry about Mona being sick at all. And that was going to start drama, and it was going to put a spotlight on Mona that she didn't want. Especially right now as she was doing everything in her power to get away from her family.

"Mona's throwing up, and it looks like blood!" Birdie told her. As expected, Birdie sounded hysterical. She couldn't possibly just say that Mona was throwing up and that it might be blood in a calm or reasonable voice, she had to make sure that her mother heard the seriousness of this possibility. She had to know that Mona was throwing up and that it was blood. And that blood was very important. That blood was something that needed to be addressed right now and taken care of. And her mother needed to see it and realize that Birdie was doing such a good job taking the situation and allowing her to know.

Mona managed to catch her breath. She rested her cheek against the toilet seat. Honestly, she didn't see a reason to try and pretend that she felt okay. Because no matter what, her mother was going to be angry.

Which was clear when she came closer to the toilet and spoke.

"Why'd you wait this long to tell anybody you were sick?" her mother accused.

"I'm sorry," Mona said.

"Yeah, well let me get your father," her mother said roughly.

Mona thought about how in the movies, her mother would have just been worried. Scared even. She would have seen the blood in the toilet mixed with all of dinner and she would have been concerned. Maybe she would have even called an ambulance right then and Mona could have told her no, it's not that serious. Or she would have gotten her father to come back there while holding her and telling her it was going to be okay. She would tell her that they were going to take her and get her checked out. That she didn't have to worry about any of it, because Mommy and Daddy were going to make sure she was okay. And then they would baby her. Because they were sympathetic to what she was feeling.

But instead, her mother used the tone that implied that Mona had hidden it for awful reasons. That it was Mona's fault that she was sick, and that could very well be true. Honestly, it probably was true, but she was still a little upset that she couldn't get some sort of sympathy from her own mother.

Mona heard Birdie's voice in the living room telling Daddy that Mona was sick and to come to the bathroom. Mona listened as his footsteps came down the hallway and then smelled his cologne as he came into the bathroom. She even heard his gasp, similar to Birdie's, as he asked, "Is that blood?"

"It looks like it, but it could just be the tomato soup we ate for lunch," her mother answered. She seemed to conveniently forget that Mona hadn't eaten lunch though. Mona had tried to avoid eating anything all day.

"I don't know, it looks kind of like blood. How are you feeling, Mona?" her daddy asked.

"I'm okay now," Mona answered.

"Maybe we should take her to the emergency room," her daddy suggested.

"I'm sure it's just stomach bug," her mother answered. "What are they going to do for a stomach bug?"

"They might put her on an antibiotic or something," her daddy said.

"Which is going to be money that we don't have," her mother answered. "I think I got some old antibiotics in the medicine box. Just give her some of those and see if it passes in a few days. She can stay in bed so that she's not spreading it around. Birdie can take over her responsibilities for a few days."

Mona could hear the contempt in her mother's voice. Like her sudden illness was just an inconvenience for every single possible person in their house except Mona. As if Mona was actually getting something from this.

And Mona realized she hated her mother. She hated her mother for the way that she hated her. Because her mother was supposed to love her. Mama was supposed to have a closer relationship with Mona than anyone else besides her father. Because Mona was her only daughter.

And yet it seemed like the only feeling that Mama had for her was contempt. The only thing she felt for her daughter was anger. And if she could manage to turn everyone else against her, then she'd be better for it. And in that way, she reminded her of Beau. If Mona had ever wanted to know where Beau got that same type of reasoning from, it was their mama.

Maybe that was the reason that her mama seemed more attached to Beau than she did either of her other kids. Maybe it was why Mama would actually stick up for Beau if she felt the need to. Beau was her baby.

And with this, Mona realized that she was going to have to escape soon. She couldn't get trapped in this house, especially now that she was feeling sick. She didn't know how long this might last or if it might just blow over in a few days like Mama said but either way, Mona couldn't allow it to keep her stuck. She was going to have to find another way to escape. Even if it meant that she would still be there when Beau got found out.

Either way, Mona couldn't afford to stay much longer.

THE BREAKING OF MONA HILL

Chapter Seven

Colossians 3:9

Lie not to one another, seeing that ye have put off the old man with his deeds.

Mona didn't say anything, but she wasn't very happy at the prospect of being stuck in bed while Birdie looked after her. It wasn't that she didn't like the idea of being taken care of. She didn't think anybody in their right mind would have a problem with being taken care of. And it wasn't even the fact that it was Birdie that was the one that was going to take care of her. She was sure that Birdie would be nice enough; she would probably take care of her and be as good of a nurse as Birdie knew how to, but Mona had plans.

Mona had things that she had to do, and she couldn't be stuck in bed. She wasn't going to just sit there and waste precious time. Because the sooner that the cops were onto Beau's trail, the sooner they could find whatever evidence there was that might link the deaths of the woman that performed her abortion and her children to Beau. The longer she waited, the more of a chance that Beau could get away with it. Evidence could wash away, or people could forget seeing him close to the crime scene. Whatever that one piece of evidence was that could put Beau away, if she waited too long, it could be gone.

And if it was gone, Mona would really be stuck.

There was no way that Beau would allow her to leave without coming after her. And there was no way that Mona would ever feel safe leaving if she knew that Beau could hunt her down and find her. The whole point of getting the police onto Beau's trail was that it gave her time to get away.

But now she was pretty much stuck in bed until she could convince her mother that she did feel better. Mona wasn't sure how she was going to do that other than faking it.

She felt awful. She felt sick and in pain. Birdie didn't really seem like she was excited about the prospect of having to take care of her, and Mona really wanted to get over this as quickly as she could.

All night she had been thinking. No matter what, she had to get out at least one more time. She had to get out of the house on her own and do something. Make a phone call or something. All night she had been going over in her head how she was going to do that. How was she going to get out of the house and find a way to get the police on Beau's trail?

She couldn't go to Owen's house and just use the phone. She had to be careful where she used the phone because she didn't want people overhearing her. They lived in a small town and small-town people talked. The last thing she needed was for someone to overhear even part of her conversation and tell her parents or Beau what they had heard. She couldn't have anyone knowing that she had anything to do with tipping off the police.

Her next option would be to tell someone that she trusted. But the problem was that Mona didn't have any friends. And with her and Owen on the outs, she couldn't really tell Owen. Plus, if her dad heard that she had been anywhere near him it would probably blow up in her face. Her daddy had already made it very clear that he didn't want her anywhere near Owen at all. And she planned to obey that for as long as she could.

Because getting away was the only thing on her mind.

She didn't have any girlfriends. Mona didn't really get along with anyone because she didn't like the idea of having to explain why she was the way she was. And friends would turn their backs on you. She didn't trust the idea of opening up even a little to someone and then finding out that they were telling her parents or her siblings or her cousin something behind her back. Or even telling other people that weren't her family behind her back. She didn't want to risk anything that would make her life more difficult.

And she feared any girl she was friends with would get a crush on Beau. Or Beau would make moves on them. It wasn't a secret that girls in school already had crushes on him. Mostly because he was unattainable, Mona thought. He wouldn't date them. So, every girl was determined to be the one to change that.

If they knew he wouldn't because he wanted his twin sister, maybe they'd change their minds.

But Beau would do something. He'd always do something to hinder her. To keep her trapped, so she played it safe, even if it was lonely.

Because the idea was that she wanted to get away as quickly as possible. Without any incidents.

She also couldn't afford for her mother or anyone to get angry with her. She knew that she was on her mother's bad side at the moment. Because anytime Mona or her siblings got sick or inconvenienced their mama in one way or another, she would always get upset with them. And she would make their life a living hell because of it.

She hadn't so far, but Mona knew that if she didn't try to act as if she felt better, her mama would start. Once she did, Mona would struggle to get back in her good graces again.

The first day after they realized that she was vomiting and sick, she did stay in bed all day. She didn't really eat much, and she drank water all day. The next day, she decided that she was going to get up and be better. No matter what, she was going to convince everyone that she was better.

And she did feel a little better when she got up. She wasn't sure that she was feeling completely healed, but she hadn't thrown up all day. And the pains in her stomach had only been slight. And that was enough for her to try and convince everyone that it had just been some sort of stomach bug. Something that was twenty-four hours long and now she was feeling fine. Now she was better and they could go about their normal lives again. None of the focus would be on her.

With this in mind, and having thought so much about Beau all night, when she got up the next morning and heard that they were going to need a few things from town, she volunteered to go.

"You need to rest as much as possible," her mother said snidely. She was washing up the pots from breakfast with Birdie. Clyde was out in the yard and doing whatever Clyde liked to do when he had time alone. And Mona was wiping down the counters.

"I feel fine," she told her mother. "I really feel completely fine now. And I didn't throw up at all yesterday or this morning."

Her mother cast a look her way. It was a gaze that made Mona feel as if her mother could tell when she was lying. She wasn't convinced that her mother couldn't. Maybe it was motherly intuition or maybe Mona was just a horrible liar, but it always seemed like her mother had a sixth sense for these types of things.

That she could just tell that Mona was trying to pull the wool over her eyes. Mona tried her best not to ever lie because of this, but she had come to realize that in order to survive, sometimes lying was necessary. Sometimes you had to break a few of God's precious rules in order to not meet Him too early.

"I guess you can go.. Birdie can go with you if she wants," her mother said.

"Yes ma'am, but she doesn't have to if she doesn't want to. I know the bathroom up front really needs to be cleaned today."

Mona knew that mentioning a room would need cleaning would put her mother into a different state of mind. Birdie wouldn't get in trouble because Mona had already said that it needed to be cleaned today, but her mother would ask Birdie to clean it now. About the only thing her mother was sterner about than the Bible was keeping a clean house. Nothing could ever be out of place. Everything had to be cleaned or put away the moment you were done with it. You couldn't put your dishes in the sink and just walk away to clean them later when there were more. You cleaned them as soon as you finished dinner. If you spilled something from the pot onto the stove, you didn't clean it when you were cleaning the rest of the house. You cleaned it up right then. Her mother was very anal about these things, and Mona knew that she could use that to her advantage.

"Birdie can go get started on that so you can go to the store. Probably won't take as long for you to get back with her not with you anyway," her mother said.

For once, Mona was glad that even her mama knew that Birdie liked to dilly-dally around and take her time when they took her somewhere. Her plan worked and Mona was able to leave the house by herself. She took her bike and got the groceries that her mama had asked for.

She did all of this in a hurry. She rode her bike into town as quickly as possible, gathered all of the groceries, and double checked to make sure she had gotten them all. She paid out as quickly as she could so that she could attempt to find the person that she needed.

She checked behind the store in the dumpsters first, but Paul and Biscuit were not there. She kept an eye out as she walked through town, thinking that at worst, she could probably come back another day and hopefully find him somewhere. But she didn't have to because when she decided to check the bridge where she had saved their lives, Paul was sitting there at the water with Biscuit. Biscuit was playing in the water, while Paul sat and watched him. When her foot slipped, making a noise which alerted them to her presence, they both turned to her. Without hesitation, Biscuit came running.

"Hey little lady," Paul said as he stood. "Making another grocery trip?"

She looked down and nodded. "Yes. But I need to ask you a favor," she said, looking back up at him.

THE BREAKING OF MONA HILL

The light easiness that had been on his face was suddenly replaced with a serious look. He nodded and came closer to her. "Sure thing. What do you need?"

"I need you to call the police," Mona told him.

Paul narrowed his brows at her. She could see that he thought she was a little crazy. Mostly she could tell that he was concerned. He looked very worried about why she would be asking this.

"Okay? What am I calling the police for?"

Mona took in a deep breath. This could be dangerous. She knew that it might not even work, but this felt like her best option. In fact, it felt like her only option. Because it was the only way she could see that things might not come back on her.

"I need you to tell the police that you saw a certain truck with two people in it the night of that fire over on Palmetto Street. The truck is a red Dodge with large mud tires on it. And a very loud exhaust. And I can roughly describe the two boys, but you have to make sure that you tell them all of this quickly," she said with urgency.

"Okay? What's going on, Mona?"

Mona took in a deep breath. She wasn't sure how honest she should be with Paul, but she figured that it was best to not lie to him. Maybe it was also best not to hide parts of the truth from him. In fact, one of the best things that could happen to her might be being one-hundred percent honest with someone. To have someone know the truth. Because Mona didn't have anybody in the entire world. And a part of her kind of hoped that maybe if she was honest, she could have somebody that she could tell what was going on and they might be behind her. Maybe they would be able to help her situation in some way.

Mona looked at him and then realized that she couldn't speak while looking at him. She looked away as she started to talk. "You heard about that fire over on Palmetto Street?" she asked him.

"Yeah, I heard about that. That lady and those poor youngins burned up in the trailer."

Mona swallowed hard. "My brother and his friend killed them."

"And how do you know that?" Paul asked.

Mona looked up. "Because he told me," she confessed.

Paul raised a brow. "Your brother told you he killed that woman and her kids? Why would your brother kill them?" he asked, and Mona could tell he was confused. She didn't blame him. She also didn't want to explain, afraid that he would judge her decisions as well, but she had to try.

Even if it was killing her to talk about it.

"I had an abortion. I went to that woman because the lady at the clinic told me it was the only way I was going to be able to get one without my parents' approval. And she was so nice to me, and her kids were so nice, and they took care of me. When my brother found out what I had done, he killed her and her kids. Because of me. Because of what I did," she said, unable to hold his gaze any longer.

When Mona looked down, she realized she was crying. And she suddenly hated herself for that. She didn't want to cry about this. She didn't want to cry in front of Paul no matter how much she was able to be honest with him. She didn't want to be this weak. She didn't want to feel so guilty. But she did.

"You think this is your fault," Paul said. It wasn't a question. He knew the answer, but she answered anyway.

"Yes," Mona said. "He wouldn't have gone there if I hadn't gone first. And if I had been more careful and thrown away the address that I got from the lady at the clinic, he wouldn't have known where to go. I am responsible for the death of her kids and my brother saw that as justice for the death of his,,,"

"What?" Paul interjected.

Mona suddenly looked away again. She wrapped her arms around herself and realized that she was starting to feel sick again, but this time not from needing to throw up or stomach cramps. It was more like she had opened her mouth to speak and now she was wishing she hadn't. Because she really wanted to take back all the words she had said now.

But Paul's eyes were kind. And when he came over to her, he touched her. And that touch was kind. His hand was rough, and he even smelled a little, but he guided her face up to look at his. She could see that there was compassion there. There was even love. But what she didn't see was guilt or lust. He didn't look at her the way her brother looked at her. He didn't even look at her the way that her father looked at her.

In fact, when Mona looked up at his face, she was struck by how much he looked like her father. Not that he resembled her actual father, but that he looked at her the way that a daddy should look at their daughter. With love. With kindness and forgiveness and understanding. Not doubt. Not guilt. It was innocent. And if there was one thing in the world that Mona wanted more than anything, it was innocence.

"It's okay. You have nothing to be ashamed about, do you hear me?"

Mona started to cry again. And when she did, she couldn't stop. And when Paul pulled her in close and wrapped his arms around her, she broke. She felt every last bit of strength just slip out of her as she broke in his arms.

And he held her, his head resting on top of hers, his arms keeping her from falling to her knees. He just held her while she shook and cried. He held her as she broke. He kept her from falling down as she let all of the things around her hit her at once. Her mama and daddy. Clyde and Birdie. The lady that gave her an abortion and her poor kids. And Beau. What Beau had done to her. What Beau would do to her. What Beau had done to other people because of her. What Beau was going to do to other people because of her. She let every single bit of it hit her and she trusted him not to let her go.

"It'll be okay," he told her. "Just let it out."

And she did. She didn't trust herself to speak. Words would have been torture, and the truth was, she didn't want to speak. She just wanted to be held. Cared for. Loved. She hadn't realized how much she had wanted all these things until she actually felt them coming from someone.

A part of her was angry with Owen because of this. Was it so hard for him to offer her even a slice of what she was getting from Paul? Even if it wasn't as innocent, he could have still shown he cared for her at times. Maybe she would have been more likely to sleep with him if he had. Maybe he could have made her feel those feelings if she genuinely believed he cared about her.

But she had never been honest with Owen, either. Maybe if she'd been more willing to confide in him, that emotion would have grown between them. She'd been just as much at fault as Owen had, she realized. She just didn't like to admit it because it made her feel better to view him as she did everyone else.

The enemy.

"Maybe we can both go to the police," Paul offered. "Tell them what is going on at home. You can tell them everything and maybe they can help you."

Mona shook her head as she wiped her eyes. She slowly moved away from him. "It would only make things worse. Even if Beau went away, I'd still be stuck at home. And my parents would never forgive me for having an abortion," she told him.

"They can take you away from there. Maybe foster care?"

"I can't deal in possibilities. And I don't want to risk being placed in a new hell to replace the old one. I have to play my cards right. I just have to find a chance to get away, but I can't do that if Beau is still around to chase me. He'll never let me go," she told him.

"You're just a kid, Mona," Paul told her, sounding defeated. "Just a baby. You shouldn't be under a bridge, talking about how you have to run away from your sick brother, to a homeless man. You should be shopping at the mall and crushing on some kid with a face full of acne that works in the food court. Not dealing with this. Not being hurt like this."

Mona appreciated the sentiment, but she knew he knew just as well as she did that life wasn't kind to anyone. Not even children. Sometimes, especially not children.

"And you shouldn't be living under a bridge getting attacked by jerks, but that's life. It's not fair," Mona said.

Paul frowned. "I have half a mind to take care of your brother and parents myself. Forget the law, what they need is a good lashing," he said. And Mona could tell he was serious.

That scared her.

"Please don't do that. They'd kill you," Mona warned him, her voice slightly frantic. "Promise me you won't ever do that. Beau would kill anyone that tried to separate us. And if you did hurt them, you'd go to jail, and I couldn't handle that. I can't be responsible for anyone else getting hurt."

"Okay, okay," Paul said, holding his hands up and speaking with a calm voice. "I won't do it. Only because you asked. We'll do it your way."

Mona hadn't realized how upset she'd been getting until he was calming her back down. The idea of Paul ending up like that woman and her kids was almost enough to send her into a panic attack.

"Thank you," she told him.

"Don't thank me. I don't like this. It's wrong. But if I'm going to do it your way, you have to promise me something," he said.

Mona raised a brow. "Yes?"

"You have to promise me that when you find that chance to run away, you do it without hesitation. Don't feel guilty. Don't worry about what they'll do. You just run and stay hidden until it doesn't matter anymore. Got that?"

Mona nodded. "I promise."

He nodded once. "Good. You deserve better than this, Mona. I hope you know that," he told her.

"So do you," she said, looking at Biscuit as she said it. He was sitting like a good boy and watching them both. If people could be as innocent as dogs were, the world would be a much better place. Mona might actually enjoy being alive if there were more people like animals.

"When do you want me to contact the police?"

"As soon as you can. The only thing I'm not sure of yet is how to escape. What to do once I have," she confessed.

Paul shook his head. "Give me a few days. I might know someone who can help you when you need it. An old friend that will help you get as far away from here as possible. She's given up on me, but a young girl like you, she'd help. Even for me," he said.

"Your sister?" Mona asked.

He nodded. "Yeah. I've done a lot of stuff that hurt her and my mom, but it's because of her kind heart that I did. It'll be crow I'm eating, but I know she'll help. You just need to be safe until then. I won't let you down," he told her.

And Mona trusted that. More than she had ever trusted anything or anyone in her entire life. She was putting an unreasonable amount of trust into Paul, a man she barely knew.

Why?

Because she needed something to make her feel hopeful.

"I need to get home. Tonight is church and my mama will really be angry if I'm not home early," she told him.

He nodded. "Get going. I'll handle everything," he told her.

Mona looked to Biscuit and then knelt to receive his wet kisses. "Goodbye, Biscuit. I'll be seeing you," she told them both. She grabbed the grocery bags and left her friends under the bridge, now moving quicker to get back home. She wasn't sure what time it was, but she was desperate to get back in her mama's good graces and getting home earlier than expected would be a good way to do that.

When she came into the house, Mama was in the bedroom. She

was just laying out her church dress, and by the look at the clock and the surprise in her Mama's voice, she was early.

"That was quick. You didn't forget anything, did you?" she accused.

"No ma'am. They had everything you wrote down," Mona answered.

Her mother nodded once and then looked over her dress. In a surprising gesture, she spoke to Mona again. "What do you think of this dress? I sewed it last week," she said.

Mona looked at it. It was Mama's normal style. A long, floral dress with the doily-looking neckline. It had a set of white, plastic buttons along the bust, doing their best to resemble pearls. The capped sleeves had white lace on them and were a little shorter than what Mama would usually sew.

"I think it's lovely," Mona told her with a smile.

Mama looked at her. Her eyes moved over Mona's body like she was looking for something. Or maybe she was noticing something. Realizing something.

"You really are becoming a lovely young lady, aren't you?"

Mona's smile faltered a bit. The words weren't a compliment, even if she tried to phrase them that way. Mona knew they were an accusation. There was an underlying issue there that Mona had suspected, but it seemed confirmed as she stood in the room with her mama.

Her mama was jealous of her.

Mona didn't know if it had something to do with Daddy or her own aging that sparked Mama's jealousy against her daughter. Maybe it was even that Beau said. Daddy thought she looked a lot like Mama at her age. Daddy wasn't intimate with Mama anymore. Maybe Mama was beginning to wonder if she had to worry about her husband trading her in for her daughter.

After all, if he could marry his sister, what would stop him from doing the same with his own daughter?

Mama's feelings toward her made more sense when Mona thought of it that way. It at least gave her a reason for why Mama treated her the way she did. But it didn't offer a solution. It gave her no way to earn her love.

"Not as beautiful as you are, Mama," she answered, but it didn't make Mama happy. She looked at the dress again instead and suddenly frowned.

"I think I'll sell this one. Sister Mathis would probably pay fifteen for it," she said nonchalantly.

Mona knew the dress was now tarnished because she had said something nice about it. Mama would never wear it now that Mona had given it approval, and in a lot of ways, that hurt. It hurt to realize her mother was growing to hate her that much.

"Go see if Birdie is done in the shower. She was supposed to be ready by now so I could braid her hair," Mama ordered.

"Yes ma'am," Mona answered. She left the room feeling defeated. Maybe because a part of her hoped that her Mama might give her a reason to not want to leave. Just one glimmer of hope. Something to make her think Mama wasn't as bad as Mona thought.

But there was nothing.

Mama didn't love her and that wasn't a secret. Mama didn't love any of them. Out of everyone in her family, Mona was convinced it was Mama that didn't know what love was or how to feel it more than anyone else. She doubted Mama had ever known love in her entire life.

She almost felt sorry for her. How awful it must be to not care about anyone. To not feel loved by anyone. She wondered if Mama had married their dad, her brother, because at least the chance of love had been there. Or was it just means of an escape? Had their father been like Beau? Had he taken a bad situation and offered a sick solution?

All it had gotten Mama was more misery. She was aged before her time. She was cruel and twisted. She wasn't a good person and used God to justify it. What an awful life she led.

And Mona wasn't going to follow in her footsteps.

She would escape. She would be happy. She wouldn't be Mama.

Mona walked through the kitchen and living room and down the hall. The shower water was on, but Mona felt the hair on her neck raise up at the sight of the door being ajar. They all showered with the door closed, house rules, but couldn't lock it. There wasn't a lock on the door.

She moved slowly toward the door. She was careful not to make a sound in case her suspicion was right. She didn't want to be right. She didn't want to think her baby brother was in the bathroom with Birdie. That he was acting the same way as Beau, but as she peered through the crack, she could see Clyde in front of the shower, peering through the curtain. Birdie's back was turned, and Mona wasn't sure if she was aware Clyde was watching her.

Even worse, she didn't know if Birdie knew he was jacking off to her.

"Get out of here!" Mona yelled at him. Birdie spun around and covered herself, but Clyde looked close to dying on the spot. He pushed the door open and stumbled into the hallway, zipping his pants.

"I wasn't doing nothing!" He started scrambling, trying to move away, but Mona wasn't letting him run. Not so he could get out of the house and think of an excuse.

"What's going on back there?" Mama yelled.

"Clyde..." Mona began to yell, but Birdie was clinging to the shower curtain and stopping her.

"Don't tell, Mona. We wasn't doing anything," she begged, almost near tears with her pleading.

Mona felt a cold chill run down her spine. Birdie knew he was there? That gave her an uneasy feeling, but even worse, Birdie wanted to protect him? Protect her cousin jerking off to her showering? Protect a cousin that would only progress to something worse. Protect a cousin that would become just like Beau.

Had he already?

Were they having sex? Had he raped her? Worse, was it consensual? Were they having a relationship together? Were Birdie and Clyde past saving too? Just like the rest of them?

"He was watching you shower, Birdie. That's disgusting," Mona told her.

"Don't say anything, Mona. I'll never forgive you if you do," Birdie told her, and her voice let Mona know she meant it.

She was serious. She was willing to protect Clyde. Because of how they were raised? Did she think it was her fault? That Clyde getting in trouble would be her fault? Or was she as complicit as he was? Did they both want to do these disgusting things?

And if they did, who was she trying to protect? They were barely teenagers. Children. Babies. Who was at fault? Who did she blame? Who was she supposed to be mad at?

These questions were swirling in her mind as Mama came down the hallway. Mona didn't have to see Mama to know the look on her face. She was glaring at the three of them, taking the scene in. Clyde outside the bathroom door, Mona in the doorway, and Birdie clinging to a shower curtain. Even before she asked, Mama knew the answer.

"What's going on here?" she asked.

Clyde and Birdie weren't going to say anything. The answer to that question rested on Mona's shoulders, and it was heavy. Because there wasn't a right answer. Not in her situation. The truth or a lie, neither helped. Neither one would save her cousin. Or her brother. Or her.

And Birdie was pleading. But Mona could handle Birdie's anger. She couldn't handle Mama's. Mama knew what the truth was and lying would only make things worse for Mona.

"Clyde was in the bathroom," Mona answered.

Birdie narrowed her eyes at Mona and set her mouth firmly. Her anger was clear as day and Mona knew she hated her. She hated Mona for doing this, but Mona hoped she'd realize she was trying to help her. Give her a chance. She hoped Birdie would realize this wasn't normal.

"Clyde Hill! You get in your room right now!" her mother screamed, her voice loud enough to make Mona flinch. "When your daddy gets home, he'll handle you. Birdie, finish your shower and get to my room now. You and I are going to have a talk."

Mona turned around, about to protest, but stopped. Mama was already walking away and there was no hiding that Birdie was going to be in just as much trouble as Clyde. Mama didn't question whether Birdie allowed it or not. Clyde looking was Birdie's fault, even if she told him to leave. Even if she had screamed for help. Mama was angry that Birdie was a girl. That Birdie bore the curse of being female. It was Birdie's fault if Clyde or any man looked at her.

"I hate you," Birdie told her. Mona looked at her, but Birdie was slamming the door. And Mona knew it was true. Birdie hated her.

She was sure Clyde did too, but he was disappearing into his room. Within seconds, she was standing in the hallway alone. She didn't feel good, even though she told the truth. She didn't know how to feel. She wasn't dealing in black and white hues. There was no clear sign of what was right and wrong in this situation, no good and bad. It was all gray. One huge gray area.

Mona walked into the bedroom and sat down on the bed. All she felt was confusion. Confused as to what she should have done. What she *could* have done. Maybe if she had been paying closer attention to Birdie, Birdie could have confided in her. Mona could have tried to get through to her about what was right and wrong.

Or maybe she could have gotten to Clyde. Maybe if she had tried to be closer to him or acted more like a big sister, he would have grown more respect for women and wouldn't want to emulate Beau or their daddy. Maybe she wouldn't have to distrust him the way she did the rest of them.

Instead, he was watching his cousin shower and Birdie didn't care.

It was disgusting. Mona wondered why she seemed to be the only one that was completely revolted by it. Her mama was angry, but only because she felt Birdie had made her son act such a way. Misguided anger. She didn't have to tell Mona for her to know that was where her anger would stem from. Her dad would be the same way.

Neither one would feel they were responsible for it. They wouldn't see how their actions, even unknown to Clyde and Birdie, could have set this up. That the way they raised them and treated them would create kids that acted out in disturbed ways.

Nature versus nurture again. Mona was tired of questioning. She wanted to know the answer.

She heard the bathroom door when it opened again. Birdie didn't come into the bedroom. She went straight to Mama's room by the sound of it. It was all the better. Mona wasn't sure if she wanted to deal with Birdie's temper tantrum. Not over this.

She grabbed the clothes she'd wear for church and took her own shower. Once she was dressed, she finally entered the living room again. Birdie sat on the couch, cheeks red and tear stained. She didn't even look at Mona as she passed.

Mama was in the kitchen and immediately put Mona to cooking when she entered. Mona had just finished when Daddy and Beau came home. Mama shut the door when Daddy came inside, to tell him what had happened, no doubt. Beau came through the kitchen, stopping at the doorway between the living room and kitchen. He looked at the couch where Birdie was sitting and then looked at Mona.

"I'm guessing someone is about to get themselves a nice whooping," he commented.

"It's Mona's fault," Birdie answered in a grumbling voice. "We weren't doing anything."

Beau looked at Mona with a renewed joy. "Uh oh. Looks like you've pissed off the little Birdie," he said with a smile. Mona hated his smile. "You know Mona has to interfere with everyone's fun. Playing holier than thou when she's just as trashy as the rest of us."

Mona glared at him, setting her mouth in a firm line as she turned her attention back to filling the plates. She knew Beau was enjoying himself. He thrived in the chaos.

"Clyde wasn't even doing anything. Looking isn't doing anything," Birdie said.

Mona couldn't stop herself. She looked at Beau. She wished she hadn't. Maybe she could have missed the look of satisfaction that was waiting on his face if she had. She could have missed the smugness and the knowledge that this was likely the result of Beau interfering. Putting his own disgusting ideas into these children's minds.

"That's right, Birdie. Looking doesn't hurt anyone. And you like boys looking at you, don't you?" he asked her, but he held Mona's eyes the whole time.

Mona felt sick to her stomach for a different reason this time.

"There's nothing wrong with it. It's not hurting anyone," Birdie answered.

Beau was leaning against the doorway, arms crossed, his face a mixture of pride and conceit. He'd implanted these thoughts into their minds. Assured them there was nothing wrong with it. Played with their emotions. And for what? Revenge? To get back at Mona? To show her he could corrupt them? To show her they were already corrupted?

He didn't care about them. He didn't care about what this was going to do to them. How it would affect them. He did it because he could. Because he wanted to. Because he liked it.

The bedroom door opened, and Daddy came out in a rage. He stormed past them, heading straight for Clyde. Mona almost felt sorry for him. Especially when the sounds of him screaming filled the trailer. The sound of whipping through the air was enough to assure them all that it was Daddy's belt that was handling this. Clyde was going to have a hard time sitting through church.

Mama came out and started getting the rest of the plates ready. There was nothing on her face. No joy or pain. It was just the way it had to be for her. Just another day in the life.

But Beau was happy. There was no denying that.

"I'm gonna get a shower, Mama," he told her. She nodded as he left. He smiled at Mona as he did, and she wanted nothing more than to knock it off his face.

They were bringing the plates into the living room when Daddy came through and stopped in front of Birdie. Mona walked in just as he backhanded her across the face, almost knocking her off the couch completely.

"Do you want to grow up to be a whore just like your mother?" he asked her. "Ain't you got enough sense to not let men look at you?"

Mona wanted to disappear. All of a sudden, it seemed like if she made the wrong move, she'd be the next one. No one was safe once Daddy was mad and they all knew it. Beau was the only one that wouldn't have to worry because Daddy would be calmed down by the time he got out of the shower.

She averted her gaze down and waited. She tried to make herself as small as possible. Blend in with the wallpaper. Become the wallpaper. Make it seem as if she didn't exist at all.

"I'm sorry," Birdie cried. Mona could hear the pain in her voice at having to say the words. She wasn't sure if Birdie even meant them. At this point, they had all apologized so much, it was hard to be sincerely sorry. When you lived in a constant state of awareness, it was hard to figure out if you were truly sorry about something you were in trouble for.

"Sorry will get you nowhere, and letting boys look at you is just gonna get you pregnant. You're lucky I'm not giving you a little of what Clyde just got," he told her.

When he moved past Mona to sit in his chair, she didn't breathe. She stood still and quiet, eyes down, just biding her time before it seemed safe to move again. When he turned on the TV, Mona began to move, holding out the plate to him.

"Thank you, baby girl," he said, changing the TV to the news and accepting his plate.

Why was the name bothering her so much? Why did having his

approval always make her feel guilty? Like he decided the best time to treat her better was when someone else was in trouble. She was the only one he did it with. If she was in trouble and Birdie wasn't, he didn't call Birdie a name. Usually, he'd get onto her too. It was the same with Beau and Clyde. Even Mama.

She didn't look at Birdie at all as she walked back into the kitchen and grabbed the other plates. When Mama came through and sat down, Mona handed her plate to her and then sat down with her own. The four of them ate, with Birdie picking at her food slowly. Mona knew if she didn't pick up the pace, she'd get in trouble for that too. She also knew her mouth was probably hurting too much to eat quickly.

"I don't think Clyde will be going to church tonight. So, you're just gonna have to take the girls," Daddy said during a commercial break.

"What about Beau?"

"Beau worked today. Ain't no sense in him sitting through service when the boy has work tomorrow," he told her.

Mona didn't trust the time Beau was spending with Daddy. She knew there was something behind it. Something that Beau was doing, and it was to get back at her. Maybe he was trying to get his own baby girl treatment. Get in Daddy's good graces and then get her in trouble.

"He can't start missing church all the time. The Devil will come for him," Mama answered.

"Don't start," Daddy warned.

Even though Mona felt bad for Birdie, if Mama had gotten slapped too Mona wouldn't have felt as bad. She didn't want Mama to get slapped or beat, but Mama was cruel. It didn't seem as unfair.

Birdie wasn't innocent, but she didn't deserve to be treated and spoken to the way she was. She was just a kid. She was only twelve and influenced by anyone that would show her attention. Mama was a grown woman and only cared about her children paying for their wrongdoings. She was selfish.

But she didn't start an argument. She ate her food and kept quiet. And when they washed the dishes and only the girls left the house, she still didn't say anything. Maybe she wasn't feeling spunky, or she was just ready for church. But she said nothing, and she went through her usual Wednesday night routine.

Birdie and Mona went to the youth service as Mama attended the normal church service. She sat right up on stage with Pastor Steve as she always did and completed her role as his church wife.

Birdie didn't speak to Mona at all. She wouldn't even look at her. Mona couldn't blame her in some ways. She was in trouble, and Mona was the one that told. But Mona had only confirmed what her mother had deducted. If she'd said otherwise, she would have been in just as much trouble.

And maybe she would have preferred that. It was a bonding moment in her trauma filled mind. If Mona had lied and gotten in trouble, that would have bonded them as sisters. Maybe Birdie would have even done the same for her if the situation arose.

Mona doubted it. Out of them all, Birdie was the biggest tattletale.

After the service, the small group of kids and teenagers went outside to wait out the normal service. Birdie went as far away from Mona as she could and resolved to sitting alone at the swing set. She moved it back and forth without any joy and annoyed the little kids by doing so.

Mona felt bad for her. Birdie was just a kid. She shouldn't have to deal with this type of abuse. She should have been a twelve-year-old.

Like Paul said, she realized. Birdie should have been crushing on weird guys that worked at the mall. Birdie should have a group of girlfriends, girls she trusted her secrets to and laughed with over silly things. The only tears she should be shedding were over silly crushes and embarrassing things she said that no one would ever remember but her.

She was a kid. She should have been living like one.

But none of them had that chance. They'd never be given that chance. Even if they were all able to get away now, none of them would ever be able to reclaim the childhood they lost. Not really. They were all broken now, and Mona just wondered how irreparable they each were.

"Mona."

"Owen?"

Mona was surprised to see that it was Owen that had called her name. Even more surprised to see that Owen was at the church. Owen didn't like church. Owen called people that went to church Bible thumpers and holy rollers. So, for Owen to be there, Mona knew it had to be something important.

"I need to talk to you," Owen told her. He was being quiet and staying out of sight of most of the kids outside. She realized this was for her benefit. She was grateful.

Mona looked around, then motioned for him to go to the side of the building. She wasn't sure if anyone had seen him, but she was hoping that they hadn't. Things would not be good if they had.

Owen had been to church with her when they had first started dating. Back when he had a shred of hope that he might win her parents' approval. Mona had thought that maybe he might, but she realized it was a dumb thing to think. Her parents were not going to like anybody that she dated. It didn't matter who they were, the only way Mona would ever be with someone was if they married her and took her out of her parents' house. If that didn't' happen, she would be stuck with them for the rest of her life.

There really wasn't a middle ground in her household.

But after a couple of incidents where Owen had almost gotten into a fight with her parents, mostly her dad, Owen stopped attempting to go to church at all. He made it very clear that they could see each other away from her family. In a way that had drawn Mona closer to him because she liked the idea that he was hers. He was her one shot at rebellion. It gave Mona a scapegoat of her own.

But she hadn't spoken to Owen in over a week. She had seen him when he tried to come to the house, but that was it. She hadn't been able to speak to him then. Because her daddy had gotten in the way.

So, she was very curious as to why Owen would risk trying to talk to her again. What was it that he needed from her so badly? Why was it important for him to talk to her?

Mona moved to the side of the building with him, and when she did, the first thing Owen did was pull her in for a kiss. Mona didn't stop him, but she was surprised at the feeling it gave her.

It was no secret that she had never felt very romantic toward Owen. A part of her was even convinced that maybe she couldn't feel those feelings. But the kiss that Owen gave her now sent butterflies throughout her stomach. It was a feeling that she didn't know existed. Something she had never felt before. And she didn't know how to explain this feeling at all. It didn't make any sense how it could suddenly overtake her like that. It felt like that feeling that people would sing about.

She didn't so much kiss back as she did stare at him. The look of shock had to be clear on her face because Owen looked almost scared. "I'm sorry," he said. "I just missed you."

But those words only made it more confusing. It made her feel even more strange. Because she believed him. Maybe Owen wasn't the best at knowing exactly who she was, but whoever she was to him, he really did miss. When he said those words, Mona truly believed that it was exactly how he felt.

She didn't say anything back. She wasn't sure if she missed him. Honestly, she had kind of thought that she might not see him again. Because her daddy made it very clear that he didn't want him around, and she wasn't about to start sneaking around behind his back just to see Owen. Especially when she had been convinced that Owen didn't want to be with her anymore. She had never been broken up with, nor had she ever been in a relationship before him, but it seemed like someone being ready to hit you and then telling you just to leave was a clear sign that they didn't want to be with you anymore. All of it was very confusing and she wasn't sure how she was supposed to take any of it.

"Are you going to say anything?" Owen asked.

"I don't know what to say," Mona confessed.

"You can say anything," Owen answered, smiling a bit.

It was easy to see that the smile was just to make her feel better. Owen was nervous. Mona wasn't used to seeing him be nervous. Owen was the one that always seemed so confident. He always seemed to not care what anyone thought. Including her. He was just who he was. You either accepted that or you left.

The only person he showed any sort of restraint around was his mom. And the only reason he did that was for the same reason that Mona showed restraint around anybody.

Because his mom was the one that ruled with an iron fist. She was the one that he had to worry about. Because no matter what there could be repercussions.

Mona figured that it was best to get whatever it was that was on his mind out in the open. "What are you doing here?" she asked him.

Owen rubbed the back of his neck. He looked away from her, a clear sign that something was weighing heavy on his mind. He refused to look at her even as he spoke.

"I've been thinking a lot lately. About all kinds of different things. About us, about this place, just everything that's been going on and I really just wanted to talk to you."

"My dad doesn't really want me talking to you anymore," Mona confessed.

"Yeah, I kind of got that hint the other day," Owen answered. He sounded a little bitter as he said it, but Mona didn't blame him. "I just. . . I can't leave things like they were. I mean if you don't want to speak to me, that's one thing. I would understand. But I just don't think that that's the case. I don't understand what's going on in your head, but I would like to think that you don't hate me."

Mona felt small again. And she didn't have to think about her response. "I've never hated you, Owen. Why would I hate you?" she asked him.

"I haven't been a really good person," Owen answered. His voice was low, as if he was embarrassed to admit this to her.

Maybe she could understand why someone would be

embarrassed to admit it to anyone, but she was still very confused as why he wanted to admit that in the first place. And especially to her.

"I was going to hit you the last time we were together. I'd understand if you hated me. I expect you to hate me, but I hoped you didn't. Because I realized something that day. Something huge," he told her.

"What?"

"I love you, Mona."

Out of everything she expected him to say, those four words together, in that sequence, were not it. When her mouth parted, it was in surprise. Completely dumbfounded by what he had said and the fact that it seemed like he meant it.

"I don't know what to say," she confessed.

"It's okay," he told her, but there was a hint of disappointment in his voice. "I get it, I really do. But I wanted you to know. You needed to know how I feel. Because I haven't shown it. I haven't done a good job of being your boyfriend and it sucks. Because I really did start off with good intentions."

"I know you did," Mona told him. "I think I did too."

He smiled at that. "I hope so. Because you're too good for me, Mona. And I think that's why I was drawn to you. When we were working together on that stupid project, you were so calm. So smart. Anyone else and I would have sat back and done nothing. Sabotaged the project even, because I truly didn't care about it.

"But I wanted to impress you. I think I still do and there's no one else in my life I've ever wanted to do that for. But somewhere, things got messed up. I don't know if it was because I couldn't get your family to like me or all the stuff going on in my own family, but I stopped. I put you in a box of things that I owned and stopped trying to impress you. Stopped wanting to. Instead, I wanted someone I could control but I didn't realize that until you were staring at me, and I was poised to hit you. It hit me like a brick that I was about to hit someone the same way my dad used to. Because he wanted to put them beneath him. Control them. Hurt them.

"And I loved you. You don't do that to people you love, but I'll confess. I have no idea how to love you the right way. It's not like we have great role models to show us," he told her, smiling.

She smiled. "No, I guess we don't," she answered, then looked down.

He was quiet for a moment, but not too long. "How do you feel, Mona?" he asked, but the question was soft. He kept his tone quiet and hushed, as if he were asking a very vulnerable and scary question.

And it was. To Mona, it really was.

"I don't know how I feel," she confessed.

He smiled and shrugged. "I expected that."

"I'm sorry."

"Don't apologize," he told her. "I'm not hurt. I'm not mad. I just want you to think about it, too. Figure out how you feel and then let me know. Because I'd like to give us another try if you're willing."

Mona's throat felt thick. Even if she did think about it, it would never happen. She wanted to be gone. She would be gone. She wasn't staying here, not even for Owen. Even if she woke up and realized he was the love of her life, which she knew he wasn't, even that wouldn't stop her from leaving the moment she had a chance.

"Let me have a few days to think," she told him.

He nodded. "You've got it," he told her.

When he moved toward her this time, Mona was prepared for the kiss. When he leaned down and kissed her, she kissed him back. It wasn't as exciting as the first, but she couldn't deny she felt something.

"I'm gonna get out of here before someone sees me," he told her, pulling away.

She nodded. "Probably a good idea."

He smiled and backed away. Mona thought that smile looked different too. Brighter. Innocent. Happy. Things she was convinced that she'd never seen on his face before. Not in this light. Not this purely.

There was definitely a change that had come over him, and Mona couldn't deny she was intrigued by it. Maybe it would be nice to start over fresh with Owen. Start dating each other without the walls and fall in love. It might be nice to know what that felt like.

But as she turned around to rejoin the others, she knew that would never happen. Not when Birdie was the first person she saw. Not when Birdie was glaring at her because she had seen her talking to Owen. There was no way she could have missed him.

"I can explain," Mona started.

"Uncle Ray said you weren't allowed to talk to Owen anymore," Birdie snapped.

Mona knew exactly what was going through Birdie's head and she hated her for it. She didn't care that Mona talking to Owen wasn't bad. Not like your cousin watching you shower. She only cared that Mona was doing something wrong because she could get her in trouble. She could have her revenge for Mona getting her in trouble, even if the situations were vastly different.

"Telling on me won't change the fact that what Clyde and you were doing wasn't right. You just want me to get in trouble," she told her.

"Beau's right," Birdie said, frowning as she rolled her eyes. "You really do think you're better than everyone else. It's about time you fell off that pedestal they have you on."

As Birdie spun around and stomped away, Mona was left dumbfounded. A pedestal? Was that what she thought? Because Daddy called her baby girl sometimes? That was just to rub salt in their wounds. Not to shower Mona with special privilege.

How many times had Birdie gotten a bag of peas for her face after Daddy smacked her? How many times had she watched

Mona get cut and bleed after being hit with a switch over and over? How many bruises had they shared? How many punishments?

A pedestal?

It was a cage.

And they all had one.

No, this was Beau. Beau was getting in her head just like he was with everyone. He was trying to turn all of them against her. But why? So her life could be even more miserable? So they'd hate her?

Or so she'd hate them?

Maybe both. Because if she hated them and they hated her, she'd want to leave. Eventually, she'd have to leave or resolve to living a life that gave her nothing and took everything. At least, that was Beau's way of thinking.

He didn't realize that he wasn't going to be able to run away. He was going to be in jail. Rotting for killing those kids and that woman. He'd never see the light of day again outside of prison if she was lucky. For once, he'd be punished for all of the bad he'd done. A real punishment for him, where he couldn't hurt anyone else.

But for now, she only had her own punishment to look forward to.

She knew the moment Birdie told her mother because Mama refused to speak to her. Not that Mona was trying, but Mama was completely silent and Mona knew it was because of Birdie. Because they both were excited to get home and watch her get into trouble.

And she was starting to feel sick again. She couldn't explain the sudden dizziness she felt. Or the nausea. It seemed to creep up on her and then explode. It was all she could do to not close her eyes and try to sleep on the way back. That would give Mama something else to tell Daddy when they got home.

And when she walked inside, the first thing Mama did was tell Daddy.

"Birdie caught Mona talking to that boy," she told him. "She says they were making out behind the church when she was supposed to be with the other kids."

Mona started to protest, but there was no point. The moment she opened her mouth, Mama's hand swung and connected with her cheek. Mama's backhand wasn't as strong as Daddy's but Mona wasn't feeling particularly strong. Mama's hit knocked her against the living room wall and then to her knees.

"Don't you even try to start with that smart mouth. I saw you too," she told her.

But Mona knew that was a lie. It was a lie to make sure Mona got in trouble. Because Birdie might just be trying to save her own skin, but Mama? Why would Mama lie?

"I thought I told you not to talk to him anymore?" Daddy said, standing up. Mona looked up from her place on the floor to see he was taking his belt off. He was ready to strike her with it, probably give her worse than what Clyde had gotten.

But she didn't feel right. She didn't feel like she was even attached to her body in that moment. Even as she looked up and saw Beau standing in the hall with his arms crossed. Even as she knew she couldn't trust him. That somehow this was still his fault. Every problem led back to him.

She couldn't focus on that because her entire body suddenly didn't belong to her. Her entire body began to convulse, and Mona was nothing more than a trapped victim in it.

"What's happening?" Daddy asked, in a voice of fear and shock.

"She's just acting," Mama said. "Trying to get out of a whooping."

But Mona wasn't acting. Not that she could tell them that. Her mouth wasn't hers anymore. She couldn't control it and that scared her. She couldn't stop her body from convulsing. Couldn't stop her eyes from rolling backwards as her brain struggled to focus on any one thing.

She heard words. Words that stuck out. Seizure. Tongue. Swallow. Hold her down was a thing that she felt. Not that she knew who was holding her down. The only thing she knew was someone had her spread eagle and her body was fighting against them.

Then someone was opening her mouth. They were sticking something cold and hard inside, against her tongue. As the jerks began to subside, she realized it was a spoon she was gritting against. A spoon to hopefully stop her from swallowing her tongue.

But as the seizure began to fade, the only thing her body wanted was to expel everything. She rolled to the side and vomited dinner and blood. Her face half lay in it as they moved from holding her and she curled into a ball on her side.

"Faking it?"

"You know these kids. And she had a whole car ride to worry herself sick," Mama told him.

"I think you have to make her an appointment. After last week with the vomiting and now this? This ain't normal, Ann," Daddy answered.

"It was one little thing. Maybe it's epilepsy or something. You know my grandma had epilepsy. It ain't nothing to worry about," Mama said.

"Isn't that caused by strobing lights or something though?" Daddy asked.

"Well, how would I know? I don't have it."

"Then how can you know that's what she has? Either take her to the ER now or make an appointment tomorrow. I'm not playing anymore," Daddy said. "And clean up the mess, Birdie. Beau, carry your sister to the bedroom and put her in bed."

Mona wanted to protest, but Beau lifted her easily. She was too tired to fight it, even if his very touch felt like bugs crawling along her skin. She wanted him to let her go, but she wouldn't say that. If he did, she had to walk and at the moment, she doubted her legs could support any weight. If they were anything like her neck,

THE BREAKING OF MONA HILL

they'd feel like jelly.

Beau took her into the room and laid her on the bed. He pulled the blanket over her with more tenderness than Mona was used to. It was also more than she ever wanted from Beau. But she was in no position to make that known to him.

He lingered after he pulled the blankets up. His eyes just looked down at her, boring holes into her. A part of her wondered if he was going to

Rape

Take advantage of her situation. She hated to admit it, but if he did, he'd find no fight. In that moment, she had no fight left in her. It would be easier to let him get what he wanted and go.

But he didn't. Instead, he met her eyes and a small smile pulled at the corner of his mouth. "Aren't you sick of it all yet?" he asked. He left the room, leaving Mona in the dark.

Chapter Eight

Psalm 50:19

You use your mouth for evil and harness your tongue to deceit.

Mona's dreams consisted of disjointed moments, memories, and possibilities. She tossed and turned in her sleep and kept waking herself up. Her life was a nightmare, but her dreams were tiny different nightmares she could wake up from. There was no crueler punishment than to wake up and realize the nightmares never truly ended, only to fall asleep and find a different nightmare waiting for you behind your eyelids.

And Beau was there. Beau was always at the center of her nightmares. But in these, all she heard was his words replaying.

Aren't you sick of it all yet?

Was her sudden sickness because of him? Was he doing something to her? Causing all of this? Was he referring to something else? Like his time with Daddy? Or his brainwashing of Clyde and Birdie? Was he cooking up a plan or was one already in motion?

Was Beau punishing her?

Or was God?

Mona couldn't help but wonder if all of this was a punishment from the man upstairs. She hadn't been sick until after the abortion. Maybe it was guilt eating her up inside. A slow revenge for her for killing his child. God could be wrathful.

But she hated to point out how hypocritical it would be for him to punish her for killing one baby when he'd killed millions over his time. But as a Christian, she wasn't supposed to point that out. That was almost blaspheming.

But Beau could be doing it for the same reasons. Maybe he was drugging her or something. She wasn't sure how, but she didn't doubt it. Beau was sneaky.

But Beau could also be trying to kill her.

Or it could be nothing. Maybe she was just sick and there wasn't anyone to blame. Not even herself. It was just something that happened, and the timing was coincidental. It had nothing to do with Beau or God. It had nothing to do with her abortion.

Either way, when she woke up, she knew she had to get out of bed. She had to get dressed and put on a front. There was no time to waste anymore. She couldn't wait around for herself to get sicker and be stuck at home. She had to see Paul soon and get away from there.

But she was lightheaded when she woke up. No matter how she tried, getting out of the room and pretending wasn't going to be an option. Even if she did, she'd never convince everyone she was okay to leave the house. She changed quietly and resolved to getting back into bed. She was about to fall asleep again when Daddy came in the room.

She knew it was time for him to leave for work. He walked in as quietly as he could as to not wake up Birdie and sat beside her on the bed.

"How are you feeling, baby girl?" he asked her, touching her forehead. He'd find no fever. Mona wasn't sure why she was sick, but it definitely didn't feel like a cold or the flu.

"Better. Just tired," she confessed.

"I'll tell your mama to let you rest today. We'll see about getting you to the doctor soon too," he told her. "But when you get to feeling better, we're going to have a talk about that boy. You understand?"

"Yes sir," Mona answered.

"You know, it disappoints me the most when you do something you're not supposed to. I expect it from the rest of them, but you…" He brushed her hair away from her face. "I expect more from you. You're my good girl. Always have been."

Mona realized that this was as close to tenderness as she'd ever get from anyone in her family. Daddy was the only one that might care for her, but she didn't trust his intentions. It came from a place of possessiveness very similar to Beau's. Daddy just wasn't trying to have sex with her.

"I'm sorry," she told him.

"Just don't let it happen again. That boy isn't any good. He'll knock you up and then leave you. That's the only thing boys like him know how to do. Ruin a good girl's life. You don't want that, do you?"

"No, sir."

"Then get some sleep. And forget about that boy," he said, then kissed her forehead. "I'll see you when I get home tonight. I want you to stay in bed. I'm gonna tell your mama the same thing."

Daddy stood and left the room. Mona had no problem following his orders. She fell back asleep easily and only woke up when lunch time came around.

Birdie shook her awake and gave her a plate with food and a drink. She said nothing and left promptly. She was still angry with Mona, but Mona didn't care anymore. It hurt to not care, but she realized she had to in order to survive. She had to stop caring if she was going to leave.

Mona knew after she was gone, she'd call someone to come and take Birdie and Clyde from her parents. Maybe they'd be able to help them. They'd both need a lot of help to make it out in the world after living with her parents and Beau.

She realized the risk that would come for them too. It was the same risks she knew would happen if she called the police for herself. The foster system wasn't always the best. There were no guarantees.

But Mona couldn't be trapped again. She had to get away and be alone. Birdie and Clyde needed someone. They needed someone that could help them, and they wouldn't get that running away with her. Mona couldn't give them that.

This was the best she could do for them.

She barely touched her food. She drank her glass of tea and then fell back asleep until Daddy came into the room. She couldn't believe she had slept through the day.

Mama came in the room with him and stood behind him. She looked angry. Upon closer inspection, Mona could guess why. The red welt on her face was a good indicator.

"How are you feeling?" Daddy asked.

"Better," Mona lied.

"That's good. Your Mama forgot to make you a doctor's appointment today," he told her. He didn't look at Mama as he said it, but Mona did. Her face remained solemn. If anything, it became emotionless. "We can take you to the emergency room if you want. But I'll let you decide."

Mona shook her head. "I feel better," she lied again. Honestly, she felt awful and like she was dying, but she wasn't about to tell anyone that.

"Okay. Want to eat dinner with us?" he asked.

Mona nodded, even though she didn't. She knew staying in bed wasn't going to help. She needed to see how she'd feel after sitting up for a while. She planned, come Hell or high water, to find Paul tomorrow and get as far away from Beau as she could.

She got out of bed and waited a moment before standing up. She was determined to work through whatever dizziness came over her. She would prove to them that she felt better, just like before.

All of this was just another obstacle in her way. Another hurdle to jump over, but she would do it. Her determination would get her there. In the end, her determination would get her away.

When she stood to her feet, she didn't feel as bad as she thought she would. She still didn't feel okay, and it was hard for her to look at her parents and offer a smile, but she did it. She walked ahead of them as they left the bedroom and went toward the living room. She sat down at her normal place on the floor and Daddy, of all people, brought her a plate to eat.

It was because of this that she knew they were worried about what was wrong with her. It didn't pass over them that she was sick. That something was wrong. She wouldn't get the sympathy or caring that most parents would give their children who were really sick, but they couldn't deny that she had something wrong with her.

And that only made it more important that she get out of that house as quickly as possible.

Birdie made it her mission to not look at Mona at all. It wasn't just because Mona was responsible for her getting in trouble, Birdie was definitely mad at the fact that Mona hadn't gotten into bigger trouble. There was jealousy rising there, and Mona really wanted to avoid it.

Clyde was basically the same as always. It wasn't as if Clyde ever pretended that Mona existed. Out of all the years that he had been alive, he'd always treated Mona sort of like a vase. Most days, he was content to just walk past it and not even register that it was there. But there were some days that he walked past, and she knew he was thinking about knocking it over. Just to see it break. That was how she felt Clyde viewed her. One day he would push her just to watch her shatter on the ground.

But Beau, he watched her. She was used to this. Beau watched her a lot. She was always aware of it, but she was even more aware of it now. Aware that he was studying her. Or maybe he was just watching her as usual. Maybe she was paranoid. Paranoid that Beau was the one causing her to be sick. That Beau was doing this to keep her there.

There was no way that Beau could know that she had made plans to leave. There was no way that he could know how close she was to being gone. That the moment he was out of sight she could go. That she could have him questioned about those deaths. There was no way he could know that she had all this planned.

But he wasn't stupid. And maybe it was just a natural reaction to her situation, or maybe it was a twin thing, but he had to know that she wasn't going to stay around for long. If impregnating her was his way of getting her to run away, maybe pushing her to the brink of death was his way to get her to stay until she decided to run away with him.

The worst part of it all was that she couldn't tell either way. Although she had said for many years that she would not like to know what was going on in Beau's head, right now, she would have made the sacrifice.

They ate dinner without any excitement. Mama was quieter than usual. It was almost peaceful. Daddy was more talkative than anyone, but the only people he could really get to engage in conversation with him were Beau and Clyde. Mama and Birdie were sulking, and Mona barely joined conversations even when directed at her.

After they finished dinner, things went as normal. The only difference was that Birdie assumed all the cleaning duties that she and Mona normally shared. Mona was told to get a shower and go ahead to bed. She didn't argue it, but it wasn't going to help her Birdie situation.

She couldn't worry about Birdie though. She couldn't worry about any of them too much. She just had to survive without any other incidents like the night before. No more Owen. No risky meetings. No chances for someone to get her into trouble.

She was asleep before Birdie came to bed and awake before everyone in the house. If she wasn't worried about someone waking up before she could get home, she would have left then to find Paul. But she would wait. A time would always arise.

And it did.

After everyone woke up, Mona did more than her usual share of chores. She was sucking up in a lot of ways. Trying to ease tensions between her and her mama and Birdie. If she couldn't get on their good side again, she could at least placate them for a little while longer.

The day went on as it usually would. No one asked her if she was okay. They cleaned the house and did their chores. Birdie and Mona helped Mama sew a few dresses, and Mona managed to sit up without feeling too awful. Her head didn't feel like it was attached to her body anymore, but she faked it as best as she could.

It was around three when Mama mentioned delivering a few of the dresses. She offered Clyde and Birdie to make the run, but Mona volunteered.

"You don't want to push yourself too much. We don't want another episode like the other night," Mama said scornfully.

"I feel okay. And if we split the orders in two, neither one of us will be out too long," she told her.

This was a good thing to offer because they all knew Clyde would take the rest of the day to deliver one dress. Clyde did nothing past a speed of slow. He only got slower. He was the king of dilly-dallying.

"If Mona handles half and I handle half, we'll be done in time to cook dinner tonight so you don't have to," Birdie said. Mona didn't expect Birdie to chime in on her side, but she welcomed it. It seemed to put Mama in a better place.

"Okay, but I expect both of you home before five," she told them.

Both nodded in agreement. Mona was surprised that Birdie didn't act snappy toward her, even when she asked which packages she wanted. Birdie just separated them and went on her way. Mona couldn't believe her luck.

She delivered her packages quickly. Despite her own words about Clyde, Birdie could also be slow. Mona liked that, but she wanted to be sure. She'd never ridden her bike as fast as she did to deliver the dresses. She worked quickly so she could look for Paul.

She didn't see him in town, but she'd already known her best bet was the bridge. That was his *home*. It was exactly where she found him too, but she could tell things were wrong before he even realized she was there. She could smell the whiskey the moment she walked beneath the bridge.

Biscuit ran up to her and she scratched his head as she walked closer to Paul. He was half asleep, it seemed. It wasn't until her foot hit one of the bottles and it clinked against another that he turned to see her. He smiled, but there was a far off look in his eyes. When he spoke, her suspicions were confirmed.

"Monaaaa. I didn't suspect to see you," he said. She doubted he meant to say 'suspect' but the way his words were slurring, he probably didn't have much of a choice. He was drunk and Mona was worried.

She'd never been around people that were drunk. No one was allowed to drink at home. There wouldn't have been an argument. Mama would pour it down the sink. She'd never tolerate it.

Beau drank. Only once to Mona's knowledge, but there was no telling what he and Jerry did while they were out. But Mona was never around. She didn't know what to do around someone that was intoxicated, or what they were capable of.

"You're drunk," she stated.

"You're correct," he said, pointing his finger at her. "You're a smart girl. Very, very smart girl." He said this to himself as he nodded and rested his head against the concrete again.

Mona moved closer to him. She was sure if she stayed too quiet, he'd fall asleep. She didn't have time to waste on waking him up again.

"Paul, wake up," she demanded.

He opened one eye and looked at her. When he closed it again, she was tempted to slap him. She decided she didn't like Paul when he was drunk. He wasn't as nice as the sober Paul.

"Paul," she said again, this time louder. He opened his eyes and looked at her, and that was about all she could ask for. "Did you call your sister? I'd like to leave as soon as I can."

He shook his head. "Didn't."

"You didn't?"

He was taking another swig from the whiskey bottle in his hand. "Tried to call my sister. Couldn't do that because she's got a new number. Guess she didn't want me bothering her no more."

"You could go to her house. Maybe she couldn't find you to give you the new number," Mona suggested.

"I did," he said. This time, the look he shot her was closer to a glare. "Saw her from the road. She was dancing in the kitchen with a baby. She had a baby and I didn't know. She didn't even tell me. She didn't give me the new number. She doesn't want anything to do with me."

"Did you ask her? Maybe she…"

"She hates me. When I knocked, she put the baby away. Wouldn't even let me inside. Wouldn't let me meet my niece or nephew. She said I wasn't allowed to hurt her child. I wasn't going to come in and out of their life like I did hers and Mama, she said. Not until I proved I was different."

"You are different."

He laughed. It stung Mona to hear it. "No the hell I'm not. And you wouldn't know anyway. You don't know me, kid. My sister is right to keep me away. She's right to hate me."

Mona felt helpless. She couldn't talk to this Paul. Not to offer possibilities that weren't as awful as he thought. He was convinced his sister hated him and it was likely why he was now drunk. Drinking away the pain.

"I can leave without your sister. When did you call the police, so I know how long I have?" she asked, but he was shaking his head again.

"Didn't call them."

"Why not?" Mona asked, unable to restrain the pain in her own voice.

"Why should I?" he asked, laughing. "Who's gonna believe some homeless drunk like me, Mona? Hell, they'd probably think I did it and throw me in jail instead. Gotta protect myself. Can't be getting caught up in this mess."

"Mess?" Mona questioned, tears prickling in her eyes. "What about being a kid? What about helping me? You promised me you'd help."

"I lied, kid."

"I trusted you."

Paul looked at her. There was a moment she thought she could see him sobering up. A moment she was staring at the Paul she knew again, but he forced the bottle up again. He drowned himself again.

"You shouldn't have done that. Don't you know? I'm only good at letting people down," he told her. Those words seemed both easy and difficult for him to say.

But Mona was hopeless. And yet, not surprised. This was what happened to her. Things didn't work out for her. They never would. Not if she had to rely on someone else. She couldn't trust anyone to help her. She could only be let down.

"I guess it looks that way," she said, looking down and wiping the tears from her eyes. She was frustrated and hurt, but she refused to keep crying in front of him. As far as she was concerned, he could stay under the bridge and keep drinking. She would figure something else out.

She wouldn't make the mistake of waiting on anyone else.

She turned around and found Biscuit looking at her. His ears were back. She knew the dog could tell she was upset. Dogs were pure. You could trust them, but they couldn't trust humans. Still, they did so. Mona wished she could have that love they possessed.

"Be a good boy," she told him, scratching his head and walking away. She didn't bother looking back at Paul. She realized she needed to cut him out of her mind as well. Not care the same way she knew she'd have to do with Birdie and Clyde. Caring about them would only hurt her in the end.

It seemed like caring about anyone ended that way.

Maybe it was why everyone was the way they were. She judged her family so harshly, but maybe they had already reached this point. Maybe they were just smarter than she was. She was still foolish, thinking people could be good and honest. She was stupid to still hope.

But she didn't want to be like them. That was the issue. She didn't want to lose that hope. Because what was the point in living if you didn't have a single shred of hope left? How could anyone settle on life being awful and ugly and continue to live it?

But she wouldn't deny that it was hard to keep hoping. To keep believing. It hurt. It would only continue to hurt more if she kept thinking about it. She couldn't afford to dwell on it. She'd deal with those feelings once she was safe. Once she found her place and, maybe, found people that helped her not feel like a fool for trusting them.

She waited at the place she and Birdie had decided to meet at. Birdie came along about a half hour later, and they made it home long before five. They had enough time to take it easy coming home, which Mona was thankful for.

She felt weak. Her entire being felt drained. She was sure it was mixture of emotional and physical exhaustion. To lift her arms or even keep her head up seemed like it required every ounce of strength she had.

But she couldn't dwell on that either. She had to keep going. Keep thinking until she could find another way to get away. No matter what it took, she had to find some way to escape.

As she cooked dinner, she thought about women's shelters. Maybe if she could get away to a new state at least, she could go to one. She could lie about her age. Tell them her abusive husband kept her ID. She was sure she could make herself look older. Girls her age did it all the time.

She did worry that her face would get plastered as a missing person. People like that, if they came across something like that, they'd feel morally responsible for returning to teenager to her family. Even if she told them the truth, kids were different than abused spouses.

But teenagers did it all the time. They would run away and live on the streets. Risks came, but at this point, she had to deal with those risks. She'd start figuring out a way to protect herself and just go. She needed to learn how to handle herself anyway.

Mona would be lying if she didn't admit to feeling hopeless. As the days passed, she found herself feeling sick on and off. Her mother even made mention of it to the pastor, and he offered to keep her in his prayers. She'd accept them if she could feel better again.

At church, Birdie was with her. Mona guessed it was to make sure she didn't meet up with Owen again, but he hadn't spoken to her.

She didn't hear from Owen until one night he came tapping on her window. It was the day after church, making it almost a week since she had last seen him.

At first the sound didn't bother her, but when it persisted, she sat up in bed and looked out to see Owen standing outside. He used his cell as a flashlight and waved for her to come outside.

Birdie was asleep, but Mona was very afraid to go. She feared waking anyone up, but she also was afraid of someone seeing him outside if she didn't go out. She wasn't sure which would be worse. She slowly crawled out of bed and slipped out of the room. Birdie didn't turn or move at all. Mona walked down the hall cautiously, worried about making too much noise. She thought she was doing fine until the floor creaked.

Mona stood completely frozen in fear. She closed her eyes and waited, counting seconds down until someone came out or said something. She was rifling through her head for an excuse of why she was up. She was getting a glass of milk. She heard something in the kitchen. She was getting toilet paper for the bathroom. Anything that would save herself from getting in trouble and Owen from being seen.

But no one came.

Everything remained silent around her. She took another step, and the floor didn't creak again. She took that as a chance to quickly get out of the house and out the back door. Mona took her time closing the door so as to not make a sound and then walked slowly around the trailer to where Owen's light was.

He smiled as she came up and wrapped his arms around her in a hug. It reminded her of old friends that hadn't seen each other in a long time. It was a little weird coming from her boyfriend.

"What are you doing here? My daddy would shoot you if he finds out…"

"That's why he isn't going to find out," Owen answered. "Come on."

Owen started pulling her with him, and Mona followed, but she was confused. "Where are we going?" she asked him.

He was using his phone to see where they were going. He was also being very quiet, so they didn't wake a neighbor. "I figured we could go for a little ride. Maybe talk," he told her and turned around to look at her. "That'd be okay, right?"

Mona swallowed hard, looking back at the trailer. She guessed if no one woke up and checked her bed, things would be okay. She worried though. She was scared of what would happen if someone found out she was missing.

"We won't be gone long, if you don't want to," he said.

Mona looked at him again and saw that he knew exactly what was holding her back. She wasn't sure if she liked that. She much preferred the Owen that saw nothing beyond himself. The fact that it felt like he was paying attention now bothered her.

"Okay."

He smiled in the darkness. He led her out of the trailer park and to his car. He had parked right outside the gates. Owen opened her door for her and waited for her to get in before getting in himself and starting the car. Mona slipped her seatbelt on as he began to drive and found herself nervous.

Was he going to kill them both? Maybe he just wanted to get her alone to

(Rape)

Pressure her into having sex. Maybe he just wanted to finish what he didn't a few weeks before. Get a good hit in, put her in her place.

Or maybe he really did want to talk. She was beginning to wonder as they drove if he really did want to just spend some time with her. He didn't seem tense or angry. Maybe not completely relaxed, but not ticking like a bomb ready to explode. Mona didn't feel like she should walk on eggshells when speaking to him.

"Where are we going?" she asked.

He looked at her. He bit his lip nervously and then turned his eyes back to the road. "Anywhere you want," he said. "Pick any place in the world and we'll go."

Mona furrowed her brows. "Owen?"

"Seriously. Name a place and we'll go right now."

Mona was confused and a little wary. She was unsure of how to answer, so she named the park. Owen looked at her and narrowed his brows. He looked ready to object completely, like she was missing the point, but instead, he pulled the car to the side of the road and parked.

Mona didn't know what he was going to do. She was a little frightened by how he was acting because she was unsure of what was going on. She didn't know what he had on his mind.

"Not the park. Not a restaurant or a grocery store. Not even a town or two over. Name any place in the world you'd like to go. Just one," he told her.

Vulnerable. That was how he was making her feel and she hated it. She hated it because she didn't understand. She was used to being vulnerable, but in ways she understood. She didn't understand this.

"I don't understand what's going on, Owen."

"Let's run away."

"What?" Mona asked, unable to hide the shock in her voice at all. The last thing she expected to hear was the one sentence she had always hoped to hear.

"Let's run away. I have to get out of this town and so do you. Once we're gone, we'll figure it out from there. Maybe we'll finally be free enough to go our separate ways and find some sort of happiness. Maybe it'll all change and we'll actually be happy together. Either way, we'll be gone. We'll be free, Mona," Owen told her, holding her hands in his.

She could almost feel the excitement sparking in them, jolting her veins with life. They sparked something inside her. A hope she had long forgotten.

"We couldn't."

"Why not?"

"Beau will find us. They'll kill us if we leave."

"Mona, we'll die here. Maybe not all at once, but that's what makes it worse. It'll happen slowly, day by day, draining us and changing us until we become mirror images of our families. That day you snapped at me, when I went to hit you, you didn't even blink. There wasn't a single ounce of fear on your face. And I realized it was because you were used to it. You expected it and worse than that, you expected it from me. And I was going to do it. I was going to hit you just like my mom hit me and my dad hit her. I was going to hit you so hard and not feel bad about it. Not really. And you were going to be hit and not even flinch. Not even care at that point.

"And I realized that I didn't like that. I felt ashamed. I don't want to be like my parents. I don't want to be like yours. And despite how you feel about me, I can't stand the thought of you going through your entire life being okay with being treated like that. Not by me or anyone.

"If we don't leave, things will just get worse. We will get worse. We'll become copies of them and treat people the same way. If we have kids, the cycle will continue. It never stops unless you stop it and I want to stop it," Owen told her.

She could see in his eyes that he did. He was serious about everything he was saying, and Mona believed him. She didn't know how she could so easily trust him, especially after what had happened with Paul, but she did. She trusted him. She knew he was serious.

"How are we going to run away? And where would we go? The cops would be on us so fast," she told him.

"Not if we changed our identities. We could be anyone we want. And we could go anywhere we want. I have money saved. A couple thousand. I was saving it for a trailer to move out of my mom's house, but I'd rather disappear completely and take you with me," he told her. "Now, I'll ask again. If you could go anywhere in the world, where would you go?"

Mona didn't have to think about it. She knew. She had thought about it so much within the last few years that no other place in the world would be suitable for her.

"Alaska."

Owen grinned. He then laughed and leaned forward, kissing her forehead so tenderly that Mona wanted to cry. "You really are full of surprises. But Alaska sounds perfect and about as far as you can be from Alabama without moving to another country," he said with a laugh.

"We don't have to go there…"

"We're going. We'll leave now. No turning back, no regrets, and just be gone."

"What about clothes? I'm in my pajamas, Owen," Mona reminded him.

"We'll get new clothes. Nothing to stop us, Mona. No second guessing. We decide we're going, and we go, okay?" he asked.

She was unsure. Mostly, she was scared. Scared to say yes. Scared to think that this was really going to happen, that she might actually escape this place and go away. Run away. She was afraid to get her hopes up.

Owen seemed to sense her hesitation. "If not, I'm leaving tonight. But I really want you to be with me. Let me do this for you. Let me do this one thing for you, Mona. No strings attached. I don't expect anything in return. Just let me help you," he said.

Mona nodded. She almost couldn't believe the movement, nor the words that came out of her mouth next, but they were hers. "Okay."

"Okay?"

"Let's do it," Mona said.

Owen grinned and pulled her close. He kissed her. He really kissed her. With meaning and purpose. Happiness and excitement, and Mona found she liked that. For once, she actually liked being kissed. It gave her a twisting sensation in her stomach and set her nerves on fire. It was exciting and she liked the feeling.

But that feeling slowly subsided as Owen pulled away. He was smiling, still holding her. When she pushed him away, it wasn't because she didn't like it. The bile that rose up from her stomach was quick and violent. She had barely turned and opened her door before she was throwing up. Some of her vomit got on his door panel, but she could barely focus on that as her body lurched forward as far as it could and expelled everything in her stomach.

The seat belt was the only thing holding her back, but she was kind of happy about that. Had she not been wearing it, she might have fallen out of the car. Owen's hand was pulling her hair back, and that might have stopped her too.

She waited for it to pass before sitting back up. The world was spinning. She closed her eyes. Owen helped her lean back against the seat. When she looked at him, he looked scared.

"Is that blood?" he asked.

Mona looked forward into her mirror. Her nose was bleeding. There was blood inside her mouth too. She could taste it and it burned. It was the absolute worst time for her to get sick, but it was coming back.

This time, Mona unhooked her seat belt and stumbled out of the car. She got on her knees outside the door, away from where she had vomited before, and began to gag again. Her throat was burning, and her stomach was contracted like an overworked muscle. She even felt lightheaded, like she had been feeling the last couple of weeks.

In the midst of her sudden sickness, she had barely noticed the headlights that pulled up beside them. She heard Owen when he rolled down the window and told them everything was okay. A car door opened, but Mona was focusing on not passing out. Her fingers dug into the dirt and grass. She closed her eyes.

She heard the footsteps as they came closer to her. At first, she thought Owen might be coming around to help her back into the car. Maybe suggest a hospital, which she'd decline because they'd never manage to run away if they stopped at a hospital.

Mona heard the gunshot. Her ears rang because of it, and she started to turn around, but a swift kick came from her side and connected with her ribs. She lurched again, clutching her stomach as she fell to her side. Her entire body seemed to explode in pain and when she coughed, the metallic taste of blood came back into her mouth.

She knew who it was before the shoes stopped in front of her face. Mona didn't have to look up the jeans to know who waited for her. She didn't have to hear his voice to know.

It was a twin thing.

"Going somewhere?"

She only had time to see his smile before his boot connected with her face and everything went black.

THE BREAKING OF MONA HILL

The Beast, The Whore, And The Dragon

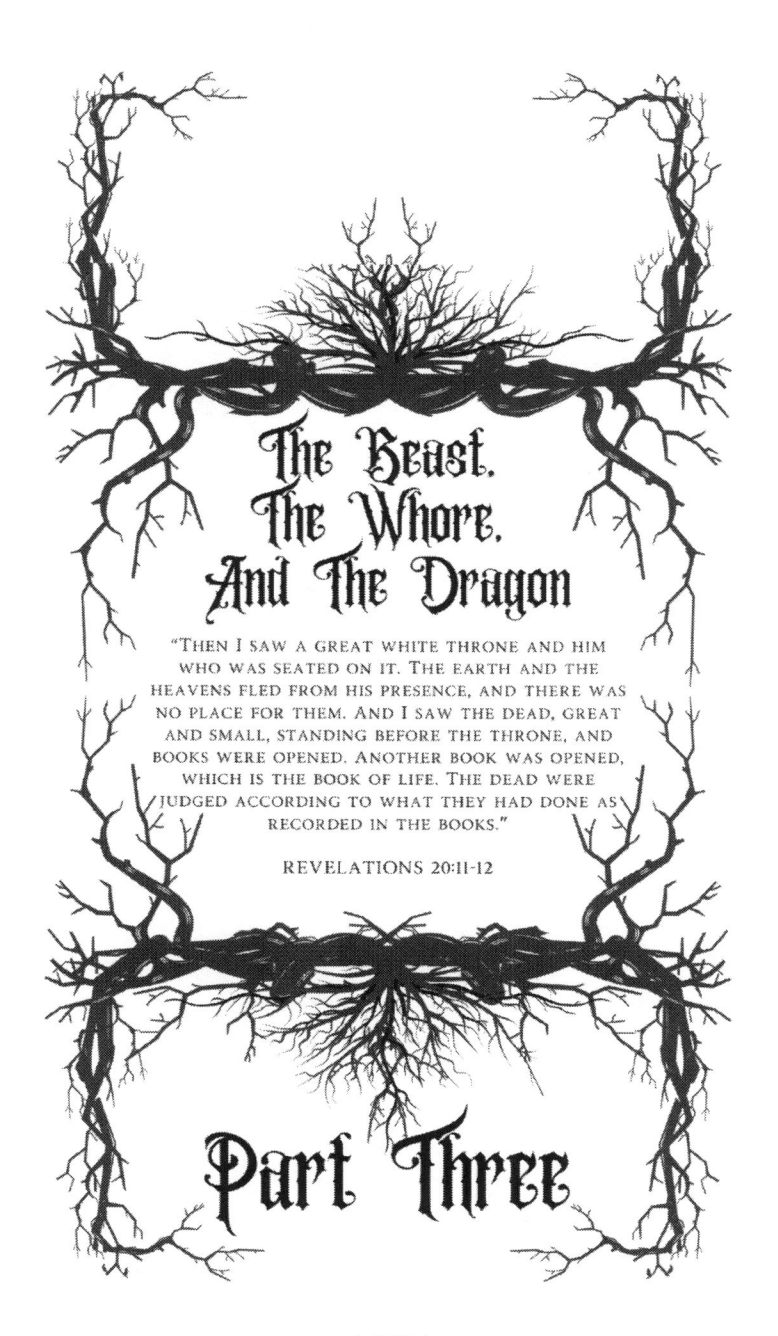

"Then I saw a great white throne and him who was seated on it. The earth and the heavens fled from his presence, and there was no place for them. And I saw the dead, great and small, standing before the throne, and books were opened. Another book was opened, which is the book of life. The dead were judged according to what they had done as recorded in the books."

REVELATIONS 20:11-12

Part Three

THE BREAKING OF MONA HILL

Chapter Nine

Mark 7:30

She went home and found her child lying on the bed, and the demon gone.

Mona often wondered how different she might be if she'd had a different life. When she was born, if her parents had been different people, not related, not cruel, not the man and woman she knew as Mama and Daddy, would she be a different person?

It was more than just wondering how her life would have been. No one's life was perfect. She didn't have some grandiose fairytale idea of how happy and carefree she would have been in someone else's life. Even Jill from the clinic would have bad days and bad people that came into her life. No one escaped life.

She wondered if she would be a different person altogether. One small change. Different parents, not Beau's twin, born in a different town, on a different day, a different year, if just one tiny thing had been different at her conception, would she have been fundamentally changed? Smarter or dumber. Extroverted or introverted. Kind or evil. Selfish or selfless.

How much did those circumstances influence who she was as a person? Was being born on a Thursday an indicator to how ugly you could be? Were Sunday babies prettier? Maybe Tuesday babies were smarter. Did it affect anything in your personality to be born on a different date or time?

Mona knew about the zodiac signs. When she was in the third grade, some girl at school told her she was a Capricorn. When Mona mentioned it to her mama, she slapped her and told her not to ever mess around with that witchcraft again. Astrology was one of the Devil's tools.

Mona never looked into anything else about it, but she wondered. She wondered if the way the stars were aligned on the day she was born had any bearing on who she became, different personality traits she might have had from being born during that specific time frame.

Or was it environment? Was being born in the south something that caused her to be one way or another? Maybe the humidity or the amount of sun in her life would push her toward different routes. Different mindsets. The weather had effects on plants and animals. What if it had one on humans too? Especially during their developmental stages.

But she also wondered about simply being born a twin. Were their fates entwined when she and Beau shared the same womb? Did Beau and all the possible outside forces that could affect him have a butterfly effect in how she developed as well?

Was she born bad?

That was the question she thought about the most. Was she simply born the way that she was? Predetermined to have certain thoughts, reactions, and feelings? Was it something she didn't have control over because her fate was decided long before she took her first breath?

Or had her first heartbeat?

The Bible spoke of free will, but God was also omnipotent. He was all knowing, all seeing. If he knew and saw all things, did you really have a choice in anything? Not just the choices you made, but in who you were as a person too? Did anyone have a choice in whether they were good or bad?

And if this was true for her, if she was simply born the way she was born and there was nothing she could do about it, was that true for Beau too? Could he not help himself being cruel? Being bad? Was he gypped of free will just like she was?

Were they really all that different in the end?

Beau was driving. It didn't make any sense, but she was sitting in the passenger seat. Was this a dream? Had she told Beau she would leave with him? Were they running away to live out Beau's disgusting fantasy? Was she trapped in a nightmare?

No. She was going to run away with Owen. She had been in his car. They were going to run away to Alaska and be free of everyone around them.

But she had gotten sick. She could still taste the blood and vomit in her mouth. There was a shot. A gunshot behind her. It had to be Owen. Maybe Beau had shot him or maybe it had been her daddy or Clyde. Either way, Owen looked down the barrel of a shotgun and she didn't know what happened to him.

And then there was Beau. She remembered seeing him before his boot connected with her face and the world turned black. She could feel that pain in the center of her face. She was trying not to move her nose too much. It felt sore at the slightest twitch. He could have broken it.

But how did he find them? How had he known?

The creak in the hallway.

Mona had waited for someone to come out, but now she was sure Beau had been waiting instead. His eyes watching after she walked out of the house, giving her just enough time to get away, to get in a position to get in trouble, before alerting their parents and setting out after her.

What had they thought? And Owen. Was that part of the plan?

Was he dead? Did they kill him because she was going to run away with him? Had they really gone that far?

She wasn't sure why she questioned it. Beau had killed the woman that performed her abortion. Her and her kids. There was nothing Beau wouldn't do when it came to getting what he wanted. There was nothing he wouldn't do when he was angry and looking to hurt someone.

And now, she was hurting. Not just her face from him kicking her, but all over. She felt like she had been scratched by a cat or had run through some briar bushes. Tiny little stings of pain seemed to be all over her body.

She looked down at her bare legs and saw tiny little cuts all over them. All of them were upside down crosses. She groaned but lifted her shirt to see the carved crosses there too.

"Oh, look who's awake," Beau said, looking over at her. There was a grin on his smug face and it angered Mona. Had she not been in so much pain, she might have hit him.

She reached for the door, but Beau laughed. He had already locked it. He had thought ahead, and it wasn't working in her favor. He pulled into the trailer park and up to their trailer. He parked but didn't turn the truck off. He let it idle, and that somehow felt worse.

"Owen is dead. Daddy and Clyde are out pushing his car into the swamp. They're gonna be figuring out what to do with his body too. His head exploded," Beau said with a laugh. "His brains look like Jell-o on the windows. I thought Clyde was going to barf."

Mona restrained herself from crying. She used that restraint to scowl at Beau as he laughed about killing someone for no reason. In her head, she told herself she was going to kill him. For Owen. She was going to murder Beau and rid the world of one more evil person.

"Daddy told me to bring you home. When he gets here, things aren't going to turn out so good for you, Mona. I doubt he'll kill you, but death isn't the worst thing that can happen to a person now, is it?" he asked.

"What do you want, Beau?"

He smiled. "I thought you'd never ask," he said. He leaned toward her, his smile going ear to ear and too smug for anyone. "I've got the truck. Daddy's wallet is in the glovebox. I snagged Owen's too. We could go. Drive away. Run away the same way I know you were going to do with that little twit you dated. You can avoid all of what's going to happen to you if I have to drag you in there."

"Screw you."

Beau sighed, nodding. "That's right. Keep that anger, Mona. It's going to help me sell my story," he told her.

He opened the door and unlocked hers. Mona struggled to open the door and tried to get out and run, but Beau slammed her against the truck. She crumpled to the ground and felt herself get lightheaded again. While dazed, Beau grabbed her and carried her into the house, bridal style.

When he opened the door, Mona heard her mama's gasp in the squealing inside her head. She heard the shock in Birdie's voice as she got close to them.

"What happened to her?" Birdie asked.

"She was spasming again and these marks just started cutting themselves into her skin! Mama, she was foaming, and her eyes were rolling back into her head," Beau told her, his voice shaky and scared. He sounded terrified.

But he was also lying straight through his teeth and they both knew it. She knew he had cut them into her. She didn't know what the endgame was, but he was lying.

Mona began to push against him, trying to get away from him, but his grip got stronger. She scratched his face and he shrieked and dropped her. Birdie moved into the corner, scared to death.

"Mona," her mama said. Mona turned to see her slowly coming up beside her. "It's Mama. Everything is going to be okay. You have to tell us what's going on."

She looked at Beau. He was smiling at her. That conceited, awfully smug smile, and Mona couldn't stand it. She lunged at him, striking him across the face, but he threw her to the ground and pinned her arms down as he got over the top of her.

"Let me go!" Mona screamed at him, fighting with every ounce of strength she had against him but not doing much. He was too strong.

"What's wrong with her?" Birdie asked in fear. "She's acting crazy!"

She looked to her mama, but she looked at a loss for words. Mona would have given anything to know what was going on inside her head. To know what she was thinking as she stared at Beau pinning her down.

"Mama," Mona pleaded. "Mama, help me."

There was sympathy in her eyes. For a moment, Mona wondered if she was thinking about it. Did she consider helping her daughter? Did she think about doing something to save her? Mama had never looked at her with compassion, but it was there now.

"I don't think this is Mona," Beau said.

Both Mama and Mona looked at him. It was Mama who spoke though. "What do you mean, Beau?"

"Think about it!" he told her. "The unexplainable bruise. She's been sick and vomiting blood. That weird seizure. Snapping at people, acting crazy, attacking me just now, this isn't like Mona. And then these marks on her now?"

"What are you saying?" Mama asked.

"What if she's possessed?"

Mona laughed. She couldn't help herself. Birdie and Mama looked at her with confused shock, but Mona was looking at Beau. Beau and this ridiculous idea he was trying to sell them.

She was possessed? That was the thing he was going with? This was his game now? It was stupid and they were never going to fall for that.

"You're so stupid," she told him. "Now let me go."

"Who are you?" he asked, his face serious and stern. "Who are you and what have you done with my sister?"

"Go screw yourself," she told him between gritted teeth.

"Mona," her mama whispered. There was actual fear in her voice as Mona looked at her. She looked scared and Mona realized that Beau had planted a seed of doubt in her mind. A 'what if' type of thought. Just the tiniest doubt that caused Mama to really look at her. To think about what he said.

But Mama had to be smarter than that. She couldn't believe this stupidity that Beau was trying to spew. It was dumb and there was no way she could believe that. No one was going to believe something like that.

"Mama, he's lying. You know he's lying," Mona told her.

Mama came closer to her. She got down on her knees beside Mona and touched her cheek. She could see it. The doubt. Doubt that she was her daughter, but also doubt that Beau's 'theory' was true.

The scream that escaped Mona's throat was shrill. The pain in her wrist that caused the scream was sharp. Mama fell back, moving closer to the kitchen counter on her butt. She stared at her in confusion. She looked terrified and Mona only felt pain.

"Mama! Your cross!"

Mama looked down at her necklace and clutched the tiny silver cross between her thumb and pointer finger. She looked at Mona in terror, convincing herself that what Beau was saying was true.

But that wasn't what caused Mona to scream. Her wrist was where the pain was coming from. The scream came from whatever Beau had done to her wrist.

"Oh my God," Birdie said throwing her hands over her mouth. "She really is, isn't she?"

"I'm not!" Mona screamed. "It's Beau. Beau is the one doing all of this!"

"Get out of my sister!" Beau screamed at her, lifting her wrists to slam them back against the floor. Mona yelled again at the pain. Part of her wondered if he might have dislocated her wrist. She began to kick at him, trying her best to get away from him again. But all of her struggles only seemed to cement the idea even more into Birdie's and Mama's minds.

"Get her in the bedroom!" Mama said. She stood up and clutched her necklace even tighter. As if it was going to help her against this so-called demon that was inside of her daughter. She chose to do this, rather than just look and see that her daughter was not possessed. That it was Beau. Beau was the one doing all of it.

Beau kept his hands around her wrist but stood up. "Birdie, get her feet," Beau told her. "We've got to keep her from injuring herself."

Birdie moved to do exactly what Beau said but Mona was trying to twist out of his grasp. She kicked Birdie when Birdie went to grab her feet. She didn't need them carrying her to the bedroom. She had to get away. And if Mama wasn't going to believe her, she had to get away from her, too.

"Ow!" Birdie yelled. "She really is possessed, isn't she?"

"I don't know," Mama said. "Just get her into the room for now. I'll go get some rope and we can tie her to the bed until Daddy gets home."

"No!" Mona screamed. "Mama, please don't do this!"

"Birdie, stay with Mama so you don't get hurt," Beau instructed. "I'll get her to the bedroom, y'all just find me some rope or something."

Mona struggled against Beau as he dragged her through the living room and down the hallway to the bedroom she shared with Birdie. He closed the door behind them and then let go of her wrist. He all but slung her onto the bed.

Mona propped herself up, finally seeing what Beau had done to her wrist. She was bleeding. Beau had cut her with his fingernail, it seemed. She had a narrow slice across the bottom of her palm.

"You should have listened to me," Beau told her. "Now you're going to get everything that you deserve."

"I'm not scared of you," Mona told him.

Beau laughed. "Of course you are. You're not Mona. You're the devil."

Mona got up to go after him. To attack him. Scratch and claw and bite and do whatever she had to do to get away from him. To give all the fight that she had in her body against him and get away.

But Beau was quicker and stronger. He grabbed her and threw her up against the wall. He used his grip on her shirt to throw her against the other wall. Then he threw her down against the floor, and he kept hitting her head against the it over and over and over.

Everything was swimming inside of her head. Mona felt like she was going to pass out, but she knew she couldn't. She had to get away. She had to muster up some sort of strength and get up.

But all of her strength seemed to be gone. She had nothing left. Even as she felt Beau pushing her head down against the floor even harder, she couldn't lift it. Mona felt as if her head was too heavy in the first place. Like trying to lift it was like trying to lift a hundred-pound weight. And her neck lacked the strength.

She heard the sharp metallic click. She opened her eyes and saw that he had his carpet knife out. His utility blade was pushed out and against her forehead.

And he dragged it down.

Mona screamed as she felt the blade cutting into her skin. He made two lines. One going down, and the other one going across. And she knew what he had done. He cut another upside down cross onto her face. Just like he had done all the ones on her body.

And she knew why, even before Birdie and Mama ended up coming in the room. With his blade put right back in his pocket, he began to sound scared and shaky again.

"I watched it, Mama," he told her. "She got away from me and started throwing herself up against the walls. When I got her down again, she had another mark. It looks bad!"

"Let's get her on the bed while she's not fighting," Mama told them.

And Mona wasn't fighting. When they lifted her, she let her head fall back. She groaned, even as they laid her on the bed. She tried to pull her wrist away as Beau tied it, but he was able to keep it in place with minimal effort. She just couldn't find any strength to fight back when everything was blurry and her head was pounding.

Beau tied her wrists to her bed posts. He tied her ankles and then tied the rope to the legs of her bed since it only had the headboard. Birdie put her pillow behind her head to let her lift it slightly. Mama stood at the foot of the bed, holding her cross in her hand and staring at her daughter.

Before Mona allowed herself to close her eyes, she saw Beau's triumphant smirk.

Chapter Ten

Matthew 15:22

And, behold, a woman of Canaan came out of the same coasts, and cried unto him, saying, Have mercy on me, O Lord, thou son of David; my daughter is grievously vexed with a devil.

Mona wanted to believe it was all a dream. Open her eyes and find out she hadn't woken up for Owen. Owen didn't come over. She didn't sneak outside to see him. He didn't suggest running away. He wasn't dead. She wasn't tied to a bed and being portrayed as demon-possessed by her vindictive twin brother.

But when she opened her eyes, her shoulder was sore. Her wrists wouldn't move much farther than the bed posts themselves. Her feet had more movement, but not much. Her neck had a kink in it.

She looked around the room. For the moment, she was alone. She didn't know whether that was a good thing or not at this point.

The thing she did know was that she had to find a way out of there. There was no question, she had to get free and escape. She would catch the first car coming through and hitchhike as far as she could until she was gone. Until there was no way they would find her. She'd shave her head. Change her name. Become a completely different person. She'd stay far away from them.

But she had to get free first.

Mona adjusted herself, sitting up as much as she could. Her head felt so dizzy. She was happy that she couldn't stand with the ropes. She would have fallen down the moment she did, of that she was certain.

She didn't have much room to pull either way. The ropes were tight, but Mona was able to tell that the ties against her left wrist weren't as tight. When she looked at her wrist, she saw the smeared blood from Beau's cut.

Blood was slippery. Mona twisted her wrist back and forth and then pulled down. Despite the slickness, it wasn't coming out of the rope. They were tied too tight, and she had almost no room to work. She couldn't reach to untie herself. She couldn't move.

She had to do something. She couldn't lay here and let Beau's twisted game play out. She had to find some way to get herself free, no matter what it took.

And what made him think this would work anyway? It was a far-stretch to convince people she was possessed. She didn't know how to explain her sickness, but the crosses, he drew on her. Cut them himself. Clearly, she wasn't possessed. And he knew that.

She heard the footsteps coming down the hall long before Daddy threw open the door and stood in the doorway. He looked at her, his brows furrowed and his face angry.

"Just what the hell is this?" he asked.

"Daddy, help me," Mona begged him.

He walked further into the room, looking out into the hall where Birdie and Clyde stood, staring in with fear and hesitation. She saw Beau and Mama pushing past them and coming toward the bedroom, but she focused on Daddy.

"Please let me go. I need a hospital, Daddy. I'm hurt really bad," she told him, almost struggling to even speak.

"I'm gonna help you, baby girl. Just let me untie you," he told her.

Mona relaxed against the headboard. Daddy wasn't stupid. He wasn't going to fall for Beau's theatrics. He knew she wasn't possessed, and he was going to free her from their ropes. Maybe he'd even take her away and they could both escape. She could worry about getting away from Daddy when she was away from everyone else.

"Don't do that, Ray!" Mama yelled, bursting into the room and pulling his arm. "It's just fooling you!"

"What is?" he asked, shoving her away. "A demon? Our daughter is not possessed by some God-forsaken demon, Ann! I don't know what kind of fairy tale you're living in, but we're not keeping our daughter tied to a bed."

"She is possessed! We all saw it," Birdie said from the hall.

"You'd do best to shut up, young lady," her daddy snapped.

Mama pulled even harder on him. "Just stop! You have to hear us out!"

Daddy swung and hit Mama. She landed on the floor, and he turned to look at all of them. "I swear if another one of you come any closer, I will hurt you," he told them.

"You mean you'll kill us," Beau spoke.

Mona looked up to see him as close to the doorway as he could be without coming in. His eyes were on Daddy, but Mona's were on him.

Daddy glared at him. "You watch it, boy. I did what I had to do," he told him.

"And we did what we had to do. You know Mona hasn't been herself for weeks now, Daddy. Throwing up blood, seizures, mood swings, and when I got her in the truck, she was spouting off something crazy and all those crosses started showing up on her," Beau told him.

"He cut them on me, Daddy. It's all Beau," Mona pleaded.

"How would I make her sick? How would I cause her to throw up blood and go into those violent fits?" Beau asked.

Mona didn't have an answer for that. All she knew was that she wasn't possessed. There wasn't a demon inside her. It was her inside. Her alone. This was some sick and stupid plot Beau had come up with off the top of his head to get his revenge.

"There's an explanation for all of that. We'll take her to the hospital, and they'll find out what was causing that," her daddy said. He went back to untying her. Mona watched him, but she couldn't focus on him for long.

Beau was the one pulling the strings now. He and Daddy were fighting for control, but it was Beau in control for the moment. And she knew he wasn't going to quit until he planted doubt in everyone's mind. Until he got his way, one way or another.

And that was the look he was sharing with her now. She wasn't going to get free, even if he had to kill their daddy right here and now. The only way anyone was going to help her now was if he helped her, and she hadn't learned her lesson yet.

She had to stop him.

She looked at the rope and realized her daddy had loosened it dramatically. All she had to do was pull with some force and her hand would slip through. She jerked her hand down and it slipped out. She rushed to get her other hand untied, but it was her daddy that grabbed her hand.

Mona met his eyes. "Daddy, please."

"You barely touched those ropes," Beau said. "With as weak as Mona's been, do you really think she'd have the strength to get out of those alone?"

Her mama was clutching her necklace so tightly, Mona was sure she'd cut herself of the metal. "You saw that with your own eyes! You see that she's…"

"I don't see anything but a scared little girl surrounded by a bunch of crazy people!" her daddy yelled. "You're all acting insane right now. That church has been poisoning your minds and now y'all can't even give one rational thought to…"

"There's something else. Something you don't know," Beau told him.

He looked at her. That glimmer of malice in his eyes seized Mona's chest. She knew what he was going to tell them. Her eyes widened. "No!" she screamed. "I swear I'll kill you, Beau. I swear it on my grave, I'll kill you!"

Daddy's grip tightened on her wrist. He was looking at her, and she looked up to plead with him, but his eyes looked toward Beau. She didn't know whether it was her outburst or Beau's teasing information that caught his curiosity more, but Daddy wanted to know.

And nothing would stop Beau from telling him.

From telling all of them.

Mona could see that they were all curious. None of them would know what was coming. None of them would see it coming for miles, and it would work in Beau's favor.

"What is it, Beau? Because right now, you're looking at not being able to walk for a month for these shenanigans you're pulling," her daddy answered.

"Mona had an abortion."

Mona felt tears slip from her eyes and down her cheeks. They came without warning. She hadn't been aware of how close she had come to crying until she was. Until her secret was out and she knew she'd be forced to hear of how shameful her act was.. She held her breath to keep from drawing attention to it but watched helplessly as Beau wove his web.

"You're lying."

Beau pulled out a piece of paper from his back pocket. Mona watched him hand it to their daddy and then move away as Daddy read over it.

"What is this?" Daddy asked, narrowing his brows and looking angrier by the second. He wasn't into Beau's little games and Mona was hoping this would work in her favor.

"It's the place she went. I found it in the bathroom a couple of weeks ago. I remembered her being down that way because Jerry and I passed her. But she told everyone she was babysitting for her boyfriend's mom. So, I decided to check it out myself and the woman was a freak, Daddy. Dead animals hanging around in her house, upside down crosses, it looked like a place you sacrificed animals to. I asked her if she knew Mona, showed her a picture, and she said Mona asked her to kill her baby. Word around town was that she performed abortions and Mona had been to a clinic the day before," Beau told him.

Mona was suddenly confused. How did he know about that? She had been so careful, even more careful than normal, when it came to the clinic. She'd done everything she could think of to keep anyone from knowing she had been there.

Her daddy asked the question for her.

"How do you know that?"

"Jerry's cousin was there. She took her kids that day and recognized Mona because of how Jerry pines over her," he answered. Mona couldn't miss the way his voice tightened as he said that. She wondered if everyone else had noticed it too, or if the word abortion made them deaf to anything else. "She said Mona was there, acting nervous, and went to the desk but never in the back. Like she couldn't get what she wanted to get. I looked it up. You have to have a parent with you to get an abortion at the clinic."

Mona could feel the judgment coming from all of them, but it was hatred coming from her mother. She could feel it radiating from her in waves, getting worse, uglier, as it came at her.

"How could you?" her mother asked, looking away from her.

"Mama, I…"

"Is it true?" her daddy asked. Mona looked up at him and saw he wasn't looking at her either. The truth wouldn't set her free.

Not with Mama or Daddy.

She was feeling sick again, maybe from the stress, maybe from anger, but all she wanted was to be set free. To get loose from them. To run.

"Is it true?!" her daddy asked again, this time his voice raised.

"No. It's…"

Mona felt it when it hit the back of her throat. When she threw up, it burned her nose most of all because she tried to stop herself. The last thing she needed was to get sick. The sickness was just another one of the tools Beau was using to get his way.

"She's lying. That's why she's sick," Beau said.

"Are you lying to me?" Daddy asked.

But Mona couldn't answer. She could only throw up, vomit getting on Daddy and the bed. Not only vomit, but the blood too.

"Of course she's lying!" Mama yelled. "You may not want to believe it, but something is wrong with her! She's been getting worse for weeks."

"Ever since the abortion," Beau said.

"I'm going to kill you," Mona croaked. Her voice was hoarse, her throat burning from the days and days of vomiting. Her eyes were watering, and her vision was blurring. She was seeing red.

Literally.

Birdie gasped. Her Mama fell to the floor and began to recite a Shepherd's Prayer. Daddy let go of her hand and fell back onto the floor. Clyde's eyes widened to the size of dinner plates.

But Mona knew something was really wrong when even Beau looked surprised.

Mona reached up to touch her cheek. She pulled back with blood on her fingertips. She was crying blood? Blood was leaking from her eyes?

It scared her. She even looked up to Beau to see if this was part of his plan, part of his game, but Beau looked just as confused as she did. Not afraid like the rest of them, but surprised.

Unnerved.

Pleased.

But Mona was scared. What if he was right? What if this is what he wanted to happen? He kept saying it and saying it until she was possessed. She had done so many things against God, maybe lying had been the last straw. Maybe the truth really would set her free. Maybe she was being possessed.

"Just tell the truth, Mona. I know you're scared, but just tell the truth," Beau told her.

She wasn't comforted. She wasn't sure about any of this. She was scared, so scared. She didn't know what was happening to her.

"Did you?" her daddy asked again.

"Yes!" Mona shuddered as the word left her mouth. She fell back against the pillow, squeezing her eyes closed and feeling exhausted. Her entire body felt so heavy, but she felt so lightheaded at the same time. She was scared of what was going on inside her body. Scared that Beau might be right.

Maybe she was possessed.

But it wouldn't make any sense. None of it made any sense. She was alone inside her head. She hadn't made any deals with the Devil or even heard voices. The only time her body did things involuntarily was when she was sick. She didn't feel any presence of evil.

She didn't even feel the presence of good.

She didn't feel much of anything other than exhaustion and sickness. She didn't even feel the shame or guilt she had been so accustomed to before and after the abortion. She didn't feel relief from finally admitting it to the people she had been the most afraid of. She didn't feel fear. She just felt empty.

It was Mama that spoke. "How could you, Mona? You killed a poor innocent baby," she said, tears streaming down her face.

Mona wanted to tell her that it was a fetus. A baby could live outside the womb. A baby was the thing that was born, not the clump of cells inside feeding off like a parasite. She wanted Mama to know that, but she wouldn't say it. It would only make things worse.

"Beau raped me," Mona said, her voice low. It was barely even a whisper, but Daddy heard her. And Beau heard her.

"Is that true?" he asked her, but he looked at Beau.

"Of course not!" Beau answered, as offended as one person could sound. "I would never hurt my sister like that. It's the demon lying to you again."

Mona wondered if Beau might cry blood or throw up for lying. Maybe if he lied enough, he'd suffer the same fate she was, but he seemed fine. She could almost believe what he was saying.

"So, it's Owen's?"

"Maybe," Beau shrugged. "I don't know. All I know is when I went to that woman's house, she had places set up for sacrifices. She told Jerry and I as much too. That she used the aborted babies to sacrifice to her gods. I can't help but wonder if maybe Mona was vulnerable. There was no God in that place. Maybe that's when it happened. She stopped wanting to see Owen right after, started getting sick, and then tonight..."

Mona could see her Daddy falling for it too. Just like Mama and Birdie. He was starting to fall into Beau's game too. Starting to believe it.

"Everyone has been doing things, doing things because of Mona. Birdie and Clyde with the shower. I killed that woman. I didn't want to, but something told me to. Something for Mona, like she was trying to get in my head to kill her dirty little secret. Like I had to do it. Even you, Daddy. You killed someone tonight. You didn't plan to. It wasn't something you thought about doing. But you did it."

"Because of Mona," her daddy said softly. "My baby girl."

"She's been fooling all of us. Playing us for weeks now. Weakening us. Playing on our doubts and our lack of faith. I think that's why Mama hasn't been affected. Her faith has always been the strongest."

Fair play, Mona thought. He could play on everyone else's doubts and insecurities, but Mama's pride. Because everyone knew Mama had no doubts about her faith, but Daddy? Daddy walked a fine line of being a believer and doubting. Daddy had weak spots and Beau knew them. Beau knew them because in a lot of ways, he and Daddy were similar.

"That's not my sister in there. She's been teasing us. Taunting us. Giving us all impure thoughts. I know you can feel that too. She's been trying to make us feel things we're not supposed to because then it can get in our heads. That's not your daughter, Daddy. That's not Mona."

Mona looked at him, but she could barely muster up the strength to do that, let alone try and plead with him. She could see that he was believing it. Falling into the palm of Beau's hand.

And when his hand reached out and touched hers, it wasn't out of love or kindness. It was opportunity. Opportunity to tie her wrist back up to the bedpost. To restrain the demon in the room again. To keep them all safe.

But it was Mona that wasn't safe. Staring around at the eyes that bore holes into her, she realized they were all terrified of her. Scared of what was inside her and what that thing would do, but it was the same for Mona.

That fear prickled at the back of her neck. She was in a room with a group of people she knew to be cruel. All of them were in their own ways. All of them in different ways. All of them were scared and fear made people do crazy things. It made them act in ways they might not normally act.

So, what would happen when people that were already abusive were afraid?

They were in a position of power, whether they were aware of this or not. People in power rarely did good with it. And if someone in power, like Beau, could use fear to motivate others, you could see the worst humanity had to offer.

Mona was trapped with people filled with fear, under Beau's power, and she was afraid of what they would do to her.

"What can we do?" her daddy asked, moving away from the bed. He held his head in his hands and pulled his knees to his chest. "How do we get that thing out of her? How do we save my baby girl?"

Everyone, including Mona looked at Beau. The difference was, Mona knew exactly what Beau was going to say. She saw his plan unfolding before her. She knew what you did when people were possessed. They all did, and yet, they still looked to Beau.

To be sure.

For guidance.

Beau tried to look worried about what he was going to say, but Mona could tell it was bringing him nothing but joy to say those two little words and seal her fate.

"An exorcism."

Chapter Eleven

1 Corinthians 9:18

What is my reward then? Verily that, when I preach the gospel, I may make the gospel of Christ without charge, that I abuse not my power in the gospel.

Everyone left the room again. They didn't want the demon to hear their conspiring against it. Beau told them that they had to be careful around her. The demon was always listening, even if Mona had moments of clarity. You couldn't trust her.

Mona sat in the dark, in the silence of the room around her and tried to stay awake. Her eyes felt heavy, but sleep wouldn't bring her rest. She feared she would be surrounded by them in her dreams too.

Right now, she had quiet. Not peace, but close enough for the moment. No one's emotions or fears drowning her. No unwanted feelings being forced at her. Things were better when people weren't around her. She could focus on what she was feeling.

Empathy. But more than that too. A lot of people could be empathetic if they wanted to. It was different than that. Different than just relating to someone, understanding how they felt, and emulating that feeling in yourself.

Paul said his mama could just tell things. Just when he walked in the room. Not see what he had done, not like a psychic, but *feel* that he had done something he shouldn't have. Women's intuition, but stronger. Able to pinpoint the thing that was wrong by the way the other person's energy came off them. How it smelled. How it felt. How it looked. His mama called it her knowing.

Mona wasn't sure about it, but she knew she could feel exactly what they were feeling. And all of them at once, all their fear, all of their conflicting emotions and thoughts, was going to drown her. She couldn't sort through their feelings and manage her own at the same time. It became difficult to know which emotions were exactly hers.

And then Beau with his vengeful retribution. His pride. It all rolled off him with a sickening taste. It was the strongest. Maybe because he was her twin. Maybe because his feelings were more pronounced than theirs. The only thing she knew for certain was

Beau choked her. Everything about him and what he was feeling got stuck inside her throat and made her want to choke. Suffocated her.

This wasn't normal. She knew Beau was behind all of it, but there was a tiny part of her that wondered. What if she was possessed? What if there was some truth in what Beau said? Maybe he had made a deal with the Devil. Her soul for her body. He'd give the Devil what he wanted if Beau could have what he wanted. Sure, Beau was throwing in some showmanship, but what if there was a demon inside her? What if that was the reason she was so sick?

Nothing made sense. No explanation she could think of seemed to work for her. She didn't feel like there was a demon inside of her body. She wasn't hearing voices. She felt alone. Mona might welcome a demon if it came to her, but there was nothing but silence around her.

No God.

No Devil.

Just silence.

For once, she wasn't sure how she felt about the silence. She wanted to hear someone. Prove they were real, God, Devil, or both. Talk to her. Show her they existed. Give her something to believe in. Someone to call to. Someone that would help her.

But there was nothing. Nothing but the sounds coming from the rest of the house. The sounds of people talking softly. Sounds of plates. Sounds of Bible verses. The sound of a car door. The sound of the front door. A welcoming voice. Not for Mona, but for Mama.

When the bedroom door opened and Pastor Steve walked in alone, Mona felt her heart sink. She knew why he was here. Pastor Steve would be worse than they were. As a pastor, he had an itch to confront the Devil. They all did. Each one wanted an exorcism, whether they admitted it or not.

What better way to show your true devotion than to go toe to toe with the King of Lies?

"My God," he said under his breath, staring over her. If he had any doubts before, they were wiped away when he saw the crosses carved into her skin. He'd never believe that Beau had done them. They were all the proof he needed to confirm that a demon was inside of her.

Beau, Daddy, and Mama walked in behind him. Birdie and Clyde were at the end of the hall, but they were trying not to be noticed. Mona could see that from her place in the room.

"When did it get this bad?" Pastor Steve asked. "On Sunday she was just sick."

"Tonight. They just appeared on her," Daddy said.

Mona realized he wasn't going to mention Owen. Not that he had killed him. Not that she was running away. Not that Beau was the cause of all of it.

"Beau cut them on me tonight," Mona said, but her voice was dry. Her throat was sore, but she wasn't sure if that was because of the vomiting or the blood.

Pastor Steve looked at her and then over her body. "Why would your brother cut them on you? Don't you know he loves you?" Pastor Steve asked.

Mona shook her head. "He did it to punish me. Because he wants me to be with him," she told him. "You have to believe me. Someone has to believe me."

"Believe that your brother wants to be in a relationship with you?"

"He raped me," she said.

They all looked at her with surprise, except Beau. He didn't even look scared. Or bothered. It was almost like he was waiting for it.

"The demon lies still," he said. "I love you, Mona. I would never hurt you like that."

"Why are you lying?" she asked him, struggling to even keep her breath against the panic welling in her throat. "You raped me. Impregnated me. Because you wanna be like Mama and Daddy!"

This time, her parents paled. Pastor Steve and Beau looked confused, but only Pastor Steve's was genuine. Beau knew exactly what she was talking about because he was the one that told her.

"What do you mean?" he asked her.

"You know what I mean," she told Beau between gritted teeth.

"Then tell me," Pastor Steve said, but the soft nature of his voice was only for effect. He wasn't genuine. None of them were.

"They're brother and sister. They got married and ran away and that's what Beau wanted to do with me. But he knew I wouldn't, so he got me pregnant."

"Owen got you pregnant. Or someone else. I'm still a virgin," Beau told her. "Is that what Owen was trying to do? Did he impregnate you so you'd run away with him? When that didn't work, he came here and kidnapped you to go with him?"

She wanted to laugh at Beau's claims of virginity, but she was angrier with the way the rest of them looked at him as if he'd unlocked all the secrets. That this Owen explanation was exactly what had happened.

"No!"

"I bet when he discovered you had an abortion, he knew he'd have to if he wanted you to leave with him. You really were just protecting her, Dad," Beau said, looking at him.

Daddy looked sheepish. He didn't want to discuss any of it, it seemed. Not about his relationship with their mother and definitely not about the teenage boy he shot in the face. Not in front of the preacher. Not in front of a man that was as close to competition as he'd get for his wife's affections.

"An abortion?" Pastor Steve asked. His hand clutched the cross he was holding in his hand tighter. It was the equivalent of a woman clutching her pearls and it angered Mona. Out of everything she'd said, that one singular word stained all of it.

"I think that's where she was possessed at. The woman was some sort of occultist or something. I think she used the aborted baby to sacrifice to Satan," Beau told the pastor.

It was funny that they would all believe it so easily. Mona had seen what the fetus looked like. It was barely a thing at all. A clump of cells. It didn't look like a baby. It wasn't a baby. Why would Satan want something like that to begin with? It would be the smallest sacrifice anyone could offer.

"And you killed her," Mona accused him.

"I was trying to protect you," he answered.

"You're a liar."

"No, the King of Lies is in you," Beau said. There was so much indignation in his voice, it was almost cheesy. No one else seemed to share that sentiment though. Only Mona found him silly and cringe-inducing. The rest of them were eating out of the palm of his hand.

"Will you help us?" her mama asked the pastor. "Will you perform the exorcism?"

Pastor Steve looked over her again. His eyes were full of judgment. Self-righteousness. Get in the ring with the Devil? Go to battle for God? His answer was already set in stone.

"Please, Pastor Steve," Mona begged. "Don't do it."

He shook his head. "I'm afraid I have to Mona. For your soul," he told her.

"I'm not possessed!" Mona screamed.

"Shut her up!" Mama yelled. She covered her ears with her hands and squeezed her eyes closed. Mona wasn't sure why her screaming was bothering her, but she kept doing it. Maybe if she screamed loud enough, someone would hear her. They would never perform an exorcism on her and keep her quiet. Someone would hear her.

Daddy jumped on the bed and placed his hand over her mouth. His grip was strong, and his hand was wide. It covered almost the entire lower part of her face.

"How will we perform an exorcism with her screaming so much?" Mama asked. "We can't have anyone involved. They'll never understand that we're fighting for her soul."

"We can duct tape her mouth," Daddy suggested, but Mona was shaking her head furiously. She was fighting against him as much as she possibly could.

They couldn't take her voice.

"Who's going to hear her?" Beau asked, and Mona stopped. A slow, sinking realization came over her as Beau confirmed her fears. "The only person around that might hear her is the old lady and she's practically deaf. And besides, no one is going to come over here and do anything about a little yelling. We scream louder when Daddy gets the belt and no one ever comes."

"We'll still duct tape her mouth if she doesn't stop though," Daddy suggested.

"So she can choke on her vomit?" Mama asked.

"Well, what do you suggest, Ann? Let her scream until she goes into another seizure?" Daddy snapped back.

"This isn't the time for arguing," Pastor Steve told them both.

"The Devil feeds on animosity. And if your sin is like she said, the last thing you need is to give the Devil another reason to come in. We want to get him away, not invite him in."

Both of her parents went quiet again. Her daddy looked ashamed. Her mother looked indignant. Mona wanted them to squirm. She wanted to hear them admit it.

"Is it true? We all know the Devil lies, but he also will use the truth to shame you into doing nothing," Pastor Steve explained. "If we do this, I'm going to need you to be honest and repentant. I'll need as much help as I can get, and it will have to be all of you."

"You're not going to tell the church?" Mama asked.

"I'm not telling anyone outside of this trailer. Not about anything. If I do this, no one can know about anything that has happened or is going to happen. Mona's eternal soul is more important than idle gossip, but also, it's more important than anyone trying to stop us. We can't wait," he told them. "So, I need to know the truth."

Daddy's grip seemed to be even tighter on her mouth. Her jaw was starting to hurt, and she had stopped trying to scream. She was afraid if he squeezed too hard, he might break or dislocate her jaw.

"It's true," Mama finally said.

"Ann!" Daddy snapped.

"No, Ray!" Mama yelled back. "We did this to our daughter. Our sin caused all of this. I knew she was suspicious and tried to bury it, but our sin always comes back to us. I thought God had forgiven me for what I had done, but look at her! We're finally being punished for what we did."

Mona looked from Mama to Daddy. Daddy was livid. Angry at Mama and Pastor Steve, and he was taking it out on her face.

"We made it right. We got married. It's no different than the Bible," Daddy said.

"You can't make a sin right but by the Blood of Christ. Have either of you asked God to forgive you for your iniquity?" Pastor Steve asked, but he was looking at Daddy when he said it. Even he knew Mama had probably asked for forgiveness every day of her life.

Daddy gritted his teeth but said nothing. He didn't have to. Everyone knew Daddy had never asked for forgiveness for anything. And especially not for something he saw nothing wrong with. Their marriage was enough to fix any issue as far as Daddy was concerned. Mona knew how his brain worked.

"I have," Mama answered. Her voice was so weepy. Mona couldn't remember ever seeing her look so weak in her life but answering to Pastor Steve about this secret seemed to wipe Mama out. "I've begged and begged, but it's always loomed over me like a dark shadow. I've never felt cleansed."

Pastor Steve came to her and stood over her. Mama got down on her knees and stared up at him. Although the scene before her was one Mona knew, it didn't look like Mama was about to repent and be saved. It looked almost sexual, and it struck Mona as odd that she'd never noticed how much it did before. How getting on your knees for the preacher felt submissive in a sexual way rather than one of grace.

"You have to believe that God has forgiven you, Ann. When you pray for forgiveness, you must believe He has forgiven you and wiped your sins away. Then go forth and sin no more," he told her.

"How do I do that when we're married?" she asked. "I can't divorce him."

"No, you shouldn't do that. But Ray should be saved. If you're both saved, your marriage will be equally yoked and God will recognize your marriage and forget your sin," he told her.

"Y'all are all so stupid, it actually surprises me," Daddy said. Mona almost laughed, especially as his hand eased up on her mouth. "If we want to be forgiven, we have to jump through a bunch of imaginary hoops to please some man in the sky? What we did isn't even wrong in his book! Look at all the inbreeders in the bible. How are they any different than us?"

"They married out of necessity. You married out of shame and lust."

Daddy looked ready to clock the pastor. For once, she and Beau might have agreed on something. They might have both enjoyed seeing it, but Daddy was controlling his temper better than Mona had ever seen with him.

"You can see what it's done. Look at how it has affected your children. Your daughter is possessed, Ray. Your daughter! Do you want her to stay in this state of torment? Do you want to be responsible for her soul being sent to hell? For her being damned for all eternity because you don't want to admit you did something wrong in the eyes of the Lord?" Pastor Steve asked.

"Think about Clyde and Birdie, too," Mama answered. "And even Beau. Look at how all of it had been bothering our children. You let one sin in and they all swarm like flies. Our family stinks of our sin, Ray. I love you, but what we did was wrong, and our children are the examples of that."

There was a feeling that washed over Mona as Daddy looked at Mama. A secret lost between them. A truth he wouldn't share. A blame he would bear. She didn't understand it.

Daddy looked ashamed, but Mona looked at Beau. Beau and his desire to do exactly as they did. Because for once, she genuinely believed her parents were feeling something. Shame, guilt, remorse, things they'd never shown before. Being confronted with their secret was causing them to react in ways Mona had never seen.

But Beau just looked disgusted. Disgusted at them or disgusted at the way they were acting, she wasn't sure, but if she had to guess, she knew it would be the way they were acting so shameful. Because Beau still believed they would be different. They would be better than their parents. The very thing that made their parents feel shame wouldn't happen with them.

Why? Mona didn't know. Maybe because they were twins.

Maybe because Beau just wanted to believe it. The only problem was, Mama actually wanted to be with Daddy. Mona couldn't stand Beau. She hated him.

"I love you," Daddy told Mama. "Why do I have to feel guilty because of that?"

"You don't if you're forgiven," Mama said. "Only God can judge you. That's why you feel guilty right now. That's why you feel shame. Because you know he's judging you."

"If you'll just give your heart to Jesus, you'll be relieved of that shame. And you'll help Mona too. I know you want to help your daughter, Ray. I know you love her," Pastor Steve said.

He seemed convinced, but Mona was still unsure. If he loved her, he'd realize she wasn't possessed. He'd see Beau for the disgusting pervert that he was. He'd see that it wasn't the Devil doing this to him and his family, but Beau.

But he looked to her and like everyone, he saw what he wanted to see. For now, it was his daughter possessed by a demon. That was what everyone saw when they looked at her now. The Devil. The Whore. The Sin.

"What do I do?" he asked.

"We'll pray a prayer of repentance. You'll give your heart to Jesus, and he'll make you new again. But you have to believe it or it's for nothing. Faith is the only thing that's going to keep the Devil out of your heart and allow you to cleanse him from Mona's too," Pastor Steve told them.

Daddy nodded and finally released Mona's mouth. Her jaw hurt when he did, and she took a moment to adjust it as he got down on his knees in front of Pastor Steve.

"I'm not possessed, Daddy," Mona told him. "This isn't going to help me. You have to let me go. Don't you hear me?"

"Beau," Daddy said. He didn't have to tell Beau what to do. Beau was on the bed with her and keeping her mouth closed with his own hand this time. The only difference was, he made sure to keep her head firmly placed to watch their parents get saved. Some sick part of Beau was enjoying this too.

"Repeat after me and believe it," Pastor Steve instructed. "Heavenly and Almighty God."

"Heavenly and Almighty God."

"I come before you humbled and sorrowful."

"I come before you humbled and sorrowful."

"Aware of my sin, and ready to repent."

"Aware of my sin, and ready to repent."

"Lord, forgive me for I have sinned before you," Pastor Steve said, looking at Daddy and Mama. Mama repeated with no issue, but Daddy looked hesitant. Even so, he repeated the words as well.

"Lord, forgive me for I have sinned before you."

"Wash away my sin, purify me, and help me to turn from this sin."

"Wash away my sin, purify me, and help me to turn from this sin."

"Lead me to walk in your way instead, leaving behind my old life and starting a new life in you," Pastor Steve said. When Mama and Daddy said it, he anointed their heads with holy water and pushed back. "You are forgiven for your sins. Amen and Amen. You are made new by the Lord, our God."

They didn't look any different. Both Mama and Daddy still looked like two inbreeders, guilty of their relationship. They still were. No words would get rid of a fact. It wouldn't change that they came from the same womb.

"Now what do we do?" Daddy asked.

Pastor Steve looked to Mona. The rest of them followed his gaze. They all stared at her, and Mona couldn't help but feel like an ant beneath a magnifying glass, and their stares were the sun. There were no true good intentions in their gazes. Only disgust. Only fear.

"We perform an exorcism."

THE BREAKING OF MONA HILL

Chapter Twelve

Acts 16:18

She kept this up for many days. Finally, Paul became so annoyed that he turned around and said to the spirit, "In the name of Jesus Christ I command you to come out of her!" At that moment, the spirit left her.

They left the room even as she protested and screamed. Mona wasn't sure why they left, maybe to discuss things without the 'demon' hearing them, but she knew her screams were falling on deaf ears. No one in the house or outside of it was listening to her. She ceased to exist anymore.

Only the demon was there.

She was listening in the silence. She listened for the demon. She was scared she'd hear one despite convincing herself of the facts. Beau cut the crosses. Beau raped her. Beau was the one pulling the strings. Not a demon.

But what about the vomiting blood? The seizures where she lost control of her body? Crying blood? Was there truth in it? Did Beau make a deal with the Devil to get his revenge?

Maybe being possessed wasn't living with a demonic voice but having no control over your body. Maybe her mind was hers, but her body was not.

She had to find a way out. She'd watched an exorcism in a movie once. There was a lot of disturbing things going on like floating in the air and convulsing. They contorted their bodies in strange ways and random wounds appeared on their bodies.

But they were possessed. She was not. She couldn't be.

Still, she feared what was going to happen. She feared a demon might take a chance and get inside of her now. Maybe she was an empty vessel, prime and ready for the Devil to get inside. For the Devil to come to stay inside her heathen heart. What if that was exactly what Beau had done? Made her as a sacrifice to the Devil?

Her head was messed up. That wasn't real. That wasn't something that could happen. She wasn't possessed any more than her parents were suddenly saved. Saying something didn't make it true, no matter how many times you said it.

But wasn't she doing the same thing?

But what would happen if they performed an exorcism on her while she wasn't possessed? Would she still act the way the person in the movie did? Would it hurt her? Or would they just be words, and she'd lay there unresponsive?

Maybe if that happened, they'd see she wasn't possessed. If there wasn't any response, they'd have to see that they were reciting scripture and throwing holy water on someone that wasn't possessed. Maybe they'd see how stupid it all really was.

Unless she was possessed. Then, she'd know, and she wasn't sure what she'd do.

When the door opened again, everyone walked in, but they were doing stuff. Beau and Clyde grabbed Birdie's mattress and carried it out of the room and Daddy began to unscrew the bolts to her bed. He carried out the rails and posts and Birdie and Mama cleared out her clothes and belongings.

"What are you doing? Where is Birdie going?" she asked, straining to sit up and see what was happening.

"You're not going to poison her mind like you have been," Pastor Steve answered. "You won't continue to hurt this family, demon."

"I am not a demon," Mona snapped. "The only one poisoning her mind is Beau. Beau is doing it to all of you and you're not paying attention!"

But no one was listening to her. They were busy clearing Birdie completely from the room and setting up the room for an exorcism. This included bringing everything Mona knew to be Mama's religious knickknacks into the room. They began to hang crosses and pictures of Jesus. The figurines Mama had of Jesus were placed on the nightstand.

When the room was cleared of Birdie and filled with Jesus, Pastor Steve told Mama, Birdie, and Clyde to leave.

"I want to be here with her," Mama told him. "Why do I have to leave?"

"Because it was woman that first sinned," he told her sharply. "Eve committed the first sin, making her the weaker of the sexes. You and Birdie are more susceptible to the woes of the Devil because of this. It'll be safer for you to leave the room and pray."

"Why can't I stay then?" Clyde asked.

"I need you to watch over them and guide them in prayer. You're too young to be faced with this," Pastor Steve answered.

Mona could tell this displeased Clyde, but he wouldn't argue. When Mama and Birdie walked out, he slowly followed them and closed the door.

"What do we do?" Daddy asked.

"You're going to read with me from the Bible when we start. I'll need you to focus on the words and not anything the demon says. Neither of you will interact with the demon. It will try to distract you, to spout lies, and to prey on your weaknesses. You'll have to be strong and stay with the Word of God. Focus solely on Him," Pastor Steve answered.

They each pulled out their Bibles and then Pastor Steve began to search through his pockets. He patted himself down and then looked around the room.

"Where is my holy water?" he asked.

"I think you left it in the kitchen when you were getting ready," Beau answered.

"Could you grab it for me? Pastor Steve asked. Beau nodded quickly and left the room, leaving only Pastor Steve and Daddy in the room with Mona. Pastor Steve might be a lost cause, but Daddy wasn't irrational. Not completely. She knew he still had his doubts.

"Daddy," she pleaded. "I won't tell anyone about any of this. I'll never speak about it ever again, I swear. Just let me go. You know I'm not possessed. There's an explanation for everything that's happened. I can prove all of it, I know I can."

Daddy didn't say anything. He looked down at the closed Bible that he held. It looked so foreign in his hands, clutching it so delicately, like it'd turn to ash at any moment. He wasn't magically a different person because he said the words and had water on his forehead. Even Mona knew, if all of it was real, you had to truly believe it.

Daddy had doubts.

"Please listen to me, Daddy. I'll accept whatever punishment. I know I was lying a lot, but I had to. I knew you wouldn't believe me about Beau if I told you. I was scared," she told him, trying her best to get his attention.

The way he purposely wasn't looking at her was why her anger began to boil again. He wasn't going to meet her eyes because he would see how wrong it was. He knew this was wrong. They all did. They had to. No one could be that blind. They all knew she wasn't possessed, and they wouldn't look at her because they'd be faced with the truth when they did.

"Will you just look at me?!" she snapped.

And he did. Daddy looked at her and she could see the weakness. She could see how close he was to untying her. There wasn't even anger on his face from her yelling. Just guilt. Doubt. Pain. It was the most human she'd ever seen Daddy look.

"Look away from the demon, Ray. That's not your daughter," Pastor Steve warned.

"Leave him alone!" Mona yelled at him. "I am his daughter. There is nothing inside me and you know it!"

The door flew open, and Beau came inside, closing it behind him. He handed the bottle to Pastor Steve and then took a step back, holding his Bible like it was actually important to him.

"You are a liar," Pastor Steve said. He looked to her Daddy. "This is not Mona. I know she's preying on your doubts, but you'll see. She's not Mona."

"Yes, I am!"

"Silence, demon!"

Mona wasn't worried about the holy water in his hand. Even as he lifted it to throw on her, she wasn't worried. It was water. She was not possessed. There was nothing that a vial of well water could do to her, blessed or not.

Then it began to sting.

Then it burned.

Mona screamed in pain and moved her body away from the water. She couldn't focus on much more than the stinging pain around her wounds. Each splash made her skin feel tight and her body tense.

"See! Do you need more, Ray? Do you need to see more to know that the thing in this room is not your daughter? Or do you want to continue to live in the dark?" Pastor Steve asked.

"She's not Mona," Daddy said softly.

"Of course not! But your daughter is still in there. But we're never going to get her out if you continue to doubt the Lord and what he can do."

Mona didn't understand it. She wasn't possessed. She knew she wasn't possessed.

So why did it burn?

"Are you ready to start now? Is everyone ready to start?" Pastor Steve asked.

"Yes," Beau and Daddy answered in unison.

"Good. We'll get started with a prayer then. Just follow my lead," Pastor Steve said. "Lord, Father, Almighty. We come to you tonight in the name of your precious Son, Jesus Christ. We ask for

Your Holy Guidance and Protection against the dark forces that look to devour our souls. We ask you to guide our hands and our mouths to send these demons back where they came from. We ask you to protect us and to protect Mona. We ask you to forgive her sin and guide her back to your Holiness again. We ask all of this in the name of Jesus Christ. Amen and Amen."

"Amen."

"Amen."

Mona was beginning to feel the stinging subside a little. But now, she was afraid. If the water burned her, would the Bible hurt her too? Were they right? Was she possessed?

"Have you ever performed an exorcism before?" Beau asked.

"No, but I've watched videos on it. The church doesn't like to talk about exorcisms anymore, but I've always known this moment would come," Pastor Steve answered. "I've always known I'd go toe to toe with the Devil."

It was laughable. Mona could see Beau struggling to hold back his laughter. If she was possessed, Beau wasn't aware of it. He wasn't the one to have her possessed.

Maybe her abortion had done it. Mona feared that when she had the baby removed, maybe it had left an open space for the Devil to slip in. Maybe it really was wrong. It was her fault. Maybe she had invited him in when she killed one of God's children.

"Let's begin."

"In the name of Jesus Christ, our God and Lord, strengthened by the intercession of the immaculate virgin, Mary, Mother of God, of Blessed Michael the Archangel, of the blessed Apostles Peter and Paul and all the Saints. And powerful in the Holy Authority of our Ministry, we confidently undertake to repulse the attacks and deceits of the Devil."

Was she actually possessed? Was it just the reaction to something Holy? Was she going to feel something now? As he read some prayer in his Bible? Something scratched on a piece of paper, probably taken from a movie or web search.

"God arises: His enemies are scattered and those who hate Him flee before Him. As smoke is driven away, so are they driven; as wax melts before the fire, so the wicked perish at the presence of God."

Her head was beginning to pound again. She felt like her ability to focus was getting weak. She knew what was about to happen this time and it only scared her even more.

"Hold her down!"

Things began to feel disjointed again. Her body began to convulse without her control, her eyes were rolling backwards, plunging her into darkness. She could feel things in moments, then moved to the next sensation. Hands on her wrists, then over her body, something in her mouth, something on her feet, touching her body then moving.

"We drive you from us, whoever you may be, unclean spirits, all satanic powers, all infernal invaders, all wicked legions, assemblies and sects!"

The stinging was there again. This time, not just over her body. She felt it in one center place. The upside down cross on her forehead. It was deep there, erupting a scream from somewhere in the midst of her seizure. It ran down her forehead, into one of her eyes. She saw the room again, but only briefly as it burned and sprung new tears trying to flush it away.

"Be gone, Satan!" Pastor Steve yelled. "I said be gone of this child!"

But his words weren't stopping the shaking. And they didn't stop her from vomiting. She felt it come up and she tasted it in her mouth. It tasted mostly of blood.

"Come back, Mona," Beau said in a soft voice. She felt him touch her forehead and she moved away from him. His touch was the last thing she wanted to feel.

"Maybe we should stop for now," Daddy suggested.

"We can't stop anytime she looks in pain. The demon has to come out."

"We don't want it to kill her on its way out though," he answered. "And I'm tired. I know that's wrong, but ain't I more susceptible to the Devil when I'm tired too?"

Mona felt herself relaxing again. She turned her head the other way. She didn't want to lay in her vomit.

"Okay. We'll get some rest and start again tomorrow. Get Ann or Birdie to come in and clean Mona up while I'm in here though,"

Pastor Steve instructed.

The weight on top of her was gone again, but Mona was closing her eyes. She was tired. Suddenly drained, it seemed like no seconds passed between her eyes closing and her body passing out. She had nothing left to give in that moment.

She woke up for a moment when Mama came in and began to cut her pajamas off of her. She felt exposed, but sleep dragged her under again. Her eyes lids were heavy. Her head was pounding, when she fell asleep again, she knew she slept for hours.

The next time she opened her eyes, Beau was in the room. He had a glass of lemonade in his hands and bread. No one else was inside the room, but Mona found she didn't care. He had a drink, and her mouth was dry. He had food too. Mona hoped if she ate or drank it might get rid of some of the blood and vomit taste in her mouth.

She also knew Beau would be honest in the room with just them. No one to impress here. He could assure her that she wasn't possessed. He could squash that doubt in her mind.

Because that doubt was flooding most of her thoughts.

Beau brought the glass to her lips and Mona drank slowly. At any moment, she was afraid she'd start throwing up. So, she took her time as her stomach flooded with the drink.

When he pulled the drink away, she saw she had drunk half of the glass. He ripped a small part of the bread and put it to her lips. Mona took it and chewed at a slower pace. Solid foods hadn't been her friend for a while now.

But Beau wasn't saying anything. He was being so silent during all of this, and she was unsure of the reasons why. Beau liked to gloat. Beau liked to brag. He'd pulled the wool over everyone's eyes. Didn't he want to laugh about it to her? Didn't he want to let her know who was in control?

Instead, he was taking care of her. He was providing for her in silence. When she'd eaten most of the bread, he stood and turned to leave.

"This is never going to work," she told him. "None of this is going to make me change my mind."

Beau looked at her. "I don't know what you're talking about," he told her.

Mona narrowed her brows. "You can do all of your little parlor tricks, it doesn't change anything. I'm not going anywhere with you," she told him.

"Parlor tricks?" he asked innocently.

"I'm not possessed," she said.

"Aren't you?" he asked.

Her stomach began to turn again. She felt it coming and her entire body tensed in revulsion. When the vomit came up, Beau walked out the door, leaving her alone in the dark with her sickness and her demons.

Chapter Thirteen

Acts 19:5

When they heard this, they were baptized in the name of the Lord Jesus

Mona didn't sleep even after she stopped gagging and throwing up all over herself and the bed. She sat up in bed and focused on the pain in her stomach. If she focused on the different places of her body that felt physical pain, she found she could focus on an anger of her own.

She wasn't used to anger. She wasn't even used to feeling her pain. For so long, she'd buried both in order to keep going. Holding onto pain and anger made a person bitter, and bitter people couldn't survive abuse. They became abusive. They became like Beau. Mona never wanted to be like Beau.

But she was stuck here now. Strapped to a bed, sick, possibly even dying, possibly possessed. That nagging fear that Beau had somehow gotten her possessed was crawling all over her skin. She hated the doubt it caused. She hated that sinking feeling that maybe this was his plan of revenge all along.

And she had to use the bathroom. It was such a strange thing to try to ignore. She had to pee badly, but she didn't want to pee the bed. She'd have to lie in it until someone woke up if she did. Even after they cleaned her, it would still be in the bed. She'd be stuck with the smell and that made her start gagging again.

What would she do when she had to do the other? When she couldn't hold her bowels anymore and went in the bed? It was dehumanizing to her.

Her biggest problem now was trying to stay lucid enough to find out what was going on. She didn't feel like she did before a seizure, but this was worse than throwing up. Her head was swimming, and she wasn't sure if she could trust her eyes or ears.

At one point, she knew she heard voices, but they seemed so far away. They sounded like echoes in her mind. Like she was in a cave and they were at the opening while she sat in the back against the wall.

"This could take a while. If we're going to do this, we'll have to dedicate most of our time to it, but we can't alert suspicions either. Especially now that you have a body to add to the list."

That voice was Pastor Steve's.

"He was stealing my babygirlllllllllll," said her daddy's voice, but it dragged on like a song stuck. She tried to focus on one word at a time when other people spoke, but they all sounded garbled. Like radio static was coming through their mouths as she listened.

"I'll talk to the church. . . vacation to exorcise the demon. . . gotta get rid. . . gotta be here. . ."

"Work. . . still gotta pay bills, Ann! Can't afford. . . like some. . ."

"Stay. . . be home to help. . ."

"You. . . work. . . Clyde is here. . ."

Mona fell asleep again, her brain playing the words over and over, putting them together like a jigsaw puzzle. Filling in missing words while her eyes relaxed. It was almost like her brain could finally think once it wasn't focused on the other senses.

And now Mona was waking up, but she was no longer alone. The room was spinning, but Clyde was there in the spinning room. He was standing in the doorway, just watching her. For a moment, he was a bird watching a worm lay on the dirt. She was the worm. Like the vase, Clyde didn't want to just look.

Mona closed her eyes and opened them again. This time he was next to her. She wondered if she might be dreaming with the way he was looming over her. When she looked up at him, his face was distorted. Everyone had screamed demon at her when she convulsed or vomited, but Clyde's face was no longer human. It was contorted into slanted eyes and rows and rows of sharp, crooked teeth stained yellow and red. When he opened his mouth to speak, flies flew from his lips and into her face.

She screamed. She felt them crawling up her nose and into her ears. They buzzed inside her ear canal as she thrashed about, begging them to get out. The sound of them rattled her brain and made her entire body feel like it was under attack.

"Shut up!" Clyde yelled, his voice twisted into a deeper tone, but underneath, it was still a prepubescent boy's voice. "Stop it now!"

There was a hand over her mouth. This one didn't envelope half of her face like Beau or Daddy. It was Clyde's hand, and he was trying desperately to get her to be quiet.

His other hand was somewhere different. It was under her nightgown. It was touching her through her underwear, and it had claws. They were stabbing her sex, hot irons attached and burning the inside of her flesh. The Devil's hands. Clyde had the Devil's hands, she decided, because Clyde was the Devil. They all were the Devil, and she was the new toy.

The Devil was inside her. The Devil was coming inside her. She could feel him snaking his way into her body, here to possess all of her, here to take what was his. If she wouldn't be Beau's she would be Satan's.

"It's okay, Mona. Stop fighting. Mama said you weren't really my sister right now," Clyde told her. "There's nothing wrong with it now."

Not the Devil's hands. Clyde's. Clyde is touching you.

Mona stopped screaming. When she opened her eyes again, there were no devils. No birds or flies. Just her baby brother with his hand in her underwear.

The Devil isn't responsible for his hand any more than he is for your 'possession'.

"Stop touching me!" she screamed at him, thrashing about the bed as much as she could. She was trying to stay focused. Her brain felt like mush inside her head. If she blinked, things transformed. She couldn't trust her eyes to tell her the truth.

"You're not my sister. It's fine!" Clyde yelled at her, trying to stop her from moving. His hand moved from her panties and moved onto her thighs. He was trying to stop them from moving, and it was working, but not because of him.

She felt so weak. Delusional even. What if this wasn't real? What if she was dreaming and hadn't woken up yet? Maybe this was a memory. Or just a nightmare. She couldn't trust her senses to let her know what was real.

Maybe she wasn't his sister. Maybe she was just a vessel for a demon now. Beau's words were echoing throughout Clyde's head, only this time to make him feel better about touching her. Because she wasn't his sister, right? She was the Devil.

Focus.

That rational voice in her mind, a voice belonging to her, knew. It always knew and that was why Mona hadn't listened to it for so long. That voice didn't live in the wallpaper with her. It lived behind the wallpaper, suppressed from being seen by anyone. Because no one needed to know how ugly the walls were behind the pretty wallpaper. But those ugly walls also kept the paper from withering, so it was necessary to keep it too.

But the paper was peeling now. Mona could feel that, and keeping her hidden wouldn't last long. She needed her now.

She focused. It was Clyde. His smell, his voice, his touch. He was alone in the room. She didn't know if they were alone in the house, but if Clyde was in the room, they had to be.

Her legs were spread. Clothes were still on, but Clyde's hands pushing her thighs apart were a sure sign that they wouldn't stay on for long. Clyde was going to follow right along in the footsteps Beau had laid out for him, only this time, he had their parents and Pastor Steve's words to go with too.

She wasn't his sister.

"Get off of me now!" she screamed at him.

"Shut up, Devil," Clyde told her.

She couldn't fight him. With her wrists and ankles tied, and her already diminished state, fighting anyone off was pointless.

But there was nothing wrong with her lungs.

Mona began to scream. She released the most primal, high-pitched scream her body could muster and kept it. It hurt even her ears for the sound to be released. She could only hope that someone in the trailer park might also hear her. Maybe if she screamed loud enough, someone would come busting through the door and save her.

And someone did, but they weren't going to help her.

"What are you doing?" her mother asked. Clyde was pulled backwards by his shirt collar and yanked from the bed. Mona stopped screaming and watched Mama glaring down at Clyde on the floor.

"She made me!" he yelled. "I couldn't control myself."

"He was trying to rape me!"

"Everyone just wants to rape poor Mona, don't they?" Mama snapped. Mama didn't even look at her. She clutched the necklace around her neck and focused on Clyde alone. Afraid her demonic daughter would get into her head too.

But her words stung Mona. Their callous and cold tone made her feel ashamed. And for what? Because of the implications? That Mona was making things up? That she might even be responsible?

"Out of this room now. All of us," she ordered.

Mona realized it was fruitless to continue on with Mama. Out of everyone, Mama and Pastor Steve would never help her until the 'demon' was gone. They were as much prisoners to their religion as she was to them.

She could see Birdie down the hall. She was holding grocery bags, but Mona would never get her help either. There wasn't even fear on her face now. At that moment, Birdie looked green with envy. Probably because Clyde had been with her. And in a strange and twisted way, Birdie saw Clyde as hers.

And she saw Mona as a harlot trying to take him from her.

The door closed and she was left alone again. Mona had no way of telling time other than the light outside, but she didn't guess anyone would be back in the room until around dinner time. No one was allowed until Pastor Steve and Daddy got home. They were all vulnerable.

She had no doubt they would attempt another exorcism too. This time probably more intense. At this point, an exorcism was just another way to torture her. A way to cause her pain and anguish at Beau's own pleasure. And if she was possessed, things would get even more intense.

She didn't know if she could trust falling asleep, but she decided to try. She'd need as much rest as possible to handle it. She needed to have her guard up as much as she could.

She also needed to try to heal. She needed to try to conserve as much energy as possible. She would have to find a way out of the ropes and to escape. And when she did, she'd need to be rested to run and not stop.

There were no other options now. Hitchhike, live on the streets, whatever she had to do, she no longer had better options she could wait on. Owen was dead. Paul was too busy drinking and no longer cared about her. The police wouldn't come for Beau. She had no one to help her other than herself.

So, she slept. She slept until she heard the sound of car doors and the front door. They slammed and then the unmistakable sound of Daddy stomping came through the house. The next sound was a hard thud, likely Clyde being thrown to the floor or into a wall.

"You just can't learn no better, can you?" Daddy yelled.

"She made me!" Clyde cried.

"And you were weak enough to fall for it, were you? Maybe if I make you eat that Bible in there, you'll learn not to touch your sister?"

"You said she wasn't my sister!"

"That doesn't mean you try to screw her!"

It was Beau's voice that interrupted Daddy and Clyde's exchange. Beau and his own anger, one rivalling Daddy's. She was surprised she didn't hear Clyde get hit again at the sound of the rage in Beau's voice.

But she knew his wasn't because of Clyde's actions alone. It was because someone had tried to sleep with a person he considered his. No different than Daddy with Owen. She was nothing more than property to both of them.

But you belong to no one.

She wasn't sure if that was true. It sure seemed like she'd always belonged to someone. Her parents. Beau. God. Pastor Steve was convinced the Devil owned her now. Even Owen had viewed her as someone he owned. It was the way her world worked. It was the way it had always been.

"It's not my fault!" Clyde cried again.

This time, there was another sound. The sound of things crashing. Mona lifted herself to see if she could peer between the crack in the door, but she couldn't see anything. She could only listen to the sounds of things being broken and Mama screaming at them to stop.

And then it stopped. "You need to go cool off," Daddy said in a deep voice.

"But…"

"Get out of this house for a while," Daddy instructed a protesting Beau. "We don't need this type of conflict going on when Pastor Steve gets here for the next exorcism. You know what he said last night about all of this."

Beau grumbled something, but Mona couldn't make out what he said. She just listened to the sound of the front door opening and closing.

The next thing she heard was Clyde crying and screaming again. This time because the sound of a belt whipped through the air over and over. Daddy was tearing his butt up and Clyde was crying and in pain. Each lash he got, Mona could feel it. She could feel his pain calling out to her innermost being. She knew he was hurting.

And for the first time, Mona found it didn't bother her.

Chapter Fourteen

Ephesians 6:1

Children, obey your parents in the Lord: for this is right.

When Daddy and Pastor Steve walked into the room, Mona wasn't sure what she was planning to do. She was happy to see Beau wasn't with them. Beau couldn't rig anything to give the illusion that she was possessed if he wasn't in the room.

The problem was, she was feeling at her absolute worst. Her hallucinations with Clyde still seemed to be lingering around too. It seemed like she would blink and they would be in a different place, wearing different faces. She couldn't trust her eyes to see what was real again.

It wouldn't be too much before she was throwing up again. At this point, she hadn't eaten all day. She hadn't had anything to drink either and she wasn't sure if that was some sort of exorcism technique or just Mama and Birdie being too afraid to come into the room and take care of her. If she threw up, there wouldn't be any food in the mix.

But the lack of food was making her feel weaker. Her eyes didn't want to stay open, and she had a strange feeling in her chest. Her heart wasn't racing, but more like the opposite. At times, it felt like her heart was beating too slowly.

Her shoulders were sore from being spread apart all night and day. She had a little slack, but she wanted to lay them down. She worried over the ropes cutting her circulation. They were already rubbing her wrists raw. Each time she moved them one way or another, they burned. When she looked at them, the skin was already red and starting to bleed in places.

"Are you ready to get started?" Pastor Steve asked.

"No."

Maybe he wasn't asking her, but Mona answered. She laid her head against the wall, trying to sit up for this exorcism. A part of her wanted to fall asleep instead, but a part of her hoped she might be able to convince them she wasn't possessed. If they went through the process and there was no reaction, maybe they'd see she was just sick. Sick and in desperate need of a doctor.

Pastor Steve looked at her. Every time she spoke, he looked disturbed. It was almost funny, but Mona wouldn't laugh at it. She could only try to reason with it.

"I need to go to a doctor," she told him. "I don't feel right."

"It's the demon, baby girl," Daddy answered.

"No, I need a doctor," she told them.

She could see Daddy thinking about it. Considering it.

But Pastor Steve opened his bible. "John, chapter eight, verse forty-four. *'You belong to your father, the devil, and you want to carry out your father's desires. He was a murderer from the beginning, not holding to the truth, for there is no truth in him. When he lies, he speaks his native language, for he is a liar and the father of lies.'* Believe nothing that comes from her tongue, Ray. Her tongue is controlled by Satan, the father of lies. We must remain diligent," Pastor Steve instructed.

The doubt erased from her Daddy's face, and he nodded. He opened his Bible and stood just behind Pastor Steve. Mona rested her head against the bed post to watch them both, her head beginning to feel heavy.

"In the Name of the Father, and of the Son, and of the Holy Ghost, we ask for your forgiveness for the sins we have committed against you. We ask you to cleanse us of our impurities and protect us from the wiles of the Devil as we cleanse your child of this demon," Pastor Steve began.

When he looked at Daddy, he pointed to a place in the Bible, a piece of paper Daddy had opened to, and said, "Read from this with me. Do not stop for any reason, even if I do."

Daddy nodded and looked down at the page. Mona had never seen him follow anyone's orders so well. Not Daddy, the man that always had to be in control. This was unlike him.

"In the Name of Jesus Christ, our God and Lord, strengthened by the intercession of the Immaculate Virgin Mary, Mother of God, of Blessed Michael the Archangel, of the Blessed Apostles Peter and Paul and all the Saints. Powerful in the holy authority of our ministry, we confidently undertake to repulse the attacks and deceits of the devil. God arises; His enemies are scattered and those who hate Him flee before Him. As smoke is driven away, so are they driven; as wax melts before the fire, so the wicked perish at the presence of God," they said, almost in unison. Daddy was a little slower, reading from a page, while Pastor Steve seemed to have memorized this prayer completely.

Pastor Steve lifted the holy water and began to throw it on her. It burned as it seeped into the cuts, even with their scabs now on her. But not like they did before. She just flinched as they touched her skin.

Pastor Steve's voice grew louder, angrier even, while Daddy continued to read at a normal voice. "We drive you from us, whoever you may be, unclean spirits, all satanic powers, all infernal invaders, all wicked legions, assemblies and sects!" he yelled, throwing the water even harder.

The only thing he was managing to do was wet Mona and the bed.

"In the Name and by the power of Our Lord Jesus Christ, may you be snatched away and driven from the Church of God and from the souls made to the image and likeness of God and redeemed by the Precious Blood of the Divine Lamb.

"Most cunning serpent, you shall no more dare to deceive the human race, persecute the Church, torment God's elect, and sift them as wheat. The Most High God commands you! He with whom, in your great insolence, you still claim to be equal!"

Mona felt like she might accomplish something. Nothing he said was making her feel worse than she already did. The Holy Water burned, but it didn't hurt any worse than her wrists or ankles. The words he said didn't make her feel sick or like she'd start convulsing. It felt like it really was just three people in the room. No supernatural forces at play.

She was sure this was part of the reason he seemed to be getting angrier as he spoke.

"The Power of Christ compels you! The Power of God compels you! The Power of the Holy Ghost compels you! Come out of this child, demon! Reveal yourself to us, followers of Christ, blessed by the Most Powerful God. Give us your name!" he yelled at her.

Mona didn't expect him to come closer to her. She didn't expect the amount of rage that was on his face. She couldn't be sure if it was coming from a place of religious indignation, or if this phony exorcism was just a way for him to release some pent-up anger. She didn't know if touching a 'possessed' person was part of the exorcism, but Pastor Steve grabbing her face was part of his.

"Reveal your name to us, demon! The Power of Christ compels you to give us your name!"

"You're hurting me!" Mona yelled, but he only squeezed her face harder.

"God is hurting you! He will drag your name from these lips because He possesses that power!"

"Pastor, are you supposed to…"

"Don't question me!" Pastor Steve yelled, letting go of Mona and spinning on her daddy. "Don't you dare start questioning me now. This is not going to be easy to watch or do, but we have to fight for her soul, Ray. We can't start acting sensitive now. We're not dealing with your daughter."

"You've lost your mind," Mona told him, and she meant it.

When he turned around, he grabbed her nightgown and yanked her forward. It pulled the ropes taut as he jerked her closer to him. She cried out in pain from the sudden movement in her shoulders and the tightness of the rope around her wrists.

"You dare to speak to a man of God that way?"

Mona looked up at him as he glared down at her. The look in his eyes was almost deranged. She'd never seen Pastor Steve look that way, not even during his most powerful sermons. She was scared of the look on his face. It was that same unhinged spirit as Beau.

The same as Clyde earlier that day.

Maybe they were all possessed. Maybe everyone but her was. This seemed logical as horns began to grow from Pastor Steve's forehead. They broke through the skin and twisted as they rose high above his head and curved downward like a mountain goat. The hand holding her nightgown was still human, but his other hand, the one lifted and ready to strike her looked like a hoof.

"You're no man of God," she told him. "You're the Devil."

Wasn't he? Weren't they all? God wasn't influencing their choices. The Devil was here, and it was walking amongst them in this trailer.

You're imagining things again.

"You have no dominion over us. You have no power in this room, demon. You are inferior and not welcomed in this house of God," Pastor Steve said.

Mona wanted to laugh. She feared to laugh. The last thing this trailer had ever been was a house of God. They said it was and Mama tried to act like it was, but it wasn't. The only power this trailer knew was the one of control and torment.

Worse than that, she was starting to feel sick. When Pastor Steve yanked her forward again, she felt the vomit at the back of her throat.

She desperately wanted to not throw up again. She was tired of throwing up. Her throat was sore, her stomach and the muscles around it were tight and in pain. Her body was sick of being sick.

But when Pastor Steve pulled her forward again, likely to tell her something else about being a demon, Mona vomited on him. Blood spewed from her mouth and onto his face and shirt. He released her in disgust, and she fell back. Her skin felt tight and cold, prickling with goosebumps as she laid against the bed.

"God commands you, demon. He can make you sick as He pleases," Pastor Steve said, wiping his face with his shirt. "When we come back in here, you will give us your name."

"We're stopping?" Daddy asked.

"I want to clean up and find Beau. I might even have Ann come with us for the next one. If Ann can handle it, I can keep going during the day when you go to work too," Pastor Steve told him.

"Is that safe?"

"I trust in God to protect her," Pastor Steve answered. "Your wife is the holiest woman I know."

Daddy nodded, but Mona wanted to laugh. They both knew he was jealous of Pastor Steve being alone with Mama. Daddy couldn't hide that jealousy, even if he was trying his hardest.

"I'll go and find Beau while you clean up," he said gruffly.

"Send Birdie in here to clean her as well," he said, looking at Mona. "I don't know if I can stand that smell again. And we need to be sure we're taking care of the body as much as possible. The flesh is weak."

"Is that safe to send her in alone?"

"She can leave the door open. I'll tell her what to do to be safe," he said, and walked to the door himself. Daddy followed closely behind, and Mona watched them walk away. She wasn't feeling good at all. She really wanted them to leave her alone and let her go to sleep for a while. While Beau was gone and it was night, she just wanted to sleep.

Instead, Birdie was coming into her room cautiously. She looked scared to death and was now sporting a shiny new cross necklace around her neck. Mona had no doubt that Mama had given it to her.

Birdie placed a small bowl with a rag beside her. She looked at Mona for a long time before she reached inside and wrung out the rag. Mona knew she was trying to determine whether Mona was going to hurt her.

But Mona wouldn't. If anything, Birdie seemed to be the only one she might have a chance with. The only one that might have a chance outside of this family too. Birdie might be able to still be saved.

She began cleaning Mona's face. She was gentle and worked slowly. Mona was appreciative of that, but she needed to speak.

"Birdie," she said softly.

"I'm not supposed to talk to you," Birdie answered, her voice just as quiet. "You're a demon."

"Birdie, you know that this isn't right. I know that you do. I'm not possessed by a demon," Mona pleaded with her.

I can't be.

She hoped she wasn't. God, she really hoped they weren't right. She feared they were, feared she was filled with something awful. She feared God really was punishing her, filling her with a demon to replace the baby.

She really wished that Birdie would look her way, meet her eyes, but Birdie wasn't. If anything, Birdie looked ashamed to look at her at all. Not so much fear, but guilt. And that was why Mona knew that Birdie knew that this was all wrong. Birdie just had to know that what they were doing wasn't right. She had to realize that.

And if she did, Mona could finally talk her into doing something. She could finally convince her of the thing that Mona hadn't been able to convince herself of.

They could be free. They could rid themselves of her family. Birdie deserved a chance too. There was still time for Birdie's life to change and for Birdie to change. Just because she was acting like them now didn't mean that she would be that way forever. She could easily change her entire life if she would just do the right thing.

And that was the thing that Mona wanted to play on.

"Birdie, you're not like them," Mona told her. "You've never been like them. You were given a bad hand. Your whole life has just been one bad thing after another, but you can change it. We can leave here. You and me. We'll leave and make a new life for us. One that is better. One where we don't have to act the way that we do in order to stay safe. Where we're not just surviving. All you have to do is untie me."

Birdie looked at her and Mona saw a shift. It wasn't shame that was on her face. Not the type of shame that Mona had hoped. She did look guilty, but it was sort of indignant. Like even Birdie didn't think that she should be feeling the shame that she felt. Despite feeling it, she didn't think she deserved to feel that. And it confused Mona.

"I am like them," Birdie said.

"No, you're not! You're better than them," Mona told her.

"You're just saying that because you don't want me to be part of this family!" Birdie yelled at her.

And that was where Mona realized that the shame Birdie felt was because of how she felt about Mona. Not about what they were doing to her. The only shame was about how she viewed Mona in general. Even before this nonsense. Before the abortion and the possession. Birdie didn't like that she felt a certain way about her at all.

"I've always been more of a daughter to her than you have! You've always had all of it, Mona. You always had their love and their approval. You were the daughter. I didn't have any of that. And now I do. And now that you're acting this way, I think that she might actually like me even more than you. And I know God is going to think that I'm evil because of that, but it's true. I wish the demon would just go ahead and take you so that I could have your place."

Mona looked shocked. She felt shocked. But even Birdie looked shocked at what she had just said. Like she didn't mean to actually say it out loud. Because it was one of those thoughts that people just didn't say. But Birdie had just confessed that she was hoping Mona would die. Someone that had done nothing but try to be there for her. Someone that had tried to love her. The one person that existed in this world that had tried to do what she could to help Birdie not end up like the people they were around, and she was hoping that she would die? Almost counting on it even.

It made Mona feel awful because she didn't understand how Birdie could want to choose them, to choose the very people that ran her down and beat her and made her feel so bad. She'd rather have that than a way out.

But then, Mona realized that Beau had offered her a way out. As sick and twisted as that way out was, she was still choosing to stay.

But on the other hand, when Owen offered a way out, she took it. She was going to go with him. Because it was her chance to get away from all of them.

But when she looked at Birdie now, she no longer felt sorry for her.

"You're making me say awful stuff, demon. Lord, please forgive me," Birdie said, folding her hands in prayer.

"I didn't make you say anything," Mona told her. She wanted to believe it too, but at this point, she wasn't sure. People said so many things when they were around her, things that they normally wouldn't say. She wasn't sure if they were just awful or if there was something inside her that compelled them to speak in such a way.

"Yes, you did," Birdie said, her voice indignant and proud. "You're a filthy demon and you made me say something awful. But it's okay. Because God will take care of you, one way or the other."

The only thing she could do was feel an intense hatred coming from Birdie and she wanted to direct that back at her. She also wanted Birdie to know just how much she hated her as well.

So, tell her.

No matter how that little voice in her head tried to make it sound rational, Mona wasn't going to tell Birdie that it wasn't Birdie's fault. She was being manipulated into this family. She couldn't help the way that she was being raised. If you were raised the same way for long enough, you couldn't be too different than them.

You were raised by them too, and you're not strapping anybody to a bed and performing an exorcism on them.

And maybe that was true, but Mona just couldn't find it in herself to admit that Birdie was just like them. She still wanted to hope Birdie was different. That there was time for her to change.

This was the time for her to change.

Mona looked at her as she wiped the vomit and blood from the rest of her skin. She watched the look of disgust on her face as she did. The resentment she didn't bother to hide. Like Beau, Mona wasn't even sure if Birdie believed the demon talk. At her core, she was just glad to see Mona being hated. She was glad to have an outlet, a logical reason, to hate her too.

She's just as bad as the rest of them. Irredeemable.

She hated to admit that to herself. Couldn't anyone be saved? Wasn't there always a chance for people to change? Even people like Beau?

No. She refused to believe that Beau could ever change. He was beyond help. Beyond forgiveness. Beyond Grace. Beyond hope.

Maybe she was too.

Maybe they all were.

Chapter Fifteen

1 Corinthians 10:23

"I have the right to do anything," you say- but not everything is beneficial. "I have the right to do anything"- but not everything is constructive.

Mona was thankful for thin walls. She could hear when someone had pulled up, and she knew that that meant someone unexpected was in their yard. Someone that could possibly mean help. She was also able to hear the police radio. The flash of red and blue lights that filled the room and then vanished gave her hope.

Maybe Paul had done exactly as she had said and got the police involved. Maybe he had managed to put those names on their radar. And now, they were here, and she could be saved.

"Help! Help me!"

She had barely had time to get the three words out of her mouth before Birdie's hand was over her mouth. She bit her, causing Birdie to move away and grab her hand.

Her bedroom door flew open, and Clyde came into the room. They were both frantic, but Clyde jumped on top of Mona and placed his hands over her mouth roughly to keep her from screaming loud again.

"Quick, grab a sock," Clyde instructed Birdie, who looked as if she were about to have a panic attack herself. It seemed as if they both knew, or had been told, that if the police found Mona tied to a bed, they wouldn't understand it. Because they would know that she wasn't really possessed by a demon, and they would rescue her. And when they did, that would mean trouble for everyone else.

Mona fought and tried to scream past Clyde's hands, but the sounds were muffled. She even tried to bite him, but he just pressed further down on her face and nose until she stopped, to give herself some relief.

When Birdie brought the sock over, Clyde took about two seconds to shove it into her mouth and grab the duct tape that was on the bedside table to tape her mouth closed. With that safely done, he got off the top of her and looked at Birdie with a finger pointed at her accusingly.

"If she makes a single sound, you'll be the next one tied up to a bed. So, make sure that she doesn't make a peep," he instructed.

Birdie nodded and looked frightened at the idea of being stuck alone in the room with Mona.

Hate her for it.

They had been stuck in this room together so many times before and it had always been Mona that wanted to get as far away from her as possible. But now Birdie looked at her as if she were trash that could kill her. And Birdie looked positively afraid and slightly annoyed that she was the one that had to stay with Mona.

But Mona decided that maybe her best option was to stay quiet at the moment. Because it could be that the police officer was coming to arrest Beau. And without Beau, she stood more of a chance with everybody. She could be more convincing or have a better chance of finding a way out if Beau wasn't there.

She needed to be quiet so she could hear what was going on.

"Come on in," she heard her Daddy say. She could tell that they were at the kitchen door, and once again, she thanked God for thin walls. She also thanked God that everyone and her family seemed to be really loud talkers.

"Thank you, sir," a new voice answered. It was clearly the police officer, seeing as she knew every other voice in the house.

"So, what seems to be the issue?" her Daddy asked.

"I'm out here checking on a possible lead. Does a Beau Hill live here?"

Mona wished that she could see them all. She especially wished that she could see Beau. See Beau as he heard his name and realized that he was in trouble. Watch his face as it crossed his mind why the police officer was there. To watch that fear come up for a moment that would remind him that he had done something awful. Something that was considered more awful than her rape. He had committed murder. He killed five innocent people. Because of his stupid mistake. Because of his awfulness.

Mona was almost thrilled at the idea of what his face might look like. And her only regret was that she wasn't in the room to see it.

"That's me," she heard Beau's voice. He was back in the house now and cooled off. She was a little sad to hear how confident he sounded. She didn't like the fact that he didn't sound worried. Most people would sound worried. But obviously not Beau.

No, never her brother. He was only sure of himself and would stay sure of himself until the end.

But Mona knew this was it. This was her chance. All the officer had to do was arrest him. Take him away and arrest him.

"My name is Officer Meyers. I wanted to ask if you might know something about the house fire that happened a couple weeks ago. Off Pritchard Street, out in the boonies."

The officer sounded nonchalant. Mona didn't like that. She wanted him to sound rougher. More hostile even. He was talking to someone that might have possibly killed four children and one woman. Was it too much to ask that the man act a little mean? He was dealing with a possible murderer after all. But instead, he just seemed as if he was asking how Beau's day was.

"I was hanging out with a friend for a while, got drunk, and came home and got a whooping," Beau told him and he even laughed a little.

Mona's skin began to crawl. How dare he laugh at what he had done? How dare he even lie? He was responsible for a murder

It was as if the cop didn't even care. And Mona should have known that maybe they wouldn't. She should have guessed that Beau would be able to charm his way out of this. Because Beau was always able to charm his way out of anything.

And it seemed that he was going to charm his way out of murder.

"Do you have someone that can corroborate your alibi?" the officer asked him.

"I was the one that gave him a whooping," her daddy answered and even laughed. It was the laugh that got under Mona's skin the most. That stupid laugh as if what he just said actually happened. What he said was true and it was kind of funny because *'my son couldn't possibly be out murdering anyone'*. Because *'he was too busy at home getting a belt to his butt'*. And it was just so funny. Just a big laugh in everyone's face. And they would all pat each other on the back and get going. And all the while Mona would be back there stuck in the bed. Stuck and left for dead.

"What about your friend?" the officer asked.

"Jerry?"

Yes! That was the way he needed to head. Maybe Mona was wrong all along. Maybe the officer was just trying to establish a rapport with her brother and her dad. He was just trying to give them the false impression that everything was okay. That he would completely understand. And all the while he was just urging them on to see if maybe, just maybe, they might slip up. Because he knew more than what they thought he knew.

Beau didn't just need an alibi. He would need something solid to prove that he wasn't there because the officer found something that would link him to the crime. Beau wasn't going to get away with it. Because they already had the evidence they needed. They were just hoping that Beau would come quietly. It was exactly what was going on.

"What about Jerry?" Beau asked. "I can't remember the last time I even spoke to him."

Liar! Mona screamed in her head. It was frustrating. Frustrating to hear them all lying straight to the officer's face. Frustrating to sit there and not be able to move. So, Mona was moving. She was slowly moving her wrists back and forth, hopeful that she could just get one out. Just one would be enough to rip the duct tape off her face and scream. Scream as loud as she possibly could. If she could just do that, if she could just get out one big scream before that officer left, maybe she'd be saved. Maybe she would be okay. And she would be free, and they would be in jail.

There was still hope.

There was still a chance.

And it was these tiny little chances that Mona kept holding onto. They were the only thing she could hold on to. When she was in the position that she was, it wasn't as if she could cling to anything else. Hope was the only thing she had left.

"Well, we have a vehicle matching your friend Jerry's description at the property that night. Now, I've been by Jerry's house, but it seems like no one can find him. And I've heard from some people around town that he is your buddy. So, I'm just trying to clear up some facts," the officer said.

Did Paul call them? Mona wasn't sure. They didn't mention any tips, but maybe they were just trying to draw Beau out. Maybe they just had evidence on him instead.

"Well, Jerry was who I got drunk with that night," Beau told him. Mona could even hear that he was trying to sound a little embarrassed about it. But he wasn't nervous. That was thing that was bothering Mona so much. Beau didn't sound nervous at all. He didn't sound scared. He sounded as if he knew he was going to get out of this. Like he just knew they only had to keep playing along. That this officer was going to believe whatever he said. The officer didn't have any other reason not to.

"So, when did you leave Jerry?" the officer asked.

"Well, I got him to bring me home pretty late, but Jerry was still pretty wasted. I tried to talk him into just staying, because it was bad enough that we drove to my house drunk, but Jerry lives on the other side of town. Jerry was complaining about that he had some things he had to do. I don't know what he was going to do, but all I know is that he told me he couldn't stay here. Which is fine because Jerry was making some awful advances toward my sister," Beau said.

"I made it very clear to Beau, after I heard, that I didn't want Jerry anywhere near my daughter."

It was her father that spoke. And it was Mona that was confused. What were they getting at? Were they trying to say that she and Jerry were having some sort of fling together? Were they really trying to pin this all on Jerry?

And why even bring her into it. Why would they risk even saying her name?

"Is your daughter here?"

Yes!

Mona began to try and scream through the tape, which scared Birdie. She tried to pull out her hands and wrists, but it was too tight. Between the rope and the duct tape, they weren't budging fast enough.

"Hush," Birdie said in a rough but low voice. "You have to be quiet."

Mona glared at her and made sure not to mask any of the hatred in her eyes. She didn't want Birdie to have even a moment of doubt that she absolutely hated her. She didn't want any of them to doubt that she hated them. She saw no point in pretending otherwise anymore.

But she continued to try to bend her head to her tied hand to pull at the duct tape. She could almost reach enough to grab the edge. If she could just pull it enough, she could scream, she thought, until Birdie came up to her side and slapped her across the face. She wouldn't have expected such force from her thirteen-year-old cousin, but it was strong. And it stung. It was almost on par with the slap that Beau had given her at church.

Her eyes immediately began to water, and her head started to swim. For a moment, Birdie had what she needed. Mona was struggling, but not against her restraints now. She was trying not to throw up with the sock duct taped over her mouth instead.

"Mona has been missing for a few days actually," her daddy answered.

Mona struggled against the rope, but only slightly. Mostly, her head was spinning, and she was feeling woozy. Too much movement and she might throw up. That would be awful. She'd probably choke on her own vomit with that sock shoved into her mouth. She didn't need that.

Or could it be just what she needed? If she threw up, Birdie would have to take off the duct tape or let her choke. All she had to do was wait long enough for her to get it off and she could scream.

"Have you reported it?" the officer asked.

Mona forced the back of her tongue even further back. With the sock in her mouth, that wasn't difficult. She gagged. When she did, she did it again. She looked at Birdie with wide eyes, scared eyes even.

"I hope you don't think we're bad parents about this, but this isn't the first time," Daddy lied. "She runs off with some boy and then comes back home a week or two later. We're just lucky she hasn't ended up pregnant."

Birdie looked scared, but not willing to remove the tape. Mona knew she was going to have to actually throw up before Birdie would act. She had to throw up and take the risk. This could be her only shot at getting out of this room alive.

"That's the thing about this woman that was killed," the officer said. "She was apparently performing abortions from her home. It was suggested that the person that killed her and her kids might have been an angry dad that decided to take matters in their own hands."

She kept on until she finally felt the vomit come up. What she didn't expect was to actually start choking on it. Some of it came up and went into her mouth, pushing against the sock and going back down her throat. She was only able to breathe from her nose and she wasn't able to breathe fast enough. Her airways blocked and the vomit in her throat went down, then back up.

"Well, officer, we're a Christian home here, and murder is wrong, no matter what the reason," Daddy said.

Mona felt genuine panic as she found she couldn't breathe. She looked at Birdie to show her this was real, and she was in trouble. She could see the fear on Birdie's face as she struggled to think of what to do.

"I'm the same sir, but I'll tell you a little secret. No one is too bothered by this case getting solved," the officer said. "After all, someone just stopped her from killing more babies. Spare one life to save hundreds. The only thing that has them sending me out on leads are the kids that were killed too."

Mona couldn't breathe at all from the choking. The vomit was in her nose as well, dripping down and burning all her airways. She was already so light-headed and now she couldn't breathe. She couldn't free the blockage in her throat because of the gag and it only made her try to gag more. If she could breathe, she would have been hyperventilating.

"That's awful. And you really think Jerry had something to do with it?" Beau asked.

"Well, it's a lead. But I'll just say, I doubt, even if he did, that anyone would charge him," the officer said with a laugh.

Mona couldn't even focus on the nonchalant way the officer was talking. Or even the fact that he was revealing the information that he was. Because she was convinced she was about to die instead.

"Oh, God. What do I do?" Birdie asked out loud. Whether she was actually asking God or hoping someone else would come in and tell her, Mona didn't know.

Tears were falling from her eyes as she began to see black spots in front of her. After a while, the pulling on the restraints grew less and less. She wasn't going to be helped. Birdie was going to let her die. She didn't have to worry about the officer at all because she was going to die while he was just down the hall. What a cruel joke it would be. To die while help was feet away.

But maybe that was better. Better than going through anymore exorcisms. No more dealing with Beau. No more living with people that wouldn't help her. People that enjoyed seeing her suffer. Maybe the only way she could be free was if she was dead. Maybe it was the option she should have considered all along.

Is dying the worst thing that could happen?

It wasn't like she had much of a choice now. This was it. She was going to die. She was *dying*. The best she could hope for was that it wouldn't hurt too badly. Or that God would accept her. That death would offer peace. All she wanted was peace.

She was somewhere between unconsciousness and lucidity when the tape was removed, and Birdie took the sock from her mouth. She yanked it free and then started pulling Mona up. When she pulled her into a sitting position, Mona found she couldn't keep her head up. It fell backwards and she had no strength to lift it back up.

"You die can't me on," Birdie said, pulling her head forward to slump over. "Killed they you think I. No believe me one will."

These words were just sounds going into Mona's ears. She wanted to focus on them, but they seemed to disappear just as quickly as they came to her. They jumbled in their sentences and made no sense. Like Birdie was speaking gibberish.

When the spots in front of her finally merged and became one black blob, she didn't hear any more words. No sounds. She didn't feel Birdie shaking her. She didn't hear her saying her name. Everything was gone and there was only darkness around her.

For a moment, long enough for the thought to come and go, she wondered if she was dead.

Then everything came back. The lights of the bedroom coming from the ceiling fan. The feel of someone pressing down on her chest. The smell of vomit still on her pillow. The sound of someone telling her she wasn't allowed to die. The taste of someone's mouth breathing into her own.

She sputtered and choked. When they turned her to her side to hang off the bed, she was able to move her arms. Someone was holding back her hair as the rest of the contents in her stomach came up and landed on the floor.

"She's alive," Beau told them.

"Thank God," her mama exclaimed. Mona could see her feet dancing on the floor like it was some miracle. God had brought back her possessed daughter.

And why?

So they could torture her some more?

She didn't know what lay in the darkness, but it was more peaceful than here. She was still alive. Maybe she had been dead before, maybe she was dying. Maybe if they had left her alone, the light would have come at the end of the tunnel like they said. Heaven would have opened up for her and she would have been welcomed in to feel nothing but peace and forget what they had done.

Or maybe the pits of Hell would have opened up and swallowed her whole.

Being back in this room, she was convinced that was exactly what happened.

"Praise Jesus! He didn't let her go to Hell. This means He wants us to save her soul," Pastor Steve proclaimed and began to speak in other tongues. When he did, Mama followed.

When Mona finally looked up, she saw Mama and Birdie dancing and Birdie doing her best to speak the same way. Clyde stood by Daddy, both about as white as a ghost could be. Pastor Steve was smiling and waving his hands up in the air to celebrate this wonderful victory in the name of the Lord.

But when she turned her head and looked at Beau, she knew the only victory that had been had was his. Because he was still here. No officer was in the room. Beau wasn't being carried away. And she was still alive. The smile on his face was smug because things were going his way.

When Mona punched him, she made sure to aim for his nose. There wasn't much strength in her throw, but she was hoping she wouldn't need much to break it. To cause him pain. In that moment, hearing him cry out was equal to the sounds of angels singing.

Clyde and Daddy were on her quickly as Beau moved from the bed, holding his hands over his nose. The blood beginning to seep through his fingers brought a smile to her face as they tied her hands back to the bed. She couldn't stop herself from laughing a little at his pain.

"Oh, baby. Come here, let me see," Mama said, going to him and pulling his hands back. Blood was coming from his nostrils, and it looked like his nose was crooked from where Mona laid. That made her happy.

"I think it's broken," Beau said.

"Birdie, go get a few wet rags," Mama told her. "Ray, come look at his nose."

Daddy left to go to Beau. Clyde finished tying her hands to the bed. He looked at it from a bunch of angles before slowly nodding. "I think it'd dislocated. I should be able to pop it back into place," he said, reaching for it.

"The hell you will," Beau said, moving away.

"Watch your mouth," Mama ordered.

"You've got to. It's going to be more painful to leave it like that," Daddy told him. "It'll be quick."

Birdie came into the room with her wet rags. Daddy held out his hand for one and then looked at Beau again. Mona was excited to watch it, to watch Beau squirm. To watch him be in pain. He deserved that and so much more.

"Quick," he said.

Daddy nodded. He moved in front of Beau with the rag. It took less than two seconds for the rag to close over his nose and for Daddy to pull. Mona knew exactly when his nose popped back into place by the howl of pain from Beau. It looked like he was inches from punching Daddy, but he spun around with the rag and held it over his bleeding nose.

Mona began to laugh. Mostly because it was funny. She was also feeling a slight bit of joy at seeing Beau in his condition. Those were the normal reasons. They made sense to her.

But she was also laughing at the absurdity of it all. Here she was, tied to a bed, believed to be demon possessed by her entire family except for the one person that was currently holding his bleeding nose and probably thinking it was the worst pain he had ever felt.

All the while, she had just been brought back from the brink of death and was still slowly dying in this bed. She wasn't allowed to die, and yet, she was dying either way.

"Quiet, demon."

This demand from Pastor Steve was cold, but Mona wasn't bothered by the tone. She didn't respect him. She didn't respect any of them. She hated them. She hated all of them.

They deserve to die.

It was a sobering thought, but not one she disagreed with.

"Why isn't he in jail?" Mona asked. Her voice was raspy. It barely even sounded like her voice anymore. Just one more sign for them to think she was a demon. One more doubt for her to believe it too.

"Because he doesn't deserve to be in jail. He didn't do anything wrong," Pastor Steve said.

"Beau killed that woman and her kids."

"He killed a killer. And God protected him for it," he answered.

"He tortured them. And you all know it. All of you lied for a murderer. All of you are just as guilty as he is. You might as well have killed her yourself," she told them, her eyes looking over all of them.

"The demon is just trying to play on your emotions," Pastor Steve told them, turning to the rest of her family instead. "If you had needed to feel guilt over this, God would have punished Beau. The police officer would have taken him in and arrested him. He had every reason to. But God used his Mighty Hand to protect Beau, and why? Because he did the Lord's work when he killed that woman. The number of unborn babies she killed is horrendous, including your grandchild. Beau saved thousands of future babies from dying at the hands of that demonic woman."

Mama actually looked proud. Clyde and Birdie looked to Beau with admiration. Even Daddy looked pleased once Pastor Steve explained it that way. It made Mona sick.

"Hypocrites. All of you are hypocrites," she told them, unable to keep the scowl from her face as she looked at them. "I can't stand to look at any of you. All of you are murderers and you will reap what you sow."

"I already have," her mother answered. Pastor Steve attempted to stop her, but Mama shook her head. "No, I have a confession I need to make. Because it's been weighing heavy on my heart. I believe the Lord wants me to tell the truth so that I can be set free of it."

"Okay. Say what you need to say, Ann," Pastor Steve allowed.

"What Ray and I did was wrong. I knew it even then. But I found God while I was pregnant. I prayed He would forgive me. And He did. Because he is a loving and forgiving God, but that didn't mean I could escape punishment.

"When I gave birth to Beau, it was easy. He came out without much pain. A beautiful little boy, handsome like his father, blessed by God, a sign of His Grace," she said, looking to Beau with a smile. "He's always been a light in my life. A sign that God is merciful. God is good.

"But I couldn't escape punishment. When I gave birth to you," she said, looking at Mona. "I never felt a pain so horrible in my life. You ripped me open. I almost bled out with you. I held you once you were born and knew I didn't want you. Because you were a mirror of my sin. Every time I look at you, I'm reminded of what I did. I never wanted you. I begged Ray to give you away, but he loved you. Because he loved his sin. But I was ashamed of it. You were a constant reminder of it hanging over my head."

Mona watched her mama say this without any compassion. No regret. No pain. If anything, Mona doubted it was a truth she had to speak for God. It was a truth she wanted to say. For herself. For Mona. If there was ever a time to confess your hatred for you daughter, when she was strapped to a bed and being tortured was the best time possible.

"I hate you," Mama said. "And I wonder how long that demon has been inside you. I wonder if that was the ultimate punishment from God. I wonder if I'll be able to love you once you're cleansed or if there isn't any hope for you."

Pastor Steve walked to her and put his hand on her shoulder. He was comforting her, smiling gently as she leaned into his embrace, hand to her mouth like she might cry. Like this was difficult for her to say in front of everyone.

"God hears your pain. But you're not responsible for this. You can't cause someone to be possessed because of your sin, Ann. She made herself vulnerable to the Devil. She allowed him inside. You're forgiven," he told her, and she nodded as if it were true.

Mona narrowed her eyes, feeling the rage build up inside her. It had never felt more pure than it did in that moment. If what they said was true, how dare Mama be forgiven for hating her child and treating her the way she did, but Mona was punished and hated for not allowing one into the world to live the same life. Was God angry because she wouldn't become her mama? The risk of her treating her child that way would have been great. Mona was convinced she'd never love it because of what it stood for.

But her mama was forgiven and washed in the blood of the Lamb. And Mona was the sin. Mona was hated. No one would forgive Mona.

"You're a horrible person," Mona told her.

When Mama looked at her, Mona couldn't hide the hatred. Not that she wanted to. It was about time Mama knew how much she hated her. It was about time that Mama was knocked from her high horse.

"You never loved me because you can't give something you don't have. How can you give your heart to anyone when you don't have one?"

"The demon taunts you, Ann."

In that moment, Mona didn't even care if a demon was making her say it. If the Devil was controlling her tongue, let him. If a demon was the reason she was suddenly aware of her anger, fine. Mona didn't care.

"You didn't love me, because you were jealous of me. Jealous of the way Daddy looked at me. Jealous of the way Beau tried to be around me. I think you might have even been jealous of Birdie's relationship with me. Because I serve as a reminder that I have a chance to be better than you. Because I'm not like you. I'd never be as ugly and cruel as you, Mama," she told her, her mouth set firm and her eyes not leaving Mama's.

She could see the anger in them. Not hurt. Not shame. Anger.

Because Mona was telling the truth and everyone in the room knew it. They could lie and pretend Mona was just possessed. That her words were lies from the Devil, but they all knew it. They knew Mama was just as rotten as whatever demon was supposed to be inside Mona.

"God cursed my womb when he placed you inside of it," Mama said slowly. Venomously. She intended her words to hurt, and they did. Mona tried to deny that they did, but it didn't stop them from doing so. The pain was there, and she felt it. "You were a temptress to everyone you came across. Flirting your way through life, teasing. I watched you with your daddy. Watched you trying to lure him into your trap…"

"You're sick," Mona snapped, but Mama was continuing.

"…the way you acted around him, the way you teased him, trying to get him to screw you like the little whore you are. The same way you did with your own brother. Even if it was true and Beau did rape you, impregnate you, who could blame him? You can't put trash in front of a raccoon and expect it not to eat. But I could see you for what you are. The Jezebel, the Great Whore of Babylon, a slut living in my own home, and I hate you," her mother said, then spit on her. It landed on Mona's face, and she turned her head in disgust.

She tried to wipe it off until Mama grabbed her by the chin and turned her face to look at her. Mona hated her being so close. She hated the feelings she felt when she could see the hatred unhidden.

She wouldn't bother to hide it now. Not here where she was among like-minded people.

"It's no surprise there's a demon inside you. If it has a cock, you'll let anything in, won't you?"

In that moment, Mona wanted nothing more than to kill her. She didn't have a moment of shame in that thought. She wished her dead. If that wouldn't come naturally, Mona found she wasn't afraid of the idea that she could do it. The thought wasn't one she was scared of. Not one she found remorse for.

"Unlike you, I guess I have better options than my brother," she told her.

Mama squeezed her face. She looked ready to break every bone in it. Break her prettiness that she was jealous of. Break her confidence. Break her mouth. Break her.

"Ann," Daddy said, grabbing her arm. "Come on, Ann. You're getting too involved."

"Don't tell me what I'm doing!" she snapped, looking at him. "You've always coddled her. Lusted after her. You're the one that was getting too involved!"

It wasn't a surprise that Daddy looked guilty as she said that. It wasn't even a shock that he couldn't look at her, couldn't stop his own wife from hurting their daughter when she said something true. He lusted after his daughter the same way he had lusted after his own sister.

They were all sickening.

"Ann, it's just the demon getting to you," Pastor Steve said from behind her.

"No, it's her."

"The demon is playing on your guilt," Pastor Steve told her. "It's trying to make you do something you'll regret. Can't you feel how strong it is right now? Don't give in to it."

But the only thing Mona could feel was the hatred spilling from Mama in waves. It was the only thing Mama felt when it came to Mona, even as she pulled away and nodded for Pastor Steve. She hated Mona, demon or not.

"I'm sorry," she muttered.

"It's okay. You're forgiven."

Forgiven. The words slipped so effortlessly from his mouth. Just like that, she was forgiven. She wasn't possessed. She wasn't wrong. She wasn't damned. Forgiven. A word no one would give to Mona. A mercy she would never know.

"Why don't you take Birdie and Clyde and make some food for everyone? I think we've all been locked in this room with the demon for too long, and it won't be pretty if we allow our souls to become weak and weary," he told her.

Mama nodded, then looked scathingly at Mona. "What about her? Do I make something for her? She hasn't eaten since early yesterday," she asked. Apparently, no one was aware of Beau's visit.

"No," Pastor Steve answered. "During the exorcism, it'll be best if she fasts. Make the flesh weak and keep at her with the Word of God, the demon will flee. We can give her water if needed, but we need to make her body uncomfortable for the demon."

Mona felt her heart sink as she heard it. She was starving, slowly becoming sleep deprived, and weak. How long would these exorcisms last before she died of dehydration or hunger?

When she looked at Beau, she could see that he knew exactly what she was thinking. His face was starting to bruise around his nose. He was in pain, yet he was content. Because he knew it was starting to dawn on her what the options were. The exorcisms, this torture, would last for as long as she was alive unless she went with him. That was his entire goal. If she wouldn't choose him, then she had to choose death. Demon possessed or not, he was still her best option. In fact, he was her only option at this point.

Chapter Sixteen

Proverbs 12:10

Whoever is righteous has regard for the life of his beast, but the mercy of the wicked is cruel.

Mona wished she could sleep. Go to sleep and dream a dream that was better than her current reality. Be transported to a new place, where things were better. Where life wasn't the same as it was here.

But she couldn't trust her dreams. Every time she'd closed her eyes, she hadn't left. The abuse continued behind her closed eyelids, making her dreams as bad as her reality.

If she could sleep and have a good dream, she would love it. And she wished she could. But since she couldn't, she enjoyed the alone time.

It was the middle of the night now. She could hear someone snoring in Beau and Clyde's room. She wasn't sure if it was either one of them. She knew Birdie was sleeping on the couch, but she wasn't sure where Pastor Steve was sleeping now.

With Mama if he could.

And this was why she was okay with not sleeping. She could think while everyone else slept. She could be alone with her thoughts and focus on them. Sometimes it wasn't fun, but it helped. It helped her to prepare for the rising sun.

She wasn't completely sure if being left alone with her thoughts was a good thing, but it helped her. And as long as it helped her, she figured there was no reason to doubt it. Nothing else was helping her. No one was going to help her.

Thinking allowed her to ignore the hunger pains. Her body felt like it would explode into pain if someone pricked her. Like she'd cry if any type of force was given to her. Sometimes, she'd gag, but nothing was coming up now. It was just dry heaving, which made the muscles in her abdomen feel sore. She was tired of the waves coming and going.

The sickness had been going on for a couple of weeks now. She was already weak when they tied her to the bed. She had now been tied for over a day. It seemed like a lot longer than that with the way she felt. At this rate, how long would she last before she was dead or giving in to Beau?

She was stuck. She was stuck here in this room alone with no one coming to her rescue. That was the way things would stay now. Owen was dead. The cops had come and gone, believing her parents' stupid story about running away. Even Jerry, though she doubted he could have helped, was either missing, dead, or laying low. She had no idea where Paul was or what he was doing. She wasn't even sure if he'd been the one to call the police or not. Either way, Beau had managed to cut her off from everything and everyone.

This was the way things were now.

The only way she was going to escape was to free herself. That was the main thought circling in her head now. If she wanted to be free, she couldn't wait for someone to come for her rescue. She had to get out while she could by any means necessary.

Mona pulled at the ropes around her wrists. Clyde had tied them back after she nearly died. Though they were tight, they were nowhere near as tight as they had been before. She could move her wrists up and down through the rope.

She jerked her arm down, but the hole was still too tight to slip over her hand. Not to mention the pain she felt as it rubbed over her already irritated skin. The skin around her wrists was red and bruised. Tiny droplets of blood were prickled along her skin.

She wondered if the blood would help the rope slip over her hand. There wasn't enough there to make a difference now, but if she managed to make herself bleed more, maybe she could use it to slip out. If not, maybe the sight of blood would help her family untie her and give her a chance.

Making herself bleed wouldn't be easy or without pain. She knew this. She'd hurt, but she'd hurt worse if she stayed here.

It was worth the pain.

Mona pulled her wrist tight against the rope and began to rub the already irritated skin against the rope. The rope was coarse and scratched her, but it rubbed raw with every soft movement. With a fast and rough twist, it cut.

She squeezed her eyes closed as she twisted and pulled with the rope, rubbing her wrist against it like she was trying to create a fire with it. Fire was a funny choice because that was the exact feeling in her skin. It was burning. Each twist felt like she was ripping her skin off the bone.

She stopped to look at her wrist. Blood was smeared around, but not flowing. She pulled down again, then up, repeating the motion as she tried to wet her hand with the blood, as well as the rope. Each pull hurt not only her wrist, but her arms and shoulders too. She'd been in her spread-eagle position for so long, her arms ached.

But it was working. Her hand moved farther down in the rope. She pulled it taut, squeezing her eyes closed as she used her strength to keep pulling. When her hand landed against the bed, she opened her eyes. Her hand was free.

She lifted her hand, but it felt like dead weight. Pain spread throughout her arm as she moved it, lifting it in small bursts. First to her lap, then to her shoulder, then she moved her hand to the rope. She tried to untie the rope, but it didn't want to budge.

She glanced around her, looking over the table beside her. Rags and a bowl of water sat on it. Part of her wanted to drink the water because of how thirsty she was, but she'd wait. Wait until she was out of the house and gone.

Instead, she looked at the figurine of Jesus on the cross. Her bedroom was filled with a bunch of crosses and Jesus figurines, but this was the only one within reach. It was porcelain and very precious to Mama.

Mona grabbed it and slammed it down on the table. The top part of the cross and Jesus broke into a few pieces. The part still in her hand also broke. Mona laid it on the bed and picked up the largest broken piece. She took the sharp edge and began cutting at the rope quickly.

Then she heard the creak in the hallway.

Someone was coming. Mona clutched the broken porcelain and slipped her hand around the back of the rope and held it. If she didn't move, maybe they wouldn't look hard enough to see the rope wasn't wrapped around her wrist.

Her heart was racing as the door opened. It was Beau that walked in. His nose looked swollen and bruised. He didn't look like it felt good either and Mona loved that.

What she didn't love was the way he was standing in the doorway, staring at her. His eyes were boring holes into her, looking at her closely, examining her face.

He didn't say anything, but she knew her breaking the figurine had woken him up. She knew the broken pieces of Jesus were on the floor too, but he wasn't looking down. He was just watching her.

When he decided to speak, he sounded tired. "Are you ready to leave yet?" he asked.

"Not with you," she told him defiantly.

"I'm your only option, Mona. You wanna be free, you've got to be mine," he told her, leaning against the footboard of the bed. "Life with me wouldn't come close to this. I'd never treat you like this again. I'd spend my whole life proving that to you."

His words made Mona feel sick. It wasn't because of the words themselves. She'd heard this from Beau so many times before.

It was the sincerity. She hated that he genuinely felt this way. It made her sick to know how poisoned his brain was on this. He truly believed they'd be better off together. Living like husband and wife. Loving like husband and wife. He was sick and he wasn't even aware of how sick he was.

"I will never be yours," she told him.

He stared, anger boiling under the surface. "Then you'll be

theirs," he said.

Mona wasn't sure if he meant their family or the demons. At this point, she wasn't sure if Beau even knew what the truth was. His reality and fantasy were just as mixed up as hers was.

She was silent, hoping he'd turn around and walk out. It looked like that was exactly what he was going to do too, but as he turned, his eyes landed on the floor. He looked at the broken Jesus and Mona knew her time was up. Beau came around the bed, ready to grab her hand, maybe tie her back up, and Mona slashed the broken porcelain along his arm, causing Beau to cry out in pain. He fell back, hitting the nightstand and falling against the floor.

The sound made the lights come on. Mona could see Birdie sitting up on the loveseat from the doorway, but Clyde and Pastor Steve were coming from the living room and the bedroom. Pastor Steve saw her free hand and yelled for her Mama and Daddy.

She moved the shard back to the rope and began to cut furiously. She had to risk it. She had to try. No matter how unlikely her odds were, she couldn't sit there and let them keep her tied up.

Beau was getting up. His arm was bleeding pretty badly. Beau looked at her and attempted to grab her hand. She held the shard at him and kept her eyes glued.

"Come closer to me and I'll slit your throat like the mangy dog you are," she warned him.

Holding his bleeding arm, he glared at her. He had her strapped to a bed, cut and bruised, but she had also managed to slice his arm open and break his nose all in one day. She was feeling powerful, and she wasn't scared of him or what he would do.

And he could see that. Fear had kept her in place. Fear had kept her quiet. Beau knew how to control fear. But Mona wasn't afraid of him. She wasn't sure why, but the only emotion she was finding anymore was pure, unadulterated anger. Rage. Loathing. It kept her warm at night as she thought of his pain.

But Beau would never take it lying down. She knew that. For each little victory, there were repercussions. And Beau wouldn't let those past. He'd just get crueler.

"Don't let her get loose!" Daddy yelled, coming down the hallway.

It was a fool's game. She knew it. She couldn't cut herself out and get out of the trailer. Even if she got her wrist cut from the rope, her ankles were tied too. If she somehow managed to cut herself free, she wasn't even sure if she could walk. She was tired and weak. Even holding her head up now made her feel lightheaded. She couldn't fight Daddy and Beau to get out.

And Beau knew that. He wasn't moving any closer to her, but he knew she was thinking about this. About how far she was willing to go to get free. She had him nervous with the shard, but could she hurt Daddy? Could she kill him if she needed to if it meant she could get away? Birdie? Clyde? Could she?

Beau moved to the end of the bed and slammed the door. He separated them from the rest of the family, even as they banged and yelled to be let in. He slammed his hand down on the doorknob, breaking it off and locking them inside. He just stared at her, watching her with a slight smile to his lips.

"Do it," Beau challenged.

Mona didn't move. Not her gaze or her body. She just stared at him as he moved a little closer to her. Daring her, holding up his pocketknife as he moved it closer to the rope on her other wrist.

Was he going to cut her free? Was Beau about to let her free? If he did, it wasn't for her. It was for him and his benefit. Everything was for Beau's benefit.

"Kill them," Beau said softly. It was barely over a whisper. She doubted anyone heard it at all. Not between the yelling and banging.

It was an invitation. That was what this was. He'd let her arms loose, let them free, but kill them all.

"We can do it together. Kill all of them and leave. Get our revenge. Not just mine, but yours too. Don't you want to make them suffer?" he asked.

And she did. God, she did. The thoughts of what she'd do to them if she could swirled in her head. How she'd kill all of them. How she wanted to do it. It was a powerful thing, revenge. It poisoned her the same way Beau's lust poisoned him.

It was a test. She'd be no sooner free if she did. Beau wouldn't let her leave just because she killed their family. He just wanted to see if she could do it. If she would do it. How badly did she want her freedom? Was she willing to kill anyone other than him to do it?

You can.

"I'll start with you," she told him, digging the porcelain into his side. It was sharp enough to pierce his ribs, but not to cause any real damage.

Beau gritted his teeth and cut the rope on her other wrist and moved back, leaving the pocketknife on the bed. Mona grabbed it and held it firmly. He jerked the porcelain out of his skin and then glared at her. "You're gonna regret that," he said. The door flew open, splintering as Daddy busted through, just as Beau put on his game face. "Kill me, demon. But come out of my sister. Take me instead!"

"No, Beau!" Daddy yelled.

Beau didn't do anything to her, but Daddy lunged at the bed. His hands grabbed her wrists and pinned her down, squeezing the one with the knife until she cried out in pain and released it. It fell from her fingers as Daddy kept her beneath him as she fought against him.

"What's going on?" Pastor Steve asked in alarm.

"Beau tried to get the demon to go into him. He tried to let her kill him," Daddy said.

"I'm tired of it hurting my sister," Beau said in a fake defensive voice. "It can have me instead. It can hurt me."

"That's not how it works," Pastor Steve said.

"Y'all can worry about that later, I need to restrain her again," Daddy told them. "Go get me some rope."

Mona fought against him as best as she could, but Daddy was an immovable force both physically and mentally. He didn't have to struggle to keep her there while Clyde ran out of the room to get more rope.

"Let me go!" Mona screamed. But he wouldn't. They wouldn't ever let her go.

"How did she even get free?" Pastor Steve asked.

"I think she managed to get her hand free," Beau told them, then pointed to the broken Jesus. She was trying to cut the other one when I came in. That's when she stabbed me and cut me."

His side was bleeding, but his arm was worse. She'd cut a deep gash in his arm. She wished she would have gotten his side deeper. Maybe stabbed a lung. He deserved it.

"How would she do that? She'd not strong enough to do that," Daddy said, staring at the bloody rope.

"It's the demon," Pastor Steve said. "The demon is strong, Ray. It can do whatever it likes when it chooses."

"Then what's the point in trying to tie her up?" Daddy asked, exasperated. "If she can just break free whenever she wants to, why even try?"

Beau just stared at her as she struggled. His eyes were looking at her wrists and then to the bed. She could see the wheels inside his mind turning. There was a plan concocting in his head and Mona wouldn't be on the good end of it.

"Pastor Steve, what is that thing that happens when the marks show up like they did when Jesus was crucified?" Beau asked, looking at the pastor.

Pastor Steve narrowed his brows. "Are you talking about stigmata?" he asked.

Beau snapped his fingers and nodded. "Yes! When they show up on people, it's said they're touched by divine power or something, right? Like they have favor in the eyes of the saints and God, right?" he asked.

Pastor Steve shrugged. "I guess so, but that's more a Catholic belief than a Pentecostal one," he said.

"What are you getting at?" Daddy asked.

Beau looked at Mona one last time before meeting their eyes. "Mona has marks of the Devil all over her. She's been touched by him. Maybe if we marked her by God, we could help her and keep her from breaking free again," he said.

"Like the power of God would hold her in place," Pastor Steve said.

Beau nodded. "And maybe it'd make her more favorable in His eyes too."

"You're suggesting we nail her hands to the bed?" Daddy asked, a little shocked, it seemed. His voice certainly gave the impression that this sounded crazy, even to him.

And Mona knew it was crazy. Beau was just spouting stupid

things off at a whim now. Anything that he could twist into the slightest hint of being biblical, whether it was or not. He had a captive audience with very few questioning members.

"Yeah. We don't know how much strength this demon inside her has. Shouldn't we do everything in our power to weaken it?" he asked.

"You're absolutely nuts!" Mona yelled at him. "And y'all are just as stupid if you go with anything he says. Can't you see how twisted he is?"

Her questions were at Daddy specifically. Cursed by his sins and emotions, maybe, but there was still a rational being somewhere inside. Mona hoped, at least. Someone that was just caught up in the madness, like a vulnerable person in a cult. He was told not to question, but he did. He knew it was crazy.

"There's no rope outside," Clyde's voice yelled as he came through the back door. He came into the room and stood at the doorway as Daddy's mind seemed to spin in front of her.

"Daddy, please," Mona begged.

But Daddy wasn't looking at her. Maybe he couldn't look at her. Maybe if he did, it would break him. Maybe it was the thing that would make him see the truth, so he refused to look at her. He refused to acknowledge her existence as he gave the next order.

"Grab the hammer and some nails."

"No!" Mona screamed, fighting against him again.

"I know where they are," Beau said and left with Clyde. Mona watched him leave the trailer before realizing she had a few precious moments to try to convince someone.

"Daddy, please. Don't do this. You know this isn't right," she told him. "Please just look at me. I'm begging you."

"The Power of Christ demands you be quiet, demon. You can't prey on us just because we're weak and weary. We won't be victims to the wiles of the Devil," Pastor Steve preached at her.

"Oh, shut up!" she yelled at him. "Let me go now! I am not a demon! And the only Devil in this room is with you! Because I don't know any other reason y'all would willingly do this!"

She looked at Daddy again. He was staring ahead of him, out the window. She could feel the tension in his body. He was the only person in the room that was as weak and weary as she was.

"I need help, Daddy. I know you know that. I know you know this isn't right," she told him softly, hoping he'd listen. Hoping he'd really hear her. Hoping he'd help her.

"Pastor Steve," Daddy said.

"Yes?"

"I need the duct tape and something for her to bite down on. She'll scream something bad when we do this," he told him.

Mona began to cry. "No. Please. I'm begging you," Mona pleaded, fighting and writhing beneath him but to no avail. Daddy wasn't budging and he was turning as cold as steel.

"All of the nails were small, but I found these from the Easter display we made for the church," Beau said as he came into the room.

In his hand were two railroad spikes. They were smaller than the normal size and the ends were worn down to the same size as the heads of the spikes, making them without a real nail head. They were covered in rust and grooves from years of use.

And he wanted to drive them into her hands.

"I guess we'll have to use them then," Daddy answered.

"Please," Mona begged again. "God, please don't do this."

"Cover her mouth," Daddy said, ignoring her. I'll hold her hands while Beau nails them in."

His voice was dull. Lifeless. Automatic. Every ounce of emotion had disappeared and there was nothing but a shell over her. He wasn't listening because he couldn't. If he did, he'd break.

Pastor Steve came to her side with a rag. The duct tape was still beside the bed from when the cops came. She turned her face, refusing to open her mouth and help them, but Pastor Steve squeezed the sides of her jaw until he could shove the rag into her mouth and secure the tape over it.

Mona began to scream through the rag. It was uncomfortable in her mouth. Too big and it didn't want to readjust, but the spikes were coming toward her now. Beau laid one on the table and held the other in his hand. He looked at her with a smirk as Daddy lifted her right hand and held her wrist against the bed post.

"Do it quick," he told Beau.

Mona tried to pull her wrist away. She tried desperately to move her hand around enough that it wouldn't work, but Beau held the spike in the center of her palm. In one moment, she stopped moving, her eyes watching him draw the hammer back. Time slowed for only a second as she caught that glimmer of joy in his eyes.

Then the hammer came down and the first part of the spike went into her palm. Mona screamed as the pain exploded, but he didn't give her time to focus on that first burst of pain. His hits with the hammer came quick and hard, not failing to drive the stake into her hand a little farther each time.

Each time it drove the stake into her hand, Mona's entire body seemed to explode in pain. She screamed against the gag as tears fell down her cheeks. She couldn't bring herself to even attempt to close her fingers because of the intense pain in her entire arm. She didn't think she'd ever felt a pain as intense.

"That's far enough," Daddy said, and his hand let go of her wrist. The weight of her own arm naturally lowering seemed to set every nerve in her hand on fire. She stared at her bloody hand and the stake sticking out of it. It was at least half an inch thick and now coated in her blood.

Beau grabbed the other stake. He crawled onto the bed, with Daddy moving away to hold her wrist still again. This time, she tried to close her fingers into a fist, but Daddy pried them open and held them in place.

When Beau began to hammer in the railroad spike this time,

Mona screamed until both the sound and the pain faded into darkness. When her body decided to go under from the pain, she let it.

THE BREAKING OF MONA HILL

Chapter Seventeen

1 John 3:1

"See what kind of love the Father has given to us, that we should be called the children of God and so we are."

Evil wore a face, and that face was not ugly. It was never ugly. Not true evil. Evil had a way of looking beautiful or kind, not bad. If Evil was ugly, if it was hideous to look at and disgusting, people wouldn't do evil things. People wouldn't want evil things. Some people could see that it was and still wanted it, but most people could justify everything. Because it was desirable, and Evil had a way of tempting people with that desire. People didn't always believe that, but it did. Mona believed it.

She had seen it.

A month ago, she might have said differently. A month ago, the only thing she knew to be completely evil was the Devil and Beau. In her book, they were one and the same. The Bible said so, as did Pastor Steve at church each Sunday. The Devil was evil. He was the incarnation of evil. Every evil thing you thought or did was from his influence because he first sinned against God. Every time you allowed him to make you sin, you were being evil too. You were driving another nail into Jesus's hand.

Nails had been driven into her hands too. After a while, that pain had numbed into a slow pulse. She tried not to move them any more than she had to. Sharp bursts of pain would sprout from the fresh wounds when she did.

When she woke up after Beau had hammered the railroad spikes into her palms, the room was empty. She didn't know what they did after she passed out. Had they checked her pulse to be sure she was awake? Did anyone stop to see if Mona was okay? Clean her wounds? Wet her lips? Take care of her?

Her wrists hurt from being strapped to the bed. Those remnants still hung, but they were no longer rubbing her wrists raw. The ones around her ankles did. They burned, but compared to her hands now, that pain was nothing. It was barely even noticeable.

She was uncomfortable. In the hours she had fainted, her bladder had finally had enough. Despite getting no water or food, whatever had resided in her bladder had finally expelled itself. She woke up in the smell of piss and a wet bed that was now cold around her bare thighs and butt.

No one had come to clean her up. As the sun burned brightly outside, the house remained alive with the sounds of Birdie and Clyde doing their chores.

She was going to die here.

She had tried to escape, and it had gone down like a lead balloon. She was stuck here and fading quickly. She could feel it. Whether her body was decaying because of abuse or the demon inside, she wasn't sure. But she was dying. She knew this.

She looked at her hands. They were horrific. The skin around them was bruised. They had to be swollen. They were throbbing madly, like they had been given their own pulse. If this was what Jesus had felt, she thought him mad. There was no way she'd willingly let someone do that to her. Not for someone else. Not for people that wouldn't even care. Not for people He knew to be selfish and cruel. Not for the rapists, pedophiles, and murderers.

This had been done for worse reasons. They tried to say it was to protect her. It wasn't. It wasn't even to protect them from the 'demon'. It was just to be cruel. To torture her. To have their own sick and twisted enjoyment from watching her suffer.

Blood came in slow drips down her wrist, leaving a scarlet ribbon along her arms and onto the stained bed sheet beneath her. The urine had soaked into the mattress now but was still wet against her bare legs and panties. She was sore between her thighs from the sweat and piss that kept them wet. Sitting in it for hours had irritated and chafed them. If she had to pee again, it would sting because her skin was raw.

Her lips felt cracked. She tried not the peel at the skin with her teeth. They were uncomfortable as well, peeling and cracking as they were. <u>She was hurting enough, but she had begun to wonder if even the tiniest bit of blood might make her throat feel less dry.</u> Even her teeth felt like wool. She couldn't stand the way her teeth felt when they touched each other but breathing with her mouth open only made it feel dryer.

Breathing through her mouth had been her only option a few times now. She had cried so much that her nose would get stuffy, or snot would run down her lips. She couldn't wipe it, and they weren't going to. They didn't want to come any closer to her than the foot of the bed anymore.

Her head was splitting. She wanted to go to sleep but her racing heart wouldn't allow her to. She needed to be awake. She didn't know what would happen if she wasn't. Maybe they'd finally kill her. Maybe if she closed her eyes, she doubted she'd have the will or strength to open them again.

But her eyes hurt. They felt dry and wide. Like they were bulging from her skull. It hurt to close them. It hurt to keep them open. They were tired and strained. Too much time was passing for them to rest properly.

Time was funny. It had only been a few days since she'd been deemed a demon and confined to the room. It seemed like so much longer. Her body felt so much worse. She watched the hours tick past slowly. They felt like days. Weeks.

This was exhaustion.

This was pain.

But as the sun faded to night, no one came to spout Bible verses at her. The house had people in it, but no one came to her room. Not to clean her or feed her. They ignored her and left her alone. They talked and lived within the other half of the house. They ate dinner, they prayed, they read from the Bible, they took showers, they lived their lives as she rotted in the back bedroom alone.

"Let me go," she cried. Her voice was barely audible. It was cracked and hoarse. She sounded like the demon they claimed was inside her. Her voice scared her, but she tried to use it. All of the screaming and crying had it damaged. Dehydration wasn't helping. She didn't think she could even scream anymore. She couldn't put up a fight. Not now.

She was exhausted.

She didn't know how many days it had been. It seemed like she'd sleep in short bursts. She'd close her eyes and open them, and it would still be night, but was it the same night? No one coming into the room would tell her. The next time it was a morning, someone finally came in, but they said nothing. No one spoke to her when they came inside. They would barely look her in the eye.

They were afraid of her.

They were ashamed of themselves.

Mama and Birdie changed her clothes. They wiped her down in a rush, neither looking her way other than to clean her skin. They didn't touch her hands. Mona's voice barely worked to even ask for water. When she was able to speak, it was hoarse, but they ignored her.

They were faced with what they were doing each time they did. Mona wondered if that made them the least bit remorseful for what they had done. Were they trying to desensitize themselves so they could continue on? Right now, were they all still a little ashamed of it? Maybe nailing her to the bed was the thing that finally had them questioning it.

Mona tried to sleep, but she was afraid she might not wake up if she did. She couldn't explain the feeling that was coming over her. She was beyond weak. She was afraid, but not of them. She was afraid of what was coming next beyond this trailer. She was afraid of becoming the next body in the swamp, joining the boy that tried to help her.

And where did they go from here? How many exorcisms would they perform before they gave up? How many more things could Beau come up with to put her in pain?

How long before she chose to leave with him?

When night came, the door opened. Pastor Steve's face was the first one she saw, followed by her brother. Neither gave her joy or hope. Both only instilled fear. One seemed to feel that fear too.

One was operating from fear and pride.

The other simply enjoyed it.

Neither would make eye contact with her. She was just an object in the room. An object of their possession. One to prove they were a man of God. The other to prove he owned her.

Daddy came in too. He looked worse for wear. Daddy looked like a man on the verge of breaking. He was as pale as she felt. He was struggling like she was, but in far less pain. His pain was mental, not physical. His guilt was eating him from the inside out. His doubt was crushing him.

The pastor opened his Bible. It was a Bible Mona knew well. It was the Family Bible that sat on the coffee table in the living room. It had her great-great grandmother's name in it. It was the most valuable thing they owned, according to her mother.

Her brother opened his as well and she could see her mother closing the door behind them. There was no remorse on her face as she did. She had hoped even her mama might try to save her.

The truly ironic part was that she already thought she was.

"Are you ready?" Pastor Steve asked Daddy and Beau. They both had their Bibles open now and bottles of holy water in their hands. They both were clinging to crosses in the same hand that held their Bibles.

"Please stop," Mona begged. Tears were already beginning to form in her eyes. She felt so exhausted. She couldn't handle it again. Not another round of this. Not another night of them yelling at her. Not another night of Beau finding a way to hurt her.

"Lord, who art in Heaven, hallowed be thy name…"

"Please, no."

"Thy Kingdom come, Thy Will be done…"

"Just look at me!" she yelled at him. She wasn't sure where the spark of energy came from, but she regretted it. She jerked forward, pulling her hands as well. The nail heads went further into her palms, and she screamed through the pain. The cracking in her voice gave her wailing a deep, monstrous sound. The sound made her ears uncomfortable. It wasn't the sound that should have come from her throat. It wasn't a sound that should come from anyone's throat.

Pastor Steve did look at her then. So much conviction waited for her on his face. Some much judgment and even hatred. Disgust. Anger. Contempt. He hated her. He despised every part of her. She was a demon. The Devil incarnate, and it was his mission to rid the world of this evil. This evil that had a face, but not one of beauty.

Because she wasn't evil.

Between his gritted, yellow teeth, he said, "You are not Mona. Come out, demon. The Power of Christ compels you!"

He splashed holy water on her, almost directly in her eyes. She turned her head and squeezed them together as more tears flowed. At this point, she no longer had the will to stop them. She no longer had the will to look tough or strong, to resist, not even to spite them.

She was too weak to fight back anymore.

They began their Bible verses and Mona laid there. She just wanted it to be over. She was tired of begging them to see through Beau and his part in this. She was tired of pleading for someone to help her. She was tired of fighting against Beau.

There was no goodness in this room. No goodness in Beau. No goodness in Pastor Steve.

But when she looked at Daddy, she wondered if there was some goodness in him. There was something different about him tonight. Something different about the way he looked at her. Mostly because he *was* looking at her.

And Mona looked at him. As the three of them spouted off their Bible verses and threw holy water at her, she rested her head to the side and watched Daddy.

What was so different about him? Why didn't he look like a monster to her? When she looked at all of them, she could see there wasn't any help for them. It was a reality she'd been faced with constantly. Even the youngest of them was corrupt. She was starting to believe there was no redemption for any of them.

So why did she not think that about Daddy now?

He was so small. Daddy had never looked small. Daddy was a presence. A force. He demanded respect. He demanded you acknowledge him. Follow him.

But he looked weak. He looked fragile. She'd never seen him

look so close to shattering. One wrong move and he'd completely crash, but Mona found no joy in it.

There was something in his pain that felt genuine. Something that sparked that empathy in her. Even if he was responsible for this continuing on, there was something in her that sympathized with him unlike with the others.

He was caught up in the hysteria. It didn't excuse him, but she didn't think Daddy enjoyed any of this. Not like the rest of them. They were just living out their sick fantasies at this point. That was the thing she could see with them. They each had a reason that that wanted this to continue, and none of them were interested in helping *her*.

Out of everyone in the house, she thought Daddy was the only one that actually believed this might help her. It wasn't just an excuse to cause her pain for him. He bought the idea that these things were being done to get his baby girl back. Crazy as they were, they were helping her. She needed the help. She wasn't his little girl right now.

"The Power of Christ compels you to speak, demon!" Pastor Steve yelled. Mona rolled her head back to look at him. He must have asked her something. But she didn't know what. She didn't care either. He wanted to talk to a demon that wasn't there.

So, she stayed quiet. Beau looked at Pastor Steve, almost removing himself from the equation as Pastor Steve allowed his own self-righteousness to fester into anger. At this point, Beau didn't have to do anything to get them riled up and he knew it. He just got to sit back and enjoy it.

"I said speak!" Pastor Steve yelled. His Bible flew with his hand across her face. It made an awful popping sound as it hit her. Her head snapped in the direction it hit her, and blood filled her mouth. She spit it at the wall, along with one of her teeth.

"Stop it!" Daddy suddenly yelled, grabbing Pastor Steve and throwing him against the wall. The pastor stumbled. Beau took a step away too as Daddy stood in front of her like a stone wall.

"What are you doing?" Pastor Steve asked. "I'm trying to help your daughter, Ray. You have to let me do my job the way I need to, regardless of how it bothers you."

Daddy was silent. He stood rigid, his back to her as Pastor Steve glared at him. She could see the fragility in him but based off the way Beau and Pastor Steve were looking at him, they still feared him.

"I still want a daughter after this," Daddy said. His voice showed no signs of weakness. You'd never know how close he was to losing it by the way he spoke, but Mona could tell. She wondered how they couldn't.

"If we don't keep at it, you might not have a daughter after this," Pastor Steve answered.

"If we keep at it like this, I know I won't. If God can't get the demon out without hitting her every chance you get, maybe you don't have as much faith in Him as you think, or He isn't as powerful as people say," Daddy answered.

"You shouldn't say that! Your lack of faith is showing."

Daddy scoffed. "My lack of faith? You just hit my daughter across the face with a Bible because she wouldn't speak. How do you know she's still possessed? How will you know when she isn't?" he asked.

"We'll know..."

"How?!" Daddy asked again, this time with more force. "Because the only signs that y'all say show she's possessed haven't happened. The only time I've seen any pain is when we've caused it. So, I'll ask again. When will you know that she's not possessed?"

Pastor Steve stood taller, trying not to buckle beneath the pressure of Daddy's intimidation. "When God tells me she isn't. I actually have faith in Him and His word," he answered indignantly.

Mona stayed quiet. She watched them with mild curiosity. She wondered whether Pastor Steve believed his words, whether Daddy did, and mostly, what each of them would do because of it. What would they do at this crossroads? Who would buckle?

Daddy was the one to finally move. After looking between Beau and Pastor Steve, his shoulders slumped slightly. "Well, until then, I don't want anyone hitting her again. If you can't get the demon out of her some other way, I'll find a preacher that can," he warned him.

"Fine," Pastor Steve said. His jaw was clenched tightly, and his grip on the Bible was so tight that Mona could see the veins in his hands popping through. He wasn't happy about this new rule. Knowing that brought joy to Mona's bleak existence.

"And I want your bottle of water now. Fasting is one thing, but she's going to be dehydrated if she doesn't get some liquid in her," he instructed.

Pastor Steve didn't argue. He handed the bottle of water he had to Daddy begrudgingly. Daddy almost snatched it from him, both men standing at odds with each other.

But the pastor was the weaker of the two. Everyone knew that. And when Daddy knelt down beside Mona to tip the bottle to her lips, she watched the pastor snap in his own way.

"I'm getting some fresh air," he told them. With his Bible clenched, he pushed past Beau and walked out of the room. Mona heard the screen door slam as he walked out of the trailer too.

Beau looked a little shocked at the display, but he stayed in the room. Beau looked like a guy realizing he might not have as much control of the situation as he thought, and that gave Mona immense pleasure.

But the water in her mouth was the best thing. Daddy poured slow, but Mona's mouth was so dry, and she was so thirsty, that it didn't all stay in her mouth and go down her throat. Some of it dribbled from her mouth, wetting her lips and chin.

"Slow down, baby girl," Daddy said softly. He reached beside her on the nightstand and picked up the rag that was there. He began to wash off her face, not just from the water, but from the sweat and blood too.

He was gentle. Careful. Like she'd break if he pressed too hard. Mona wondered if maybe it wasn't that Daddy didn't know how to love, but how to love right. Healthy. Maybe he only knew possession. But he knew the motions. The feelings. He just didn't know how to execute them properly.

When he stopped, he stared at her, and Mona watched him. She could see the struggle inside him. The two conflicting traits. To love. To possess. To help. He struggled. He was confused.

She had no idea what he'd do, but this was her chance. It was probably the only time she might have to convince him, alone, that Beau and the rest of them were crazy. That this was just a sick and twisted game.

"Daddy," she started slowly. Softly. She tried to keep her voice low.

He wiped her forehead with the rag. "What is it, baby girl?"

"It's never going to stop," she told him. "He's just saying things now to torture me. There's nothing biblical about this and you know it. I know you know it, Daddy. Can't you see how crazy they've all gone? How far are you going to let this go?"

When Daddy looked at her, she could see it. He did know. He knew it would only get worse. There was something in him that knew this was only going south. They wouldn't save her.

Whether he believed she was possessed or not was a different question. One she didn't care for the answer. She just wanted him to set her free. To untie her feet and take her out of this room. To understand that this was wrong.

"They're trying to save you, baby girl," he said with just as soft as a tone. Maybe he was also aware of Beau and his presence. Aware that this wasn't allowed. He wasn't supposed to talk to Mona, to the demon inside her. Only pray and read Bible verses.

But Mona had a hook in him, and she was going to pull it. She refused to give up just because everyone was there and listening. If anything, she wanted that nagging feeling in Beau to get worse. For him to realize he was just as powerless as she was. For him to see who really had the power in this room.

"No, they're not. But you know that. Deep down, you can tell none of this is about love or saving my soul. They just enjoy the torture," she told him.

"I can't save you."

"Yes, you can. You can get me out of here. You can make them stop."

Tears welled in his eyes. For once, Mona saw her daddy, an unbreakable man, break. A flood of emotions she'd never seen before seemed to come to the surface. Remorse, regret, pain, sadness, guilt, these were things he didn't show. Things Mona was convinced he'd never felt, but here they were. Finally, they broke through his anger and cruelness, and she could see a human being beneath it.

"I'm so sorry, baby girl," Daddy said. His hand touched Mona's

THE BREAKING OF MONA HILL

cheek and when she looked into his eyes, she could tell that he really was sorry. It seemed like he could tell that what he had done hadn't been right.

"This ends tonight."

Those three words meant more to Mona than an 'I love you' ever could coming from Daddy. A weight seemed to lift from Mona's chest. This was it. Daddy was going to let her go. Daddy was going to put a stop to this. If anyone could, it was Daddy. Because he was the boss. He was the one who ran things around there. And even Beau wouldn't be able to stop him. Not even Beau could stop Daddy once he decided to do something because even Beau was scared of Daddy.

But when the gun behind him cocked, Mona felt every nerve in her body go alert. When her eyes left Daddy and looked just past him to the doorway, fear seemed to spread throughout her entire body.

Mama stood with the gun aimed directly at Daddy with a look of anger on her face. Clyde and Birdie stood behind her, watching with idle curiosity. "You let her go and I'll put a bullet straight through you," Mama warned him.

"Ann," Daddy said in a mixture of surprise and hurt. "Ann, what are you doing?"

"You're not letting her go," Mama said. "She's not going anywhere until she's not possessed anymore."

Mona looked at Mama's face. And she knew that Mama wasn't

worried about her being possessed. She could use that as a way to rationalize it, but she was just like Beau. Just like Clyde. Just like Birdie. Even just like Pastor Steve. She wasn't sure if any of them actually believed that they were doing this for her soul. Did any of them really believe that she was possessed or were they all doing this because they were getting some sort of twisted thrill from all of it?

Maybe it had started that way. Maybe at first, they all really believed it, but now? There was no way they all truly believed it now. It was just an excuse to keep playing their twisted game. A way for them to get their own forms of revenge the same way Beau was.

Because the look on Mama's face wasn't one of love or even fear. She didn't want to help Mona. She didn't want to protect her. It was a look that told Mona that Mama was getting some thrill out of this. She enjoyed being able to torture someone in the name of the Lord. She enjoyed being able to get her revenge on Mona. The confession she had made before was the truth. She hated Mona and this was her awful way of getting back her control.

"Ann, you're not going to shoot me. Now put that gun down. You put that gun down right n…"

When the gun went off just above his head, Daddy stopped talking. Mona's ears were ringing. She knew Daddy's ears had to be ringing too. Neither of them had actually expected Mama to pull the trigger.

"Don't make me do it," Mama said. "God will forgive me for stopping you."

"Ann?" Daddy said, almost as a whisper.

Mona was too afraid to move with Mama holding the gun. Because she didn't put it past Mama to shoot her too. The way Birdie and Clyde's eyes seemed to light up, they were hoping she would.

"Don't 'Ann' me. She's gotten to you. The demon has gotten to you. Don't you see that, Ray? A demon is getting in your head just trying to trick you. And you're letting it!"

"This is wrong!" Daddy told her. "All of this is wrong! And y'all know it. Y'all know it just as well as I know it. I don't know how we got this far, but y'all need to listen to yourselves. We've nailed our daughter to the bed! Look at her hands! Look at our daughter! How does this not hurt you? Can't you see this is lunacy?"

"She's gotten to you, Daddy. You've got the get out of here for a while and pray," Beau said from beside him.

When Daddy turned and looked at Beau, Mona saw a switch. Something about the way Beau was looking at him or the tone in his voice seemed to set off the alarms inside his head.

"You'd best shut up. No one is asking your opinion on any of this," he told Beau. "Kids should be seen and not heard."

"I'm not a kid," Beau said in an outrage, throwing his Bible across the room so it hit the wall with a bang. "I'm just trying to save my sister," Beau snapped at him.

But Daddy was looking at him. Really looking at him and it reminded Mona of the way he had looked at him the night before her abortion. When Beau had grabbed her thigh. That night, Mona had hoped he wouldn't notice. That he wouldn't understand, but tonight, she could see he did. He knew Beau. He knew what Beau was and what he had done.

"She wasn't lying, was she?" he asked him. He stood up, his eyes narrowing in on his son. "You were the reason she aborted it. You raped her, didn't you? You were the father of that baby."

"She's getting to you, dad."

"Why would you do that?"

"I didn't."

"Did she threaten to tell on you?"

"I…"

"To tell us?"

"I di-…"

"Why did you do this?"

"Because she killed my baby!" Beau suddenly snapped. Once the words were out, Mona saw the fear on his face. The cat let out of the bag. His secret now out and confirmed. His loss of control in the situation. It was the same expression he had the night he confronted her about the abortion. That moment he realized he wasn't pulling the strings like he thought. That he was vulnerable.

"How could you do that…"

"Don't even go there," Beau said as he met Daddy's eyes

vehemently. "Don't you dare say that while your sister is over there with your ring on her finger. Mona is mine. We were meant for each other. I love her."

Daddy looked at Mama. Mona followed his gaze. There was no change on her face. She didn't look disgusted. She didn't look bothered. She didn't look upset with Beau. The only person still receiving her death glare was Daddy.

"You hear this, don't you? You have nothing to say?" he asked her.

She glared at him, still holding the gun and pointing it at him. "The demon inside her made him do that," she told him. "She killed an innocent baby. She needed to be punished."

"A baby from her brother!" he snapped. "He raped our daughter, Ann. How does this not bother you?"

"She's your daughter. She was never mine," she answered.

Mona met her eyes for only a second. Just enough to feel the hatred rolling off her. If she could feel it, Daddy could too. He had to know she really meant that. Whether he loved her or not, he couldn't deny how cruel and ugly his wife had become.

He slowly nodded. "You're right. She is my daughter. And if you think I'm about to sit here any longer and let the two of you torture her because you enjoy it, you're out of your mind," he told them.

"No one enjoys this," Mama told him. "Not a single person is enjoying this. We want to save her just like you do."

"The only way she's going to get the help she needs is if we get her to a hospital."

"You're not taking her out of here," Mama protested.

"The hell I'm not," he said. "You will have to shoot me, Ann. And you better hope like hell you don't miss because I'll snap your neck on the way out, I swear it."

Even though Mama had the shotgun in her hand, and in most ways had the power, her hands were shaky. Whether that was years of abuse or some part of the love she had for Daddy keeping her from pulling the trigger, Mona didn't know, and she didn't care. Because Daddy was going to save her. Daddy was choosing her. And Mama wasn't going to stop him.

"So? What are you going to do?" Daddy asked, holding his hands out. "Come on now. Shoot me, Ann. Pull the trigger now."

Mona narrowed her brows. "Daddy?" she questioned. She couldn't understand why he was prodding her. Why he was trying to get her riled up. If she shot him, where would that leave Mona? If he wanted to save her, why was he trying to get himself killed?

And when Mama's hands stopped shaking and she lifted the gun, Mona flinched. She squeezed her eyes closed, wishing she could close her ears too. She refused to watch him die. Refused to watch him get shot like Owen.

But there wasn't a loud bang. Just a single click. One pull back from the trigger, but no bullet to come out of the gun. No shot. No blood.

Daddy knew there was only one shell in the gun.

But he looked at Mama in disappointment. He scoffed, shaking his head as he lowered his arms. "You're just as bad as your son. Maybe you should tell them how we ended up married, Ann. Maybe you did. Maybe that's why Beau did the same thing you did. He's just like his mother, isn't he?" he asked her.

There was shame on Mama's face for only a moment before it was replaced with righteous anger. She threw the gun down and narrowed in her gaze on him. "Don't act like you're some innocent party in all of this. Don't act like you didn't sleep with me of your own free will," she told him.

"You're right. I'm sick. I'm disgusting. Watching all of this has proven that to me. I'm an awful person, Ann. And I've done awful things. And I'm ashamed of them. Are you?" he asked. "Are you ashamed of what we're doing now? Are you ashamed of the kids we created? Are you ashamed of what you did? Your part?"

She didn't say anything, but Mona was confused. Watching them at this standoff, she didn't understand why Mama suddenly looked like the one that needed to be shamed.

Daddy turned to look at Beau and Mona. When he did, Mona could see that Daddy had his own secrets. Ones he didn't share. Ones he might have taken to his grave if the circumstances hadn't been what they were.

"You should be glad she aborted that baby," Daddy answered. "That's what we should have done. That's what I should have insisted on when your mama came up pregnant. The only difference is, I didn't rape my sister. She raped me."

Beau scoffed. "Yeah right. You told me…"

"I don't remember what I told you," Daddy interrupted. "I'm sure it was something about marrying my sister or being attracted to her. Both are true. I had feelings for her. I knew it was wrong, but I wasn't the initiator."

"Stop it," Mama suddenly said, watching Daddy with fear on her face. "Stop it now."

"What? You don't want them to know the things you did before you 'found God'? You don't want me to tell our kids about the way you kept sneaking into my room, getting me off under the covers, even when I begged you to stop? About how our daddy would say I was a faggot if I didn't like it. That you'd tell him I messed with you if I did anything?"

Mona looked at Mama, but then her gaze landed on Beau. Because the confusion she felt was the same that she saw on his face. The only difference was, it also looked like betrayal was taking up residence there, because this wasn't what he'd known. This wasn't how the story was supposed to go.

"You're lying," Beau told him. "You're just trying to make yourself look better now. Trying to make it seem like you're a good person."

"No, because I'm not. I did lust after her. Long after everything happened. We had Clyde, didn't we? We've stayed married. But the two of you, I didn't choose that. Your mama was right about one thing, y'all were a sign of our sin. The only difference is, I always knew it was you that I'd need to keep an eye on. Because Ann was wrong. I tried my best with Mona because I knew she was a good kid. Not because I wanted to screw my daughter. Definitely not because I saw Ann in her. It was always because she was the complete opposite. I didn't want her to ruin that," he said.

When he turned around to look at Mona, he shook his head slightly, giving a shrug in a defeated, remorseful way. "I have so many regrets. I know I went about things the wrong way. But I was always trying to protect you the best way I knew how. I'll never be able to take back the things I said and did, and I'm not trying to pretend I had a good reason for those things. But I do love you. I'm so sorry I couldn't love you the right way. The way a daddy should," he told her.

Mona hated the tears that sprang to her eyes. Because he was right. He couldn't take back the things he said and did. All of the beatings, the harsh words, the times he'd knocked her against the wall or slapped her across the face, he couldn't take that back. Couldn't erase the memory.

And yet, she didn't hate him for it. That was the awful truth that kept replaying in her mind. Out of everyone around her, she didn't hate Daddy. It confused her because she hated Beau. She hated Mama. She even hated Birdie and Clyde. She knew what that hate felt like. It was pure. It was unbridled. No matter how they apologized, she'd never forgive them.

But not Daddy. She didn't hate him. For once, she finally felt like she understood him.

When he turned to look at Beau again, Beau was angry. Jealous even. He looked like he was on the verge of going off the rails, but that didn't scare Daddy. Daddy didn't shrink under Beau's rage.

"The night your mama came into my room and had sex with me the first time, I was drunk. She knew I was because she was the one that picked me up and got me home so I didn't have to call our parents. I don't even remember it, but I remember her the next morning telling me about it. And I definitely remember six weeks later when she said she was pregnant. She told me that if I didn't marry her, Daddy would kill me. If I told our parents, she'd kill herself. I should have. Maybe we'd all be spared if I had, but I loved her. A part of me thought if we did leave, if we got married, one day I might forget she was my sister. One day, we would just be an old married couple and maybe she'd even change. Out of our parent's house, maybe we'd have a shot.

"But I was wrong," he said, looking at Mama. She was staring at him now, but there wasn't any love on her face. No remorse. Like Beau, she only showed anger. "You only became worse. I know it's my fault that the Ann I grew up with is gone and replaced by this. All of this hatred and ugliness. I helped create that. I'm sorry."

Mama didn't cry at the apology. Her emotions shut off completely. It was eerie the way she closed down so quickly. The coldness that rolled off her as she stared at him.

But Daddy didn't care. He had said his piece, his truth, and now he was done. He was over it. "This stops tonight. All of it. No more exorcisms. No more torture. No more. It ends now," he told them.

The room was silent as Daddy turned around to Mona again. His eyes looked over her but went to her hands. Like he had to remind himself to focus on the task at hand. Not to dwell on the result of their tortures. His first task was getting her hands free.

It was Mama that finally moved. Mama that finally did something. Mama that finally said something.

"I should have divorced you," she told Daddy. Mona watched him turn stiff as she said it. "I should still divorce you. I need a godly man like Steve. Someone that loves me."

Daddy turned around. Mona watched his whole demeanor change. He seemed small again, hurt.

"I do love you."

"Do you?" she asked. "If you loved me, you wouldn't let a demon get in your head that way. You'd know I'm trying to help her. That everything I'm doing is to save her, and why? Because I love you."

Mona knew she was lying. She wasn't doing this for him. She was doing it for herself.

"You're a monster," Mona told her.

Mama's head snapped to her. Her gaze was venomous. "You're the only monster in this room. You deserve ever bit of this. I don't care how you got your daddy wrapped around your finger. I don't know how this started, when you were possessed, but I know one thing. You deserve it. You can only hope the exorcisms might actually help you," she told her.

"You know I'm not possessed," Mona told her between gritted teeth.

"I know you're not innocent," Mama answered. "Maybe by the time we're done, it'll teach you a lesson."

The front door slammed, and they heard feet running through the house. When Pastor Steve ran into the room, he was out of breath. "I heard a gunshot and..." He stopped. He immediately looked at the standoff between Beau, Mama, and Daddy. Only Daddy looked less likely to do something now. "What happened?"

"The demon was getting in his head again. He wants to choose it over his family," Mama said.

"I want to help my daughter," Daddy pleaded. He was down on his knees, head in his hands. "I'm so confused. I just want to help her."

Mama got to her knees too. She lifted his face to hers and kissed him. Mona couldn't remember ever seeing them do anything romantic together, but it was clear the kiss meant a lot to Daddy.

"We are helping her," Mama told him. "You just have to be patient. You just have to trust me."

"Liar," Mona said in a low voice.

But it no longer mattered what Mona said. It didn't matter what truth she tried to tell. She could see that even Daddy didn't care about the truth. He only cared about what furthered his own wants. Apparently, he still wanted Mama.

There was no one in the house that wanted the truth. No one that cared about it because she wasn't getting out of this room. No one was going to set her free. It didn't matter what she said. It didn't matter what she did. She would never convince anyone to help her. There was no one left to save her from the tortures and pain they would have planned for her now. No one to be the voice of reason. No one to listen. No one to set her free.

Except Beau. But that was just exchanging one death sentence for another.

Mona would die in this room before she lived as his wife.

Chapter Eighteen

Romans 14:8

"If we live, we live for the Lord; and if we die, we die for the Lord. So, whether we live or die, we belong to the Lord."

She wanted to die. Mona used to think she was stronger than that. Thought she had more willpower to get through life. That nothing they did, nothing the people that were supposed to love her did, would ever hurt her enough to want to die.

She thought she was a survivor. A part of her had clung to a hope that she was going to escape and get as far away from them as possible. When she did that, she would never want to die again.

She would be able to handle any of life's normal problems. She'd be able to find something good in it. She would always keep hoping, keep dreaming, and she'd survive.

But she didn't want that anymore. She didn't dream now. Not good dreams, at least. She used to have such beautiful dreams. Dreams of faraway places. Dreams filled with possibilities. Of the future, both of her and her life. Dreams where she hated to wake up because they were heavenly. Dreams that made her feel happy, for even a fleeting moment. Dreams that gave her a purpose.

She didn't have those dreams now. Only nightmares. Life followed her into sleep, when she managed to fall asleep, and she only dreamed of her own life. A constant loop, never ending, never changing, day in and day out, over and over, and it was never going to stop. After years of life coming at you and never stopping, you began to realize that this was just how things were.

She wanted to die. She began to yearn for that instead. Because at least it was an escape. Maybe it was an escape into something worse but having a change of scenery might be nice.

She'd even be okay with nothing. Going out, like a light, and just nothing. Not heaven or hell, just cease to exist completely. Like a glitch, she had been here, and then she could be gone. She would love to be gone.

Because living was just a cycle of gaining hope and losing it. And each time it happened you died a little more inside. You would keep cutting away parts of yourself until the end of time or the end of you. Until nothing of you existed. Not even a shell. You just were and they would still demand more from you.

Because people never stopped wanting more. It was in their blood, coursing through their veins. They were conditioned to only want and take. And when they found people they could continue to feed off of like a parasite, like a fetus forced inside by a man who wanted something, they would feed until they had drained it. Like a leech with blood, they would suck every ounce of hope, every ounce of you, out of you until you were completely drained.

Mona was drained. When she was alone, she had no emotions now. Long gone were the days that she had hope.

What was hope?

Faith was the substance of things hoped for, the evidence of things not seen, so what was hope?

Mona was convinced it was a tool. A tool used to keep people blind. To keep them in their place. To keep them in line. You couldn't take all hope away. People wouldn't do anything without motivation. Hope was the motivation. If you gave people just enough for a long time, they would do almost anything you wanted them to.

But once that hope was gone? People became unpredictable when they no longer had hope. Unpliable. Without hope, people were barely that. Because they barely existed. What was a human being without hope?

Mona wanted to die. A small sliver of hope was still there.

Because it would have to be for her to think death would even be an option. Death was a kindness, and she wouldn't get any kindness in this life.

Still, she hoped. She hoped each time she closed her eyes that they wouldn't open. To blink. To pass out. When she opened them, she hoped they might see death coming. She repeated the cycle. She stayed on the hamster wheel and kept moving forward like a good little soldier, allowing that hope for death to keep her in line.

In her case, it kept her in bed.

Sometimes when she opened her eyes, someone would be there with her. They had their own complicated hopes and dreams. None of them wished for death. Sometimes, they wished for hers. So, they didn't have to look at her anymore. So, they didn't have to deal with their own guilt that came from being around her. Knowing she was there, a dirty little secret in the back room. Their hatred for her. Their burden of dealing with her. They wanted her death more and more every day.

But not Beau. His hope was that she would have enough. Change her mind. Go with him. Be his wife, lover, soul mate. He hoped she would choose him.

Each day his hope grew smaller. Mona could feel it and she fed off of it. She hoped she could be alive just long enough to see it all drain out of him and him realize it was never going to happen. That he had lost. That he didn't and wouldn't possess her.

When she opened her eyes again, Mama was beside her. She was scared. She was rocking a little, but she was blurry. Mona's eyes didn't want to adjust on her. They wanted to go to sleep.

"That thing is killing her," she told someone. She sounded so convinced, but there was a part of her that knew she was part of it. A part of her that knew she was trying to convince herself of it. Convince herself that there was a demon to alleviate her own guilt. They were the ones killing her. No matter how self-righteous or prideful she was, she *knew* it was her fault her daughter was dying.

"At this point, we're fighting for her soul," Pastor Steve said. Mona hadn't realized he was in the room. She didn't see him, but her eyes were closed now. She didn't feel like opening them. "We have to worry about where she'll go on the other side if she does die. We can't give up."

"Why isn't God helping her? Why is she going through this?"

Mona almost couldn't stand the amount of bull crap that was coming from Mama. It left a bad taste in her mouth and she wished she could close her ears the way she could close her eyes.

"This isn't God's fault. She made her choices. Those choices landed her here, but God is showing her kindness. He is helping her now. We just have to have faith in Him. He is here with us," Pastor Steve said with such conviction and purpose that Mona laughed.

She didn't have to open her eyes to know they were looking at her, but she did anyway. Just so she could see their faces. Because they looked so surprised and frightened by that tiny little laugh. It made her smile. Filling them with terror, unnerving them, it made her laugh again. Knowing that she knew something they didn't, knowing how stupid they were.

"God isn't here. God's never been here," she told them.

Her Mama gasped and then began to sob. Pastor Steve held her, more than just as a comforting friend. The lust he had for her was potent. At this point, Mona could almost smell his boner and it made her sick with the stench of it. Daddy would strangle him if he were seeing the same thing Mona was.

But Daddy wasn't in the room now. He hadn't been back in for days.

"The demon lies," Pastor Steve told her mother. "Don't listen to it."

Mona laughed again. This time louder, more unabashedly. She didn't even care how crazy she sounded. At this point, there was nothing she could say that would change their minds. It was like arguing with a wall. She wasn't going to get anywhere trying to convince them that they were wrong.

Might as well drop the façade.

Drop all of it.

She had made peace years ago with the idea that she was trapped within the wallpaper. It was best to blend in, to behave, but now? What was the point? She had nothing to be afraid of anymore. She wasn't going to escape. They had stopped that. She wasn't afraid of being punished. She was already being punished, in ways worse than she could have ever imagined. Her body was in so much pain, she wasn't sure if they *could* inflict more.

Why blend in with the wallpaper when she could spend her last days (maybe even hours) being a mirror?

"The only liars in here are you," she said, looking at both of them. "You're so horny for my mama, you'll tell her I'm breathing out smoke and spitting literal fire to have a chance at catching a whiff of her panties. We all know it. Daddy knew it. I even think Mama knows it and she likes it."

Pastor Steve moved from the embrace he had been holding her mama in. He moved to the bed, clutching his Bible. "You speak lies to get in our heads, demon. But we are children of God. We…"

"You're a fool," Mona told him. "She was never going to leave him for you. I know you think she would, but the exact reasons you love her are the exact reasons she'd never leave him. Her devotion to that stupid book. But now, she still won't. Because she's incapable of love."

Pastor Steve brought the Bible to his chest. But she knew she was right. He did too. It didn't take a demon inside her to see. To know. Or maybe it did. Maybe her entire life had been spent with a demon inside her. Maybe that was the thing that gave her the ability to know. Maybe it didn't even matter what it was.

She was right. Maybe that was all that mattered.

"Both of you preach about what God wants. Then you use that

book as proof. Proof of what, exactly? Of things He did? Accounts of people saying they were doing the Lord's work? Men wrote that book, some really awful men sometimes, and I'm sure they wrote it to use the same way you do. To be the judge and executioner. To tell people what they can and can't do while waving God's Word in their face, failing to mention all the stuff you choose to overlook because it doesn't fit your own ideals. Morphing the words inside to fit whatever narrative *you* deem holy.

"You see, being strapped to this bed by y'all has taught me something. There are no good people in this world. Not a single one. Yet, everyone spends their entire life trying to provide proof that they are. Like an accumulation of all the good things they do will prove they themselves are good, but your book even preaches against that. *'Who can say "I have cleansed my heart, I am pure from my sin?"'*. You reek of your sin. You all do. None of you are good. None of you are doing God's work because if there is a God, He isn't talking to you. You'll cry His name and He'll ask who you are. You'll tell him the things you did in His Name and He'll be ashamed of you. And then you'll go through the same things you've put me through," she said, glaring at them.

She could see they believed that. They feared it. Everyone in the house seemed to be full of fear.

No one would be looking for Owen. But they were still afraid if someone did, they might trace him back to them. And how long would that take? How long before someone came snooping?

But unlike them, Mona didn't think anyone would. Why would they? If they did, her family would lie their way out again. Just like with the lady that gave her an abortion. There was no justice in the world. Only pain. Only cruelty. The only people that had things go right for them were the bad people. No one would come for Owen, not until after Mona was dead. Because no one was coming to save her.

"The biggest mercy you could give me would be to kill me," she told them.

"God is going to save you…"

"GOD ISN'T HERE!" she screamed at them. When she did, she jerked forward, driving the stakes further into her palms. She cried and screamed at the same time, throwing her body back against the bed. She threw her head back, hating the sudden onslaught of pain that spread throughout her entire body. Her arms were sore from being held open so long. She could barely feel her feet at times. Her body was useless. Damaged.

While she cried and sank into the bed again, they both began to pray. Exorcism prayers. That was why they were in the room. It was time for their daily exorcism. Their few minutes to make themselves feel holier than thou.

Mona had come to a realization while being stuck in the room under the care of 'God'. When you gave people the power to play God, they became the very thing they hated.

She saw this especially with Mama. Even now as she stared at her, reading from her Bible, trying to actively convince herself that her daughter was possessed while knowing she was only doing this from a place of jealousy and rage, Mona had never seen a bigger hypocrite in her life.

"I hope when you go to hell, they rip you apart limb from limb," Mona told her as they prayed. Mama stopped to meet her gaze. Mona saw the fear in her eyes as she continued to speak, cursing her mother with her own wishes. "I hope you get raped over and over again. I hope the Devil himself finds you and rips your filthy cunt completely out and shoves it in your mouth. Maybe after an eternity of it, you'll finally see how awful you are. I hope you spend the rest of eternity realizing that no one ever loved you. That no one could ever possibly love someone as hideous as you. You deserve nothing less."

"Shut up."

"Why?" Mona asked. "Because you can't stand the truth being forced down your throat? Can't stomach the idea that you are the reason for your own pain and everyone else's too? I hate you, Mama."

"I said shut up!"

"I hate you! Everyone hates you! God hates you!" Mona screamed back. "But no one hates you as much as you hate you. You will *never* be the person you pretend to be. You are everything that is wrong with the world. You are the one that shouldn't have been born. You're the whore. The possessed. The disease. You..."

Mama slapped her and Mona laughed. Mama slapped her again, her hands flying at Mona's face as she unleashed her attack. An attack from a place of hatred. A place of denial. A place of shame. Mama went after Mona like she was attacking her own image.

And Mona just laughed. She couldn't do anything else at this point. Laughing was where she was at. She was past pain. Past hope. Now she was at acceptance. Humor. Delirium. What was the point? Why did she bother?

"Ann, stop!" Pastor Steve yelled, grabbing her by the waist and pulling her backwards. Mama was still fighting to get back to Mona, to keep hitting her, but Pastor Steve was keeping his grip. She couldn't fight him.

"Let him screw you now, Mama. Daddy isn't in here to stop you. Your God won't judge you now, will He?" she asked, then looking at Pastor Steve. "Go ahead. Shove that pathetic cock in her and make her an honest woman. Get your rocks off like you've always wanted. God will forgive you, right? If he can forgive you for what you've done to me, he can definitely forgive you for a minute of sloppy sex."

"Shut your filthy mouth!" Mama screamed at her.

When the door opened, Birdie and Clyde looked inside. Mona looked at them, watching fear spread through their bodies as she did. She had power right now, power she had never known before. Maybe that was what happened when you gave up. Maybe that was where strength finally came from. At your weakest physically, you found your strength. Your hatred. The deep, unfiltered anger that resides in the core of every human being. Mona could tap into it, and she found she liked the taste. God, she loved it. She was addicted, wishing nothing more than to linger in it forever, or at least until she died.

She hoped that was soon.

"I hope every single one of you finally screw each other like the sick, twisted inbreeds you are. No sense in denying Clyde anymore, right? Right, Birdie? Or were you ever denying him? You're worse than your mother. At least she got paid to get screwed," Mona told her.

Birdie scowled at her, but the look of childish guilt said it all. She had. She had probably let Clyde do whatever he wanted. And she had enjoyed it. Maybe she didn't know any better, but maybe she did. She wasn't too much younger than Mona. Why was Mona held to a higher standard than her when they were both children? Why wasn't Birdie held responsible, but she was?

"God hates you. He hates all of you, but not as much as I do. I hope I'm in Hell to see you get tortured. I hope I get to torture you. I hope I get to do everything you did to me to you. To every single one of you!"

"Get out!" Pastor Steve yelled at the kids.

"Why? You're trying to protect them now? Now?!" Mona asked, then began to laugh. Her throat was dry, and the laugh was hoarse. She could see the way the sound bothered them. It unnerved them in ways she could only enjoy now. Because they needed to be unnerved. They needed to see how she had been affected.

"Be quiet, demon. You speak lies and cause pain. Will you not leave this poor girl? What purpose do you still have here?" Pastor Steve asked. And he asked as if he believed it. She hated how much he sounded like he believed his own lies. His own fairytales.

"I'm not POSSESSED!" she screamed.

And she screamed. She cleared her lungs with the scream and began to cough. The coughing led to dry heaving, and that made her feel lightheaded. It made her feel so weak.

And for what? What was the point?

"God, why won't you kill me?" she asked, looking up at the ceiling. She prayed to see a face, His face, in the popcorned texture, but there was nothing. No devils, no angels, no God. There was nothing to answer her, nothing to calm her, she was alone.

"Is that what you want?"

"I want to die," she said, softly.

"You want to kill her?"

"I don't know why you won't just let me die."

Pastor Steve's voice was as close to God's as she could find in the room. And like God, he answered in ways she didn't want. "We're not going to let you take her soul to Hell. We'll keep fighting for her until God decides to take her."

Mona closed her eyes. She couldn't cry now. She was too exhausted to cry. Too angry.

"Mama," she said, her voice barely above a whisper.

Mama said nothing, but when she opened her eyes and laid her head to the side to look in her direction, she could see that Mama was looking at her. She was waiting. Waiting for Mona to say what she wanted to say. Waiting for Mona to do something else. Something that would make her feel less guilty. Something that could spark her anger.

"Mama, if you ever loved me at all, you'd kill me now. No one would be mad at you for doing it. I swear, I wouldn't hate you for it, I'd take it all back. I'd take back everything I said if you'd just kill me. Just let me die in peace, please," she pleaded. Her voice cracked and broke as she begged, the words choking her emotionally.

Because she meant it. She would. God, she would forgive her mama for everything if she'd show her that mercy. If she'd just let it all end. She'd forgive everything Mama had done if she would end her pain.

Mama moved toward her. Her movements were soft, careful. Pastor Steve said her name gently, but Mama didn't listen. She came closer to Mona, her hand touching her cheek. Her skin was warm, unlike Mona's. Mona felt so cold. She leaned into Mama's touch, relishing it.

For a moment, she could pretend it was love.

"I will never let you go," Mama said, but the words weren't spoken with love. With care.

They were vindictive. Meant to cause pain. And they did.

Mona hated her.

Mona wanted to kill her.

Mona spit in her face. Mama jerked back in disgust, wiping away the spittle and glaring at her. The hatred was genuine for both women.

"I hope you rot in hell," Mona told her. "I hope you all rot in hell for what you've done for me. I hope you get shown no mercy the same way you've shown me none."

They were silent, and that was fine. Mona preferred the silence.

THE BREAKING OF MONA HILL

Chapter Nineteen

1 John 4:21

"And He had given us this command: Whoever loves God must also love his brother."

"You had a very eventful day today," Beau's voice said through the cloud of unconsciousness. When Mona opened her eyes, she almost thought she was dreaming. Maybe Beau wasn't actually in her room. Maybe she believed that he was because reality and dreams were not the same anymore.

Honestly, nothing she did now would have a consequence,

would it? There was nothing worse they could do to her. Nothing at all. She was determined that they could cut off her fingers now and it wouldn't matter She literally had nails driven through her hands. They could pull her body apart limb by limb and it would just be another pain. Just another injury. Another little moment in time where she would feel something other than complete hopelessness. The pain was just subjective at this point. She could choose to feel it or not. She guessed that when your body was in extreme agony, but your mind also was, it learned how to prioritize what it wanted to feel and at what time.

Because every moment where her hand felt something, she'd feel it and let it pass. She didn't want to move them or think about them at all. When that would happen, she would immediately turn the thought over and tell her mind that it was fine. Because she was also in pain all over her body.

Her stomach felt like a it was the most sensitive part of her body. Her throat was so sore that she was determined if she spoke another word it would feel like glass coming up through her mouth. And she didn't even want to think about what it would feel like if she would have vomited again. She imagined it would feel something like throwing up lava. The burning pain was just as bad as the pain in her hands, but if she thought about her hands, she didn't think about the burning and vice versa.

And if she thought about the complete loss of these people that had at least shown her some sort of kindness, she barely felt any of the physical pain. If she chose to focus on the fact that Owen had died trying to save her, she would think that her body wasn't in any sort of torture. If she thought about the woman that performed her abortion, she didn't think about her pain. She thought about her children as their bodies burned up and hoped Beau had at least killed them all before setting the place ablaze.

They were all at peace while she lived with their deaths and her pains.

And when all of these things were dismissed all together and she just thought of the hatred that she felt for her family, she didn't think about any of it. She didn't feel any of it. It was all nothing. All of it was nothing and she could focus on that, and it helped. It helped smooth things over for her.

But now she was looking at Beau, and that hatred was the only thing that she could think of. There was no other thought in her head. No other feeling in her body. All she saw was rage. And with no reason to fear what would happen if she let that rage boil over, she didn't stop it.

Why would she? There was literally nothing they could do to her now that wouldn't maybe give her some sort of relief. Honestly, the only thing that they could do to her now was kill her. And she wasn't so sure if that was a bad thing at this point. Death would be a release and she could really do with a release right now.

"Not looking so good," Beau said to her.

Mona managed to laugh. "I wonder who's responsible for that," she said, hearing her own voice. She hadn't heard her voice for a few hours, ever since they all had heard her screaming during another exorcism. After she had made sure to tell each of them exactly how she felt. It was hoarse and it was rough. It didn't sound like her. More accurately, it didn't sound like the voice that she had used for fifteen years. She didn't sound like a little girl that was scared to say anything. She didn't sound like a meek little mouse. In addition to her voice was hoarse, and she was possibly even losing it, due to either the screaming or the pain stressing her vocal cords, there was no sign of the voice that she had used her entire life. That was gone now. Any chance of innocence in her life was gone. Purity was all gone. None of that girl was left.

"The demon, of course," Beau said, rolling his eyes. Mona stared at him, and after a moment he grinned. "Wait? Are you starting to believe it too? Isn't that just a treat!"

Mona didn't say anything. She had nothing to say. A part of her truly wondered if something was inside of her. Maybe it was why she felt so bad. She could use it to explain so much, or to not take accountability. Whether Beau realized it or not, she could be truly possessed.

"I honestly didn't think it would be this easy to convince them," Beau said, sitting at the edge of the bed. "I didn't realize I could even convince you."

She just glared at him. Most of her was annoyed he was in the room. Part of her was ashamed that she wasn't snapping back. Part of her knew he wanted to talk, and she actually wanted to hear it. She wanted to know what was going on inside his head.

"Don't feel like talking?" Beau asked. When she didn't answer, he laughed. "I guess not. You've never been big on talking. Always listening though, right? You hear everything and never forget any of it. You just tuck it away. I guess when you're surrounded by so many people that can hurt you, the only thing you can do is listen, but that's not how it is with us, Mona. I see you. You don't have to be afraid with me. You can always be yourself with me."

He waited. Mona knew she wasn't going to say anything. Even though he was the one responsible for her not being gagged, she wasn't going to speak. She didn't want to waste her breath on the likes of him.

When she didn't say anything, he leaned back. "You really don't want to talk? You're not even just a little curious as to how you ended up here? How I did it? I really want to tell you. There's no telling how much longer I'll have to tell you," he said, smiling as he looked toward her. With how light and cheerful his smile was, one might have thought he was a lover talking to his girlfriend about their future.

"Maybe you can just listen then. Since you're so good at it," he teased her. "Because I know you want to know how this all happened. How a few weeks ago, you were fine, and now you're bound to a bed, crying blood, having seizures, vomiting so much, even being burned by holy water, just not yourself at all. Granted,

I didn't know the bloody tears would be a thing, but it worked out so wonderful, didn't it? That really added the cherry on top for this whole charade."

Mona looked at him. She didn't want to, she didn't want to give him the satisfaction, but he was right. She was good at listening. Really good, and he had her full attention.

"When I found out about the abortion, I was mad. I snapped that woman's neck without even thinking," he told her.

She flinched on instinct. She could see it. She could see that poor woman that had helped her, been kind to her, probably begging for her children's lives, and then SNAP! And Beau, angry, self-righteous, and satisfied. No remorse. Just anger.

"Does that bother you?" he asked her. "That's the thing that bothers you? That murdering whore getting her neck snapped like a twig? It doesn't bother you that she ripped apart our baby? She mutilated it but that's okay?"

"It wasn't a baby."

"It was my baby," he hissed. "Ours. Our escape. Our second chance."

Mona reverted to steely silence. Beau expected her to fight. He wanted her to fight. She wouldn't give him the satisfaction.

After a moment, he relaxed again. He went back to his tale. As much as she wanted to hear it, he wanted to tell it. Emotion could come later.

"Jerry was so shocked, I think he almost pissed himself, but I was angry. After we handled that whole situation, I went off and got drunk with him, just trying to go over and over in my head what I could do. I couldn't stop you from getting another abortion if it came to that. But you needed to pay for what you had done, and I needed you to have another reason to get out of this place with me.

"After Daddy finished his 'discipline', he left the house for a little while to cool down or something. I was on the kitchen floor, wondering if I was even going to be able to get up, and just seething in my anger towards you.

"Because I couldn't tell anyone," he said, looking at her. "It's as much my secret as it is yours. Or was. I guess the cat is out of the bag now, but it doesn't even matter. Daddy won't do anything to me. And you knew that even then. But I figured, if I couldn't tell anyone but still wanted to shift the focus to you, I had to make sure you were unreliable."

Mona just stared at him, unwilling to speak, unable to ignore. He wanted her to listen, and that was what he would get. She didn't know why he felt he had to tell her, but she would give him an audience, even if it only meant she was finding a final insight into his head.

"Our parents are idiots. Our brother, he's basically clay. Whoever has their hands on him can mold him into whatever they want. He doesn't have a backbone. And Birdie, well, she's just willing. I guess that's a hereditary trait passed down from her mama. She doesn't care what it is, as long as she's included. She'll do anything because she doesn't have any real emotions. I just had to find something that would turn them all against you.

"When I confronted you at the church, I knew you weren't going to tell anyone. You were going to be afraid that I would. But I had nothing to fear. Not from that. The only thing I had to worry about was if you left because I could tell you were thinking about it. Planning it. I think you've always wanted to just run from this place, which is why I never understood why you wouldn't run away with me. Anything is better than here."

"A cage is a cage no matter who has the key," Mona finally said.

Beau seemed to consider this. He shrugged. "Some cages are better than others. I would take care of you. Give you a place to be who you are," he told her, looking at her as he said it. "I love you, Mona. I understand you because we're the same."

Mona turned her face, choosing to go back to silence rather than argue.

He seemed almost hurt by her reaction, but again chose to speak instead. To tell his story.

"Anyway, when we got home that night, I was in my room with Clyde. You know how Clyde is. He just talks about anything to get conversation started. He'll even lie if he thinks someone will take interest. He was talking about something, but I heard the word when he said it and stopped him. All I heard was 'possessed'. He told me that one of the kids at the church told him that their mama said anyone with tattoos was possessed by devils.

"Just that, that singular little thought got me to thinking, Mona. What if I could use this, use all of this, to make *you* look possessed? If I could convince our hyper-religious mother that you were possessed, the rest would fall in place. Everyone would slowly start to follow along. I thought it would take longer than a few hours but look at them," he said with a laugh. "Even our miserable old man, that holy water trick really got him. I thought I'd have trouble with him. I even thought about killing him when he was alone with you and let everyone think you'd done it, but hiding bodies gets risky and I can't trust them to do it right. Even your boyfriend, I hope they weighed him down in the swamp like I said, but you can't rely on anyone."

Mona wanted to cringe. She was trying desperately not to think of Owen. Owen, just another messed up kid from a messed-up family trying his best to change things. Trying to get away and start fresh. If he had just left without her, if she had told him she'd never loved him at church, if he hadn't stopped to get her, he'd be on his way to somewhere new.

He'd still be alive.

"Even with our mama and that exorcist-happy preacher, I couldn't just tell people you were possessed, right? No one would believe that without proof. Even if I told them the story about that woman with the abortions being some sort of Devil worshipper, they'd need to see something that they couldn't explain.

"That's where I started looking. Symptoms of demonically possessed people. Then I looked up stuff that could cause some of those symptoms. Do you wanna know what I found? Because that's the biggest question, right? That's the one you can't answer. The one missing piece to assure you that it's me and not a demon, right? But we both know better, don't we? The Devil isn't inside you anymore than the light of Jesus is in any of them," he replied, laughing as he moved closer to her.

Mona moved away, but she was curious. If he told her, maybe she could use that to her advantage too. To let them know what was going on.

Then again, if Beau was confident enough to tell her, he was also sure it wouldn't matter if she told anyone. And if she did decide to tell everyone, he knew they wouldn't believe her. He'd have some other trick up his sleeve. Some sort of scapegoat.

"I know you wanna know, Mona. You're dying to know. Funny enough, I could kill you. I could have killed you. But I'm still hoping you'll see my side of things and give in. I was kind of hoping when you first started feeling sick, you'd give in then. I would have never done it again. We would have left, you would magically get better, and we'd be away from this place," he said. "But no. You just made plans to leave with Owen instead."

"I didn't make plans to leave with him," she told him. "I didn't want to leave with Owen any more than I do with you. He was just a better option."

"Well, now he's alligator bait," he said, smiling, with a shrug.
"So, it's looking like I'm your best option."

Mona looked away again.

"I keep getting off topic, though. It occurred to me after Daddy said something that I had an option to cause you some trouble inside our house. Something that no one was going to realize was gone because we were told to spread it out anyway," he said. "Did you know that just enough rat poison ingested can cause seizures and vomiting blood?"

Mona looked at him again, a cold chill spreading through her body. He was smiling, pleased with himself and the reaction he was getting.

"Too much for too long and a person can die, but small doses? Well, that can make someone violently ill. It can cause all kinds of different things, and I was surprised at how many were similar to signs of a person being possessed. And it can work quickly! I was surprised how quickly. I heard you up and throwing up that night. It took everything in me not to get people to notice it then," he said.

"But how?" Mona finally asked. "How did I take it? How would you get that in me without me knowing?"

He smiled again. He was really proud of himself with that. Beau couldn't hide how pleased he was with himself with the whole process, but this was where most of his pride lay.

"That's the funny thing. It was just there. Something that only you would touch. I couldn't risk someone else getting a dose and getting sick too. Then it becomes an illness and not a possession. Possessions aren't contagious, so only you could get sick. And there's only one thing that you do that no one else does. No one else touches it," he said. "Everyone else likes to drink out of a can."

Her lemonade. Mona could have kicked herself for drinking something different, something made. Beau had spiked her pitchers with his rat poison, and she had drunk it without even noticing. Without even wondering.

"I just had to add some poison to your lemonade and then wait to see how you reacted. Some days you drank a lot, some days none at all. And your symptoms just went all over the place. That first seizure though, I actually thought I might have gone too far. You may even have some permanent damage now, but that's your fault. If you'd just gone with me when I asked, none of this would have needed to happen," he reminded her.

"Why would I want to be with you, Beau?" she asked.

"Because I love you."

"So much that you'd kill me?"

"Well, if I can't have you, no one can," he said. "You were made for me. From me. We came from the same egg, split from the same cell. We were made from each other. We're as close to being soulmates as any two people can be. We were born together, from the same womb, on the same day. I don't understand how you can deny it."

Mona laughed. She almost felt bad for laughing. Especially when she knew this was coming from a genuine place.

"What are you laughing about?" he asked angrily.

Mona stopped, but she was still smiling as she watched him. "That's what you think? That we came from the same cell? The same egg? That's not how fraternal twins work. We are just two siblings born on the same day," she told him.

His face fell a little and she found herself unable to stop the giggle. "You honestly thought we came from the same egg? This whole time? That's what you've believed this whole time?" she asked, but his embarrassed anger was the answer. "You're just as stupid as the rest of them."

Beau frowned, glaring at her as she calmed her laughter down to a quiet smirk. He shook his head, staring at her. "You can make fun of me all you want, but it doesn't change anything. You're the only person in the world for me. I love you. I don't know why you don't love me back."

"Because it's disgusting!" she yelled at him. "You're my brother! Not my lover. Not my husband. What you want is immoral."

"Immoral only if you believe in someone that can punish you. If God isn't real, morals don't exactly mean anything," he told her.

"That's what someone like you would say. A way to excuse something you know is wrong."

"I know nothing," he said. "It's not wrong. No more than sex out of marriage or drinking is. People just say so because some guy in the sky supposedly told a bunch of equally bad people it was. They wrote it down in a book, probably when they were drunk or high, and people ate it up. Because people like rules. They like guidelines to make themselves feel better. A book they can use to judge everyone else that they deem bad. The Bible is nothing more than the biggest circle jerk in history, and they'll all just keep tuning it down to whatever they want to cum on until they all rot away."

"You're no different than they are. You're just living by some messed up set of rules you've given yourself. It's wrong for me to have an abortion for a baby I didn't want, but perfectly okay for you to rape me. Poison me. Abuse and ridicule and do whatever you want because *you* want it. You have such a problem with God because you think you are one and you're not," she told him.

She lifted herself up, even though she felt dizzy and weak doing so. She wanted to be level with him. She wanted him to see she meant what she was about to say.

"You're nothing but a sad little boy trying to pretend you're something special, but you're not. You're just as bad as Daddy and Mama. Just as easily manipulated as Birdie or Clyde. Just as eccentric as Pastor Steve. Just as delusional as all of them because you honestly believe I'd ever want to be with you. I can't stand you, Beau. You repulse me," she hissed through her words, and when she spat in his face, he stood abruptly.

Her triumph was met with a backhand. If she wasn't nailed to the bed, she might have hit the wall. Instead, it just jerked her against the nails. She couldn't reach up and hold the spot. It had free rein to spread the pain out across her face.

But she forced herself to look at Beau. If he wanted to play this game, she wasn't going to back down. Not now. Not ever again. He had awakened something inside her. Opened a window in that room with the yellow wallpaper, and she was going to embrace the burning sunlight that came through.

If he wanted to be cruel, she found she could be defiant.

"Yeah, you're right, Beau. We wouldn't be like Mama and Daddy," she told him.

He drew in his brows in anger. He wiped away what little bit of spit was still on his face. When he looked at her, it was pure rage on his face. "You'd rather die here than even try? You'd rather rot in this bed and die than be with me? Do you really hate me that much?"

"Yes."

But Mona wasn't sure about that answer. She really wasn't. Did she hate him? Did she hate him at all?

"You're withering away, Mona. You don't even look like yourself anymore. You'd rather lay here and endure all of this than leave with me?"

And when Beau was staring at her, she could see that he could tell. His remarks may have been on her appearance, but that wasn't the only thing he was seeing when he looked at her.

Mona started to laugh. And her laugh made Beau go cold. He

furrowed his brows and even looked a little scared.

"What's so funny?" he asked her.

"You are an amalgam," she told him with slow deliberate words. She sounded each of them out syllable for syllable. And she smiled the entire time that she did that. Despite how it hurt her mouth to smile, how her cracked lips just seem to break back open the wider she grinned, and how her teeth felt like felt paper against her lips because her mouth was so dry, she wouldn't stop.

Because this gave her joy. Seeing him like this gave her joy.

"What are you talkin' about?" he asked her.

"I'm talking about you. It's not me that you're looking at right now. The only thing you see right now when you look at me is yourself."

Although Beau looked at her as though she was spouting nonsense, it was clear that her words held truth. Whether he wanted to admit it or not, and he could hide it all he wanted, he knew that she was on to him.

"We're twins. And you're right. Out of everyone in the world that could exist, you are the only person that could ever be as connected to me as possible. We shared the same womb. We are interwoven into each other and I used to think that we were that old cliché; a bad twin and a good twin. I used to tell myself that I was the good twin. Because I obeyed. I didn't fight back. I didn't make a scene. I blended with the wallpaper while you were bad. Every single part of you was bad. You had no goodness in you at all.

"And I truly believe that. I believe you're evil. And everything you do only further cemented in my mind that there was not a single ounce of good in you, Beau," she told him, watching his face remain solemn as she spoke. Her words were sitting with him, but he was refusing to show how they affected him.

But she knew.

"But you were right. We are the same. I could sit here all day and say that you are evil and completely bad and there's no good in you, but I could never say that I was completely good and that there was no evil in me. I couldn't look at myself in the mirror most days because I knew that I had that same evil in me too. Because that's where I had it wrong. You are a bad person, Beau. But so am I.

"I think that somewhere, sometime in your life, you had goodness in you too. Because I had it in me. I think we both had that same good and evil inside of us, and I think we both have been constantly fighting one way or the other against it our entire life, but you sucked it out of me. You erased any good that I had left in me, and you can see that. You see what you've done to me. Because I think part of you that actually had some sort of good intention was the part of you that saw that goodness in me. I think that some part of you that concocted this disgusting plan saw that goodness in me and you wanted to protect it. You wanted to save me.

"I'm not sitting here and pretending that you did that with unselfish intentions because at the end of the day, you wanted to save that goodness. I think a part of you hoped you could get a little bit of it for yourself. Because the only thing worse than being good is realizing that you are evil and wishing you had some good."

"It's so easy for you to sit there and try to judge me, isn't it?" Beau asked, twisting his mouth scornfully as he narrowed his gaze at her. "It's easy for you to make all your assumptions. Your accusations. Did it ever occur to you that maybe I love you? That everything I did is because I love you?"

"Love? Do you know what love is, Beau?"

Beau watched her, his face full of indignation. She was making him angry. She was fine with that. It was about time everyone else was angry for the right reasons. She was past the point of trying to remain calm. Of trying to remain rational. She wasn't here to make any of them feel better about what they had done.

"I love you, Mona," he said between gritted teeth.

"Why?"

"What do you mean why?" he asked, raising his voice. At this point, she was sure Beau didn't care if anyone knew he was in the room with her or not. Daddy wasn't here to stop him and no one else would dare.

"If you love me, why do you love me? Just one reason, Beau. Just one would be enough for me. Tell me why you love me, and I'll leave with you right now," she told him, and she meant it. She was almost sad to admit it, but if Beau gave her a real reason, she would.

But she knew he wouldn't. Because Beau didn't know what love was. And Beau didn't love her.

"Because you're mine. You're a part of me," Beau told her.

"Possession."

"What?"

"That's not love," she said. "That's possession. Just like Mama and Daddy. Just like the demon you say is inside me. Possession. That's what most people claim is love, isn't it?"

Beau shook his head. "We're not like them. We'll be better than them. I'll take care of you…"

"Oh, shut up!" Mona snapped. "Just stop it! You're delusional, Beau. Delusional to think that your sick obsession can be anything more than that. To think that this, that wanting to screw your sister, is normal! This isn't a star-crossed lovers romance. I'm your sister. Your twin. You have beat me, raped me, impregnated me, poisoned me, killed innocent people, and you think that counts as love? You think that's normal?"

Beau was fuming, but there was something new on his face. Was it guilt?

"I was trying to save you."

"Then let me die," she told him. "If that's what it takes to save me, I'd rather die. Drown. Burn. Just leave me alone to rot."

"Nothing will ever be enough for you," he said, his shoulders dropping in defeat. "Nothing I do will ever make you love me. I'll never convince you that I love you. That I'd do anything for you and have. You'll never care about any of it."

And there was pain on his face. So much pain and it was genuine. It was because of that that Mona began to laugh. All of it was suddenly hilarious to her. Everything suddenly felt so much easier when she could focus on his ridiculous pain. The stupidity behind all of it.

"It won't. And I'll tell you why, Beau. Do you wanna know why?" she asked.

Beau didn't answer. It didn't matter. Mona was going to tell him anyway.

"Because I've been thinking a lot. That's all I've had time to do. Being nailed to this bed has made me question everything around me. Christianity. Religion. God. Family. Love. Forgiveness. On the forefront, these are all good words, right? That's what we were taught. That's what we were told to believe, or we'd go to Hell.

"But if I died right now after everything you've done in the name of 'love', I'd go to Hell because I wouldn't forgive you. But you could wake up tomorrow and beg God for forgiveness and go to Heaven after everything you've done. Because that's what it says in the book. If you're sincere, your sins will be wiped free, but if you're not saved, you're damned to Hell.

"You have raped me. You have killed innocent people. But that's forgotten. Forgiven. Because Jesus died on the cross for that.

Because he died on the cross for people like you. Because that's the flaw in the design. That Heaven will probably be filled with more murderers and pedophiles and rapists than good people. Because good deeds alone won't get you into Heaven, but bad ones won't keep you out either.

"I tell you this because there's been a question that's floated in my mind for years. A question I've never had an answer to. At what point does a person become irredeemable? Is there a limit to the things someone can do and be forgiven? Is it a certain sin? But that's not it. That's not right.

"Because the only time a person becomes irredeemable is at the point when they die, Beau. Until that last breath is breathed, you can be saved. You can be helped. That's the hope that keeps people alive. The hope that keeps people going, and I'm tired of going. I'm tired of hoping. I have nothing left. You've taken everything from me, Beau. The only thing there is left to take is my life," she told him.

"I won't kill you," he told her.

"You've already killed me."

Beau's hands shook. At least that answer was genuine. He didn't want to.

"Just leave with me. I'm going to get a truck tonight. We'll pack our things and leave. We'll never talk about this again. Please, Mona," he pleaded. "I'm begging you. I don't want you to die. I don't want you to leave. I can't live without you."

And she wondered how true that was. When she was dead, what would Beau do? Where would he go? How would he survive? His entire life, he'd lean on her. He'd bear his full weight on her, even though she didn't want it. Without her there, what would become of her twin brother?

No matter how sick he was, the one thing she knew for a fact was that Beau believed everything that he said. He believed he loved her. He believed they were the same. He believed she was his.

"No."

"Why?!" he snapped. "Why won't you just leave with me? Just let me save you!"

"Because you disgust me," she told him. "You're the worst person I've ever met. You're a disease. An infection. An inbred…"

"Shut up."

"Why? You don't like the truth? Don't like hearing how inadequate you are?" she asked.

"I said shut up," Beau told her through gritted teeth.

"Maybe now is the best time to tell you how disgusting you are. How awful you have to be to rape a girl in order to get some at all. Couldn't perform with other girls, could you? You can only get your pathetic dick hard when you control it because you can't have anyone questioning your manhood. The bottom line is you're just a little boy trying to be a man."

"I said shut up!" he yelled, hitting her across the face, but Mona only laughed.

"I don't have to say another word. You know it. You see it every time you look at me," she reminded him. "And you always will. No matter what you do. No matter where you go. You'll see me in every woman you ever meet. Every woman you ever screw. You'll think of me. And it'll make you angry. And it'll make you sad. Mostly, it'll remind you that you will never be enough. You've never been enough. You are and will always be nothing."

Beau stood, glaring down at her. A part of her relished it. She hoped he was angry. She hoped he would wrap his hands around her throat and squeeze. Squeeze until her eyes popped from the pressure and splattered across his face. Squeeze until he snapped her neck and crushed every bone inside.

But he didn't. When he left the room, he slammed the door behind him. He no longer cared if anyone knew he was in the room with her. She wasn't sure if Beau cared about anything anymore.

She certainly didn't.

THE BREAKING OF MONA HILL

Chapter Twenty

Ecclesiastes 5:7

"Much dreaming and many words are meaningless. Therefore fear God."

I have to get out of here.

Like an alarm going off in her head, Mona opened her eyes. The room was dark, and when she looked toward the window, she could see it was dark outside too. It was night, but she didn't know what night. She struggled to even remember when the last time was that she was awake at all.

Maybe I'm dead.

If she was, she was definitely in Hell. The pain was constant. It felt as normal as breathing at this point, but more noticeable. It was intense. If she was dead, she was in Hell, reliving her worst moments over and over. She knew she had a lot of them but being nailed to the bed and having exorcisms performed on her seemed to be at the top of the list.

I'm not dead yet.

That was right. She wasn't dead yet, but if she didn't get out of here, she would be soon. At some point, her body was going to just give up. She was starving. She was hurting. She was tired. Her body wasn't going to hang on much longer and if she didn't do something fast, it wasn't going to be able to help her escape.

How do I get free?

It was a question she had asked herself for years. She still wasn't sure how she would now, but she would. She was going to find a way out of this room and be gone.

You know what you have to do.

She looked at her hands. Her fingers felt stiff. She curled them and wanted to cry. The nails in the palms of her hands were thick, but the head of the nail wasn't much bigger than the width of the nail itself. Whatever damage was done to her hands when they had driven them in wouldn't be much more when she pulled them out.

It's going to hurt like hell.

The only way it was going to come out was to pull her hand forward hard and fast. Pulling her hand out of the nail, or through the nail, was going to be extremely painful. She might even pass out from the pain. She had before. When they drove them in.

You can't pass out if you want to escape.

She also couldn't cry out. If they heard her, it would all be for nothing. If she was really going to do this, give herself one final chance to escape before they really killed her, she had to be silent. They would come into the room and do something worse. No matter how good they said their intentions were, Beau was the one pulling the strings. The only thing he cared about was inflicting as much pain on her as he could. And when something did happen to her, because Beau was going to see to it that something did, Beau wouldn't care. He would just finish the job and move along.

Stop.

Mona breathed in.

Get the rag.

Mona looked next to her on the pillow. Mama left the rag she had been cleaning her forehead with. She moved her head over so she could just grab the edge of it with her mouth. She pulled it toward her and maneuvered it with her teeth until she had enough of the rag in her mouth to bite down on. She needed enough thickness to not accidentally bite through her tongue or injure her mouth.

Now do it.

She took one more deep breath through her nose and held it. She jerked her hands forward, both at the same time. She felt every agonizing second as her hand moved over the roughness of the nail and through the rest of her skin. One hand, her right one, came through. She felt it slip over the head of the nail and then land against the bed. Tears streamed down her face from the pain, but the biggest pain came from the other hand. Mona looked toward her other hand.

No.

She closed her eyes and pulled it forward again. She could feel it pass through her palm. The nail head had been in the middle of her hand. She felt it pass through the muscles at a slow, painstaking pace. When her hand came free of it, Mona finally let go of the breath she had been holding and spit out the rag.

Get out now.

Tears fell willingly down her face. She sobbed but kept in mind how loud she was being. She knew without a doubt that they would come back in and drive those nails back through her hands again if they heard her. Or they would kill her. Maybe they would finally give up and just kill her and the demon.

Maybe I want to die.

She didn't. With her hands free, Mona realized she didn't want to die. Had she wanted that, she would have just stayed. She wouldn't have put her poor hands through that. If death had ever been a real desire, she would have given up long ago.

You want to be free.

She did.

Then set yourself free.

But she was scared. Because what did that mean? To be free? Free of her family? How did you do that? Was it just a location thing? She would leave the room, run away, and then she'd finally be free? That didn't feel right. It wasn't that easy, and they would be after her. If Beau realized she was gone, he'd search for her. She'd never get far with the condition she was in.

So, make sure they can't come after you.

But how would she do that? No matter what way she went, they could always come after her. They could always try to seek her out, follow her to wherever she went. She would constantly be looking over her shoulder no matter where she went.

Unless they're dead.

The room fell silent. She no longer heard the air conditioner in the hallway. Clyde's snore coming from his bedroom disappeared. The wind blowing outside was gone. The only sound she could hear was the pounding of her own heart as it began to beat faster.

Because imagining them dead excites you.

No.

No, the thing that really excited you is the thought of killing them yourself.

Mona swallowed hard. She sat up in the bed and worked her hands back and forth, squeezing them in and out like she was holding a stress ball. She focused on the amount of pain they caused. How functional were they going to be?

Will you be able to squeeze the life from them?

She waited for another voice, one that was morally good, to

interject. To remind her that she couldn't do that. She waited but received only silence. No voice of good spoke.

Because they need to pay for what they've done.

They needed to pay for what they had done to her. Retribution. That was the word in her mind. Revenge. They couldn't get away with it. They couldn't continue to live their lives or die peacefully after what they had done. They needed to feel the pain. They needed to know what it was like to hurt.

Give them hope and rip it out of them.

She finally sat completely up. She waited a moment, allowing the room to spin on its own time. Her head felt heavy, and she felt sick to her stomach, and if she wasn't careful, she'd pass out. She needed to take her time, gain her wits, see how much of her body she could use.

First, you need to untie your ankles.

This would be a great way to see how much use she had of her hands. Could she untie two knots? If she couldn't do that, how could she hope to kill them? She needed her hands. How else would she slice their throats or strangle them?

Take it slow.

She moved her fingers for a bit. They would move. The pain was intense, but they would coil and uncoil. When she touched the ropes, she was able to grip. That was a big sign. A good sign. If she could grip them, she could open a door.

Don't overdo it.

She moved slowly with the ropes. She pulled with deliberation rather than in a hurry. As the first knot came undone, she rested. She let the tingling in her hands subside and then worked on the next rope. Unlike her wrists, the ropes around her ankles hadn't pulled too tightly. The knots weren't stuck, and she didn't have to cut them off.

Curl your toes.

Pins and needles seemed to poke at her feet and legs as she did. Circulation was slow and painful, but she moved her toes. She moved her feet. She had to take time with them. She didn't plan to run, but she needed to be able to stand on them. Standing was her biggest fear at the moment.

When she moved her legs over the side of the bed, she placed the soles of her feet to the floor and waited. She applied a little more pressure, slowly over several minutes. She listened as she did, waiting for sounds outside the room, but the loudest sound was snoring coming from the room next to hers. She couldn't hear any other movement.

When she finally had her feet firmly on the floor, she lifted herself up. She gripped the nightstand for support, waited for the spinning to stop, and then lifted her hand to stand. Her body felt like it was one misstep from crumbling completely, but she was standing. She was moving. Slowly, but surely, she was still alive.

Repeat that.

"I'm alive," Mona said. When tears sprang to her eyes, she said it again. "I'm alive. I'm alive. I'm alive."

Now do something about it.

Mona looked at the nightstand. A Bible, the hammer, and one of Mama's crosses sat on the table. The thought was funny to Mona because it seemed like they had laid these items in front of her to choose their deaths. Take your pick and come kill us, it seemed.

You need to be careful. You don't know who is awake and where they are.

She did know someone was sleeping in the middle bedroom. She assumed Clyde because of the snoring, but there was a possibility that Beau or even Birdie was in there, too. If two people were in the same room, things could get dangerous.

I know you want to torture them, but it's better to be safe. Save your energy for Beau.

She couldn't be sure Beau would even be there. He wanted to leave. He wanted her to leave with him, but he could have left already. Maybe he had decided tonight was the night.

No.

No?

He'll be back. You know he will.

And she did. Maybe it was a twin thing. Maybe it was something else, but she knew if Beau was gone, he was going to come back. One last time. Whether to kill the rest of them or even take her body with him, he'd be back. Maybe even to be sure she wasn't alive. He'd come back one last time.

And you'll be waiting.

But first, she was going to get rid of the problems.

She grabbed the random rags laying around the room from the times they had cleaned her and wrapped one around each hand. She searched around the room until she found the roll of duct tape on the floor and wrapped it around her hands too. Covering up the wounds helped her grip the hammer better when she picked it up.

She squeezed it as hard as she could, testing her grip. The pain was excruciating, but bearable. It had to be. If she wanted to make it out of the house alive, the pain had to be second to anything else.

What she wanted was the gun. Shooting someone was easy and quick. Loud, yes. But if things went wrong, it would be easier to handle it. It was a good back up.

But she knew the gun was probably in her parents' bedroom. After everything that had happened over the last little while, it was probably loaded, so that was good, but that bedroom was on the other end of the trailer. It would be safer to work her way there and just try to be quiet.

In her blood and vomit-stained nightgown and bare feet, she finally walked to the bedroom door. She turned the knob gently, scared that they might have her locked in, but it opened. She pulled it slowly, careful not to make a sound. She peered through the opening to see if anyone was waiting, but the lights were off.

Clyde's door was open. From her bedroom, she could see him sleeping on his bed, but not if someone else was in the room. Beau could be sleeping in his bed, but she wouldn't know until she got there.

Birdie was on the couch. She could see her head on the arm rest, her mouth gaping open as she slept on in her dream world. She almost looked innocent when she was sleeping, but Mona knew better. Birdie was just as bad as the rest of them. She deserved it just like they did.

She inched her way out of the bedroom. She knew to watch her steps down the hallway. She stayed close to the wall and took her time. She kept her eye on Birdie most of the way.

Mona closed the bedroom door slowly, carefully. She didn't want any of them to know she was out, just in case they woke up.

As she got close to Clyde's door, she decided he would be first. Rather than go into the living room and then back to his room, she'd slip inside and handle him. He was knocked out. Even if it didn't give her the satisfaction she sought, he would be the easiest to kill and not risk a big struggle.

Mona peered inside before she walked in. No one was in the other bed, Beau's bed. She wondered if that meant Pastor Steve was sleeping in daddy's chair or on the floor in the living room. He was another big threat that she had to worry about.

But Clyde was asleep. He was snoring loudly as she walked into his room. He didn't even turn in his sleep. He just continued dreaming peacefully.

As she stood over his bed, staring down at him, she hesitated. The hammer gripped in the palm of her hand, raised above his head, and she began to wonder. Did he deserve it? Her baby brother? Did he deserve to die when he was young? When he was still a kid? Was this right?

Did he care about what was right when he tried to molest you?

No, but there was still a chance for him, wasn't there? He could still change. He could be a good person. Maybe if he was free of Beau's influence, he might become something better.

Is that what you want? For him to be redeemed after everything he's done? After everything he could grow up to do?

No. She didn't.

At what point does a person become irredeemable?

Mona slammed the hammer into his skull. The snoring stopped immediately, but Mona didn't give him a chance to wake up. She slammed the hammer into his face again and again, allowing no breaths to be taken in between each hit. His death would be quick. Merciful, even. Even if none of them had afforded her the same privilege, she would do that for them. Do that for Clyde.

But she was reminded of him with the squirrel outside of the library. That twitching, dying squirrel and how eager he had been to smash its skull in. Now he was a twitching, dying squirrel, and she was putting him out of his misery.

She realized she only stopped when she heard the creak down

the hallway. Mona moved away from Clyde, stumbling back toward the bed. She didn't know who was coming down the hallway, but she had to get out of sight.

She moved along the bed to get behind the door. She was scared to peer through the crack in the hinges but couldn't resist. She needed to know who was coming. She needed to know who she had to worry about.

Birdie was walking slowly toward the bedroom. Mona was thankful she had closed her bedroom door now. Birdie wouldn't know for sure that Mona was out unless she went into the bedroom, but it looked like she was going to check Clyde's room instead.

Maybe she was going to sneak in with him. Maybe Mona had been too loud while killing Clyde, but the reason didn't matter. The only thing that mattered now was that Birdie was awake and Mona had to be quick. She had to surprise her and not dilly dally. She couldn't stop to think about it.

It was do or die.

As Birdie came in the doorway, Mona heard her gasp. She wasted no time. She threw the door away from her, slamming it into Birdie. In the next moment, she smashed the hammer forward, not bothering to look where she was aiming. She just needed to hit Birdie. To try and contain Birdie.

She hit her face and Birdie hit the wall. She was already making too much noise, but as Birdie tried to scream, Mona realized that was the sound she needed to worry about the most. Birdie falling on one end of the house was risky, but not a deal breaker. Her screaming was a surefire way to wake up anyone else.

Mona dropped the hammer and quickly shoved one of Clyde's socks into Birdie's mouth. Birdie fought, but Mona got on top of her, one hand holding the sock inside her mouth while the other tried to reach for her hammer.

But Birdie wasn't stopping without a fight. Despite the bleeding gash at the top of her head, she was struggling hard against Mona. Maybe if she wasn't as weak as she was, it would be easier to hold Birdie down. She was tired. She was in pain.

But she had no other option. She couldn't let Birdie scream.

Instead of reaching for the hammer, she wrapped her hand around Birdie's throat. She used her thumb and index finger to press into the center of it, applying as much pressure as she possibly could. If she couldn't kill her quickly, she'd try to cause as much damage to her vocal cords as she could. Just long enough to figure out what she was doing.

You're killing her.

The voice was one of reason, but not of substance. Of course she was killing her. The issue was how. If someone heard her fall to the ground, if Pastor Steve or Daddy, or even Beau happened to be in the living room too, this was going to spin out of control. She might have a bullet shot through her back any second.

If not, she had to keep them from hearing. She had to kill Birdie

THE BREAKING OF MONA HILL

quickly. Quietly.

And she could see the panic in her eyes. Birdie knew that was the plan. Birdie knew her time had come. The consequence of her actions.

And a small part of Mona felt bad. Not for killing Birdie. Birdie deserved it. She didn't deserve a chance to change and make a better life, not after what she had done to Mona.

But she felt bad that Birdie didn't take the chance when she was given it. That she didn't get another family to take her in. That she was doomed from the time she was born and never found a way to get out of it. To be better than the people around her. Mona felt sorry for the little girl that never got to be.

You have that same little girl in you. She didn't care about that.

Mona removed her hand from Birdie's mouth. She watched the moment Birdie had a bit of hope. Hope that Mona wasn't going to kill her. Hope that Mona was about to let her go. Hope that she wasn't about to die.

That hope was still there when Mona lifted her head and twisted, snapping her neck in a swift jerk.

She rested Birdie's head against the floor and slowly moved from the top of her. She stood over the body of this little girl, but in that moment, she didn't see Birdie lying dead on the floor. She saw herself. Broken. Dead. What she would have been if she let Birdie or Clyde live. What she could still be if she let any of them live.

She knelt and picked up her hammer. It felt right in her hand.

She slowly walked out of the room, prepared to hit anyone that might be waiting for her, but no one was there. When she walked into the living room, no one was in there either. There was a blanket and pillow folded at the end of the love seat, but no one was lying there.

So, where was Pastor Steve?

She knew he was staying with them during the exorcism. He had people convinced he was on vacation. She assumed he was sleeping in the living room too. The blanket was there.

But where was he now?

Not knowing where he was bothered her. What if he was waiting for her? What if he was in the kitchen? Outside? Waiting to attack her. To end her life. To ruin her chance.

Focus.

The panic had been building inside her chest. She took a deep breath, then another. She had to take it as it came. Keep going until something happened. Room by room, kill them all.

She moved through the living room slowly. When she got to the kitchen, she looked out the window. Pastor Steve's car was there. Daddy's truck was too. That bothered her. Beau would have taken Daddy's truck to leave, wouldn't he? That could mean Beau was still here, hiding somewhere. Waiting.

She couldn't focus on that though. She had to be sure everyone was dead, especially for when Beau did show. She couldn't have any distraction when it came to Beau.

THE BREAKING OF MONA HILL

When she looked around the kitchen, her eyes landed on the knife block. She moved quietly, placing the hammer on the counter and pulling one of the knives out of the block. She looked at her blurry reflection, then turned it sideways. This felt better. The knife felt more personal.

Because Mama was next.

Mona came to her parents' door. She expected Daddy to be inside, the one sleeping close to the door, but as she creaked the door open, it wasn't Daddy. The lights were out, but the glow from the nightlight outside glowed clearly on the man sleeping in Daddy's spot.

Found Pastor Steve.

He wasn't wearing a shirt. He was sleeping under the blanket, lying close to Mama, and comfortable. He was in Daddy's spot. He had done Daddy's job. Out of everything she said, he had actually listened when she told him to screw Mama.

Mona was angry. And she found it hilarious. And she gave it no thought at all as she pulled back his head and slid the knife across his throat. Blood sprayed across Mama, but Pastor Steve couldn't mutter a sound. He moved, his hand clinging to his throat, but Mama only stirred as he turned to look at Mona.

Mona wanted to relish his dying, but she had to focus on Mama. Because she was moving, and Mona didn't want to kill her quickly. She didn't want to slice her throat and just let her die. She wanted painful. Slow. So, she moved quick, moving to Mama's side of the bed and grabbing the gun against the wall.

Mama wasn't even fully awake when Mona hit her in the head with the butt of the gun and knocked her out.

Pastor Steve stopped moving and Mona saw that this was it. Mama was the only person now besides Beau and Daddy. She was the only other person she wanted to have fun with. To make them feel it.

Mama was knocked out, but that wasn't enough. Mona wanted her to wake up. As she stared at her, she realized exactly how she wanted Mama to wake up.

Mona left the room. She went back into the bedroom she had been in. She grabbed the Bible and then looked at the nails in the bed.

Mama thinks she's Jesus, right?

Mona went back into the kitchen, leaving the Bible on the table. She grabbed the hammer and went back to the bedroom. She worked with the spikes until she pulled them out of the wood. She left with both of them laying in her hands, taking them to the kitchen with her when she noticed the front door was open.

Someone had come in.

Mona put the nails down and raised the gun. She walked slowly into the room, prepared to end things quickly if it was Beau, but it wasn't.

Daddy had his coat and shoes on. She hadn't heard the truck, so she wondered if he'd been outside. Maybe going for a walk? Either way, she wasn't going to ask him now. He was standing inside the bedroom, staring at Pastor Steve and the bloody mess Mona had left. When she got to the doorway, he turned to look at her.

"Baby girl? What did you do?"

"What does it look like?" she asked him. "I saved myself."

Mona knew he wanted to do something. She could see it. He wanted to help his wife, but he couldn't. Mama was as good as dead.

And when Mona lifted the gun and shot Daddy, he was too.

Out of everyone, his death was a mercy. She'd give that to Daddy, even if he didn't really deserve it. Blowing his brains out across the bedroom wall was better than what she was going to do to Mama. It was better than what Beau would do to him if he came home.

She looked over at Mama to see if she was waking up, but if she was, it was slow. Mona rushed back into the kitchen, grabbing the nails and hammer again. She then grabbed the alcohol and matches from the cabinet.

She carried all the supplies into the bedroom. Mama was still lying there. She wasn't moving except for the steady rise and fall of her breathing. Mona set up her supplies beside the table. Because she knew the moment she started, she'd have to be prepared.

Mona lifted Mama's hand. She raised it up above her head to the post of the bed. She'd only need one to start with. She placed the spike to her palm and then with as much force as she could muster, she drove the nail through her skin.

Mama jerked, suddenly coming awake, but Mona hit it again. Like Clyde, she didn't pause to react. Getting the nail in, at least one was crucial. And with three hits, it was through Mama's hand and into the bed post.

Mama screamed and Mona slapped her. Her head jerked to the side, her grogginess at having just been wakened doing her no favors. When Mona grabbed her other hand and stretched it across to her nightstand, Mama attempted to pull it back, but lacked the full comprehension to do so.

And Mona worked fast. She jammed the stake into Mama's hand and then swung again. Mama jerked her hand, and began to scream, but it didn't bother Mona.

"Scream as much as you want. No one will hear you!" Mona told her, smiling as she swung the hammer down, driving the nail into the nightstand.

"You little whore! You let me go now!" her mother screamed, but Mona only smiled. Tears were streaming down Mama's face and Mona enjoyed that. Tears of pain. They brought Mona joy.

Mama tried to pull away from the stakes, but like Mona, she realized quickly that it only caused more pain. She cried out each time she moved them and eventually stopped pulling at them. Mona waited patiently for that. She wanted that same look on Mama's face that she had seen on Birdie's.

THE BREAKING OF MONA HILL

She knew she was going to die.

"Some saint you are. Decided to bone the pastor, huh?" Mona asked, smiling. Seeing Mama's shame and fear was the most exciting thing Mona had ever experienced. She loved it. Wanted more of it. Mama would die too quickly no matter what she did.

"Let me go, Mona. Let me go now," she ordered her.

"No," Mona said. "I'm gonna kill you. Just like I did Clyde. And Birdie. And your precious pastor."

For the first time, Mama looked over at Pastor Steve's body. Her eyes widened as she saw blood-covered body. His slit throat. Mama began to cry.

"Tears for him, but not for me?" Mona asked, grabbing her face and jerking it back to her. "Did you care at all? Ever? About anyone? Why Pastor Steve? Why does he get your tears? Because you'll never get screwed again?"

Mama tried to kick her feet, to move her legs to get at Mona. Mona let her go and stood. She grabbed the hammer and brought it down on Mama's knee. When Mama began to howl in pain, she did the other knee.

"Don't worry, Mama. You'll get screwed again. I'm sure your precious demons down in hell will do all kinds of unimaginable things to you. I sure hope they do. I hope you never know a day without pain ever again for this," Mona said, grabbing the Bible and ripping pages out of it.

She started throwing them on the bed, around Mama. She took

her time. She waited as Mama watched her, weighing her response.

"Mona, please. Think about what you're doing," Mama said, her voice suddenly soft and cautious.

"Like you did?" she asked. "You might not want me to think about it. If I think about it, your death will be slower than this."

"You can let me go. With them gone, you and I can leave. We can start new. Both of us. I can make you forgive me. Maybe I can finally love you the right way with a new start. With no one around to know what we were before."

"What you were," Mona answered. "I was never a whore like you, Mama. Just your inbred daughter that you didn't love."

"I do love you!"

"How awful did those words feel coming out of your mouth?" Mona asked, laughing.

She picked up the bottle of alcohol and began to pour it over mama. Mama moved but cried out when she tried to move her legs. And when Mona sprayed the alcohol on the palms of her hands, she writhed in agony.

"I've got something to take away that awful taste. After all those years of you shoving the Bible down my throat, I figured it was only fitting to do the same to you," Mona said, grabbing Mama's jaw and pouring as much alcohol as she could inside. She then began shoving wads of the Bible pages into her open mouth. She forced as much as she could inside.

Mama tried to spit it out, but Mona held her jaw closed. She watched the taste, the burning sensation, spread through Mama. She grabbed the box of matches beside her. Mama saw them and knew instantly what Mona was going to do.

When Mona removed her hand and struck the match, she didn't hesitate to light the paper in Mama's mouth.

Mama's entire body lit up in flames, but watching it fill her mouth was exciting. It was justified. Mona moved away, grabbing the gun and moving toward the end of the bed to watch Mama writhe and scream. Broken knees and nailed hands didn't help her, but she jerked and moved them as much as possible. Their pain didn't match the pain of being burned alive.

And Mona watched. And she grinned, not taking her eyes off the dying woman in front of her. She thought about every slap. Every hurtful word. Every glare. Every chance she had to change things and didn't. Every chance she had to help Mona. Every chance she chose to hurt her daughter instead.

And she felt no remorse. No pain. No guilt. Mama deserved this.

Mama wasn't the only thing that lit up. The bedding caught on fire, and it spread. The fire moved to Pastor Steve's clothes. It caught the paneling on the walls, the wallpaper, and Mona knew the house would become engulfed in flames quickly.

But as headlights poured into the room, she knew this fire was only just beginning for her.

She reached into Daddy's side of the nightstand and found another bullet. She cocked the shotgun and replaced the one she used for Daddy, then moved away.

The house around her burned and she waited. Mona was used to waiting with the flames of the world around her. Her entire life, she had been wallpaper on a mobile home wall. Yellowed from the sun and faded. And the house was on fire. It melted the old paper, making it roll down the wall in the same sheets it had been rolled up on.

Her entire life, she thought she had to stay on the wall. Stay glued to it to stay safe, but that wasn't the case. It didn't keep her safe. It had never kept her safe. It kept her trapped.

But the fire blazing around her wasn't something to be feared. She never had to fear the fire. The flame. The way it danced across the room was the way it danced inside her mind. Inside the pit of her stomach. When she allowed the fire to consume to wallpaper, she became one with the flame, and she danced. She danced inside the flame and let the fire burn away the remnants of her old self.

And now, she sat within the walls of the trailer, her home for fifteen years, and she enjoyed the fire building. She waited for it to draw her in, to consume her. It burned her lungs. But she wasn't going to be here long.

Because the door opened. The front door. And she knew where he was. She knew his exact movements. Beau would come in. He'd smell the fire burning, know it was coming from their parents' room. He would come to the door. The knob began to turn as he started to open it.

Mona pulled the trigger, close enough to the door that she was right in front of it. When she aimed at the area around the doorknob, she relished the sound of his howling pain the moment the bullet shot a hold through the door and into his hand.

She pushed the door open, coming out to see Beau staring down at the mutilated remains of his right hand. There was blood on his left side too, most likely a mixture of the bullet and the blood splatter from his hand, but it was the hand that gave her delight. His fingers completely gone or split open, the blood pouring from the remains of his hand, the agony he was in, that gave her joy.

He looked up at her, holding his arm as he stared in shock. Shock of the wound or shock from her being out of bed, she didn't know. Maybe it was a mixture of both, but the color in his face completely drained as he stared at her.

"You're free?"

"Surprise," Mona said with a sing-song voice, waving the barrel of the gun at him.

Beau seemed too shocked to even speak. He just stared at her as he stumbled backwards, pulling the dish towel from the stove handle and trying to wrap it around his bleeding hand.

Mona just held the gun up. Pointing it at him. She had no intentions of shooting him. No intentions of letting him out that easily. She didn't want his death to be quick.

But he didn't need to know that.

Her mind played over all the different scenarios. All the

wonderfully horrible things that she could do to him. And she wanted to do so many. There were so many possibilities when it came to ways to torture Beau.

She wanted to cut off his penis and rape him with it. Stick it on the end of a knife and shove it inside him over and over again as he cried and screamed. She wanted to force it in his mouth and make him eat it. Choke him on his own cock and watch him die humiliated. She wanted to nail all his limbs to the floor and then shoot each one of them off.

She wanted him to beg her to kill him. Beg her for mercy. Mercy she wouldn't give him.

He needed to understand that his life meant nothing. That he was nothing.

But first, she had to figure out how she would do that.

This was all going by the seat of her pants. She didn't plan any of it. Shooting Beau's hand was a plan, one that worked beautifully, but it was just a way to even the playing field. In the end, there was a part of her that was still scared of him. A part of her that was afraid he'd get the upper hand like her always did. A part of her that said to play it safe and just kill him. Death was enough.

But it wasn't.

He needs to suffer.

"We're the only ones left, Beau," Mona told him. "Just you and me. But only one of us is leaving this house or neither of us are."

Beau drew in his brows and looked her over. Maybe he was

trying to tell if she was lying. Looking for some sign that this was a joke, but he wouldn't find it. Their blood joined everyone else's on her skin.

"You killed everyone?" he asked, shocked, but also proud, it seemed.

"Everyone but you," she answered. "Guess who's next."

Beau held his arm up to his chest. He looked nervous. He knew he wasn't in control and Mona loved every second of it. She enjoyed watching him squirm for once. She loved the power she held over him.

Maybe this was how he felt. Maybe this was why he liked it so much.

"Don't you see, Mona? We can really leave now," he told her, swallowing hard as he tried to sell his offer again. "No one can stop us. We have no family. We can leave now. Make a new life."

"I intend to. Right after you're dead."

"We can run away, Mona."

"You're never going to run again," Mona told him, grinning as she lowered the gun toward his legs. Beau backed away, but he was cornered against the stove. He had nowhere to run if she decided to shoot.

Cornered animals fight harder.

And Beau was no exception. Maybe he knew he had no other option, just like she did. Because when he lunged at her, she didn't expect it so quickly. She shot the gun, but it missed Beau and went through the wall instead.

With no other bullet to fear and pure strength, Beau made contact with her. He knocked her onto the floor, ripping the gun from her hand and grabbing a fistful of her hair. Mona reached for that hand out of instinct, but he used it to bang her head against the linoleum floor.

The world began to spin as he hit her again and again. When he finally lifted her up, he used his fistful of hair to throw her onto the kitchen table.

And he loomed over her. This wasn't the Beau from earlier. He wouldn't feel bad killing her. He wasn't going to offer her another chance. He intended to kill her.

"Only one of us is leaving this house, right?" he asked. His hand grabbed her throat, and he began to squeeze. His hand was large enough to close around her throat.

And as she stared at him this time, she refused to let him win. She couldn't. Beau didn't get to live. He didn't get to win. Not this time. Not ever again.

As one of her hands gripped his hand, the other reached to the side. When her fingers gripped the handle, she didn't hesitate, driving the knife into the side of his neck. In fact, she felt she couldn't do it fast enough.

Beau reached for the knife, and Mona used the chance to kick him. He fell backwards, gurgling on the blood filling his throat as he tried to pull at the knife.

"I wouldn't do that," Mona told him, catching her breath as she sat up. She slowly got off the table, gripping the counter for balance as she watched him struggling. "You pull that knife out and I guarantee you you'll be dead instantly. And we both know you're not gonna want to miss the finale," she told him.

She got on her knees and opened the cabinet. The house was filling with smoke now, and she didn't have time for any of the lovely things she would have loved to kill Beau with, but maybe she had the chance to have some poetic justice.

When she found the box of rat poison, she shook the bottle at Beau. "Small doses made me sick, right? But big doses, well, that'll just kill someone," she told him.

Beau's eyes widened and he started to move backwards along the floor. A trail of blood followed him. Mona was quicker than he was. She got on top of him and shoved her knee into his mangled hand. When he opened his mouth to scream a gurgled scream, she poured the rat poison down his throat. She held his head back as she poured the entire bottle down his throat, watching him unable to stop himself from swallowing it.

His mouth began to foam as he choked. Mona grabbed the handle of the knife and pulled it out, allowing his head to fall against the floor as he twitched beneath her. He began to convulse, tears streaming down his face, so much fear replacing that once indignant attitude.

And out of everyone, there was a sense of loss here. Beau was a part of her. Perhaps he would always be a part of her. She'd have to live with that. She would learn how to.

She leaned down, her lips coming close to his ear. "I'll see you in Hell," she told him.

She picked herself up and stood over him. The whole house was beginning to burn around her. The flames were now into the kitchen, moving fast along the wallpapered paneling. But she took her moment to enjoy his death. To watch him die completely. To know there was no chance he would walk out the door behind her.

She gripped the knife and shoved it into his foaming mouth. The tip broke as it reached the back of his skull, but Beau stopped moving.

He was dead.

Mona had killed him.

Now get out.

She looked at the front door. The fire was moving into the living room, but the door wasn't on fire yet. Mona moved quickly, getting to the door and throwing it open as she stumbled out of the house.

She slipped down the trailer steps, but it didn't matter. None of it mattered now.

She was free.

She was out of the house. The people that could come for her were dead. Nothing was chasing her. No one was going to hurt her now.

"I'm alive," she said, getting to her knees, staring at the sun as it began to rise. "I'm free," she whispered.

THE BREAKING OF MONA HILL

Chapter Twenty One

Ecclesiastes 3:17

"I said to myself, 'God will bring into judgment both the righteous and the wicked, or there will be a time for every activity, a time to judge every deed.'"

Wake up.

Mona opened her eyes to the popcorned ceiling above her head. It was the same ceiling she fell asleep under every night, the same ceiling she had known since she was a small child. She wasn't free. She was barely alive. Her hands were still nailed to the bed and the people responsible were still alive.

THE BREAKING OF MONA HILL

Mona was cold. There was a soft, summer night's breeze coming through the crack in the window, but not enough to cause this coldness. This was in her bones. This was deep in her soul, a freezing cold she'd wasn't able to shake.

Her heart was racing. It was beating too fast as her vision got blurry. She threw up. The vomit laid cold against her face. It was dark outside. It was freezing inside. Her body was cold and stiff.

Am I dying?

The room was filled with silence.

I don't want to die.

But she was. She didn't know how she knew it, but she did. There was a nothingness that was washing over her. A complete stillness. Mona wondered if the was any peace there. Maybe there was no greater sense of peace than nothingness.

"God?" she whispered into lonely space of her bedroom. A room she had so many bad memories in, ones that stained the walls long before she was nailed to the bed. They played like snapshots in her mind, one after another. Every slap, every word, every punch, every punishment, over and over, blurring from one to the next from the moment she was conscious of living until now.

And there was no answer in the silence. No calming words from the man upstairs. No love. No peace. Just pain. Just cold. And it was spreading.

She began to cry. To really cry. To feel more than anger. To feel every emotion. All the pity she had for herself, for the little girl lying in the bed. She imagined standing over her body. Her poor, frail body. Her weight was gone. She'd never been big, but her skin was starting to cling to her bones. The nightgown was several sizes too big. It looked like a blanket on her broken body.

Bruises, cuts, scars, blood, they covered her skin. She no longer looked human. She was nothing. A broken thing laying in her own vomit and piss.

You can be free now.

But Mona didn't understand how that could be possible. She couldn't even move her arms, let alone pull them through the nails like in her dream. She couldn't even feel her feet. They were numb. How would she ever walk on them to escape?

You would never walk out of here. Not after what they did to you.

Mona sobbed. She sobbed because she knew what the voice meant when it said she could be free. It never meant she could escape. It never meant she could live.

The biggest mercy that could be given to her was death.

She looked at her hands as her eyes began to go blurry. She stared at the mutilated remnants of her palms. They no longer bled. The skin was black and spreading. They were swollen beyond anything Mona had ever seen. Like mitts rather than once delicate hands. Even if she pulled them out, they would never be used again.

She was broken. A once fragile little girl was now a broken thing. And yet, this was the biggest mercy that could be given to that little girl. A little girl named Mona that never had the chance to truly exist in the world. The only thing this world had ever done for her was break her.

Her heart began to slow.

I'm free now.

She closed her eyes one last time and prayed they would never open again.

THE END

ABOUT THE AUTHOR

Christy Aldridge writes books. That's it.

ACKNOWLEDGMENTS

Each time I find myself at this point of the book, I always feel so nervous. I don't want to forget anyone that helped turn a book like this into a reality. I also don't want those people to think I don't truly feel blessed that they were apart of it.

Isn't it funny that now I find myself at a loss for words?

First and foremost, I want to thank God for not judging me too hard for this book. You wouldn't do that, right?

Right?

I want to thank my mama for seeing this cover and falling in love with it. You also need to be thanked for the amount of food you supplied me with during the entire process. I'm ten pounds heavier, but one book finished.

Uncle Johnny, you push me to be the very best that I can be always. Mama tells me I can do anything, you tell me how. I appreciate your honesty and bluntness more than you know, as well as the love behind it.

To my penguin, Tony. You will never understand how very special you are to me. This book felt like torture at times to write, but all of it was worth it for you to tell me you thought it was my best work. You would know, wouldn't you? This book, like so many others, would not be the book that it is without you.

Cody, without you, who would I complain to? You know all of my books simply by my complaints. You never have to read them because you're my puddle after I've pissed out the story to you.

Richie and Amy, I just love y'all and the distractions you bring. My biggest cheerleaders ensuring I reach all of the people I can. I am truly blessed as a sister.

Heather Miller, you did the Lord's work in editing this monster. I am so truly thankful that you took on this book and helped get her into shape. My readers and I thank you for that.

Judith Sonnet, not only are you such a talented writer, you were one of the first people to get super hyped for this book. I said brutal and you lost it. Thank you for everything you did to help get this book out there and recognized.

To all of those who blurbed and read my ARC copies, thank you for helping me with the launch of Mona. It will not go unnoticed and is not unappreciated. Without you, I'm just publishing into the void and hoping someone peers in. Y'all helped push people inside. Thank you.

And as always, I have to thank the furbabies for their willingness to distract me at all hours of the day and for truly being the masterminds behind everything I do. A woman's got cats and a dog to feed. Y'all make sure you get your cut.

And thank you to you, my darling. For reading. For sharing. For hating. For reviewing. For judging. For loving. Thank you.

Christy

DON'T FORGET TO FOLLOW ME

Facebook: ChristyAldridgeHorror

Instagram: Christy_aldridge

Goodreads: Christy Aldridge

Blog: www.wordpress.com/christyaldridge

You can also support me on Ko-fi

www.ko-fi.com/christyaldridge

THE BREAKING OF MONA HILL

Trigger Warnings:

Graphic physical and sexual violence

Animal cruelty

Abuse

Gore

The Breaking of Mona Hill Playlist

Scanning this QR code will take you to Spotify to a playlist of songs I listened to while writing this book. I think they capture the feeling I was trying to convey while writing it.

Made in the USA
Columbia, SC
21 March 2023